The Trouble with Inventing a Viscount

Oscar began to prowl the room, ensuring that all his belongings were where he'd left them. Frowning, he slipped the book of poetry into the inner pocket of his coat and cast her an accusatory glance. "Find what you were looking for?"

"Where you're concerned, I'm only interested in one thing."

His brow arched rakishly, and his gaze swiveled to the bed.

Honoria huffed. "I meant your untimely death."

He clucked his tongue. "Not here to fulfill your promise of breaking your fast on me, then? Perhaps another time. Although, if you are planning to return under the cloak of darkness to do your evil deed, then I feel I should warn you." He paused to shrug out of his coat. "I sleep in the nude."

When he began to unbutton his waistcoat, she wondered if he intended to prove it to her right then and there. He seemed to be under the impression that all debutantes were missish creatures. Clearly, he hadn't been paying attention when she'd explained that she'd spent a good deal of time disguised as a man to infiltrate their world. Hardly anything shocked her now.

Except for the fact that he didn't remember their kiss.

"I highly ⟨...⟩ ⟨...⟩ighting a candle for," ⟨...⟩ ⟨...⟩e score.

And yet ⟨...⟩ ⟨...⟩vas unabashedly i⟨...⟩

Also by Vivienne Lorret

The Liars' Club
IT HAD TO BE A DUKE

The Mating Habits of Scoundrels Series
LORD HOLT TAKES A BRIDE
MY KIND OF EARL • THE WRONG MARQUESS
HOW TO STEAL A SCOUNDREL'S HEART
NEVER SEDUCE A DUKE

The Misadventures in Matchmaking Series
HOW TO FORGET A DUKE • TEN KISSES TO SCANDAL
THE ROGUE TO RUIN

The Season's Original Series
"The Duke's Christmas Wish"
(in ALL I WANT FOR CHRISTMAS IS A DUKE and A
CHRISTMAS TO REMEMBER)
THE DEBUTANTE IS MINE • THIS EARL IS ON FIRE
WHEN A MARQUESS LOVES A WOMAN
JUST ANOTHER VISCOUNT IN LOVE (novella)

The Rakes of Fallow Hall Series
THE ELUSIVE LORD EVERHART
THE DEVILISH MR. DANVERS
THE MADDENING LORD MONTWOOD

The Wallflower Wedding Series
TEMPTING MR. WEATHERSTONE (novella)
DARING MISS DANVERS
WINNING MISS WAKEFIELD
FINDING MISS McFARLAND

The TROUBLE
with Inventing
a
Viscount

THE LIARS' CLUB

Vivienne Lorret

AVON

An Imprint of HarperCollinsPublishers

THE TROUBLE WITH INVENTING A VISCOUNT. Copyright © 2024 by Vivienne Lorret. All rights reserved. Printed in the United States of America. No part of this book may be used or reproduced in any manner whatsoever without written permission except in the case of brief quotations embodied in critical articles and reviews. For information, address HarperCollins Publishers, 195 Broadway, New York, NY 10007.

First Avon Books mass market printing: September 2024

Print Edition ISBN: 978-0-06-335247-6
Digital Edition ISBN: 978-0-06-335246-9

Cover design by Amy Halperin
Cover illustration by Judy York
Cover images © iStock/Getty Images

Avon, Avon & logo, and Avon Books & logo are registered trademarks of HarperCollins Publishers in the United States of America and other countries.

HarperCollins is a registered trademark of HarperCollins Publishers in the United States of America and other countries.

FIRST EDITION

24 25 26 27 28 BVGM 10 9 8 7 6 5 4 3 2 1

This book is dedicated to my friends.

*You probably don't know them.
Then again, you might.*

*They're the kind of friends who understand
the importance of plying an introvert with
caffeine to get her out of the house. They can
have an entire conversation using movie quotes
and song lyrics from the 1980s. They'll meet you
for breakfast and help you choreograph a fight
scene for your book by using the salt and pepper
shakers, silverware, and a napkin dispenser.
They'll text random memes to let you know
they're thinking about you, even though it has
been months since your schedules have allowed
you to see each other. And they are the kind of
friends that, no matter what, will always be there
when you need them.*

To JuLee, Tracy, Alicia, April and Gwen

The TROUBLE
with Inventing
a
Viscount

Prologue

～

$\mathcal{O}$SCAR FLINT RAKED the razor down the hollow of his cheek, dispensing with the beard that had been part of his identity for the past six cities.

He would become someone new. Again. Someone refined, cultured and wealthy. Someone who looked like he belonged at the Count du Maurice's gaming tables.

After all, how could he resist such a temptation? Word had spread as far as Prague about the deep pockets of the reckless aristocrats on the invitation list. And there was nothing he enjoyed more than taking the fortunes of other men.

Oh, and he would take them.

Ruthless when it came to cards—and everything else—he knew what it took to win.

It took knowing what it felt like to fight a rat over the core of a rotten apple. Or how to ignore the rapacious gazes from the toffs who'd paid a farthing for a pretty boy to shine their buckled shoes, then being prepared to do whatever came afterward for a sixpence so that his sickly mother could eat.

It took having nothing left to lose. And that was why Oscar always won.

In the mottled mirror that hung cockeyed on the wall of this dank lodging room on the fringes of Paris, his flinty gaze tracked the movement of the door.

Without knocking, Ignatius Cardew strolled in, his teeth clenched around the stub of a cheroot. A curl of smoke rose up past a pair of wizened gray eyes and a Caesar of short white hair to disappear amid the water-stained ceiling.

"The forgery is flawless, if I do say so myself," Cardew said while surveying the parchment in his hand with a self-satisfied grin.

Wiping the blade against a square of flannel, Oscar gave the page a cursory glance. "Never doubted you."

According to the self-canonizing mythology of Cardew, he'd been mastering languages and *appreciating* the great artists since he was old enough to hold a brush. And when there'd been no money left to buy canvas and paint—usually after spending it all on wine, women and song—he'd turned to other forms of replication.

He could copy a man's signature as well as his voice and bearing. And he was good at it. So good, in fact, that he'd developed a reputation. Which didn't bode well if a man traveling with him ever intended to spend time in one place for long.

"Of course, I had to weather the paper to make it appear as though both you and the invitation had traveled far and wide," his mentor said with a familiar edge of accusation.

Oscar slapped the razor against the strop and waited for the rest. Waited to hear the harping of how he hadn't applied himself enough and, *with one iota of effort*, he could have become a truly exceptional charlatan.

But in the seconds that followed, the expected shower of castigations did not come. Pleasantly surprised, he lifted his chin to scrape the sharpened blade upward along his throat.

In the mirror, the tip of Cardew's cheroot glowed orange on another drag. "Although, if you'd ever bothered to be precise in your elocution in any language, I wouldn't need to take such pains."

Aaand there it was.

"Eight postmarks. *Eight.* And all because your French sounds as though it spent a night of debauchery in a Florentine brothel with a Scot and a Spaniard."

"If the best lies contain a kernel of truth, as you say, then why should I force my tongue to disguise the fact that I've spent my entire life roaming from one continent to the next?" Oscar asked.

"*Entire life.* You're still a cub, barely eight and twenty. Why, I was older than that when I first met your father."

"And just how old were you then?"

Cardew exhaled a curtain of smoke. "Older than your left boot."

It was a familiar retort between them. This time, it was tossed over his shoulder as he crossed the room toward the bottle of brandy waiting on the sill. While conceit kept him from ever revealing his true age, with his timeless aristocratic features, tanned by the sun, he could pass for any worldly gentleman between the ages of fifty and seventy.

In fact, Cardew had looked the same for as long as Oscar could recall. He'd been about seven—hungry and already jaded after his father had abandoned him and his mother—when Cardew had first come to the door.

He'd doffed his tricorn with a flourish and claimed that he was sent to look after them until his friend could return. Though, calling himself a friend of his father's did him no favors. John Flintridge—or whatever name he was currently using—never had any luck staying in one place for long. Sooner or later, the creditors came a-knocking.

Even so, Cardew had seemed like a savior, sweeping in and rescuing them from a rat-infested hovel to provide a sense of security.

But Oscar had soon realized that nothing was ever too permanent with Cardew.

The forger's fortune often altered in the span of a single night. But, to his credit, he'd always managed to keep them fed, clothed and with a roof over their heads. Whether that roof would be in the same location from one day to the next, however, remained to be seen. But Oscar couldn't hold that against him. Risk was just in his nature.

Though, no matter what flaws he might possess, Cardew had been the one constant fixture in his life.

"My left boot was once an ancient cow who roamed the earth at the dawn of civilization," Oscar said in flawless French as he toweled off his face.

His mentor narrowed his eyes. "Ah. So the cub possesses proper elocution, after all."

"I prefer to let the cards speak for me."

Cards, and numbers for that matter, had always made more sense to him. The moment he'd first spied a pair of blokes hunched over a gaming table, everything clicked into place. Without any effort, he could remember every ace, king and queen laid and could anticipate which card would follow.

He hadn't known at the time that his abilities were considered cheating. Not that it mattered. Cheating, lying and stealing were all tools of the trade. All tools of survival.

Even so, Cardew had helped him disguise it with a few simple tricks. And, over the years, he'd learned to hone his skill into an artform until *he* was the one who kept a roof over their heads.

But now, food and shelter weren't his only motivators. In the years since his mother had died, he'd only wanted one thing: to hunt down his father and make the bastard pay for what he'd done.

"I suppose you'll do," Cardew said, his gaze appraising. "With your lean face all smooth-shaven and those high shirt points framing that mulish jaw, you nearly look the part of haute society."

"*Nearly*?" he scoffed, buttoning the stiff collar. "I could pass for nobility."

"Hmm . . . perhaps. There's just one thing missing."

Cardew tossed back the amber liquor and crossed the

room. Reaching into the open neck of his shirt above a snuff-colored waistcoat, he gripped the cord perpetually tied around his neck and tugged. Then he freed the black onyx ring. The same one he'd never parted with, no matter how many times they could have used the coin from selling it.

Resting in the palm of his hand, lamplight glanced off the faceted black stone, cut in a unique star shape.

Oscar frowned and lowered his arms to his side. "You don't expect me to wear that. A gambler drawing attention to his hands is asking for trouble."

"But you're not just any gambler, are you, my boy? And wearing a ring will show everyone that you've got nothing to hide. It will help to earn their trust. After all, these men are playing for high stakes." Impatient, Cardew snatched Oscar's hand and shoved the ring onto the fifth finger. "There. Perfect fit."

Oscar yanked his hand back and tried to remove it. But the bloody thing refused to budge. And the weight seemed heavier than he'd remembered from all those times in his youth when he'd asked about it, but that might have been his imagination.

Then, as if in an afterthought, Cardew said, "Oh, and you should probably know, they've posted guards at the door."

"Guards?"

Ring forgotten, a shiver snaked down Oscar's spine, like a ghost rattling its chains over his bones. Even though it had been eight years, the memory of his time in an Italian prison still haunted him.

He didn't want to know what a French prison was like. Though, considering the guillotine on display in the Place du Carrousel, he could hazard a guess that any stay at the Conciergerie would be of brief duration.

"This is all due to your arrogance," Oscar fumed, reaching for a length of pristine white silk draped over the back of a spindle-legged chair, then he faced the mirror again. "If you hadn't tried to sell one of your supposedly *lost* Titians to an infamously bloodthirsty Spaniard known as El Coleccionista, we wouldn't be in this fix in the first place."

"How was I to know that Miguel Ladrón's lovely auburn-haired mistress was also my muse?"

"Hmm, I don't know. Perhaps think twice before painting her wearing the ruby necklace and ermine cloak that she stole from his wife?"

Unbothered, Cardew wielded the cheroot like a brush, signing the air in whisps of smoke. "I called it *Venus in Winter*. The pelt was necessary. Besides, what can I say? Women are my Achilles' heel."

"Then, it's time to consider hobbling yourself to save me the trouble."

"Well, you're the one who promised to make arrears of four times the amount that he paid for my Venus. Even though she was an exceptional work of art."

"I was—I *am* trying to save our lives," Oscar muttered, taking care not to wrinkle the silk as he tied his cravat. "And to think, I'd thought Ladrón's promise of severing our heads from our bodies if I lose tonight was pressure enough. But now he's posted guards?"

"The guards aren't for us," Cardew said as if that made all the difference. "They're here for some English rose. Apparently, the Count du Maurice met her on the packet between Dover and Calais, instantly became besotted and was willing to grant her every desire, even a stake at his tables. His wife, on the other hand, decided that she didn't want her husband unduly distracted and likely to lose a fortune. To ensure it, *she* posted the guards to keep this supposed femme fatale from stealing inside."

Oscar shrugged into his coat, only to have the ring catch on a loose thread. Muttering a curse, he shoved his hand through the sleeve. "And so I'm being bloody inconvenienced because of your paramour, her possessive protector and now a jealous countess?"

"L'amour, mon fils." Cardew cuffed him on the cheek. "Someday you will understand."

No, he wouldn't. If Oscar wanted a woman, he had her. He didn't care who'd had her before or who would have her after. It was a simple matter of basic need, seduction and an exchange of services without expectations.

"In the meantime, I need to win two thousand pounds or we'll be dead by morning."

"We've faced worse. Unless"—Cardew took another long drag on his cheroot—"you're worried that you've lost your touch."

Oscar scoffed at the taunt and sank a pin into his cravat. "You know very well there isn't a man alive who can best, bluff or outplay me."

❦

THERE WASN'T A man alive that Honoria Hartley couldn't play like harp strings.

She wanted to crow. To throw her head back on a laugh that reached all the way up to the silver crescent moon hanging in the midnight sky. Oh, how she loved Paris! She wanted to twirl. To dance. To taste every decadent pastry. Drink a flagon of fizzy champagne. Marvel at the new gaslights illuminating the city beyond the ivy-enshrouded walls of this courtyard. And flirt with dozens of men she would never see again.

Then again, the flirting would have to wait until she was more . . . herself, she thought wryly, as she looked down at her aubergine velvet waistcoat and woolen Cossack trousers.

So, the Countess du Maurice thought posting a few guards at the door would keep any distracting females away? Ha!

Honoria grinned, the upward curl of her lips testing the glue beneath her broad tawny mustachios and pointed beard. But a surreptitious glance into the dark pane of the chateau's vacant conservatory assured her that the movement remained as natural as if she'd grown the whiskers herself. She knew from experience that she would have another hour before it would start to give way.

Even her father, a veteran of the theater, had said there was no one better at stage makeup than she. Of course, he had no idea she would be using those skills to sneak away from her cousin and chaperone on her first night in Paris to gamble.

Better yet, none of those men at the tables realized they'd been playing against a woman either.

A sly giggle escaped before she could stifle it. Fortunately, no one was in the garden to hear it. And yet . . .

No sooner had she drawn a breath of relief than she heard the scuff of a heavy sole on the tiles behind her.

Devil's doorknocker!

She went still and quickly assessed her surroundings: the ivied wall to her left, a fountain and lichen-speckled lion to her right, the shadows to her back and a gate to freedom twenty paces ahead.

Her first impulse was to make a dash for the gate. However, during her brief London Season as a debutante, in addition to the handful of times she'd become Signor Cesario, Honoria had learned a few things about men.

The male animal was a rather basic creature.

Much like a dog, they were forever hungry, underfoot at the most inconvenient times, and they scratched themselves without embarrassment. Additionally, they were always up for a game of fetch or tug. Send them on an errand for one glass of punch and they'd hang about, watching every sip and waiting for you to finish so they could do it again. Or carry a parasol through the park and a gentleman would soon find a reason to playfully extricate it from your grasp.

Though their nature tended toward mischief, they could usually behave for brief intervals when promised a treat . . .

Unless they caught the scent of potential quarry. When that happened, nothing could dissuade them from giving chase.

So instead of bolting for the gate, she paused to place the bronze handle of her walking stick in the ever-roaring mouth of the stone lion. Casually, she breathed on her monocle, rubbed the fog from the concave glass, then fixed it in place.

Taking up her walking stick, she ambled past the fountain, all the while keeping her senses on alert. After all, being dressed as a man did not protect her from pickpockets and cutthroats. And there had been more than a dozen men inside the chateau who'd wanted the two-thousand-pound purse she now had on her person.

When the clap of her booted footfalls on the tiles met with no responding echo of a pursuer on the prowl, she breathed a sigh of relief.

The footfall she'd heard had likely been that of a servant. Or perhaps a guest stepping out for a breath of fresh air. Not that it mattered. She was only a few paces away from the gate and the safety of her carriage, without anyone being the wiser of who she really was.

Perhaps it was that sense of certainty that made her reckless. That made her hesitate with her hand on the smooth iron thumb latch. And made her lips tilt slyly as she cast one final glance over her shoulder.

She should have known better.

Something moved within the inky shadows near the courtyard wall.

"I commend you on such a clever trick," came a man's voice.

A breath stalled in her throat as she recognized the timbre of it. Which was odd because the owner of said voice hadn't spoken more than a handful of words.

Seated at the far end of the gaming table, his responses to the dealer's questions had typically been a nod, an almost imperceptible shake of the head or a double-tap of his fingertips on the table. To the footman serving drinks, his manner of speaking was economical, as though every word cost a shilling. And yet, there had been something undefinable in his tone that seemed to reach across the space between them and caused her skin to tingle with gooseflesh as if draped in a length of raw silk.

Honoria felt that same reaction now, her skin prickling as she searched the shadows and listened to the sound of his unhurried approach.

Before she replied, she cleared the tightness from her throat. After all, it was important to keep her vocal folds relaxed when using the lower register of her voice, in keeping with her disguise as a wealthy Florentine merchant.

"I am afraid I do not know what you mean, sir." The words were in English, but heavily accented with the romantic lyricism of the Italian language.

"Never been choused by the likes of you."

She frowned, the glue of her carefully applied wiry eyebrows puckering as she shook her head in feigned confusion. But there was no mistaking that he'd just called her a cheat. "Choused? *Che cosa significa* choused?"

The man emerged, stepping into a patch of moonlight. The pale beam shone down on thick wavy hair the color of wet walnut shells that swept back from an escarpment of a forehead, above a pair of dark slashing brows that kept his eyes in shadow.

There was something feral about him. Something that strained against the layers of fine wool and silk. Like a wolf in the forest, waiting for the shepherd to lose sight of one little lamb.

His features were more angular than most of the pampered aristocrats she knew—puppies with soft chins, doughy cheeks and the fleshy promise of forthcoming jowls.

But this man's face was lean, his jaw hard, honed to a razor's edge. His nose, not quite straight, suggested a life beyond Eton, Oxford and afternoon teas. A life far removed from white-gloved dances with debutantes and talk of touring the Continent.

This man had lived.

There was something intriguing in that . . . *if* she found that sort of thing intriguing.

Which she didn't. At all. Because she was all too aware of the weight of the winnings tucked into the padded lining of her waistcoat, *and* how little she knew about the man introduced to the party as Mr. Flint.

Then again, she was also conscious of the poniard hidden inside her walking stick.

Her gloved hand tightened around it. Though, as of yet, she hadn't been forced to use the blade to defend herself.

She knew how to fence—to win a match but not to save her life. In fact, most of her experience with fighting consisted of what she'd learned from her eccentric father on the family stage. So she excelled in *almost* slapping someone and *almost* running them through with a sword.

To her, the choreography of a fight was like dancing in the center of a ballroom. But this? Somehow she doubted that if this man meant to silence her or take her purse by force, he would be intimidated by her *almost* attacking him.

Nevertheless, Honoria knew she was quick on her feet. And, as her father always said during rehearsal, "When in doubt, feint."

Casually, she slid one foot behind her, balancing her weight.

"Let us leave the games behind us, hmm?" He stopped and offered a good-natured shrug. "I merely wanted to congratulate you, from one Captain Sharp to another."

Gone was the ruthless gambler she'd met at the tables as one lean cheek lifted to form a bracket beside his mouth. Earlier she'd thought he was smirking at her, which had made her immensely glad to best him at that last hand. But now, the lopsided quirk seemed almost affable. Charming, even.

So when he held out his hand, she responded reflexively. Felt his grip enfold hers. It made her feel fragile and altogether too feminine.

Honoria realized her mistake at once.

She tried to withdraw, but he held fast. And before she could blink, he removed her black lambskin glove. Simply peeled it down from wrist to fingertip!

"As I said before, you're clever. But not quite clever enough. Not even for a woman."

"I beg your pardon," Signor Cesario said with a huff of indignation and a futile attempt to free himself.

The stranger took a step closer, lifting her captive hand. "If not for these nimble fingers, you might have fooled me. The bitten manicure is a nice touch, but there are certain ways women move that men do not. It's from needlework, I think. That dainty pinch of fingertips. Nevertheless, I suggest you watch the way you lift your cards from the table in the future. If you're going to continue this charade."

"How dare—"

She stopped on a gasp when he bent his head and licked the top of her finger. Actually licked her, where she had painstakingly drawn and shaded a series of very masculine-looking hairs.

But her outrage was quickly overshadowed when she felt the heated rasp of his tongue. The sensation was so startling that it stole her breath. Her stomach gave a curious little hop.

Distractedly, she watched as the ink smeared underneath the circular rotation of his thumb, and she didn't know whether to demand satisfaction at dawn or . . .

Ask him to do it again.

"You are mistaken," she said in her best Signor voice, albeit a tad raspy since all the saliva had dried up in her mouth.

But she jerked her hand free, cradling it almost protectively.

The man grinned and wagged an accusatory finger. "And that's another tell. You're too quick to shy away. Any man, even one so much smaller in stature, would have displayed affront with his chest out, shoulders back. A woman on the other hand will make herself appear smaller, hunching her shoulders ever so slightly to protect her soft underbelly. And yet, even as she does that, her eyes will flash with ire—just as yours are doing now—while she plots six different ways to murder a man in his sleep."

"Only six?" she asked, and he chuckled. "I'm not saying you're correct. However, if you were, just what would you do with that information? Extortion? Blackmail?"

"I may be a scoundrel, but I draw the line at blackmailing a woman. Though, I'm guessing you're hardly . . ." He cast an appraising glance from head to toe, his mouth pulling at a frown.

She huffed, forgetting to lower her voice. "That I'm hardly what?"

"It would be ungentlemanly of me to say."

"I thought you were a scoundrel."

"Even a scoundrel wouldn't dare suggest that you might resemble your disguise." When her nostrils flared with irritation, it only seemed to encourage him. "For all I know your voluminous mustachios are concealing a rather hairy mole. I once knew a woman who had one in the shape of Australia. It had three hairs growing out of it."

One dark brow arched as he stared suspiciously at her mouth.

This was a novel experience, indeed. In all her life, no one had ever accused her of being anything less than goddesslike. Flattery was such a common occurrence that she took it for granted. And she'd had no idea that being called *unattractive* would cause her defenses to rally.

"I'll have you know that I'm quite pretty."

He had her so vexed that she didn't realize she'd pulled out her poniard and was brandishing it at him.

His brow flattened and his eyes—still immersed in shadow—seemed to darken even more. "I don't take kindly to threats."

"And I don't take kindly to insults," she said, refusing to back down. "Those guards inside? They're here because of me, you know. I'm *that* beautiful."

"Or *that* delusional."

He took a step toward her. She cut through the air in a warning feint. But he was quick. Too quick.

He took hold of her wrist in a punishing grip that forced her to drop the blade. "Since we've apparently exhausted all niceties, I'll be blunt. I need that purse."

"Pocket's thin from paying for your *chères amies*?"

"That has never been a problem for me. You, on the other hand, obviously cannot catch a husband because no man would have you."

Drawing her arm down, he pinned it behind her back, bringing their bodies close enough that, even through all the layers of binding and padding she wore to disguise the swell of her breasts, narrow waist and the flair of her hips, she could still feel that he was a wall of solid muscle.

She caught the scent of him, a mélange of amber, smoke and sandalwood. Drat! He even smelled as if he'd roamed several continents and lived three lifetimes before they'd met. It made her lightheaded.

Then she felt his free hand steal inside her coat and—

"Ouch!" He drew back sharply.

Knowing that he'd encountered one of the many pins keeping her disguise in place, she flashed a taunting grin. "Needlework."

She twisted out of his hold. Unfortunately, there was nowhere to go. He'd corralled her into a corner. The cad.

So she maneuvered into a defensive position, prepared

to dodge under his arm when he came at her again. "And for your information, I'm already betrothed."

"To a fellow troll, no doubt," he said crossly, examining the tiny beads of blood on the tips of three fingers.

"I'm certain my fiancé is quite handsome."

"Do you not know? Or is it that you keep him courting from a great distance to ensure that he does not see your actual face and run in the opposite direction?"

"Oh, he would most assuredly run toward me."

"Then, perhaps he doesn't want you to see his bald head, mottled complexion and woodchuck teeth?"

She refused to laugh at that. "Our arrangement has been since birth."

That stole his attention. He stopped an arm's length away. "Wait a moment. Are you saying that you've never actually met the man you intend to marry?"

"The arrangement was forged between his grandmother and mine. After eloping with an actress, his father had become estranged from the family. Since he was the youngest of four brothers, he likely never thought his son would succeed to the title. It's entirely possible that my betrothed doesn't know that he's a viscount."

"You're making this up."

She stiffened. "I am not. He is the honorable Viscount Vandemere."

"And you're simply waiting for this supposed viscount to arrive on your doorstep?"

"Obviously not, if I'm gambling to secure my future. So kindly let me pass."

He shook his head, slowly advancing. "As much as I've enjoyed our little tête-à-tête, I'm more concerned with my own future than yours. I've got a lot of living to do yet, and I'm not leaving here empty-handed."

When her shoulder blades met the wall, she braced her hands against his chest. "But don't you see? That's what I'm attempting to do as well. We only have this one life. I aim to live it to its fullest extent. And I won't let anyone stop me."

She felt the weight of the locket she kept tucked against her heart—a reminder of the promise she'd made long ago. There was no force on earth that would prevent her from honoring it.

But she saw her own firm resolve harden his expression. And she knew he wasn't going to be deterred by a few pins a second time.

Therefore, there was only one thing she could do. Only one device left in her arsenal . . .

Feminine wiles.

In a flash, Honoria took his face in her hands and pulled his mouth to hers. It was the most . . . unusual kiss of her life.

Even though she'd been kissed by a number of gentlemen, none had ever felt like this. Of course, her mustachios were a bit distracting. But that wasn't all.

There was something almost familiar about him. Perhaps it was his scent, reminding her of girlhood daydreams of far-off places while drowsing in the leather chair by the library hearth. Or perhaps it was the spicy essence on his breath, the hint of port and some mysterious flavor that curled low in her belly. Then again, it might have been the warm pressure of his lips as she angled her head, causing the ground to tip ever so slightly beneath her feet as it once had when she used to twirl around in the garden amidst the twinkling lights of fireflies.

She wasn't sure. But whatever it was, it caused a hum to purr in her throat.

A peculiar sensation swirled in her midriff. It was both hot and fluttering at once, like moths foolishly drawn to the flicker of stage lights . . . just before they burned themselves to ash.

She disconnected the kiss. Then, for good measure, she kicked him in the shin.

Caught off guard, Flint stumbled back. "What the—"

If he finished his rant, she didn't hear it because she flew as fast as she could through the gate.

Once she was safely inside the carriage, with her driver spurring the team, she let her head fall back against the squabs and thanked her lucky stars that she would never see the likes of Mr. Flint again.

Chapter One

One year later

$\mathcal{J}$TANDING IN THE FOYER, Honoria grinned as she watched her older sister dash toward the carriage to elope with the Duke of Longhurst. Then the front door of Hartley Hall closed, their ever-stoic butler unmoved by the romantic display.

Though, to be fair, Mr. Mosely usually witnessed some degree of insanity every day, such as Father scaling the trellis to reenact the balcony scene in *Romeo and Juliet*, or Mother having the servants dress in the attic costumes in order to air them out from time to time. Therefore, a mad dash to Gretna Green likely seemed little more than a commonplace Wednesday.

In fact, life in the small hamlet of Addlewick was rarely conventional.

Of course, it wasn't as thrilling as Paris by any means, but—

"Would you like me to see to the matter of Miss Hunnicutt?" Mosely asked with a passing glance down to the brass key dangling from Honoria's fingertips.

Only then did she remember that their odious neighbor was locked in the closet beneath the stairs. She pursed her lips, thinking that it would probably be best to let her out. Then again . . .

Nell Hunnicutt had always been an interfering harpy

who'd made Verity's life a misery and had tried her best to stop the elopement. So, what kind of sister would Honoria be if she let her out too soon?

"Thank you, but I'll see to it." She tossed the key aloft and caught it smartly in her hand.

Then she turned and nearly ran directly into her mother.

The smile that Baroness Roxana Hartley wore upon her lips wasn't like the beatific smiles for which she was known. No, indeed. This one was glowing. And her eyes, set within a heart-shaped face framed by a chestnut coiffure with only the barest wisps of gray at the temples, were uncommonly bright as if she'd come down with some sort of illness.

Considering the fact that she'd been perfectly hale a minute ago, Honoria suspected the affliction was brought on by Verity's elopement. A clear case of matrimonial fever.

With one daughter settled, she wouldn't rest until all of them were. And as the middle daughter, Honoria was next in line. Well, not if she could help it.

The last thing she wanted was for all the matchmaking attention to turn to her. So she decided to put her younger sister in the limelight instead. "Have you seen Althea? She was just here a moment ago."

"Oh, she had an idea for another play and went off to find a new ledger," Mother offered with an elegant flit of her fingers. "It has been quite the momentous morning, hmm?"

The words were spoken with a hum of delight. To Honoria's ears it sounded like the low murmur of bees, and she had the misfortune of being the only flower in sight.

Honoria took a reflexive step back. "Indeed it has. And I'm certain Verity will be quite content with Magnus. Then again, after all the moping she's done of late, any alteration would be an improvement."

Realizing that she'd stepped directly into the fan of light streaming in through the transom window above the door, she quickly sidestepped her mother . . .

Only to encounter Countess Broadbent, who happened to be Longhurst's grandmother and an old friend of the family. The silver-haired matron stood between her and the arched passageway that was her only escape from the hive.

"How right you are, Miss Hartley," the countess said in smooth, rounded tones, steepling her fingers like a cage in front of her bosom. "Your concern for her welfare does you credit. And having one's sister married so well provides a sense of . . . liberation, I should think. Perhaps even enthusiasm, hmm?"

More buzzing, Honoria thought. The bees were circling.

She darted a sideways glance to her mother to see her eyes soften, the way they did when she was listening to Father recite love sonnets. Drat! But Honoria knew that she needed to keep the focus where it belonged: on the pair who'd just run off to Gretna Green.

They were today's news, not her.

"I have every hope for Verity's happiness. She is, more often than not, ruled by her sensibilities. In that regard, I believe she and your grandson are well matched, my lady."

Honoria oh so casually feinted left, then dodged right to slyly circumvent the countess.

But Lady Broadbent was crafty. Sidling up to her, she wove their arms together to promenade down the paneled hall toward the morning room. "I admit, this was my very hope from the start. I couldn't have planned it better myself. And while I have a mind for planning, I do believe we should discuss your Season, my dear. Of course, I shall be your sponsor."

"You are too kind. Truly. However, I've already had my Season."

"Pish tosh." She clucked her tongue. "As I recall, your uncle chaperoned you and your cousin to a few inconsequential parties. Then his daughter quickly caught the notice of a colonel and was wed shortly thereafter. You couldn't have had much of society."

"Well, there was the scandal—"

"Which has nearly been wiped from your family's name, or soon will be once your sister and my grandson are officially wed. A duke in the family opens many doors. Mark my words, some handsome gentleman will soon sweep you off your feet, and you'll never look back."

When Honoria's mind suddenly conjured a vision of a night sky filled with a fingernail moon amidst a cluster of twinkling stars and a pair of dark eyes that had seemed to see through to her very soul, she knew it meant nothing. It had happened before. And the fact that her middle might have issued a moth-wing flutter during those episodes meant even less than nothing.

"Being swept off one's feet sounds rather primitive. As if men were lurking in their caves, clubs at the ready and eager to carry off the next unsuspecting female."

"That isn't far from the truth," Mother said with a laugh, falling into step behind them. "In fact, when I first met your father—"

Thankfully, Mother's story, which was often too descriptive regarding how well Father had looked in his snug buckskin breeches, stopped abruptly at the interruption of a rather irate voice coming from the closet beneath the stairs.

"Will someone *please* let me out!"

Mother stopped. "Is that . . . Nell Hunnicutt?"

That was when Honoria remembered she had the key in her palm. Met with her mother's and the countess's dubious looks, she shrugged her shoulders. "Don't blame me. Longhurst was the one who locked her in. Something to do with recompense. Regardless, it isn't as though that's the strangest thing to happen in this family."

Lady Broadbent pursed her lips and refrained from comment.

Mother nodded and held out her hand. "Better leave the matter to me, then. I'll have to smooth things over with her mother. Lady Macbeth has nothing on Elaine Hunnicutt."

"I heard that," Nell sneered.

"Did you, dear? How splendid for you." Mother took her time in turning the key in the lock.

When Nell was finally let loose—looking a bit frazzled as she pushed back a fall of straw-colored hair, her feathered hat sagging off to one side—she pointed at each of them in turn. "You all deserve to be in Bedlam!"

Then she stormed off, marching toward the front door and passing Althea on the way.

"Don't tell me I've missed all the excitement again," Thea groused, stomping her stockinged foot.

She was a beauty in her own right, favoring their mother in form and feature, with curling mahogany hair and sooty eyelashes so thick they could start a hurricane with two blinks. More than half the men in Addlewick were in love with her. But she only had eyes for her plays.

"Serves you right for leaving me alone with them," Honoria muttered. When a throat cleared behind her, she turned to the countess, who arched a rather intimidating silver brow. "Not that I mind, of course. It's simply that, with Thea at the ripe age of nineteen, all the talk of Seasons and matchmaking ought to be directed at her."

"I'd love to go to London," her sister volunteered, bouncing on the balls of her feet. "Just imagine all the stationers I could visit. Not to mention all the juicy gossip for my plays. And I'm certain that something thrilling would happen every day. Whereas, in Addlewick, my muse is dying a slow, agonizing death."

"You see? She's more than eager to go. And Mother could certainly spare her, especially after she brought the piglets into the drawing room last week."

"Only because I learned my lesson with the chickens. And besides, it gave my pastoral comedy an aura of authenticity."

Mother cleared her throat and cast a disapproving

glance to her youngest. "I'm not certain that London is quite prepared for Thea. You, on the other hand . . ."

The muscles along Honoria's nape and shoulders tightened. Another Season of being courted? Wooed with promises she didn't care to hear? Gifts that . . . well, actually she quite liked the gifts.

However, another Season meant more expectations that she had no intention of meeting. Because she had no intention of marrying. Ever.

The sound of three succinct knocks reverberated through the house, seeming to penetrate her skull as if someone were hammering down the final nail in her coffin. *Whack. Whack. Whack.*

Backed into a corner, she knew that there was only one way to win this argument. One way to drop this matter for good. She would have to invoke the name of Viscount Vandemere.

Even so, one could not simply blurt out the name of a man one has invented—more or less—throughout one's life. No, indeed. Such an incantation should never be employed lightly.

Like a well-delivered line in a play, one must speak the name with reverence as if holding on to the dream of him. One must convince the audience that, no matter what odds stand in the path of happiness, the heart will always yearn for him and him alone.

"Mother, you are right, of course. And I would be honored to have the opportunity to be sponsored by Lady Broadbent." She smiled at both of them, letting them have one last glimmer of matrimonial hope. And then she issued a perfectly executed sigh. "But I fear it would come to naught. As you know, I'm already betrothed. And Grandmother made certain that it was a binding contract which only death could sever. In truth, I cannot lawfully marry any other man aside from—"

"I beg your pardon, but there is a caller for Miss Honoria," their butler announced, his wizened eyes wide as saucers above a beak of a nose. "A gentleman."

"I shouldn't know why you appear so shocked, Mosely," Thea said on a slow exhale, the shoulders within her primrose day frock sagging with eternal ennui. "There is always a gentleman calling for Honoria. And aside from Verity eloping with Longhurst, nothing truly inspiring ever happens in this house. We might as well be living the same day over and over again."

Mother ignored their resident diva. "And does this gentleman have a name?"

"He does, indeed, ma'am. However, it seems . . ." Their butler swallowed and blinked as if to clear cobwebs from his vision.

The hesitation filled the hall with palpable anticipation. The air fairly crackled with it.

For reasons unbeknownst to Honoria, the fine gossamer tendrils against the nape of her neck lifted. A terrible suspicion skittered over her nerves. One that would explain why Mr. Mosely appeared as though he'd just spoken to a ghost.

But no. It couldn't be, she thought. *It isn't possible.*

A shadow shifted behind their usually implacable butler. It filled the archway, blocking out the light filtering in from the foyer as it limned a silhouette.

An impossibly familiar silhouette.

The weight of dread plummeted to the pit of her stomach like a stone through water. And when the figure approached, she knew . . . she just knew . . .

"Viscount Vandemere, at your service," the caller said in a voice like raw silk as he bent his dark head in a low, courtly bow.

Mother and the countess both gasped.

Thea withdrew a notebook from the pocket of her dress. "Now, *this* is interesting."

But Honoria, who usually excelled in the art of improvisation, wasn't certain what to do.

This wasn't any viscount. This was Mr. Flint, a conniving and ruthless gambler. And by the wolfish gleam in his gaze when it alighted on her, she knew he'd come to collect a debt.

Her heart faltered, stopped, then started up again, the beats too fast to count. And there was a buzzing in her ears.

This stranger knew far too much. Things her family didn't know. *Couldn't* know. Things that would plunge the Hartley name back into scandal, and they hadn't even recovered from the last one yet.

She needed a moment to think.

The problem was, everyone's attention was now trained on her as if she were center stage.

The stage, she thought. Of course!

Years ago, her mother had taught her a simple tool to redirect an audience's attention when a scene wasn't going quite to plan. "When in doubt, my dear, faint."

So that's precisely what Honoria did.

Chapter Two

꧁

HONORIA HAD PRACTICED the art of fainting countless times.

To deliquesce with the perfect blend of grace and drama, there was a proper way to arrange one's limbs to minimize injury. Bruising was inevitable, but one must suffer for one's art, after all.

And yet, as she let her bones fall slack and sank to the floor, she never felt herself hit.

Instead, she was gathered up into someone's arms. *His* arms, to be precise. There was no mistaking that strong, secure hold. No mistaking that evocative scent that transported her to a single night in Paris in one heady rush. And no mistaking the moths.

Those pesky little insects were back.

She'd tried to keep them dormant, locked in a jar . . . but they suddenly took flight.

A frustrated sound rumbled in her throat.

She heard a low chuckle in response before he murmured in her ear. "Did you miss me, Signore? Is that why you were longing to be in my arms again?"

At once, her eyes flew open. Then she shut them abruptly before anyone else saw through her pretense.

But the glimpse was long enough for her to catch the smirk on his mouth *and* for her to realize that she'd been wrong about one thing in Paris.

Flint's eyes weren't dark. They were a shade somewhere

between ethereal blue and slate gray. The color of the sky as a storm approached. She wondered what tempest he was about to unleash into her life.

A shiver of foreboding snaked down her spine.

Roxana Hartley fretted and fussed, directing the stranger to carry her poor, overwrought child into the morning room. But Honoria had little doubt that Mother was up to something. After all, she'd taught her daughters everything she knew about commanding a stage.

"Just lay her down here, on the sofa, my lord. And Mr. Mosely, would you send to the kitchens for a ewer of fresh water? I'm afraid that a fly has fallen into this one. Thea, fetch your sister's favorite pillow. We want her to be comfortable. And Olympia, if it wouldn't be too much trouble, would you accompany me while I search for a vial of smelling salts?"

"I believe I have a vinaigrette in my reticu—" Lady Broadbent broke off when Mother cleared her throat. Then, with an amateurish exclamation, she continued on haltingly. "Oh . . . dear. It seems I was mistaken. Such a pity."

Inwardly, Honoria rolled her eyes.

Flint lowered her body effortlessly onto the gold damask cushions. She paid no attention to how weightless she felt in the sturdy strength of his arms. None whatsoever. Nor did she acknowledge that her every inhale was filled with amber, sandalwood and *him*.

She had far more important matters on her mind at present . . . like how to be rid of him.

"My lord, we'll be back in a snippet for a more proper introduction after her recovery," Mother said an instant before the graceful, unhurried patter of her retreating footsteps echoed along the corridor.

And just like that, they were alone.

"Damn," Flint muttered under his breath, sliding his arms out from beneath her. And she did not, absolutely not, miss his warmth. "I was afraid of this."

Honoria's eyes flew open to see him standing over her, his dark brows furrowing into a scowl. Which was not the typical reaction she received from men. "Of what?"

"That you weren't lying about all of"—he gestured with an irritated sweep of his hand from her forehead to feet— "this."

Understanding at once, her lips curved in a self-satisfied grin. "Told you I was pretty."

She rose sinuously and stood before him. A surge of feminine power tingled beneath her skin when she saw a flare of male appreciation in those eyes as she adjusted the fall of her dress, smoothing her hands down the trim waist of the apricot chintz and over her hips. *Take that, Mr. Flint.*

A muscle jumped in his cheek. Then he abruptly turned on his heel and stalked away from her, crossing the brightly lit room to stand in the angular shadow beside the parted drapes.

"Why couldn't those mustachios have been yours? And why weren't they hiding a hairy mole the shape of Australia? It really isn't fair otherwise," he said as if to himself as he stared toward the garden, his profile etched in stone.

She narrowed her eyes. "What *isn't fair*?"

"I don't want to be distracted by you again. Your little adventure into the world of highfliers cost me more than two thousand pounds. In fact, I barely escaped Paris with my head."

"You can hardly blame me for the fact that someone wants to be rid of a man like you. I should think that would be a daily occurrence."

He cast a glare over his shoulder. "I may be a gambler, but I pay my debts. Until you, that is. Ever since I had the great misfortune of meeting you, my luck has apparently run out. So I'm here to take back what's mine."

Honoria suddenly understood why he'd arrived on her doorstep. Unfortunately, the knowledge did nothing to ease her disquiet.

"How did you find me?"

"An old friend. The same one who saved my neck." His hand reached up to smooth the folds of his cravat in an absent gesture as he turned away from the window and began toward her again. "When I let it slip that a woman swindled me out of a fortune—"

"*Swindled*," she scoffed.

"—he naturally wanted to know how such a thing was possible. So after sharing a few pints, I told him."

"You *told* him?" She blanched, wondering how many people had heard of the woman who pretended to be Signor Cesario. There were bank accounts in his name. Properties. Her entire future. The discovery of her alter ego would ruin everything.

"Not everything," he said. "After all, I firmly believe that some secrets are sacred and should only be revealed when it's of the best advantage to me."

"Be still my heart. You're a veritable prince charming."

He flashed a grin at her withering glance. "*Viscount*, if you'll recall."

"But we both know you are not."

"Do we? Strange, but after relaying a portion of your tale, my friend took it upon himself to look into this Vandemere fellow. Since you and my friend are part of the same society, he had heard mention of the name. Though, he was surprised to have never met him. Then he discovered some rather interesting information."

Honoria kept her expression impassive. She would not reveal her cards. Not to him.

"Apparently," Flint continued, "there are many tales of the world-traveling adventurer, painting Vandemere as a heroic figure of mythical proportion. If this saint isn't plagued by the need to aid the downtrodden, he is inescapably driven to conquer the next mountain. Due to these circumstances beyond his control, his trek homeward has been delayed, leaving his faithful betrothed forever waiting." He arched a sardonic brow. "In the meantime, he writes letters to her. They've passed through different port cities over the past four years. And yet, no one seems to recall ever meeting Vandemere. Though, by a strange coincidence, there happened to have been a certain merchant sailor—a man by the name of Hawk Hartley—who was in those very ports at the same time."

She swallowed down a rise of dread.

Hawk was her older brother's sobriquet. Truman had been given the pet name when he was young and his unruly brown and gold hair had stood up like ruffled feathers.

When Honoria had asked if he would keep her secret and help her with her ruse, Truman had agreed without question. Never in a thousand years had she imagined that someone would make the connection.

Flint waited for that to sink in. "My friend was intrigued by this. He just happened to know of a family by the name of Hartley and a certain scandal that ruined the fortunes of many members of the *haut ton*."

"My father was proven innocent," she said, hiking her chin a notch higher.

"Yes. I recently read about it in the newspaper. And yet, even with an exoneration in print, there will always be those who'll harbor doubts." A cunning gleam lit those stormy eyes as he stopped a single pace in front of her. "And wouldn't it be just dreadful for your family to be embroiled in another scandal? Even a small one . . . perhaps involving a daughter and a make-believe fiancé? That would certainly cast a rather unfavorable light on the Hartley name. Again."

"You and I both know that you aren't Viscount Vandemere," she hissed, keeping her voice lowered.

"The same way that we are both aware that you aren't Signor Cesario?"

She glanced over her shoulder to the open doorway, grateful to find it vacant. "If you think to blackmail me, then you'll be sorely disappointed. My family wouldn't care a fig to learn that I've dressed in costume. In fact, they've seen me wear one on countless occasions over the years. If you had done your due diligence, then you would know my family is rather famous for our dramatic ability."

Flint didn't even blink. "Be that as it may, I shudder to think what society would presume about a young woman's character when they learn she flits about unchaperoned, immersing herself in a world of men and gambling and . . . whatever else she might fancy during those midnight escapades."

He made it sound so sordid. And the results would be ruinous. One whisper was all it would take, and her entire family would be outcasts once more.

Conchobar Hartley had worked hard to repair the damage done by the scandal. Even though he hadn't been guilty, he'd felt responsible for being the unwitting voice of the true culprit.

It began one afternoon at Tattersall's, with an investment opportunity whispered in her father's ear by a friend. And it wasn't long before his silver tongue proceeded to gain more interest in this speculation.

He didn't know at the time that he was being swindled. Didn't know that every person he'd spoken with would also be cheated out of their fortunes and would soon cast the blame on him. And he most certainly didn't know that the resulting scandal would cost the lives of two men he'd known since boyhood.

Leander Warring, the late Duke of Longhurst, was one of those. Because of that, his son and heir, Magnus Warring, had sworn vengeance against the Hartleys.

At least, until he fell in love with Verity seven years later.

Then, the Fates interceded once again when the true culprit behind the swindle was revealed a few months ago, thus slowly beginning the process of removing the tarnish from the Hartley name. Not only that, but Truman—who'd been driven away by the scandal and forced to earn his for-tune as a merchant sailor—was now returned to the bosom of their family. Both he and their father were in London, finding him lodgings as he moved forward to finally begin his life as an architect.

As for her overly romantic mother, who wanted noth-ing more than for her children to find love, she would be heartbroken to learn that the reason Honoria prepared for a future alone was that she never intended to marry.

But this man—this stranger she had met only once in her life—was backing her into a corner yet again. And this time, she couldn't see her way out.

"You seem to know a great deal about me," she said coolly, refusing to reveal the anxiety roiling inside her. "And yet I don't even know your name."

"You may refer to me as Lord Vandemere, my lord hus-band, darling, dear heart . . ."

"Blackguard, charlatan, devil."

"Such lovely, sharp claws you have, Signore," he said with a grin as he reached out and grasped one of her hands.

An instant shock of sensation trampled through her, rooting her to the spot. The touch caused her pulse to sprint on a haphazard path through her veins, reminding her of the time a squirrel had fallen through the parlor chimney and darted around the room in a frenzy, looking for the nearest exit.

Reflexively, she tried to snatch her hand away. However, his hold was deceptively gentle, those long, tapered fingers encircling her wrist.

He was not about to let her get away. Not this time.

Honoria refused to think about the sensations he caused or the way the pad of his thumb moved in slow, sinuous circles over her harried pulse. And when she met the chal-lenge in his gaze, she ignored the sudden, sharp clench in the pit of her stomach.

"Just tell me what you want."

One corner of his mouth curled like the tip of a snake's tail when it was ready to strike. But instead of telling her, he did something she never expected.

Still imprisoning her hand, he sank on bended knee. This time, when he looked at her, his expression was so tender and open that it stole her breath and robbed her of speech.

"Just you, Honoria Hartley," he said. "In all the time we've spent apart, I've only been living a half life, searching for something I could not name. Yet, from the very moment we met, a sense of certainty filled me. I saw the rest of my days unfold in the heavens reflected in your eyes, and I realized that my life could never be whole without you by my side."

Her pulse started rioting again. An entire family of squirrels zigzagged through her, knocking over the jar of moths in her midriff and sending them all aflutter. And her brain was caught in quicksand, unable to make sense of this declaration.

They were just words, she told herself. A prepared speech. A soliloquy. She'd heard hundreds of them throughout her life.

And yet . . .

She knew his tell, knew the way his thumb absently drifted to the ring on his little finger. But his hold remained steady, his gaze unswerving and no longer mocking.

Had he, too, felt that uncanny shift that seemed to click something into place when their lips had met in Paris? She had tried not to think about it. Had tried for a year to keep her thoughts away from him. Away from that night, that moment, that . . . kiss.

She hated to admit it, even to herself—*especially* to herself—but ever since, she had compared all other kisses to that one. It had irritated her beyond belief. But now? Well, now she felt rather—

Her mother squealed from the doorway.

In an instant, Honoria's senses cleared. Someone might as well have dashed cold water in her face. Dimly, she heard Lady Broadbent sigh and Thea hum with delight, her pencil scratching on a page of her pocket ledger.

A coldness seeped into Honoria's veins as she caught the triumphant gleam in Flint's eyes. The liar had only been performing to his audience. She, of all people, should have known better.

But he was more skilled at the game than she'd given him credit for. And when the great pretender slipped the onyx ring from his finger and held it up to her, she concluded that the stone was as black as his diabolical heart.

Clearly, she'd allowed her thoughts to run amok. But she wouldn't make that mistake again.

So, the gambler wanted to play the role of Viscount Vandemere, did he?

Well, she'd just see about that.

Chapter Three

OSCAR RELISHED THE daggers that his cunning little gambler's gaze hurled at him.

Though, unlike in Paris, the surrounding flesh wasn't painted and powdered to provide a wizened, masculine appearance. Gone were the wiry eyebrows, the tawny wig, mustachios and beard. In their place was hair the color of sunlight spun into strands of silk and a flawless complexion of the finest cream. And in the full light of day, her irises were so blue and fathomless that they reminded him of the Aegean Sea.

In short, she had the face of an angel.

Well . . . almost.

The impish upward tilt at the corners of those eyes, along with a sinfully full mouth and a figure ripe with tantalizing curves, all suggested that her beauty was a gift from both heaven *and* hell.

It was the latter that reminded him not to underestimate her.

Then again, he didn't require any reminder. Ever since this diabolical creature had disappeared into the night with his winnings, leaving him at the mercy of Ladrón's blade against his throat, he'd thought of nothing else aside from ensuring that she paid. And paid dearly.

If it hadn't been for the timely intervention of an old friend, both he and Cardew would have been killed. But his friend had helped them escape and flee to Marseille where they stole away on a cutter bound for Spain.

Along the way, rum and rage had loosened Oscar's tongue, and he'd let a few things slip. Not about a chit dressed as a man. No, he'd never have survived the ribbing from that. However, he had mentioned a femme fatale who'd distracted him for an instant. And he'd cursed her every day since she'd slipped through his fingers.

Listening to Oscar's slurred recitation, his friend had taken particular interest in the name Vandemere. He'd heard it mentioned in passing during his life. Or rather, his *other* life. That was when he confessed that he'd been reared among the *haut ton*. Then he revealed his true identity as the second born son to the late Duke of Longhurst.

Oscar had been gobsmacked by the news. Even though he'd long suspected that there was more than met the eye with the devil-may-care wastrel, who'd always managed to be in the right place at the right time, he had never thought of Rowan Warring as *quality*. A former military officer, perhaps. But the son of a duke? Never.

However, when Warring had explained that he knew of a family with a connection to Vandemere—a family whom he despised, incidentally—Oscar's shock fell away as a plan began to form.

Suddenly, he'd known precisely how to repay Ladrón. And his friend had been more than happy to assist him with this charade.

Which brought Oscar here, pretending to be a long-lost viscount and Miss Honoria Hartley's betrothed. And he couldn't leave until he had her right where he wanted her.

Even though Warring and Cardew had compiled enough documentation to add plausibility to his claim, Oscar needed this betrothal to provide an aura of authenticity to this production.

Unfortunately and predictably, she wasn't making it easy. She dug her fingernails into her palm to prevent him from slipping his ring onto her finger. Clenching her teeth, she hissed, "I never said *yes*."

Undeterred, he stood and pressed a kiss to her knuckles. "But we both know that it is more than a mere betrothal contract that binds us. I can see it in your eyes that you feel it, too."

Murder. It was murder lurking in her eyes.

But this was hardly his first time being the recipient of such a look, so it didn't rattle him in the least. In fact, it only made him more determined to earn every ounce of hatred she could dole out.

She tugged to extricate her hand. Though knowing she would likely dash away without a backward glance and run for the hills, he was reluctant to release her. Instead, he threaded her arm through his and anchored her to his side like a besotted groom.

Then his audience glided into the room, smiles radiant, and Oscar knew that he'd just caught several fish in the same net.

Of course, he had no intention of continuing this ruse long enough to actually marry the trickster, but she didn't need to know that. The fact that he could torment and blackmail her, while being safely hidden in the wilds of Lincolnshire away from Ladrón, was simply icing on the cake.

"Dear me, where are my manners? I'm Lady Hartley. This"—she gestured with a graceful sweep of her arm to the grinning older woman—"is the Countess Broadbent. The girl scribbling in her ledger is my youngest, Althea. But you likely already knew that. Welcome to Hartley Hall, my lord. Oh, but that's far too formal. We will be family soon, after all. You may call me Roxana, and we shall call you . . . ?"

"Oscar," he said, because every good lie contained a kernel of truth.

Honoria's flaxen brows arched, her lips pursing with

anticipatory triumph. "Oscar is an unexpected moniker for a name like yours."

"My mother always called me Oscar. Though, I imagine that with a name like Manford Octavius Rutherford Fairfax, it was just easier."

For the second time that day, he saw her artful expression slip. It was the barest flicker of a frown and pucker of her brow, but he saw it. And he flashed a grin. *Ah, yes, my dear. I've done my research.*

She offered no reply. But what he wouldn't give to be an earwig crawling around inside her skull to hear her every thought. Likely what she wanted to say was unsuitable for polite society. Nevertheless, he relished watching her school her features, hearing the faint creak of her molars grinding.

"Oscar's a fine name," Lady Hartley said, beaming as her gaze slid between the two of them as if they were standing before an altar instead of beside a sofa. "And what does your family think of your sudden arrival after all this time?"

"I haven't been to the abbey yet."

When she gasped in response, he could see that he might have slipped down a notch in her esteem. And since being a convincingly devoted fiancé, who was finally ready to come home to roost was part of his ruse, he had to think quick.

Lifting his shoulders in a sheepish shrug, he tucked his chin a fraction toward his chest in the universal sign of repentance. "I suppose it was bad form. My only excuse is that, because of my father's estrangement from the family, I know naught of them. We are all strangers. Whereas with your daughter, I feel as though I know her better than I know myself." He gazed at Honoria adoringly, watching as shadows swept across her countenance like a black veil as she plotted his early demise. "As if we'd met not long ago, perhaps somewhere in a courtyard, far from here and beneath a star-strewn sky . . ."

She growled.

Lady Broadbent laid a hand over her bosom and sighed. "How romantic. And here I was ready to whisk her away to London. 'Tis fortunate that you arrived when you did."

"Well, I had to ensure that she didn't dash off and marry someone else."

"I shouldn't be too worried. Miss Hartley has rejected dozens of proposals while waiting for you."

"Well, I'm grateful to hear that. When she'd professed as much in her letters, I admit that I thought she was gilding the lily in order to make me jealous. After all, what is a man supposed to think when a woman talks incessantly of her own beauty?" He made a dubious face, earning a snort of laughter from her sister. "But I knew that, even if she had the face of a baboon, it wouldn't have mattered as long as she was my Honoria."

His captive cast him a tight smile. "For your information, the proposals run more in the vein of *hundreds*. I've rejected twelve this week alone."

"My darling, you needn't try so hard. I am here to stay. However, I realize my appearance came as quite the shock to you. Therefore, I will bid you good-day and call on you after I'm settled at Dunnelocke Abbey." He bowed to each in turn. "Until we meet again, my lady, Roxana, Miss Althea, and my steadfast Miss Hartley."

Honoria abruptly blinked away her seething glare an instant before turning to her mother and, with a beatific smile, said, "I'll just walk him out."

Ever the gallant gentleman, he proffered his arm. She accepted but only to dig her fingernails into the woolen sleeve. Considering his wardrobe was as thin as his pockets, he felt the bite of each manicured point.

As they stepped into the foyer, he noticed that the butler had recovered from his shock. Which was either a testament to his stalwart nerves or to the fact that he'd had a good deal of practice with encountering ghosts beneath this roof.

Only time would tell. And as long as Oscar was safe from Ladrón, he had all the time in the world.

When the door closed behind them and they stood between the columns beneath the portico, he breathed in a deep, satisfying breath. The warm summer air was clean, fresh and full of promise. "I think I'm going to like it here. Addlewick has already proved vastly entertaining."

"You won't think so when my brother returns from London. He knows the truth and will do everything within his power to ensure that you don't get away with this."

Oscar clucked his tongue. "It's quite interesting, the things one learns in seafaring cities about the men who sail on merchant ships. I imagine there are sailors who'd rather not have their most diabolical secrets find their way home."

"Why, you despicable arse," she hissed, paling visibly. "How dare you threaten my family. I should have stabbed you when I had the chance."

If he had a farthing for every time he'd heard those words . . . "Surely, you're not afraid of a little challenge, Signore?"

"Ha! You give yourself far too much credit. I break my fast on men like you."

She was so furious that she vibrated with it. An angel draped in tiers of quivering ruffles and puffed sleeves. And there was just something about the way she stepped forward, shoulders back and eyes flashing, that brought out the devil in him.

So before he went to untether his horse, he leaned in close. "I'll return early on the morrow, then."

⚜

OSCAR WASN'T CERTAIN when his love affair with old houses began. Whether it was during his transient childhood or while roaming from place to place as a young man, he couldn't say. All he knew was that the more rambling, timeworn and augmented from generation to generation, the more he felt drawn to it. And Dunnelocke Abbey was no exception.

She was a sprawling gray-stone giantess, lounging on her side amid a verdant blanket of rolling hills with her head pillowed on a thick fall of leafy wilderness, her feet tipping toward a lily pad–dappled lake. At her center, her hips rose three stories and hosted a plethora of slender mullioned windows and a broad recessed doorway of weathered oak.

He left his horse with a young stable hand wandering about. Then, reaching for the large iron ring on the door, he chuckled to himself. For a grand old lady, she certainly had a scandalously placed knocker. But he doubted that the monks who'd once lived there ever thought of this Romanesque beauty as a woman.

Even so, Oscar took special care in rapping on the door.

After a time, when no one answered, he rapped again. Left waiting, he wondered if all the inhabitants had gone out the backside for a frolic or whatever aristocrats did to pass the time. Rapping a third time with more gusto, he offered a silent apology to his new mistress for treating her most ill.

At last, the door opened, swinging so wide it took the hoary butler with it. The rawboned, liveried old fellow teetered off balance. Then, facing the wrong direction, asked, "May I help you?"

"I feel as though that should be my question," Oscar muttered under his breath as he stepped across the threshold and tapped the man on the shoulder. "Viscount Vandemere."

Turning around with a start, the man blinked a pair of cloudy blue eyes as if trying to bat away the mists. "I'm afraid not, sir. There's no viscount in residence for nigh on fifteen years now."

"What I mean to say is that I am Vandemere. Or rather, Manford Octavius Rutherford Fairfax," he said, unable to keep the syncopated rhythm from his delivery. But it was a substantial mouthful. One had to build up a rhythm to make it all the way to the end.

He was just reaching for a calling card when the man-servant shuffled off, disappearing behind the door.

Curious, Oscar followed and watched as the man lifted a tarnished brass ear trumpet from a three-legged stool and summarily held the small end of the funnel to his ear. Apparently, the butler was both blind and deaf.

So Oscar tucked the card back into the silver case he'd pinched in Prague and repeated himself. Thrice.

In the grueling moments of attempted conversation that followed, he learned that the butler's name was Algernon and that the family was, indeed, out the backside. Or rather, having tea on the lawn. And after that inauspicious start, he followed the butler through the entry hall.

But Oscar felt a twinge of disappointment as he took in the sights around him. He didn't know what he expected to find, but it wasn't unpolished and chalky slabs of gray-stone tiles beneath his feet or barren ash-brick walls. Weren't these cloistered monuments supposed to host elaborate tapestries, moldering paintings, threadbare rugs and gargantuan pieces of furniture that could only be moved by an army of Romans?

But this? This was like walking through a mausoleum. The stale, musty odor in the air only substantiated that thought.

Where were the vases of flowers, clove-pricked orange pomanders and lingering aromas from the kitchen that brought a sense of warmth and life to a home?

And for that matter, where were the candelabras, tea-stained doilies and pointless figurines? Even the erstwhile pickpocket in him lamented over the lack of filchworthy bric-a-brac.

His disenchantment only grew as he passed a majestic marble staircase that swept upward from broad treads and curved in a perfect arc to the railed gallery overhead. The structure was doubtlessly designed to be admired as one would a nude sculpture of the female form. However, as he neared, he noted that some villain had marred all that devastating beauty by covering the gracefully curling banister and carved newel post with lacquer. Black lacquer. And, worse, they'd glopped it on with a heavy hand, leaving it to look as though the wood beneath were weeping in fat onyx tears.

Whoever it was deserved to be flogged.

If there was one thing he'd learned from Cardew, it was that a work of art was meant to be celebrated, not concealed.

Sidling up to Algernon, he nearly demanded to know who'd committed this atrocity. But then Oscar remembered that it wasn't his concern. He wasn't the real Vandemere, and he wasn't here to stay. So he simply cast one more disparaging glance at the desecrated staircase and walked on.

After traversing through a short corridor, he was surprised when it opened to a vast, airy chamber. The echoed clap of his bootsteps reverberated up to the vaulted ceilings of the great hall where painted plaster was giving way in hollow blisters from a faded fresco.

It took no leap of imagination to discern that, at one time, this must have been a sight to behold. He also pictured the walls as they might have been, adorned with ornate tapestries providing a welcome warmth to these spartan surroundings.

The far end of the hall resembled a crossroads with arched passageways leading off toward additional wings of the house. Though, from what he'd witnessed thus far, he shuddered to think what other profanities awaited to the north and south.

But that discovery would keep for another time because Algernon kept on a steady, plodding pace, and there was no point in asking the fellow.

Toward the west end, an arched doorway stood open to a wedge of sunlight that gilded dust motes in the air. They descended three steps, the stone timeworn and silken-smooth, their centers as concave as pour spouts on an ewer. They were magnificent.

But Oscar had no time to admire them before he found himself walking into a world of color, so bright and blinding that he had to shield his eyes. It was as though he'd been walking through a gloomy charcoal sketch and stepped into an oil painting, boasting a vibrant landscape of flowers, pruned shrubs and shade trees outlining a flat green carpet of lawn. Making it even more picturesque was a wall of glossy, dark ivy climbing over ancient temple ruins in the distance.

Here, he thought, was where the current inhabitants of Dunnelocke Abbey truly lived, and he tucked that knowledge aside for later.

Algernon continued to lead the way along a flagstone path, bordered by blue and red blossoms spilling from urns and the golden-tipped tufts of tall grasses that sprouted up like fireworks exploding from the ground.

Around the corner, Oscar paused as two tents came into view. They flanked either side of the lawn, the sides tied to slender wooden supports with alabaster drapes billowing like sails in the breeze. He spied the people sitting inside on cushioned bronze chairs and chaise lounges, their attention on the pair playing lawn tennis on opposite sides of a low net.

From what Oscar had seen of the inside, he never would have imagined the inhabitants capable of taking part in a leisure activity. Then again, three of the four women remained charcoal sketches, dressed all in black from hat to hem.

The fabled widows of Dunnelocke Abbey, he mused.

Warring had forewarned him that they would pose his greatest obstacle during this charade. Of the three elder sons who'd inherited the viscountcy, none had survived or left any legitimate issue. Their widows, however, had decided to stay, none of them willing to release whatever hold they had on the place. Or whatever hold the place had on them.

Even so, the juxtaposition of seeing them amid so much color made it appear as though an artist had left the painting partly unfinished.

His approach apparently caught their eyes at the same time, for they all turned in unison. The widows and an older gentleman in gray scrutinized him in return. A low hum of curious exchanges drifted on the breeze as they speculated on whether or not anyone was expecting a caller.

But Algernon answered those queries in short order. His surprisingly resounding voice fell upon the tableau like a thunderclap. "May I present Manford Octavius Rutherford Fairfax, the Right Honorable Viscount Vandemere."

Everyone fell silent. At the net, the ball fell with a muffled thud as the younger man in shirtsleeves and the blonde woman in a yellow dress suddenly turned.

If Oscar had thought that his greeting from Honoria had been chilly, then this could have frozen the Thames.

The first of the black-draped widows to gasp was likely the eldest, if her grizzled and heavily browed countenance was any indication. According to his research, she would be Alfreda, the widow of the eldest son, Sylvester, who'd died in an opium den. Since then, she'd remarried the man in gray beside her, a Mr. Dudley Shellhorn. The two of them lived in the north wing, along with his son from his first marriage, the young man in shirtsleeves at the net. Toby was, by all accounts, eighteen and lacking the wits to attend university, or the money to buy a commission.

The second widow was sharp-angled and scowling. She looked as though her happiest moments were spent stirring a cauldron. This was likely Millicent, widow of the second son, Hugh, who'd died rather mysteriously in a hunting accident while ensconced with his mistress in the Highlands.

The third, and the only one who'd stood, must have been Babette. She bent over to shake out her skirts, offering more than a glimpse of her generous décolletage on display above the bodice of her form-flattering widow's weeds. Then, she gave him a saucy wink.

Voluptuous and flirtatious as a Titian-haired milkmaid, and likely only a handful of years his senior, she bounced across the manicured lawn and wrapped him in a perfumed, exuberant embrace. "Welcome to the family, Manford. Oh, you don't mind if I call you Mannie, do you? I always think that shortened names are so much more . . . familiar," she offered with another squeeze, her hands sliding suggestively lower.

"Oscar," he corrected and politely extricated himself from her tentacles.

Babette was the second wife of the third son, Frederick, who'd died while in the throes of passion inside the carriage on the way home from his brother's funeral. He'd been a viscount for less than a week.

It seemed that whoever held the title never lingered in the land of the living for too long.

Clearing his throat, Oscar addressed the party, including the lawn-tennis pair which he presumed were Shellhorn's son, Toby, and Cleo Dunne, niece and only blood relative of the Dowager Viscountess Vandemere.

"I realize my arrival may seem rather unexpected, especially considering we've never met," he said. "But I hope that our reunion will become a happy one in time."

Alfreda stood and crossed her arms. "You cannot honestly believe that we're simply going to take your word for it. Do you have any idea how many would-be viscounts have appeared on our doorstep?"

"Aye. Do you have any idea how many?" her husband parroted, standing as well.

Oscar shook his head with as much humility as he could manage. "I do not. Though, I apologize greatly for any hardships you've suffered due to my absence. As you know, my father died when I was quite young, and so I never had an opportunity to know much about the family from which he was estranged when he married my mother." Since the absence of a father was something he had in common with Vandemere, it wasn't difficult to sound sincere. "When she died, I was set adrift and left uncertain how I would be received. It was Miss Hartley who moored me to Addlewick, convincing me to find my way here to what remains of my family. I do hope you can forgive my delay."

"Oh, you poor darling," his buxom aunt cooed, wrapping her arms around him as she shoved his head down to her bosom. "Of course you're forgiven."

"Babette, let him come up for air. Don't smother him to death until after we have the truth," Millicent said with the faintest Scottish burr growling at the end of her words as her willowy form rose from where she'd been perched on the very edge of the chair cushion.

Oscar let those words sink in as he was released from Babette's attempted bosom asphyxiation. And for some reason he felt like laughing.

All this time, he'd thought he had to worry about Ladrón trying to kill him. But here? Clearly, he'd have to learn to sleep with one eye open.

Chapter Four

THE WAY HONORIA saw it, she only had two options.

1. Expose Flint for the fraud he was.
2. Murder him.

And since the first option held the possibility of exposing her own secrets, she was leaning more toward the second.

Normally, she wasn't at all bloodthirsty. In fact, even a spill of red silk on stage for a death scene occasionally made her squeamish. But desperate times and a sleepless night called for . . . suffocation? Poisoning? A fall from a great height?

Hmm, more food for thought.

Oddly enough, the answer had been in the betrothal contract all along. The foolproof way out of this entanglement would be for one of them to die. And since *she* had no intention of shuffling off this mortal coil any time soon, it would have to be Flint. Which was the reason she was slipping in through the servant's entrance of Dunnelocke Abbey at dawn.

She was disguised as an aging maid-of-all-work, complete with graying wig and blackened teeth. But it was the frayed eyepatch and the hump over one shoulder that truly added an air of authenticity to her character, she thought with a measure of pride. Not even her parents would recognize her.

She'd been a servant there before and knew her way around the abbey. After all, one must have a foundation in place when building the ideal viscount. So it was no trouble to blend in to the hustle and bustle of belowstairs activity that morning.

Keeping her head down, she picked up a cinder pail and broom, her ears perked.

It was no surprise that everyone was talking about the return of the viscount. Questions arose over where he'd been all this time, wondering if he'd been traveling or fighting in a war. There was also disapproval over the state of his boots, over the fact that his valet would arrive later with his trunks, and the inconvenience of having to promote a footman to the post when they were so short on staff.

Just as Honoria was scuttling past the yawning kitchen archway, she heard a pair of scullery maids debating over his legitimacy.

"Do you reckon it's true, Moll? I mean, if'n 'e really is the viscount, then why'd 'e wait so long?"

"I dunno. But I 'eard from Sally, and she 'eard from Mrs. Todd 'erself, that 'is lordship brought a letter from a cleric at the church what baptized him in Africa. I reckon that's proof enough."

"Then, why'd Lady Alfreda tell the cook to serve the lamb stew last night, when we all know it ain't fit for pigs, let alone quality?"

"Don't be daft, Gertie. It has to do with inheritance, don't it? With a viscount in the flesh 'neath this very roof, the widows can't declare him dead no more. And that's been their plan for nigh on seven years."

"If you ask me, 'e ought to be warned about—"

"Back to work, you hens! All that pecking and chattering ain't going to scrub those pots," the cook shouted.

Honoria startled with a jolt at Mrs. Blandings's booming voice. Before she was caught lurking, she scrambled up the stairs, her pail and broom rattling in the narrow corridor.

This wasn't the first time she'd heard that the widows intended to declare Vandemere dead.

Several years ago, she'd heard a rumor that the dowager viscountess had been corresponding with her youngest son's widow—the actress whose charms had led him to become estranged from his own family. Though, no one had known anything about the letters at all until they'd abruptly stopped. The dowager, fearing the worst, tearfully revealed the correspondence to one of the widows, swearing her to secrecy. Which, of course, guaranteed that the news was fleet of foot.

When it reached Hartley Hall, Honoria knew she had to take action.

She'd been sixteen at the time, and her overly romantic mother had already begun talking about the delights of marriage. Most notably the marriage bed, stating the vital importance of women being equally—if not more so—satisfied than the men they married.

Mother even performed a sock puppet play about it, which featured an illuminating account of the lisping Lord Flaccid, the robust Lord Turgid and the quivering, breathless Lady Content.

The play was quite intriguing to Honoria . . . until she learned that when Lord Turgid was in Lady Content's bedchamber, it sometimes resulted in a child being born some months later.

But she didn't want children. And since having a husband would likely ensure that she did, she wanted nothing whatsoever to do with marriage.

So she'd begun inventing stories and fabricating letters from her adventurous, world-traveling and oat-sewing viscount, essentially clinging to the betrothal contract like a shield. And now that shield was being wrenched from her grasp by a despicable, blackmailing, swindling cad.

She heard the footmen approach and slunk back into a recessed alcove at the end of the corridor. As they carried dishes into the breakfast room, they left the scents of coffee, porridge, bacon and baked breads in their wake. Her stomach grumbled, and she laid a hand over it to muffle the sound.

It was only then that she remembered she'd been too irritated and fretful to eat dinner last evening. In fact, her last full meal had been yesterday morning.

The only thing that was sustaining her was the pot of tea she'd guzzled before leaving at first light. Which, she was beginning to realize as she shifted from one foot to the other, hadn't been the most brilliant idea.

But just as she thought about stealing into one of the unoccupied bedchambers to take care of matters, she heard the parade of footmen leave the breakfast room.

All thoughts of too much tea evaporated as her plan resumed. It was now or never.

She knew that her best method of ferreting out gossip would be to hear it from the widows themselves. From her previous sojourns, she also knew that the ladies were early risers. Doubtless, they would have much to discuss this morning.

However, when she stole into the empty room, she noticed one glaring thing that might give her away.

There had been no fire in the grate. Hence no ashes to sweep.

Drat! She should have thought of that. It had been too warm of late. Even the casement windows of the narrow, paneled room were spread open to let in the morning breeze.

Casting a baleful glance down to her pail, she wished she'd chosen a different prop. But it was too late now. She could hear the sound of footfalls in the corridor.

Hastening to look busy, she kneeled at the hearth and started sweeping out the already empty grate. But realizing that her eyepatch prevented her from seeing the door in her peripheral vision, she switched it to the other side, disheveled strands of her gray wig falling against her cheeks.

To complete her portrayal of this character, she arched her back like a cat, wanting the pillowed hunch she stitched beneath her drab woolen work dress to take center stage in case gazes fell upon her. Though, she wasn't too worried on that account. Most members of the *ton* paid little attention to servants.

". . . the utter inconvenience of his arrival is maddening," Millicent Fairfax was saying as she walked in, her wand-thin figure garbed in black crepe as if her husband had died recently instead of almost two decades ago. With an irritated swipe, she picked up a plate of Sèvres china and dropped a slice of toasted bread onto it. Honoria's stomach issued a mewl of longing. "I have not endured these years simply to be thrown out of my own home."

"*Your* home?" Alfreda Shellhorn scoffed, ruffling the layered frills over the bosom of her black shirtwaist. The women looked as though they were forever in a mourning-attire competition. "Mother Fairfax promised the abbey to us all."

"Solely to keep the memories of her sons alive. I highly doubt she intended for you to bring a new husband home to roost, in addition to his eighteen-year-old son who does little more than empty the larder on a daily basis and moon over Cleo. It's revolting. She's ten years his senior."

"*Twelve*, Cousin Millicent," Cleo corrected as she, too, sauntered into the breakfast room in a plain lavender day frock. She skirted past Alfreda at the buffet, likely not seeing the squint-eyed daggers hurled at her back. "If you'll recall, I'm the same age as Babette. I believe you flung that barb at Uncle Frederick when he first brought her home. 'Why not simply marry Cleo, if you wanted a child bride?'"

As Honoria listened to the vipers of Dunnelocke Abbey, she bit her cheek to keep from laughing. They were a formidable nest, to be sure. And she had little doubt that they would make mincemeat of Mr. Flint and save her all the work.

At least, as soon as they stopped attacking each other.

"That was long ago," Alfreda intervened as she sat at the head of the table with a bowl of porridge. "And I daresay that Frederick learned his lesson."

"What was that about Freddie?" Babette asked sleepily as she toddled in, wearing a crimson-lined black silk dressing gown that did little to disguise her considerable attributes.

"Oh, nothing. Millicent was merely remarking on what a large appetite he'd had."

Babette grinned as she gave into a stretch and a yawn, making an owllike sound. "Hoo! You couldn't know the half of it. Speaking of which, I've been positively famished since dinner. How long are we going to serve Cook's worst dishes to that divine specimen of manhood?"

Honoria frowned. She had a sudden urge to dump ashes over Babette's . . . attributes.

It made no sense. First, because there were no ashes. And second, because Honoria couldn't care a fig how many women found Mr. Flint attractive. Not a single fig. Not even half a fig.

"As long as it takes," Millicent said, as adamant as a colonel ordering the infantry to starve the enemy as she slopped mulled eggs and a rasher of bacon onto her plate. Honoria's midriff issued a woeful honk that sounded like an elk in distress. "And I want him gone, Babette, not lured into your bedchamber."

The broom clattered against the pail, and Honoria hastily croaked out a raspy *Beg pardon* as she finished sweeping. Then she drew a rag hanging from her apron string and began to polish the grate.

The conversation resumed as if she weren't there.

"The fact of the matter is," Cleo said, taking the seat at the opposite end of the table, "we must deal with this interloper together. Dunnelocke Abbey was bequeathed to *my* family in the fifteenth century. It should have remained that way and would have done if not for a greedy lord treasurer who'd come along and tried to force my great-great-grandmother into signing the deed over to him. When she refused, he and his men-at-arms surrounded the abbey and tried to starve her into submission. When that failed, he kidnapped her, forcing her into marriage to make the abbey his. Which he then gave to his son from a prior union." She slammed her fist down, rattling the silverware. "It took more than three centuries before my aunt's father finally held the deed. And he swore that the abbey would never again be stolen from his bloodline and made sure of that when he drew up her dowry contract. It clearly states that, without an heir, the abbey belongs to whomever it is willed."

"Then, it is settled," Alfreda added with a note of finality as she lifted her teacup. "We shall work together to expose this fraud and keep our home."

Babette draped herself over one of the side chairs, a scone clamped between her teeth, as each of them lifted their teacups in turn. "Agreed."

No sooner had they made their pact than the very interloper appeared.

Honoria's breath caught. She didn't expect him to be up and about at such an early hour. Surely that accounted for the sudden quickening of her pulse. After all, a man such as he was supposed to keep shadow hours and lurk in dark places to hide his evil deeds.

"Speak of the devil."

"And good day to you as well, Aunt Alfreda. Aunt Millicent. Aunt Babette. Cousin Cleo," he said baring his teeth in a grin before he turned to lift a plate from the buffet.

He never once let his gaze fall to the maid at the hearth. She was invisible. And since the last thing she wanted was to gain his notice, she finished up her work and scuttled toward the serving room that lay beyond a concealed door in the corner.

"What a lovely sight to encounter first thing in the

morning," he said before Honoria reached the concealed servants' entrance.

She stilled, heart thudding in her ears. Was he addressing her?

Then he continued, "I trust that each member of my adoring family enjoyed a peaceful repose last night since you all seem to be in high color this morning."

"And what is *that* supposed to mean?" Alfreda asked, her voice rising.

Shoulders—and hunch—sagging with relief, Honoria skirted into the slender passageway between the breakfast and dining rooms. She lingered on the other side to peer through the crack from a more discreet distance.

"Nothing other than each of you appear to be in the bloom of health," he said, all innocence. "And I see your appetites have improved since supper, when none of you wanted for more than bread."

Babette trailed her finger around the rim of her cup and looked at him from beneath her lashes. "And how did your night fair, Oscar?"

"Well, after that delightfully mysterious meal, I went to the stables to ensure my horse did not meet with the cook's cleaver." He paused as one of the widows coughed in her tea. "Relieved on that account, I then spent hours with your faithful steward. Regrettably, Mr. Price was unable to locate the accounting ledgers for my perusal. He did, however, inform me of the terms of the will set in place by my grandfather, which stated that—"

"Cease calling him your grandfather. And we are not your aunts. Your kinship, or lack thereof as I suspect, has not been proven," Millicent snapped. "One must wonder what you could hope to gain by this sudden appearance on our doorstep after nearly thirty years of nary a word."

"I've shown each of you the papers and, if needs must, I will have the registry from the church sent here to peruse at your leisure."

"We do not doubt that there was a marriage and a baptism," Alfreda remarked haughtily. "What I doubt is that you are he. There is nothing at all in your countenance that resembles my brother-in-law. And you carry no documentation written in his own hand stating that you are his son."

"The latter would be quite the feat, especially considering he has been dead three and twenty years. Shall I unearth his skull to summon his ghost, do you think? No? Well, then, as for the fact that I do not resemble him, you are the first to comment on it. My own recollections of him are rather vague, and he left behind no miniature for me to cling to in my youth when I was in need of his guidance."

The words fell from his lips with an insouciant air. And yet, Honoria heard the faintest strain in his voice, a trace of tightness around the vowels that only an actor drawing on firsthand experience might call upon when delivering a line.

It made her wonder how much this man might have in common with the real Vandemere.

Then again, Flint's acting ability might simply have been better than she imagined.

"I had been hoping to find his portrait hanging in the gallery. But I found none," he continued, casually lifting the silver cloches from the platters on the buffet.

Cleo issued an offhand sniff. "My uncle was a rather unforgiving sort and had every surface bearing cousin Titus's likeness destroyed when he married that . . . that *actress* and brought shame to the family."

Honoria took exception to that insult and narrowed her eye at the back of Cleo's head.

"Ah, yes, because there was no shame at all in having an opium-eater, adulterer or libertine in the family already," he said dryly.

"How dare you!" Alfreda and Millicent said in unison.

"And at least an actor could deliver a more clever line," he added, warding off their slings and arrows with a shrug.

Begrudgingly, Honoria had to give him credit for the way he'd put them in their places.

"As I was saying," he continued, lifting the plate to sniff the food and apparently believing it was edible, he moved to the far side of the table and sat down. "Grandpapa's will states that, in the event no male heir could be found, the Dunnelocke Abbey demesne would revert to the dowager viscountess as it had been before he acquired the property in her dowry contract. Though, one must wonder if dear Grandmama has mistakenly promised the property to each of her sons' widows."

"*Mistakenly?* Why, you—"

"Millicent, sit down," Alfreda said. "He's merely baiting us."

He raised his teacup. "Testing the waters, shall we say."

"Then, I will politely inform you that you're in over your head. Unless you can produce definitive proof, I'm afraid we're going to have you taken to gaol."

"Oh, dear. I think my betrothed will be quite disappointed by that."

Honoria resisted the urge to scoff.

Cleo scoffed for her. "And what, pray tell, does Miss Hartley have to do with any of this?"

"Surely you know that she and I have been corresponding for years. That is how I was able to find each of you. In her letters, she kept me abreast of all the comings and goings at the abbey and any rumors regarding my family." He reached for the marmalade. "You see, *she* was able to prove definitively who I am. I'm certain any court would take that into account, in addition to the supporting testimony of her new brother-in-law, the venerable Duke of Longhurst."

Of all the nerve! Honoria seethed. Why that rotten blackguard, using her sister's husband in order to continue his deception.

Well, there was just one thing to do—find his secrets and use whatever she could against him.

Chapter Five

❧

*H*ONORIA TOOK THE servants' passage to the back stairs and up to the second floor.

A pair of housemaids standing by the linen cupboard were ensconced in speculation over the reason the widows had put Mr. Flint at the end of the hall in a drafty old room that overlooked the stables. As Honoria scuttled by, she grinned to herself.

Served him right. The blackguard deserved nothing but misery.

Stealing inside his chamber, she closed the door with a quiet click and leaned against it, taking in the spartan surroundings.

Now what? she wondered, wishing she'd brought a venomous snake to slip beneath the moth-eaten coverlet. Or anything, really. Yet, as she stood in the quiet space where he'd slept the night before, it dawned on her that she hadn't come prepared to commit murder. Then again, how could anyone summon an appetite for homicide on an empty stomach?

She sighed and decided to search for damning evidence to use against him instead. After all, if he was going to blackmail her, then she would blackmail him right back.

Setting down her pail, she went to his bedside table and found a book, the woven red cover worn so thin that no printing or markings of any sort remained. The first leaf held the title, *Awildian Palace*, in block print, but there was no author.

Unfamiliar with the title, she was curious about what would have drawn Flint to choose this from the abbey's library. Though, considering it was on the bedside of a scoundrel, it was undoubtedly something risqué. So, of course, she turned the page.

She was surprised to discover that it was a book of verse.

The tumbledown mystic of castle walls
Amidst the hoary frost of early morn

Charmed by the beginnings of a fanciful story, she felt a grin tug at her lips. Flint read poetry? It made him seem so cultured, perhaps even idealistic . . . as if he cared about more in this world than ruining her life.

A rush of irritation filled her as she closed the book with a snap. How was she supposed to kill him now that he had depth?

Not that she could have gone through with it. But it was the idea of being able to do it that had filled her with a sense of control over this dratted situation.

"There has to be something here that I can use against him that won't damn me in the process," she muttered, absently setting down the book.

Unfortunately, her inner marauder was sorely disappointed. He had few possessions to pilfer. But she left no stone unturned.

Pausing by the washstand, she examined his razor, poked at his shaving soap. Her fingertip came away with a faint residue of froth. It had a pleasant, spiced scent that curled low in her belly. An image of him standing there shirtless at his morning ablutions drifted into her mind.

It wasn't until she caught herself distractedly dragging the soft bristles of the brush against her lips that she realized her thoughts had bolted away from her like a pair of Thoroughbreds on Rotten Row.

She abruptly reined them in and put the brush back.

Crossing to the wardrobe, she found only one change of clothes: a coat neatly brushed, trousers pressed, cashmere waistcoat, shirtwaist and cravat freshly laundered. And yet the scent of him still lingered in the fine weave, especially near the open collar and—

Suddenly, she heard a throat clear behind her. An all-too-masculine throat.

Flint. And he'd just caught her bent at the waist with her head buried inside his wardrobe.

Then again, he hadn't caught *her*. Not really. He'd discovered a maid-of-all-work. So there was only one thing she could do in a situation like this: put on a convincing performance.

Continuing her ruse, she grabbed the rag at her waist and began to scrub the wardrobe doors as she closed them.

"Beggin' yer pardon, milord," she said in the cracked voice she also used to portray the witches in the Scottish play. "Thought to shine yer boots for ye."

"I'm wearing the only boots I have at present. However, since you seem so determined . . ." Flint walked over to the small hearth and propped one booted foot on the stones.

She bristled. The very thought of lowering to her knees to perform such a menial task on that cad made her blood boil.

But what else could she do? If she refused, he could easily accuse her of trying to steal from him, take her by the arm and drag her downstairs to be dealt with. If he did, she didn't know how she would get away without revealing herself.

So keeping her one exposed eye lowered, she shuffled over. Staying in character, she issued a smattering of grunts and groans as she sank to her knees. Rag in hand, she roughly scrubbed the top of his boot.

When she made an impatient gesture for him to lift the other, he paused to consider. "Hmm . . . there's a bit more along the stitching. Work your fingernail into it. Some spit will give it a good shine."

And just like that, murder was back on the menu.

"Done and dusted," she muttered when she finished. Oh, and she was so finished with him!

Standing, she snatched up her pail and went to the door.

But just as she reached it, a hand fell on the wooden frame above her. Then a steely arm snaked around her waist and turned the key in the lock.

"You aren't fooling anyone, Miss Hartley."

"Dunno any Miss 'artley. Just goin' about me work. That's all."

His responding chuckle was low and deep in her ear and sent a shiver trampling through her as his warm body pressed against her. She drew in a breath, his scent invading her nostrils in a dizzying rush.

"You're clever." Without warning, he spun her around to face him. Before she even knew what he was doing, he slipped his fingers inside the neck of her shapeless dress and patted the pillow that served as her hunch. "But not quite clever enough."

The basting stitches gave way with the barest tug of resistance. He tossed the lopsided thing over his shoulder and onto the floor.

"Blimey! Where'd that come—"

He cut her off. "Utter another syllable of denial and I'll strip you down to your skin to prove you are no charwoman."

"I don't—"

His large hand splayed over her waist, coasted up along her rib cage and settled with unerring accuracy just beneath the gusseted cups of her corset.

She gasped, her one-eyed gaze flying up to his. Surely, he wouldn't dare. Oh, but by the ruthless gleam in those stormy depths and that slow smirk bracketing one side of his mouth, she knew that he would do any damnable thing he liked.

Or he'd try, she thought, preparing to lift her knee.

But as if he'd read her mind, he shifted to the side. Using the bulk of his left thigh and hips, he pinned her to the door. Then his large hand altered course, sliding around her ribs toward her back.

Before she'd even managed to lift her hands to his chest to try to push away, he'd already untied her gray apron. His fingers glided toward the fastenings, his touch skimming the bare skin at her nape.

She swallowed. A plethora of unwanted sensations galloped through her—none of them fear or loathing. At least, she didn't think so. The feel of his body, so hard against her, made her somewhat sleepy. A peculiar drowsiness settled into her limbs, and she had the mortifying urge to sag against him.

"Now, either you tell me why you're here," he said, his other hand flipping up her eyepatch so that she was forced to look into his stormy gaze, "or I'll continue what I've started. And I want the truth, Honoria."

She hated him. Hated the way he said her name. Hated that his tone was low and intimate and seemed to reach a place deep inside against her will. Hated that his warm breath brushed her lips as his tongue caressed each syllable in a way that made her crave the feel of his mouth on hers.

Splaying her hands over his chest, she tried to put distance between them. "I came here to murder you."

Her confession drew a pleased curl at the corner of his mouth. The crook of his finger settled beneath her chin, his thumb coasting along the underside of her bottom lip, making it feel plump and tingly. As if he could sense it, he leaned in.

She shouldn't let him kiss her. Shouldn't let him ease the unwanted ache with the firm pressure of his lips.

Dimly, she saw her own hands curl around his lapels. A breath stalled in her throat, anticipation thrumming inside her like a promising rumble of thunder when the garden was in desperate need of a quenching rain.

"Mmm . . . I do enjoy a woman who knows precisely what she wants."

"How splendid for you. But if you think I'm going to kiss you again, then you're sorely mistaken," she said and honestly tried to mean it.

His brow furrowed. *"Again?"*

"Just like in Paris." Her reminder was met with a blank stare. "I daresay I must have scrambled your wits quite soundly."

She'd heard other men declare as much after stealing a kiss from her. She, on the other hand, had always been left utterly unmoved.

Until the night she'd met this scoundrel and felt . . . well . . . *not* unmoved.

"You are delusional, madam. We've never kissed. The only noteworthy incident I recall is when you kicked me with your gargantuan foot and nearly hobbled me."

She blinked as he straightened and glanced down at her feet.

Wait a moment. Did he truly not remember?

It didn't seem possible. At the very least, the mustachios would have left an impression. Let alone the startling contact of their lips. The way they'd fit together. And there was the moment when their combined exhalations had melded and the kiss seemed almost . . .

She didn't allow herself to finish that thought. All the pleasant heat thrumming through her body turned frigid.

"Is that really the size of your feet, or are you stuffing your boots with straw?"

Was that all he could think about? Her *feet*?

Honoria refused to be offended. It didn't matter that he thought she had large feet. The truth was, she did have large feet for a woman, but she liked herself just the way she was. She certainly didn't require his approval.

"You know, you're the first man to ever comment on them. Which is a shame, really. Just once I'd like someone to be impressed—astounded, even—that I've managed to walk and dance with superior grace on these replicas of the Colossus for the majority of my life."

"Well, that is quite the feat, isn't it."

"Was that your idea of a teasing quip? I think you're better off playing the part of a wretched gambler."

A warning light flared in his eyes as he leaned in to whisper, "Be careful, Signore, or you'll find out just how good I am, at a great many things."

As he spoke, his lips brushed the vulnerable shell of her ear, the searing heat sending one last lick of sensation through her, before he took a step back and turned away.

She told herself that her knees weren't wobbling. She simply preferred to lean against the door.

Oscar began to prowl the room, ensuring that all his belongings were where he'd left them. Frowning, he slipped the book of poetry into the inner pocket of his coat and cast her an accusatory glance. "Find what you were looking for?"

"Where you're concerned, I'm only interested in one thing."

His brow arched rakishly, and his gaze swiveled to the bed.

Honoria huffed. "I meant your untimely death."

He clucked his tongue. "Not here to fulfill your promise of breaking your fast on me, then? Perhaps another time. Although, if you are planning to return under the cloak of darkness to do your evil deed, then I feel I should warn you." He paused to shrug out of his coat. "I sleep in the nude."

When he began to unbutton his waistcoat, she wondered if he intended to prove it to her right then and there. He seemed to be under the impression that all debutantes were missish creatures. Clearly, he hadn't been paying attention when she'd explained that she'd spent a good deal of time disguised as a man to infiltrate their world. Hardly anything shocked her now.

Except for the fact that he didn't remember their kiss.

"I highly doubt I'd encounter anything worth lighting a candle for," she said, feeling the need to even the score.

And yet as he peeled off the waistcoat, she was unabashedly intrigued. A warmth spilled into her midriff, settling low as her gaze skimmed over the delineation of muscles revealed beneath the fine lawn of his shirtsleeves. His torso appeared firm, his stomach flat, waist and hips narrow, lending the eye to fall naturally to the front fall of his formfitting breeches.

Then she heard him chuckle.

"You are such a stubborn creature," he said, crossing the room to his wardrobe. "I have no doubt that you would watch me strip bare just to prove a point."

"And you would do so to prove yours."

But she felt a blush creep to the surface of her skin as she realized that he was right. She would have watched him. Though, not to prove a point. Simply because she couldn't seem to help herself. Even now, her gaze followed him, admiring his finely honed backside.

Distractedly, she wondered why men wore such long coats. It seemed rather unfair.

"Pity that I have no time to indulge you. I am on my way to see the dowager viscountess and did not want to wear the coddled eggs that my dear aunt threw at me." Then he turned back, that insufferable grin lingering on his lips as he shrugged into his cashmere waistcoat. "But I'd like to thank you for shining my boots and making them more presentable. Would you like to button me up, as well? It would be good practice for when we are wed."

Honoria realized that she should have brought a knife. Or a rope. Possibly a club. After all, if one intended to commit murder, one must come prepared.

Then again, she could simply bash him over the head with her pail. *Now, there's a thought.* "We will never marry. I will find a way out of this. You will be left floundering, *without* the help of my family's connections to a duke."

"I see murder lurking in your eyes again. You should learn to quell those tendencies," he said, then lifted his hands in a gesture of surrender when she gripped the handle of her pail and advanced on him. "In my own defense, I used Longhurst's name because I needed leverage. If you think about it, I'm sure you'll realize that both of us say the things we need to in the moment. That is how people like us have learned to survive."

Like us? Honoria scoffed, appalled and ready to rail at him.

And she would have, too, if not for the flash of naked honesty on his face before he turned to close the wardrobe door. She'd been about to declare that they were nothing alike. That she only lied to ensure her own future. To protect herself. To live.

But that's what he was doing, too.

Of course, he had a more underhanded way of behaving. Yet, would her family not think the same of her if they knew how she had deceived—was still deceiving—them?

She didn't want to think about the answer.

"Leave my family out of our bargain," she said curtly. "And unlock this door."

Sliding the last button through the hole, he gave her an amused look. "I'm not the one holding the key. You are."

"I saw you take—"

She stopped when he glanced down to the pocket of her sagging apron. He couldn't have. She would have known . . . would have felt . . .

She reached in and her fingers wrapped around the filigree head of a brass key. Apparently, she could have left at any point.

Pivoting sharply, she put the key in the lock. But before she could turn it, she felt him behind her once more, his movements stealthy as a panther.

"Perhaps," he began as his thieving fingers stole over her fastenings to set her back to rights, "you simply didn't want to admit that you chose to stay in here and watch me undress. I'd be happy to oblige you next time."

"You are despicable," she said, ignoring the flush spreading over her cheeks when his breath stirred the downy hairs at her nape. She hated that her pulse quickened. Hated the flutter rising in her midriff.

Clearly, she had a stomach full of demented moths.

Skirting around him, she snatched up her hunch from the floor and tucked it beneath her arm. Then, with the dignity of a queen, she flipped down her eyepatch and made a somewhat less than grand exit.

Her plan had failed miserably. She was no closer to being rid of him than before, and she absolutely hated that he'd bested her.

She would have to redouble her efforts. All she needed was a new plan of action.

Surely, it wouldn't be too difficult to—

"Oh, and Miss Hartley?"

She nearly leaped out of her skin when Flint suddenly whispered in her ear as she reached the servants' stairs. Whipping around to glare at him only made him grin.

"Be prepared," he said ominously. "I'm going to take you on a picnic tomorrow."

Before she could utter a caustic refusal, along with a threat to tie a bell around his neck, he was gone like a puff of smoke, disappearing around the corner.

A picnic? If he thought that she would even consider an outing with a man who . . .

Her thoughts trailed off as an idea occurred to her.

While Mr. Flint may have an uncanny ability to see through her disguises, he hadn't been so self-assured yesterday in the morning room.

Hmm . . . she wondered if her best disguise was no disguise at all. He was just a man, after all. And perhaps all she needed were her natural feminine wiles to ferret out the information she required to be rid of him for good.

Chapter Six

❧

$\mathcal{T}$HE FOLLOWING DAY, Oscar knew Honoria was up to something. He'd known it from the instant he'd arrived at Hartley Hall and she'd greeted him with a heart-stopping smile as she'd sauntered down the stairway in a dress the color of seafoam. And now that they were situated beneath the elm at the top of this hill, there was something all too cunning in those Aegean-blue eyes as she arranged an assortment of tasseled pillows over a raft of fringed shawls.

The siren was, most decidedly, up to something.

All would be revealed soon enough, he thought. But she was about to discover that *he* was steering this ship. She wasn't.

In the meantime, he just wanted to relax and enjoy some edible food for a change. Or, at least, he hoped it would be edible.

His last bite of anything remotely palatable had been the single forkful of bacon he'd had yesterday morning . . . before Millicent had brought her fist down onto the table and upended a spoon of coddled eggs at him. Then, last evening, the cook served a sort of grayish fish after the first course of gray soup, followed by an aspic of something mysteriously cloudy. And he was convinced that the main course had been the sole of a boot.

This morning, the breakfast room had been empty, the widows having chosen to dine in their rooms. And beneath a cloche on the buffet had been a putrid gray sludge.

Apparently, the widows were trying to starve him into retreating. And yet, as he warily peered into the hamper of picnic fare he'd requested from Mrs. Blandings, he wondered if each dish had been sprinkled with arsenic.

Then again, a little rat poison might improve the flavor.

On second thought, he turned his attention to the smaller basket stuffed with straw. "I wonder if the wine survived. Though, if it did, it wasn't with any thanks to my driver."

"Indeed," she said, her gaze passing from Hartley Hall's hamper to where her maid was sitting near the carriage down the hill and looking a rather bilious shade of green, even from this distance. "However, it does point to the reason the widows rarely leave the abbey."

"I'm afraid that was for my benefit. Apparently, both the usual driver and the well-sprung landau have taken ill," he said wryly. "Which left the stable hand and that torture chamber we rode in as my only option. Yet another warm welcome from the widows."

"I am surprised that they didn't leave you with two lame horses, as well, so that you would be forced to shoot them and trudge back on foot."

"I doubt they would have provided me a pistol."

A smirk tugged at the corner of her mouth. "No, they wouldn't have done."

"Ah—huzzah!" he said, brushing the straw from the bottle. "Though, I highly suspect that the wine is either a dreadful vintage or the contents are merely leftover violet dye from the laundress."

"It could not be worse than mine. This will be more than half water." With a wry shake of her head, she held up the pale, faintly pinkened liquid from her own basket. "Our cook believes that we're all still children. Mother, on the other hand, ensured that these were in the hamper. She calls them Mad Dash—"

Catching the heavenly scent on the breeze, even before

she withdrew the scrap of toweling, he snatched the plate out of her grasp.

"—Biscuits," she concluded as he gobbled up the first.

He closed his eyes on a sigh of pleasure. Then he proceeded to inhale five more of the sweetly spiced, buttery bits of crumbly perfection before coming up for air. Her light laugh his attention, and he begrudgingly offered her the plate, but she declined with a shake of her head.

"You are welcome to them," she said. "As for me, I try to avoid that particular family recipe."

Mouth full, he eyed the remaining biscuits with suspicion. "Why is that?"

"Fear not. There's nothing wrong with them. It's just that Mother claims they have the power to make a couple fly off to Gretna Green."

He swallowed in relief. "Is that all?"

"I prefer to stay far afield of anything relating to matrimony." She watched him devour two more, her head tilted slightly to one side as she studied him. "How long have you had such a fondness for biscuits?"

Aaand there it is, he thought, his suspicions prickling when he saw that smile return.

Setting the plate aside, he brushed a few errant crumbs from his cravat. "I'd wondered when it would begin."

"When what would begin?"

"The seemingly innocuous small talk that leads into probing questions. Though, I hardly think the answer regarding biscuits will give you leverage over me. And that is your ultimate design, is it not? To find a way to send me packing?"

She rolled her eyes. "Oh, yes, of course. I fully intended to take the empty plate of biscuits, along with the secret knowledge I'd gleaned, directly to the magistrate. Honestly, are you incapable of engaging in polite conversation? And no, that wasn't an actual question, in case you were wondering."

Heaving out a sigh, she shook her head and went back to sorting the contents of their picnic.

Atop a sunny woolen shawl, she laid out the dishes from her basket: hard-boiled eggs, roasted fowl, mutton chops, sliced tomatoes, and assorted pastries, cheeses and breads wrapped in cloths. But she piled the congealed calf's head and various gray foods from his basket off to the side. Which he didn't mind in the least.

What he did mind, however, was that the smile was gone from her face, and along with it their easy camaraderie.

In his own defense, his deflection had been a reflex. A knee-jerk reaction.

"Tell you what," he said, trying to lighten the mood as he wrenched the cork from the abbey's wine. "I'll be first to drink this, and if I die, then all the better for you."

"Fine."

That word, spoken in that ice-pick tone was most certainly not *fine*.

Bloody hell. He supposed answering one question wouldn't be the death of him.

"Today," he said reluctantly. "Today is when I discovered I have a fondness for biscuits. There. Are you happy?"

Her flaxen brows drew together, making them appear as though they were caught by an invisible thread to form the most delicate of furrows. "You've never had biscuits before?"

He'd smelled them before. Lots of times. He remembered being chased away from a town house for sneaking up from the mews to peer through a kitchen window.

He'd been about six or seven when he'd spied a plump cook in her apron, taking biscuits out of an oven and placing the cooled ones on a plate that rested on a trestle table. When her back was turned, a boy and a girl in fine clothes, sitting on stools and swinging their feet, would steal a few and dunk them in their tea. They'd gobbled them up before the cook pretended she'd just caught them, fondly wagging her finger.

But ogling from afar was all he'd done as a lad. Confections had never been a priority. Back then, he'd known that, if he was going to steal anything, it had better be meat or money. Or something he could pawn for money.

In the years after Cardew came along, they'd stayed in places that served fancy tarts, iced cakes, and rum-soaked puddings set ablaze. And there had been biscuits all tied in a box with string. Even broken pieces served in a cone by some shops. But those never tempted him. They didn't fit the picture that had lingered in the back of his mind like a forgotten trunk in the attic.

"No," he answered, leaving it at that.

She eyed him as he reached across the shawl for the glasses she'd unearthed. "Hmm . . . It will be a challenge, but somehow I will devise a way to use that information for nefarious purposes."

"If anyone could, I'm certain it would be you."

"There's a compliment buried in that muttered statement, I'm sure of it."

After she set the empty hampers aside, he glanced over just as she lifted her arms to remove the pins from her straw hat. The action drew his attention to the graceful lines of her form, down the elegant column of her throat, over the lovely expanse of creamy skin and soft swells rising above the hint of lace peeking out from her snug bodice. And when a breeze stirred through an artful coil of flaxen curls, he caught a scent that made his mouth water as he imagined—

"How is the wine?"

Her question yanked his attention back to the bottle in his grasp . . . just in time to stop him from overflowing his cup. Muttering a curse at the few droplets that splashed onto his fingers, he then took a few thirsty gulps as if that had been the intention all along. "It'll do."

"Or the poison could have a delayed effect," she offered sweetly. "Either way, you'd be the first to go."

"Oh, but I always believe in ladies first."

Handing her a glass, he saw her bemused expression. But before she could ponder too long on his salacious double entendre, he touched his rim to hers and drank again.

Her shoulders lifted in a shrug after she swallowed. Granted, it wasn't the best vintage, but it served the purpose of quenching the palate on a warm day. Setting her cup aside, she began piling various foods on a pair of blue-and-white porcelain plates.

"With two baskets between us, we are dining in the true spirit of picnicking," she said blithely, handing a plate to him. "My parents were once part of a theater troupe, and they attended the Pic Nic Society gatherings brought here by the French. At these parties, each guest was expected to contribute to the meal with food and wine. Afterward, there would often be a bit of theater *and* a bit of gambling."

"Interesting," he said. "However, I did not bring any cards."

"Nor I, and all the better for you." She looked at him through her lashes, then flashed an impish grin right before she tossed an olive in the air and caught it between her teeth.

He felt a grin tug at the corner of his lips, enjoying her easy manner. She was a woman comfortable in her own skin, and he liked that. More than he ought. And when she sat back amidst a ripple of seafoam ruffles, she appeared every inch the siren who could lure careless men to their deaths . . . especially when the tip of her pink tongue darted out to lick the salty brine from her lips.

Oscar shifted and thought it best to change the subject to something less stimulating than the games they could play.

"You seemed familiar with the abbey. How many times have you been there in your disguise?"

"A few," she said, nibbling on the end of a broad celery stalk in a way that made him forget what he was eating. "They are forever in want of servants because no one wants to work for three demanding mistresses. So it is simple to blend in. Even though one might imagine wearing an eye-patch would only gain notice, actually the opposite is true."

"Because no one wants to look directly at a person with a disfigurement. It makes them uncomfortable."

She pointed her celery at him. "Ah, so you've worn one, as well."

"A time or two."

She smiled at him as if delighting in their shared secret, her eyes bright. And for an instant, he had the compulsion to share more secrets with her.

He wouldn't, of course. He wasn't an idiot. But the mere desire to do so filled him with a sudden restlessness, tightening like a fist in his gut.

Instantly suspicious of the sensation, he looked down to his half-empty plate. Had the roast pheasant come from his basket or hers?

Not wanting to take any chances, he decided to drink more wine instead. But when he offered to fill her glass, she put a hand over it and shook her head before reclining gracefully on one elbow.

Turning her face toward the sky, she closed her eyes and sighed contentedly.

He wasn't certain if it was the third glass of wine, the gentle summer breeze kissed with the essence of freshly baked biscuits, or the way the dappled sunlight filtered through the leaves overhead and brushed the tips of Honoria's golden lashes, but a sense of peace fell over him, dispelling that momentary restlessness.

"I saw you with the dowager viscountess yesterday," she said after a while.

Oscar was so at ease, sitting with his arm lazily propped on his bent knee and distractedly comparing the color of her lips to the last of the wine in his glass, that he didn't take exception to her spying. "Lurking in shadows, Signore?"

"*You* are far more inclined to dwell under cover of darkness, I'm sure."

"So you were hiding in the open, then?"

Her mouth quirked at the corner, and she issued a nonchalant wave with her stalk of celery. "I might know of a few secret passageways. What? You did say we were alike."

"Did I?"

She leveled him with a dark look. "Don't tell me you've forgotten that as well."

Of course Oscar remembered what he'd said in his bedchamber yesterday. A mind like his remembered everything. But he'd spent so much of his life redirecting statements of fact that evasion came as second nature.

He was always playing the game, reading his opponent, assessing their cards. And yet, as he sat on the opposite side of the blanket and saw those blue eyes harden to frozen pools, he felt a tug-of-war begin between his need to be ruthless and his enjoyment of their unusual camaraderie.

"I actually have an exceptional memory," he admitted. That was something only two other people—his mother and Cardew—knew about him.

It wasn't his fault that Honoria took it the wrong way.

"Except for when it comes to Paris," she said cooly.

Disliking the icy wall building between them, he reached across and stole her celery.

"I beg your pardon!" she huffed. But when he took a large bite out of it, she rolled her eyes. "You are such a cad."

Seeing a reluctant twitch at the corner of her mouth, he felt better. Before he eased back again, he tossed the remainder into the hamper so she couldn't torment him each time the stalk disappeared between her lips.

"Is that what you saw yesterday in her sitting room? A cad?" he heard himself ask and wished he could swallow down the words along with the last of his wine.

Just before he'd visited the dowager viscountess, he'd learned that she'd suffered an apoplexy and no longer had the use of the right side of her body. He hadn't known what reaction, if any, to expect when the nurse had introduced him. But it certainly hadn't been the smile he'd received or the tears shimmering in her eyes.

A flood of guilt and panic swept through him. Responding to the animosity from the widows had come as second nature to him. But utter unspoken joy? He had no idea how to react. The last time he'd witnessed an emotion so raw and tender had been when his mother was alive.

Therefore, Oscar did the only thing he could think to do. He'd reached out and smoothed the tears away, her flesh soft and papery as vellum beneath the gentle brush of his thumb. In response, she'd lifted her good hand to cover his, her eyes still shining in a way that made his throat tight.

Uncomfortable, he'd wanted to leave. But because she'd been in that room and left to stare out of a window for untold hours without anyone other than her nurse for company, he didn't have the heart to abandon her.

So he'd slipped the book of verse from his pocket—the only thing his father had left behind—then sat on the window ledge and read to her about Awildian Palace.

"Actually," Honoria said quietly, "I thought you were sweet to her. And patient in a way that many gentlemen wouldn't know how to be."

"My mother suffered an illness. During her final months, she was confined to a sickbed, the life slowly draining from her," he admitted, regret tightening his throat. "When I looked at Lady Vandemere, I imagined all the years she'd lived before and all the suffering she'd endured after losing four sons and a husband. Therefore, I chose to respect the life she once had, and the one she still clings to."

The instant he finished, he wanted to kick himself.

Damn it all! She had done this to him . . . using her wiles, putting him at ease, loosening his tongue. And he'd played right into her hands.

Overhead, the leaves rustled with mocking laughter, and he felt the muscles in his jaw clench. If she dared to utter a word of mockery or to use this information for her own purposes, she would soon learn how ruthless he could be.

When she gave no response, he scowled in her direction and saw that she was turned away, her face tipped to the clouds.

"My apologies," he bit out, the words like gravel between his teeth. "I didn't intend to bore you with my—"

His words broke off the instant he saw her profile and the tear that clung to the tawny strands of her bottom lashes. He didn't know why a breath fell out of him or why that peculiar restlessness returned, striking hard like a fist in the center of his chest. But he couldn't stop himself from reaching out to turn her face toward his.

She glared at him, tried to pull his hand away from her chin as he smoothed that single tear away. "It was a speck of dust, nothing more. Don't you dare harbor any thoughts that your words affected me whatsoever. You are nothing more than a blackmailer and a scoundrel, and your story earned you no favors from my quarter."

"There you go again"—he sighed with an insouciant air as he lowered his hand and leaned back on his elbow— "talking about favors when you really mean *kisses*. My dear, I do believe you are obsessed with the very idea."

"*Ha!* I wouldn't kiss you if you were the last man on earth. You are like an apple that rots from the core out. It may look perfectly tempting on the outside, but once you take a bite, you're sure to come back with half a worm in your teeth."

The desire—no, the bloody *need*—to slide his hand to her nape and draw her mouth to his was almost unbearable. But he'd be damned if he would reveal any more of his cards to her.

So he goaded her instead. "Then you admit it. You find me tempting."

She stood and brushed out her skirts with swift, agitated swipes as if they were on fire. Then she crossed her arms beneath her delectable breasts and tapped her foot. "I should like to return home now."

"And I should like you to pay me £2,000. Shall we see which one of us wins this hand?"

On a growl that would put a lioness to shame, she turned on her heel and began to stalk down the hill.

He crossed his legs at the ankle. Before she could get too far, he called out, "Oh, Miss Hartley?"

She spun around, her brows arched as if expecting him to concede, apologize or do whatever it was that an actual gentleman would do.

He waited a beat, ensuring that she was good and vexed. "Before you send the servants to collect the hampers, would you happen to have any more biscuits?"

He'd never seen a pair of eyes turn the color of a blue flame. But hers did. Incinerating him to ash with a single glance, right before she stormed down the hill.

Oscar could easily catch her.

Instead, he linked his hands behind his head and decided to call his opponent's bluff.

Chapter Seven

ꙨꙨꙨ

$\mathcal{O}$SCAR LOUNGED ON the top of the hill, knowing that as soon as he walked to the carriage she'd give him an earful. After all, someone as beautiful and privileged as Honoria was likely used to having men trail after her.

Well, that wasn't going to be him. And he didn't feel an ounce of guilt over making her wait.

Besides, with all these fringed shawls and tasseled pillows, she'd made quite a comfortable encampment beneath this tree. As he plucked a grape from a platter of assorted fruits and cheeses, his sole regret was that he'd have to leave. Eventually.

A quarter of an hour later, he decided he'd let her stew long enough.

So he stood, straightened his coat and cravat, then sauntered down the hill.

He expected to find Honoria pacing around in high dudgeon. When she wasn't, and all around him was quiet aside from the melodic burble of the creek and the low scuff of a hoof as the horses shifted in their harnesses, he wasn't worried. She was likely sitting inside the carriage, plotting his early demise. A smirk tugged at the corner of his mouth.

It wasn't until he opened the carriage door and found it empty that he felt the first beat of alarm.

He walked around to the other side and saw his driver throwing stones into the slender creek. Alone.

"Where is Miss Hartley?" he demanded.

Unconcerned, the young driver tossed another stone. "Said she was going to walk for a spell and not to bother you."

"Not to bother—" Oscar felt his jaw harden and the flesh around his knuckles tighten as his fists clenched. "And you just let her go? Alone?"

"Don't see her maid around, do you? The two of 'em went off together."

The boy couldn't have been more than seventeen or eighteen. He still had spots, devil take it! So when he merely shrugged and issued an offhand gesture down the road in the direction she must have gone, Oscar told himself that murdering him would be wrong.

Instead, he settled for taking the miscreant by the lapels of his livery coat. "You are a driver in the service of a respectable family. You do not allow a woman to walk unescorted through the countryside without informing your master."

"But the . . . the widows said you weren't nothing but a charlatan," he stammered, his copper-penny eyes wide. "They told me to make sure . . . to make sure you wished you'd never come to the abbey. Promised me a sixpence, they did."

Rage was too calm of an emotion for what Oscar was feeling. This was something darker. And the fear that shot through him only intensified it.

There was guilt, too. Because he alone knew what Honoria was capable of . . . such as disguising herself as a man to gallivant around Paris on her own.

Bloody hell, he never should have let her out of his sight!

On a low growl, he pushed away from the boy and turned to the carriage, climbing up into the perch without delay.

This was no longer a game.

He knew where he'd gone wrong. He'd been playing the wrong part. The aristocrats he'd encountered throughout his life had been pampered and self-entitled. So that's how he acted, essentially embodying the insouciant mannerisms he'd always despised.

A clear misstep. No, *worse*. Because of it, Honoria had put herself in danger without fear of consequence or reprisal.

"Please, sir. I don't want to lose my post. They told me you wasn't the real viscount," the boy called up to him, peeling his felt cap from his head and clutching it to his chest.

"That's where you are all mistaken." Oscar released the brake and took up the reins. "I *am* Vandemere."

It could be no other way.

As soon as he spoke the words, the horses spurred into motion, a corresponding vibration climbing through the ribbons. He felt their power thundering in the center of his chest.

Urging the team on with a gruff command, he scanned past the clusters of bulrushes and copses of hazel and blackthorn that bordered the winding creek, searching for a glimpse of flaxen hair and seafoam green. His gaze skimmed over verdant knolls and a distant field of golden wheat, but he didn't see her or her maid.

Spurring the horses up a rise, his urgency mounted, burning in his veins. This was his doing. His fault. If anything happened to her, he'd—

Relief washed over him in a flood the moment he crested the hill. Honoria was just up ahead with her maid.

But they were not alone.

His relief quickly transformed into something nameless and darker when he saw that she was brandishing a stick, trying to fend off the advances of two men, while a third watched from the perch of a phaeton. Her maid stood by in obvious terror with a hand covering her mouth.

Oscar stopped the horses. Pulling the brake, he bounded down to the lane.

"You, there! Stand aside!" he commanded, leaving a trail of dust in the wake of each charging stride.

The men lowered their arms warily as they watched him approach.

"Oh, there you are, Vandemere. Have a pleasant nap?" Honoria asked, swiping her stick in the air with a jaunty salute.

It wasn't until he saw the impish smirk on her lips and the victorious gleam in her eyes that he realized he'd been played. Hearing her maid giggle also told him that it was not horror she'd been stifling but amusement.

He drew in a breath to subdue the murderous red from his vision and took in the scene.

The trio of gentlemen were younger than he, the oldest no more than four and twenty. Each displayed a curly mop of sandy hair and soft chins. And each were garbed in fine clothes. Though, with their long necks adorned with lofty cravats and pointed collars so high that they came to their earlobes, they reminded Oscar of the llamas he'd once seen in Peru. And not even the adult llamas but the babies.

He noted the way the tallest one standing nearest to Honoria rested his hand on the stick at his side, the tapered end pointed to the ground as if it were a rapier, his feet positioned in an L shape. A typical fencing stance. In other words, the *attack* had been nothing more than Honoria pretending to cross swords with this pack of crias.

These observations did nothing to lessen his black mood.

"Allow me to introduce you to these fine and ever-so-handsome gentlemen," she said flashing a flirtatious grin as she gestured to each. "This is Percival Culpepper, his brother Peter, and over there in the phaeton is the youngest, Carlton. He recently injured his ankle by gallantly risking life and limb to leap off our stage to rescue my fallen hair ribbon."

Oscar was a man who found a woman's confidence utterly enthralling. And Honoria had that in spades, along with a lion's share of audacity and boldness which he found equally attractive. So as his jaw clenched, he was almost ready to bare his teeth in a grin and allow her to continue this new game of hers. Alone. As he rode on without her.

But Vandemere? Well, Oscar was fairly certain that the viscount wouldn't take too kindly to his fiancée traipsing along the countryside, where anything might have happened, only to find her coyly flirting with other men.

No, Vandemere wouldn't like it. At all.

There must have been some shred of that emotion on his countenance, because Honoria's smile faltered as he approached.

Her throat constricted on a swallow. "Need I remind you that you are a gentleman? And gentlemen do not make primitive displays."

He'd been about to offer a semblance of a greeting to the men, then politely escort her and her maid back to the carriage. Yet, after Honoria's muttered warning and the way she brandished that stick of hers, he decided to show her just how primitive he could be.

"Don't you d—*aaaare*!" she shrieked, wide-eyed as he tugged her off balance by seizing control of her sword, then scooped her up and tossed her over his shoulder.

As he carried her off, she began to beat him with her fists, striking his lower back and buttocks, all the while railing at him for being a brute. If she had even the smallest inkling of the control he was actually exhibiting, she would be grateful that embarrassment was all she'd suffer.

Wrenching open the carriage door, he summarily deposited the flinty-eyed vixen. Red-faced, scowling and cursing a blue streak, she didn't seem to realize how fortunate she was that there had been no transients or evildoers skulking nearby, looking for the perfect peach to pluck from the tree. And it was the thought of what might have happened to her that kept him from feeling any shred of remorse over his actions.

Even so, he was far gentler when handing her maid into

the carriage, leaving her with the instructions to keep the doors bolted until they reached Hartley Hall.

Climbing back up to the driver's perch, he sketched a salute to her three milk-fed admirers and set off again. And all the way to her door, he thought about how good it felt to be Vandemere.

⌒

HONORIA WAS STILL steaming the following day when the invitation arrived. And, of course, it came addressed to her mother, so there was no way to toss it into the hearth and pretend it never arrived.

"If that high-handed blackguard thinks that I'm going to take tea at Dunnelocke Abbey after the way he treated me, he can think again." Storming across her bedchamber, she flung open her wardrobe. "Tally, I've never been treated so ill in all my life."

Her maid pushed a pair of wire-rimmed spectacles up the bridge of her nose before tucking a bright red curl beneath the ruffled trim of her mobcap. "I know, miss."

"Did you see the way that he walked straight up to me and, without a by-your-leave, hauled me over his shoulder like a rug sent out for beating? Well, of course you did. You were there."

Honoria huffed as she blindly sorted through her dresses.

Thinking back to the picnic, she'd thought she'd been handling him quite well. After all, she'd seen the way his gaze skimmed over her figure when she'd performed the tried-and-true feminine lure of coyly removing one's hat, knowing that maneuver typically addled a man's wits.

Coquetry was an art form she'd learned at an early age. And it took great skill to skirt the line between flirting and being labeled a *flirt*. After all, it was wrong to lead a man by the nose but important to put him in his place should he become too bold.

In that moment, she'd had little doubt that she could manage Mr. Flint. And once she brought him to heel, she would be able to send him on his way.

At least, that's what she'd thought . . . until she'd seen another side of him. Until she knew he was being driven by a greater purpose than greed. Until she'd seen the shadows that had shifted across his gaze, like a cloud sweeping over the moon.

She knew that look well. It had lingered on the fringes of her own reflection over the years after Ernest died. She supposed that those who were haunted by the death of someone cherished were able to glimpse the ghosts residing in others.

But she didn't want to have that in common with Mr. Flint. Didn't want to remember the tender way he'd spoken of his mother or the understanding he'd shown to the dowager.

She especially didn't want to remember the way her own eyes had prickled with unrehearsed tears.

It wasn't like her to lose control and reveal what she hadn't intended for anyone to see. Then he'd had the audacity to look at her as if she were fragile, of all things. As if she—a woman who'd spent a good deal of time immersed in a man's world—needed a big, strong charlatan to hold her. *Ha!*

"He's nothing more than an antiquated barbarian."

"Well, you were surrounded by three other men, miss. *And* wielding a stick. From a distance, he might have thought you were in danger."

"From Percy Culpepper? That man would squeal if he saw a mouse."

Tally murmured a sound of agreement. "Then, perhaps his lordship was jealous. His primitive display seemed designed to ensure that the others were well aware of his prior claim."

"He has no claim over me whatsoever." Not only that,

she mused crossly, but a man driven to jealousy surely would have remembered their kiss. The thought made her growl into her wardrobe. "Where in the blazes is that ice-blue frock with the van Dyke trim that sits like epaulets on the crests of the puffed sleeves? I feel a need for armor. Oh," she said, when her maid lifted the garment she'd been holding the entire time. "Thank you."

Tally followed as she stepped behind the folding screen and helped her slip out of her morning dress. After a moment of allowing her mistress's vexation to ebb, she carefully added, "Considering the betrothal contract, the viscount may have an alternate opinion on the matter."

"*He's* no viscount." As soon as she said the words, she cringed.

Tally didn't know her secret. More than anything, Honoria wanted to confide in the young woman who'd been with the family for the past ten years. They'd practically grown up together. However, Tally was also a lady's maid to her sisters, and Honoria could never ask her to divide her loyalties.

"What I meant to say is he's no typical viscount, who exhibits gentlemanly manners and so forth," she hedged.

Her maid offered a thoughtful nod. "Though, it could be said his wilder nature might prove to be an asset in his current situation. Given that his aunts have such . . . strong temperaments and have been trying to declare him dead in order to take hold of the estate, they are likely to set obstacles in his path."

"All the better for them," Honoria said as the dress fell over her head. "Need I remind you that we aren't on his side and hoping for him to overcome adversity? We want to crush him."

But when the dress lowered, her maid offered a cha-grinned shrug in apology. "I'm not certain crushing is in my nature. And even though he overstepped, I find myself rooting for the knight-errant on his noble quest. After all, a three-headed dragon requires no encouragement."

That was the problem with living beneath the roof of a lord and lady infected with overly romantic sensibilities. Sooner or later, everyone came down with the plague.

But not Honoria. In fact, she was already thinking of another plan. And Tally had given her the perfect idea.

Chapter Eight

❧

*H*ONORIA WAS SO busy plotting ways to enlist the widows' unwitting assistance in delivering Mr. Flint from Addlewick that she didn't pay any attention to the woven hamper on the floor of the carriage. At least, not until she kicked it with the toe of her slipper.

It was the same hamper she'd taken on that irksome picnic. She was tempted to kick it again. "Whatever is this doing here?"

"Lord Vandemere returned it yesterday," Mother said absently, glancing up from the letter that had arrived just as they'd left. Considering the elegant scrawl and the winsome smile on her lips, it was likely from Father.

Honoria often wondered how her parents' love had remained so strong throughout the years. As passionate individuals, their fervent displays weren't only due to their mutual *amour*. They could also rail at each other until the roof tiles rattled. Or they could live at opposite ends of the house as if the other didn't exist. Yet, through all their trials and tribulations, they always came back to each other, stronger than before.

But what she couldn't understand was why her parents never seemed afraid that it would all be too much to take. Too much to bear. And that, one day, it would all come to an end and be gone forever.

She frowned down at the hamper, blaming it for the

dark cloud that descended on her thoughts. "That doesn't explain why it's here."

"Well, my inexplicably curious daughter," Mother began patiently, folding the letter and tucking it into her reticule, "after driving you and Tally home, Oscar retrieved the dishes, hamper, shawls and pillows and returned them to Hartley Hall. Not only that, but he'd begged an audience with our cook to extoll her with praises for the feast and, especially, for the biscuits."

"Ah. So that's the reason Mrs. Dougherty was all apple-cheeked smiles when we left."

"Indeed. She was so overjoyed that she baked a few cakes and tarts for our tea. Along with two parcels of biscuits, one of which—I am to tell Oscar—is just for him."

Honoria wanted to despise the blackguard. Not because she thought he was scheming behind her back to win the favor of her family's cook for some diabolical purpose, but because she knew he wasn't. Drat him. Just as she knew he hadn't been lying to her yesterday about those biscuits having been the first he'd ever eaten.

His tell had been the embarrassment he'd attempted to conceal. And she might have felt a small twinge in the center of her heart at seeing it.

Thankfully, he'd remedied that temporary ailment by proving himself to be a complete and utter arse.

"I daresay," Mother continued, "Mrs. Dougherty is half in love already."

"Then she falls in love far too easily."

"The first little stumble is often the easiest, and giving in to that giddy rush is so"—Roxana sighed, her eyes closing on a smile—"lovely. Then comes the falling. Oh, that wondrous plummet into the unknown! It's positively terrifying. I cannot wait until it happens to you."

Honoria slid a sideways glance to her mother. "Have you been spending too much time at the hatter's?"

She laughed. "No, dear. I'm not ready for the attic quite yet. It's just that your father and I are at an age of reminiscing. His letter reminded me of the longing that plagued us, that restless agony of being apart."

"Agony? It has only been a handful of days since Father and Truman left for London."

Reaching across the bench, Roxana squeezed her daughter's hand. "What I'm trying to tell you is that love is a sort of madness. The fall turns everything upside down. And around. And over and through. It is an ever-constant and changing thing, and all you have is each other to cling to. But that is what makes the journey so achingly beautiful. Because when you come to know the heart of that person, only then will you understand the immeasurable capacity of your own. I want that for you and for all of my children."

Realizing that her mother was caught in the current of another one of her romantic episodes, Honoria wished the postman's horse had gone lame. The last thing she needed before stepping into the dragon's lair was for Roxana Hartley at her side, offering her up as a sacrifice.

What she wouldn't give to trade places with Althea, who only had to suffer Lady Broadbent's quizzing glass this afternoon.

"Mother, surely you would agree that knowing someone— *truly* knowing them—takes time? A good deal of time in certain circumstances. Years, even."

"For some, perhaps. Not you and Oscar, of course. You already have a long history."

"We only just met," she lied, keeping every memory of Paris hidden behind a carefully bland expression.

"It has been seven years, dear. You were sixteen when you began writing letters to him, were you not?"

"I . . . suppose."

Roxana's lips curved, her chestnut brows arching suggestively. "Then, there's the matter of the sparks I saw between the two of you that first moment. That sort of animal attraction doesn't take any time at all. I thought we'd have to fetch a fire pail from the kitchen."

"I wouldn't say that there was any sort of—"

"Ah, splendid. We're here," Mother interrupted.

Honoria wasn't sure if their arrival saved her the bother of having to produce a plausible denial or if her mother had foreseen said denial like a Shakesperean soothsayer and refused to give it any credence.

Not that it mattered. Whatever initial attraction she might have felt for that scoundrel had certainly dissipated after their picnic.

She continued to tell herself that even as those demented moths in her midriff took flight when she saw him waiting for their carriage and when he handed her down. And it was surely revulsion that caused her pulse to quicken when the tip of his index finger brushed the inside of her wrist, just above the buttoned cuff of her kid glove.

"Miss Hartley," he said, bowing over her hand as the soles of her shoes settled onto the gravel in front of his.

When he did not release her, it became clear that he was waiting for her to greet him in turn. Waiting for her to address him by the title that was not his own. The title that she had practically handed to him in Paris.

At the challenge in his gaze, her temper flared, incinerating the moths in one seething breath.

It pained her—oh, how it pained her!—but she managed a taut "Vandemere."

Then she jerked her hand free as he flashed a grin. She looked forward to wiping it off his far too smug face.

After directing a footman to retrieve the hamper, Roxana stood beside Oscar and relayed the message from their cook.

For a man who typically revealed only what he wanted others to see, it surprised Honoria to catch a brief glimpse of naked, unexpected joy cross his countenance. And all because of biscuits.

Her throat tightened on a swallow the way it did on un-stirred sugar at the bottom of her teacup. She hated him for it. Hated that he quickly concealed his response as if uncertain how to react to a show of simple kindness. And hated the fact that she could no longer murder him.

At least . . . not with a clear conscience.

The widows stood in the stark entry hall, like three pillars garbed in black. Alfreda Shellhorn and Millicent Fairfax did not bother to alter their dour expressions with any pretense of pleasure in having company. Their young-est sister-in-law, however, smiled genially.

"Welcome to Dunnelocke Abbey. How lovely it is to have visitors," Babette said in her breathy, effervescent voice. But as a throat cleared beside her, she sobered marginally. "Though, Oscar was very naughty to send the invitation without informing us first."

Alfreda slid a reproving glance to him. "Indeed. It is the lady of the house who sends the invitations."

"Or *ladies*, as the case may be," Millicent said tightly, her voice threaded with the barest hint of a Scottish brogue.

Before any reply could be offered by Oscar or the *un-wanted* guests, Cleo Dunne entered the hall, the hem of her lavender skirt rustling, her blond head bent in conference with the slender toffee-nosed steward walking beside her. The pair of them stopped, blocking the path of the footman carrying the hamper to the kitchens.

Beneath a receding mousy brown hairline, Mr. Price's sparse brows lifted. Affecting a gasp, he splayed a hand beneath the foppish waterfall of his cravat. "Dear me, I did not realize that the family's cook had taken ill."

"I had not heard of any ailment or incapacity on her part either," Cleo remarked and looked with exaggerated inno-cence to the widows.

The steward swept a glance around the room and then, as if in understanding, proceeded to shift awkwardly. "Oh, I see. Though, I'm certain your esteemed guests meant no insult to Mrs. Blandings or her ability to prepare a simple tea."

Honoria bristled at his implication.

"That will be all, Mr. Price," Oscar cut in, his words sharp as teeth.

But the steward stood his ground until he received a nod from Alfreda and Millicent. Then, after an obsequious bow, he sauntered off.

"I'm afraid that our gift has given the wrong impression," Mother interjected in her famed dulcet tone, rumored to have once stopped a duel with the utterance of a single word. "Since our families have been acquainted for so many years, I could not imagine arriving without a tangible display of my elation that we are all together again after so long apart."

"Aren't you a dear," Babette said with a sighing smile. Easily swayed to the enemy's camp, she came forward and began to lead them toward the stairway. "I do hope there's cake."

Alfreda cleared her throat and gestured to the door just off the hall. "Sister, I believe our guests will be more comfortable in *this* room."

"Surely, the blue—"

"Right this way," Millicent interrupted, blocking their path, her slender arm sweeping outward like Death swinging his scythe.

They were summarily ushered into the receiving room. Not the spacious blue parlor on the floor above, Honoria noted. But instead, into a dingy yellow room with sun-faded brocade curtains, a clean but sparse rug and upholstered furniture worn thin to the brown webbing beneath. And on the walls, where paintings had once hung, lingered rectangular and oval ghosts of golden color not yet diminished.

"What a charming parlor," Honoria declared convincingly of the drab little room.

Alfreda's mouth twisted into a semblance of a smile, a murmured "Thank you kindly" seemingly wrenched from her soul.

When Oscar stepped into the room, Cleo sneered. "I did not realize *you* would be joining us, as well."

"Thought I'd get a feel for how these things are done properly. Wouldn't want to make another grievous faux pas, after all." Unconcerned, he lowered his frame into a low-backed chair on the outer fringes of the furniture arrangement.

Honoria had to bite the inside of her cheek to keep from grinning at his quick reply, especially when his statement earned lethal glowers from Alfreda and Millicent. Even though she didn't want to side with him, she couldn't stop herself from admiring the way he handled the open animosity with aplomb. And yet, part of her also wondered where such a skill originated.

How much of this charlatan's life had he been kept on the outside of things, without ever truly belonging? Did he have parents? Brothers or sisters? Other family?

Not that she cared. He was blackmailing her, after all. Therefore, he could go to the devil if he wanted companionship.

Tucking those thoughts away, she focused on removing her gloves . . . only to discover that two of her pearl buttons were already unfastened.

The scoundrel!

Her accusatory gaze flew to Oscar. He arched a brow in response. Then his gaze slid down the front of her ice-blue dress with indecent deliberateness. The wicked way his lips curved in a slow grin caused a rush of heat to creep to her cheeks, her skin tingling where he'd touched her as he'd handed her down from the carriage.

Averting her face, she rubbed the susceptible skin over her pulse to quell the unwanted sensation and vowed to ignore him for the remainder of the afternoon.

The tea arrived with great pageantry, a parade of servants toting trays of cakes, tarts and sandwiches.

Alfreda scowled from her perch on the edge of the sunken squirrel-colored settee. "How kind of you to have brought so many pastries, Lady Hartley. I'm sure my cook is quite overwhelmed by your generosity."

She'd likely planned to serve the mealy currant scones that Honoria had heard mention of from one of the sculleries two days ago as she was leaving.

"I believe you meant *our* cook," Millicent muttered beside her.

Cleo held her tongue, but her lips were pressed in white-edged disapproval as she poured the tea.

Babette, however, was too busy lifting the dome off the cake to notice anything else. "It looks positively scrumptious."

As the tea and pastries were served by one of the housemaids, Alfreda inquired about the time on the mantel clock. Assured that it had been set just this morning by the butler, she dismissed the maid.

Ignoring the not-so-subtle invitation to leave as quickly as possible, Roxana smiled as she stirred her tea. "Now that your nephew is home at last, we all have much to celebrate. You must be more than delighted by his return."

"We are happy to welcome him into the fold," Babette offered with a fond smile as she licked icing from the tip of her finger. But when her sideways glance slid over Oscar in a slow head-to-toe sweep, it seemed a bit too fond in Honoria's opinion.

"Hmm . . ." Millicent murmured, eyeing the plum tart on her plate as though it were made of toads. "Though, it is a shame he did not arrive with a considerable fortune to repair the abbey and make our fallow lands prosperous again."

"Fear not, Aunt Millie," Oscar said, his grin widening when she gritted her teeth at the moniker. "I fully intend to marry into a fortune."

All eyes turned to Honoria.

"Oh?" Cleo perked up in her spindle-leg chair. "Have you a fortune, Miss Hartley?"

"I believe your cousin was merely jesting. He knows that I have no dowry of which to speak," Honoria said and was delighted when the brief flicker of hope on the faces of the widows faded.

She had little doubt that they would put every obstacle they could summon in the way of their supposed nephew marrying a pauper. Over the rim of her cup, she slid Oscar a seething glance of triumph.

"Some might think that is fortunate for you." Alfreda Shellhorn pursed her lips as she considered a marzipan lemon. "At least you know he'll be marrying you for yourself and not everything you have, which will belong to him and to the estate the moment you reach the altar."

Before Oscar lifted his own cup, Honoria saw that snake-tail curl of a smirk on his lips.

Her blood went cold. He knew she had two thousand pounds. But that was all she had for her future.

At one time, her actual holdings had been considerably greater. Signor Cesario was quite adept at playing the exchange, after all. In fact, *he* had been rather plump in the pocket. But then there were necessary investments that had left Cesario's coffers a bit sparse.

Therefore, she knew that now was the time to bring the dragons over to her side.

"Of course, because your nephew has been out of society, he would likely require approval before being granted a marriage license. Though, I'm certain the Archbishop of Canterbury would assist in that matter." She flitted her fingers as if the legalities were of little consequence. "His Grace will likely take one look at Oscar's birth certificate, along with our betrothal contract, and have all the proof he requires. Then the viscountcy and this estate will be completely and irrevocably his."

Millicent's cup clattered against the saucer in her slackened grasp.

Alfreda spluttered her tea on a cough.

Cleo blanched. "That cannot happen."

A storm brewed in Oscar's gaze. An answering smile curved Honoria's lips.

"Whyever not?" Roxana inquired. "If the children wish to wed, then I see no reason to wait."

"What our niece meant," Alfreda interjected in a carefully measured tone as she dabbed the corner of her mouth with a napkin, "is that we have a tradition at Dunnelocke Abbey. A tradition where the male heir marries in our chapel."

Millicent nodded. "Quite true. However, at present, our chapel is in need of repair."

"Extensive repairs," Cleo added with a nod.

Honoria took a happy sip as another obstacle fell into place.

"I'm certain my husband and our tenant Mr. Lawson would be more than happy to assist. We are almost family, after all. And besides, our situation is not quite as dire as my daughter led you to believe. She does, indeed, have a sizable dowry," Mother declared, the lie rolling off her tongue as smooth as honey.

This time, Honoria nearly choked on her tea. She couldn't fathom why her mother would fabricate such a story. Ever since the scandal, there had been no dowries for any of them.

But perhaps her mother merely wished to make a grand exit. A baroness could hardly do so with a dowryless daughter in tow. Therefore, Honoria didn't give the announcement any credence.

"But that is a discussion for another time," Mother continued. "As for the wedding, I was thinking . . ."

As her mother continued on her fool's errand, the widows doggedly repeated their attempts to redirect the conversation to the nonexistent dowry. And Honoria set her plate aside to enjoy the spectacle.

"Shall we wager on which side will prevail?" Oscar asked from beside her, his hand resting on the back of her chair.

She'd like to tell herself that the sudden escalation of her pulse was due to him startling her because she had not seen him cross the room. But that was a lie. The truth was, from the moment he'd entered the parlor, her entire being had been attuned to him, to his every glance in her direction and to every shift of his body. It seemed as though his every move sent a corresponding vibration through her, as if they were tied together with puppet strings.

It was maddening. And now, he was caging her in on one side of the chair, the heat of him practically incinerating her clothes.

"No. I would not care to wager because I don't believe either side will win." Needing space and a heady gulp of air, she stood and moved toward the open doorway.

He bent to pick up the gloves that had fallen from her lap and went to her, a smug grin on his lips as he thumbed one of the buttons. "You didn't finish your cake."

"Most of it," she said as she snatched her gloves out of his grasp and began to put them on. "It was rather good cake, after all. But I never eat the last bite."

"Why not?"

The instant his brows drew together in curious speculation, she wanted to kick herself. Her reason for never finishing the last of anything—whether it was cake, porridge, partridge or coddled eggs—was not something she talked about.

The habit had started when she was little and a nursemaid had told her a fanciful tale about leaving an offering to visiting angels. Then, in the months after her twin brother had died, whenever the servants had seen her crying, they would comfort her by saying that her brother was an angel now. Ever since, she'd always left the last bite for him.

But that was a story she would keep to herself.

"It's common knowledge that one cannot have their cake

and eat it, too. Much like your biscuits, which I noticed were absent from the tea tray," she pointed out with an arched look. "Surely, you do not intend to eat all of them yourself?"

"Indeed, I do. When it comes to things that bring me pleasure, I always indulge until I'm fully sated."

Was that a thinly veiled barb concerning the kiss he'd forgotten?

She narrowed her eyes and was about to strike back in kind . . . but just then, her mother stood, drawing their visit to a close.

As if he pitied Honoria's failed rejoinder, he proffered an arm. "May I escort you, Miss Hartley?"

"I would prefer a slug to you," she hissed but smiled sweetly. She wouldn't want her mother to confuse animosity for sparks again, after all. "Especially after your primitive display yesterday. You were quite rude to the Culpeppers."

Since she needed to put on a good performance for the widows, however, she laid her hand on his sleeve and walked out with him, leaving the others a few paces behind.

"Simply playing a part, Signore. I believe you know a thing or two about that." He bent his head to whisper. "Besides, given your current obsession about kissing, I wouldn't want those slathering puppies to have any hope that you would practice on them."

"Who is to say that I haven't already?"

Oh, how she relished the dark clouds that swept over his gaze, a muscle ticking along in his jaw. And there was nothing he could say in response because the others had caught up with them.

All in all, she felt that she'd won the day quite handily.

Chapter Nine

ⴰⵎ

*T*HE STORM BLEW *the balcony doors open, and a flash of lightning lit the darkened chamber. A figure lay on the bed, pale and still.*

No . . . No . . . He couldn't be too late.

He staggered forward, the air tinged with the fragrance of olives, rain and the sour stench of illness. Another crack of lightning illuminated his mother—a shadow of what she once had been, her skin ashen, her dark hair in a tangle on the pillow.

A raw sob lodged in his throat as he collapsed to his knees. "Forgive me . . . forgive me for failing you."

Then, he felt a hand against his bent head. Startled, he looked up and saw a ghost of a smile on her pale, cracked lips.

"My boy, there is nothing . . . to forgive," she rasped. "You are here now. That is . . . enough."

That wasn't true. It was his fault. She'd been sick, and he'd been desperate to win the game. Desperate to have the money to take her some place where there would be a physician to cure her.

But desperation makes a man clumsy.

He'd been caught by the guard and sent away before he could do anything for her.

The storm began to rage, pelting the stones of the balcony. He rose to cross the room and close the doors. But then, she had a fit of coughing.

This time, he wouldn't leave her. Couldn't *leave her. Not again. So he let the rain come.*

The hard and hollow sound of her cough hit like hailstones, and the spasms left her weak and wheezing. She seemed to sink deeper into the bed, as though she were disappearing before his eyes.

He tried to hold her up, to help her drink from the glass on her bedside table, but she shook her head.

"Let me . . . speak . . . for a moment," she said, her voice threadbare. Yet even then, she tried to smile as she searched his gaze. "Sometimes . . . all we have is . . . a moment."

He held her in the cradle of his arms, her bones so frail and delicate it was like holding a bird. "I'm listening."

"Promise me," she said, her eyes fighting to stay open.

"I will. Anything."

"I loved your father . . . but he couldn't . . . She was all he could . . . see . . . but you . . . you changed that . . ." Her words were in a jumble, her breaths shallow, wet and ragged. Then she gripped his hand, her hold surprisingly strong, as if she were drowning and he were the only one who could save her. *"Must find him. Find your father. Then, you'll find your—"*

Thunder crashed into the room.

Oscar jolted bolt upright in bed, his arm raised, reaching out to take hold of her hand . . . Only to find nothing but empty air.

It took a moment to orient himself. To blink into the bleary gray light of early morning to see the snug bedchamber walls painted a bilious shade of green and the colossal portrait of Vandemere's grandsire scowling down from over the mantel.

Then he remembered.

He scrubbed a hand over his face and threw aside the bedclothes. As he dragged himself to the window, the curtains billowed with a breeze that sent a chill over his sweat-dampened skin. Hands on the sill, he drew in a deep breath . . . then regretted it the instant the rank odor of the paddock and the wormy scent of rain filled his nostrils.

Behind him, the door opened with a crack that caused his shoulders to tense. And, without a by-your-leave, his valet stepped inside.

"As I've said before, I would prefer it if you'd knock, Timms." Oscar wasn't shy by any means, so walking in the nude to the washstand didn't bother him. The man's blatant lack of courtesy and respect, however, did.

"Did you mean every day, sir?" The gangly young man with curly rust-colored hair didn't bother to wait for an answer but noisily went about the task of laying out his clothes.

Oscar gripped the handle of the ewer and splashed cold water into the chipped bowl. Since he'd arrived without a manservant—stating that his would be delayed, along with his trunks—he'd required the service of a temporary valet. So in the widows' usual manner of making him feel so very welcome, they assigned him one of their most impertinent footmen.

That caused snickering among the servants. Being promoted to a valet was supposed to be an honor. Yet, with widows spewing venom about his authenticity, it spread doubt among the servants and made Timms an object of ridicule instead of respect.

There was nothing Oscar could do about that other than continue on his course. So he would just have to manage with Timms while waiting for Cardew and news of Ladrón.

Once that was settled, he'd leave the abbey without a backward glance and return to searching for his father.

"That'll be all, Timms."

"What about your shave . . . sir?" he asked, the last word spoken with a sneer.

The fact that all the servants called him *sir* instead of *my lord* didn't really matter. It shouldn't bother him in the least. And yet, for some inexplicable reason, it did.

Shoving that thought aside, he rasped a hand over his stubble. He knew, from Warring's tutelage on the behaviors of men born into privilege, that acting like a helpless, pampered toff was expected of him. It would likely earn him more credibility with the widows, too.

However, when he looked at the horizonal red scar just beneath his Adam's apple, the memory of Ladrón's blade kept him from doing what was expected.

"Word of advice, Timms. Never let a man who doesn't respect you hold a blade to your throat."

And with that, he bent his head to splash cold water on his face again and tried not to think about what new horrors awaited him in the breakfast room.

⤙

THAT FIRST MORNING in the abbey was the last time he'd seen the widows and Cousin Cleo in the breakfast room. Collectively, they had decided to have trays sent up to their bedchambers where they were likely dining on actual food. The edible variety. He, on the other hand, was offered watery gruel and—

A foul scent assailed his nostrils when he lifted the cloche. He lowered it with a clang.

Oscar didn't know what that grayish-green dish was supposed to have been, but it resembled what was found in city gutters—some sort of offal that wouldn't even tempt a rat.

Ah, the joys of having a family, he thought dryly. All his boyhood dreams were coming true at last.

Though, if they thought they could break him, they were in for a surprise. His will was hard as an anvil. They could heap fiery coals or white-hot blades of steel on him all day, but soon enough they would find *themselves* bending.

Besides, at least there was burnt toast. Picking up a slice, he left the breakfast room and went out to the stables.

He looked forward to his morning ride. After all, the

horses never tried to starve him or plague him. They likely felt a particular kinship to him, considering the fact that they practically shared his bedchamber.

Stepping beneath the open pitching door, he strode down the sloped cobbled floor. He didn't bother to request to have his horse saddled. From previous encounters with the stable master, he knew he'd be met with the usual disregard. So he offered a curt nod to the man, who was conferring with the actual coachman over the quality of oats and fodder.

As expected, Oscar earned little more than a steely stare from both of them and so continued on to his horse's stall. But he was surprised to find it recently mucked and with fresh straw underfoot. Hermes's cloud-gray coat was even brushed and glossy, and he was currently munching on a carrot. Which was a pleasant surprise . . . until he saw the one responsible.

"You," Oscar said to that whelp driver who'd let Miss Hartley walk off on her own. "Get out. I don't want you anywhere near my horse."

The spot-cheeked boy peeled off his hat and bowed. "Beggin' yer pardon, m'lord. I thought you'd be wantin' to go for a ride this mornin'. So I aimed to get Hermes all ready for ye. See?" He gestured to the waiting tack that had been polished to mirror shine.

"Suddenly deciding to do your job properly does not excuse your actions."

The cub's brows ruckled together fretfully. Then he lowered his head in a nod. "Thought about what you said. It was unpardonable, what I did. Me father reared me to know better. Would've walloped me on the head, he would. You can wallop me, m'lord."

"I'm not going to strike you." Oscar gritted his teeth in exasperation when the idiot bowed lower, looking every inch the kicked puppy. "And stand up. Show some pride."

He did, still wringing his cap. "I aim to make amends,

m'lord. No matter how long it takes. No matter what I must do."

Apparently, he meant it because he stayed glued to Oscar's side as he saddled Hermes and walked him out of the stables.

Worried that the lad planned to trot alongside him for the entire morning, he stopped and considered his options. "What's your name?"

"James, m'lord. James Raglan."

"And you're about seventeen?"

"Eighteen last month."

"Old enough to know better," Oscar said and received a nod. "Well, Mr. Raglan, if you ever plan to drive a coach in the future, then it is your duty to ensure that it is safe and comfortable. It is a representation of your house and your self-respect. You alone are responsible for keeping it in good standing. That contraption"—he gestured to the dilapidated carriage that stood beside a landau in pristine condition—"could jar the bones out of a dead man's coffin. Make sure it doesn't do that any longer."

Without another word, Oscar mounted his horse and rode away from the plague that was Dunnelocke Abbey.

He wished Cardew would hurry along. Even though the man put them in more scrapes than he cared to think about, he was the only real family Oscar had. At least, until he could find his worthless father and keep the promise he'd made to his mother.

The bitter taste of burnt toast lingered in the back of his mouth. He swallowed it down as he spurred Hermes into a gallop, trying to leave behind the ghosts that haunted him.

It wasn't until he saw the stone Palladian mansion ahead of him that he realized he'd taken a few turns that led him toward Hartley Hall.

Stopping at the mouth of the lane, he considered simply turning around and going another way. However, since he was already there . . .

"What say you, Hermes? Should we see if the cook has any biscuits in the larder? Perhaps an apple from the orchard?"

At the sound of his favorite treat, the stallion's ears twitched, and his hoof pawed once over the hardpacked earth.

Oscar made a clicking sound at the corner of his mouth, and they trotted down the lane.

He took in the beauty of the well-situated country house. If Dunnelocke Abbey was a gray giantess lounging on her side, then Hartley Hall was a sandstone minx, supple belly on the ground, elbows bent with her chin resting on her hands, her portico greeting visitors with a come-hither smile.

It was a handsome house. The only thing that detracted from her beauty was the familiar phaeton in the semicircular drive. Apparently, the Culpeppers had also been drawn to Hartley Hall this morning.

Something that sounded suspiciously like a growl rumbled in his chest.

Who is to say that I haven't already? That laughing taunt still lingered in the back of his mind.

It was part of the game they played, of course. Even so, he couldn't stop himself from wondering if it was true. Wondering if he would have to kill all of the Culpeppers or just one.

Rapping his knuckles on the door, he told himself that it didn't matter to *him*. It was Vandemere who would have been bothered.

Therefore, in the interest of Vandemere, Oscar would make a show of staking his claim. Besides, doing so would irritate Honoria. Which would, in turn, put him in better spirits.

Mr. Mosely appeared to be completely recovered from his shock at seeing Oscar that first day and now greeted him with a bow. "Lord Vandemere. Miss Hartley and Miss

Althea are entertaining in the drawing room. Would you care to wait in the parlor while I announce you?"

He thought about it for a half second. Thought about the Culpeppers' phaeton. "Actually, no. I should rather go with you, if it's all the same."

Surely, in *haut* society, the word *entertaining* couldn't have meant *bacchanalian orgy* the way it usually did in the world he knew. Even so, Oscar wouldn't put it past Honoria to be laughing and flirting with three men at once.

He was led upstairs to the drawing room. It wasn't until he saw a pair of Irish wolfhounds growling at the door that alarm jolted through him.

Then, one of the male inhabitants inside the room called out, "I've got you now!"

"You missed," Honoria said with a tsk.

Another male voice said, "Well, I caught the little one!"

"Ow! You scratched me, you goose!" Althea cried.

"Not fair!" a third man's voice said. "You've got hold of the bird I wanted."

Oscar rushed for the door but found it locked.

Suddenly, the image of his temptress flirting coyly with her callers, only to have them turn into rapacious, clawing beasts filled his mind with a lurid tableau of her and her sister fending off unwanted advances.

He rattled the handle. "Honoria?"

In response, he heard a string of helpless shrieks.

Without waiting an instant longer, he rammed his shoulder against the door and barreled into the room . . . to find utter chaos.

And feathers. So many feathers.

Chapter Ten

❧

"CLOSE THE DOOR!" the Hartley sisters shouted in unison.

Thankfully, Mosely had his wits about him and managed to haul the dogs back as Oscar nudged their wiry snouts free of the door before shutting them firmly out.

Then Oscar stood and took in the scene.

Scanning past the harried trio of young men he'd have to deal with later, he saw downy yellow feathers everywhere, a pair of angry flapping ducks on the two window ledges, an overturned sofa, a raised dais in the corner swathed by burgundy drapes, and a wooden bathtub center stage with a half-dozen paddling chicks on the surface of the water.

As he heard the peeps that he'd mistaken for shrieks, part of him wondered if he was lost in some sort of strange dream. "What the devil?"

In a blur of jonquil skirts, Honoria disappeared behind the curtains. "Found another!"

Althea lifted a fringed pillow from an upholstered chair and glanced at him over the puffed shoulder of her poppy-red dress. "Well, don't just stand there, Vandemere."

"Rude," her sister scolded, coming out from behind the curtain to deposit another duckling into the water. Disheveled and decidedly vexed, she set her hands on her hips and blew a hank of flaxen hair from her forehead. "This was, after all, your fault. Again, I might add. And we'd just recovered from the piglet debacle. Though, one would think you'd have learned your lesson after the chickens."

"I did. This time, I made certain to lock the doors so the Queen's Council couldn't get in. Then I levered the basket of ducklings through the window."

That would explain the length of discarded rope, Oscar thought. But he still had questions. So many questions.

"And hasn't that worked out splendidly," Honoria said wryly and went back to collecting fuzzy yellow ducklings.

In the next instant, one of the adult ducks flew into the room, squawking and angrily flapping at the tallest of the three slender-necked Culpeppers. He backed away, raising an arm to shield his face.

Honoria expelled an exasperated sigh. "Honestly, Percy, just pick it up."

"But it will peck me."

Wondering why he'd thought that this llama-man might pose a threat, Oscar stepped forward and scooped up the creature, tucking it under his arm while carefully holding its beak.

"Well done," Percy said with a blink of astonishment, lowering his arm.

Oscar shrugged. "This is nothing. Try separating two doves who want to scratch each other's eyes out because one of them saw you first."

The trio chuckled.

"How did you manage that?" Althea asked, extracting a small ledger from her pocket and withdrawing the pencil tucked in her dark hair.

When Honoria cleared her throat with obvious disapproval, he turned to find her glaring at him.

He shrugged, all innocence. "Fear not, I wasn't going to elaborate."

Although, in that particular instance, all he'd had to do was promise to satisfy them both at once. And he always kept his promises.

"Well, you can just stop thinking about it, too," she muttered when he passed her on the way to the window.

He leaned in to whisper. "Surely, a woman I just found locked inside a room with three men isn't offended by the mention of a pair of birds."

"Are you certain it was just a pair and not an entire flock?" She narrowed her eyes.

There was something about the petulant frown on her lips that captured his interest and made him want to smooth it away with his own mouth. "I never kiss and tell, Signore."

"Or perhaps you just forget."

He watched her stalk off to round up more ducklings and grinned, his dark mood abruptly lifting.

An hour later, the fowl were liberated from the drawing room.

Oscar volunteered himself and the Culpeppers to deliver the baskets of ducklings to the pond. Standing near the bank and bulrushes, he exchanged a few words with the llamas. The three summarily left, having suddenly recalled a prior engagement.

As the dust settled on the lane after their hasty retreat, Oscar filled his lungs with a self-satisfied breath. For Vandemere's sake, of course. Then he made ready to depart as well.

However, before he could grab his hat and gloves, Lady Hartley invited him to tea. As if on cue, his stomach growled. Even so, he hesitated. There was the possibility that Warring or Cardew could have sent a letter with news about Ladrón. So he should return to the abbey . . .

But then she said the three words that every man longs to hear: *freshly baked biscuits.*

He stayed.

Honoria was about as pleased at this turn of events as a cat dunked in a washtub. And he relished every murderous glower she sent him when her mother wasn't looking.

Once his craving for biscuits was sated—well, for the moment—he was ready again to take his leave. In fact, he was just mounting his horse when the sound of a stampede drew his attention to the mouth of the narrow drive.

Perplexingly, the villagers seemed to be descending in droves. They started filing out of coaches, curricles and horse carts, chatting animatedly. Stranger still, they were all in costume. Haymarket had nothing on this hullabaloo. They surged forth in a boisterous stream that wrapped around the house and led to the back garden.

Curious, he followed, promising himself all the while that he would leave in short order.

But when he reached the garden, he found himself slack-jawed at the sight he beheld.

"Welcome to *the pit*, Oscar," Lady Hartley said from beside him, seemingly unsurprised by his reappearance. "Isn't it magnificent? My son Truman designed it."

The pit was an amphitheater formed from a natural grassy hill giving way to a steep slope, exposing the rock beneath. But then nature was shaped into a circular escarpment of tiered stone steps that looked as though they'd been there since the dawn of time. And across from them stood an oblong stage made of the same stone but inlaid with a pattern that gave the appearance of a wide eye staring up toward the heavens.

"It's quite something," he agreed, thoroughly awed.

She beamed at him and patted his arm. "Why don't you walk me down? You'll have a much better view from there."

"Actually, I wasn't planning to sta—" He stopped as she hooked an arm through his. "It would be my honor."

As they descended, Oscar mused that he'd been to many places in his life. He'd lived in squalor. Caroused in bordellos. Gambled in palaces. And yet he'd never witnessed anything like this.

Before his eyes, makeshift set dressing was being erected while people dug into crates for brightly colored costumes and props. Within minutes, the stage was a sea of floppy hats and windowpane pantaloons, gilded scepters and wooden swords, accompanied by strumming lutes and vocal scales.

Even though Rowan Warring had told him about the eccentricities of this family, it still took Oscar by surprise.

The villagers of Addlewick seemed to have no trouble accepting this thespian family, but he knew it wasn't common practice. After all, Vandemere's father had been disowned after he'd married an actress. Even his own father's family had not accepted Oscar's mother because she'd once been an opera singer.

How had the Hartleys managed to avoid such stigma?

While he mused over this, he watched Roxana Hartley bring the large personalities of the villagers to order. They likely didn't even realize they were being managed. Her command of the stage was effortless and graceful, while letting others believe they were in charge.

She was even craftier than Cardew. She'd definitely passed on her skills to a certain daughter who likely led a parade of men by the nose. Not him, of course. But men less worldly than he.

As for the youngest daughter, Althea appeared to run on gears that were constantly wound. If she wasn't moving from one side of the stage to the next, she was scribbling something in one of her pocket ledgers.

But as the day progressed, his attention kept returning to Honoria, time and again. It was impossible not to gaze upon her. And it wasn't because of her beauty but rather in spite of it.

She was truly magnificent to behold. With a simple shift in posture or an inflection in her tone, she embodied every character she played, whether male or female. It was . . . mesmerizing.

He had little doubt that if she had decided to play the part of Vandemere, the widows never would have doubted *her* claim.

"Come here, Vandemere," Honoria called down from the stage. "I require a victim to stab."

Oscar began to lift a hand in refusal. She was only looking to make a fool of him.

So then, why did he find himself vaulting up to the stage instead?

Yet, as he neared, he had his answer. He felt it—an irresistible pull, a force so tangible that it prickled over his skin, lifting the hairs along his nape and arms. And when he stood in front of her, looking down into her upturned face, he saw a flash of that same awareness in her eyes.

"I am yours to command, Miss Hartley," he said, his voice low.

A slow saturation of pink climbed to the crests of her cheeks, and her lips parted as if . . . as if . . .

He would never know. Because then she blinked, and it was as though she became someone else. Her mask of control fell into place so easily that he wanted to take a moment to marvel at her skill.

But then she slapped a wooden sword against his chest and backed away.

"For today's lesson in choreography, Vandemere will die," she announced brightly to the eager cast.

Describing the scene in detail, she demonstrated every move of the sword fight—parry, feint, thrust, kill. He had to admit she was good. During his years of enduring stuffy private tutors, which his mother had demanded Cardew pay for, he'd also taken fencing lessons. And he matched her fluidly, step for step, as if they were in a dance.

A fatal dance. At least, for him.

Honoria truly put her heart into it. Every time she struck the fatal blow, he fell onto the stage with a groan. Which, after the eighth time, was not an act. Then, standing over him, she'd slap his thigh with the flat of her sword and command, "Again."

Through the mask of choreographer, he could see that

the little sadist was enjoying herself. She liked having this power over him. And while the vision of her standing over him with her hair disheveled and her color high would fuel his fantasies for nights to come, she was having a bit too much fun as far as he was concerned.

So naturally, he had to take her down with him.

With her final lunge, her sword hit the mark, sinking neatly between his arm and rib cage. But instead of staggering back with the blade pinned to his side, he reached out and clutched at her hand over the hilt. Then, when he went down, sagging back against the stage to die, she went down with him.

Kneeling over his body, a heady laugh erupted from her lips. "You are such a cad."

Her fingers splayed over his chest to push away from him. But before she could, he reached up to tuck a fallen flaxen curl behind her ear, lingering in the silky strands.

"But you like me this way. Admit it."

A brief instant of confusion stitched her brows as she searched his gaze. Though, whatever question was in her mind, she shook her head in answer to it.

"'Not till God make men of some other metal than earth,'" she said, haughtily quoting the Bard's *Much Ado about Nothing*.

Applause swiftly followed.

It was only in that moment that Oscar recalled they were on a stage. Not alone but in front of half of Addlewick *and* her mother and sister. She had done it again, distracting him so thoroughly that he'd lost all sense.

He lowered his hand. She pushed to her feet.

"Splendid, my dear. Wrong play, but absolutely splendid," Lady Hartley said, gliding to center stage. Then she faced the villagers. "I think that will be all for today. We'll meet again Wednesday next, and by that time, Lord Hartley will be home again."

A chorus of *Huzzahs!* went through the crowd as they began to disperse in chatting clusters.

As the villagers departed, Oscar lagged behind to load costumes and props into the trunks that the footmen eventually hauled away. When that was done, he knew it was time to go. He wasn't one to linger, after all. Always ready to put a place behind him. Yes, that was his life.

And yet, when Lady Hartley prevailed upon him to stay and dine with them, he agreed.

He wasn't sure why. Perhaps it was because of Honoria's dark look as she shook her head behind her mother and pointed for him to take his leave. Perhaps it was because he knew that it would vex her to no end if he accepted. Or perhaps it was just that his stomach was growling and he didn't want to think about the nightmare-inducing meal awaiting him at the abbey.

So he stayed. Again.

They dined alfresco on cold meats, hunks of sharp cheese, hearty bread, ripe fruit and—*Huzzah*— more biscuits. Lady Hartley, Honoria, Althea and he simply sat on the stage, their feet dangling over the side, the day waning with the comfort and relaxation that he hadn't often found. Which was surprising because it had been the most peculiar day of his life.

"Is it always like this here?" He made a swirling gesture to the house and stage, and as he did a yellow feather floated out from his sleeve.

The three Hartley women laughed, the sound filling the high walls of the amphitheater like music.

"No," Honoria said. "When my father is home, it's much more entertaining."

Oscar could not imagine that. Then again, he was coming to learn that, where this family was concerned, he was probably better off not knowing in advance.

"He'll like you," Roxana offered, pressing her hand to

his shoulder as if she imagined he was worried. She didn't know that he wasn't planning on being around Addlewick for too much longer. But she smiled at him in that uncanny way mothers often had that made you wonder if they could read your thoughts. "I think I'll retire for the evening. Thea, would you come with me and bring that lantern?"

"It's still light out, Mother."

"I know, but night is fast approaching."

Oscar took the hint. "I'll be going, as well. Thank you for the unexpected but enjoyable day, Lady Hartley."

"How many times must I tell you to call me Roxana? We are family now." She pressed a kiss to his cheek. Then, weaving her arm through Thea's, the two of them climbed the stairs out of the pit.

He hopped down from the stage and turned for Honoria. Without thought, he set his hands on her waist to help her down. She opened her mouth as if to argue—after all, they both knew he wasn't the chivalrous sort—but then relented and placed her hands on his shoulders instead.

They were eye to eye in this position, her face framed by the stars just winking into existence through the indigo of twilight. "I remember a night sky similar to this in Paris."

"I'm surprised you recall it at all."

"Such a peevish tone, Signore. Is this about that make-believe kiss again?" At the mention, he could swear he saw the first curls of steam coming out of her ears. "Apparently, this is a rather sore point. Very well. If it will make you feel better, I will let you refresh my memory."

He slid her forward, taking his time to lower her feet to the ground. And she surprised him by staying close, lightly tracing the edge of his jaw with her fingertips and sending a shower of tingles over his skin.

"I've been thinking about that," she purred, looking at him through heavy lashes in a way that made his blood thicken.

His grip tightened on her narrow waist. "Have you?"

"Mmm-hmm," she hummed. And when she sank her top teeth into the plump flesh of her bottom lip, he nearly groaned.

He wanted that lip. Wanted to take it between his teeth, then take her mouth in a slow, thorough kiss. That would be the perfect ending to this surprising day. He was even willing to lose this round to her, to be the first one to concede.

But it seemed like he wouldn't have to, after all. Because she rose up on her toes and laid her finger against his lips, brushing softly back and forth. "And I think that you're right."

"I am?" His reply was hoarse and barely audible, his throat going dry when her hand slid to his nape. A warm shiver darted down his spine, pooling low. Every single part of him was focused on one thing—wanting her mouth beneath his.

"That kiss," she whispered, her sweet breath teasing the surface of his skin, making him ache with hunger, "never happened. Just. Like. This. One."

Abruptly, she lowered to her heels. Then she left him there, tongue-tied and more aroused than he ever remembered being. And all from a kiss that never happened.

Bloody hell.

Chapter Eleven

ᕲ᠊ᐟ

$\mathcal{H}$ONORIA WAS GLAD she hadn't kissed Oscar. Walking out of the pit with her head held high had felt like another victory.

In fact, she'd lain awake all night thinking about . . . not kissing him. And what it might have been like not to have his lips on hers without any mustachios in the way.

The following morning, however, she was a bit sleep-deprived and, according to Thea, *too curmudgeonly to bear.* After her sister trounced away from the breakfast room to write a play in which a fair-haired ogre met a gruesome end, Honoria decided she'd rather speak with someone who appreciated her.

So she went to talk to Ernest.

Thin bands of fog accompanied her sojourn over the lawn and down the hill beyond the hedgerow where the walled garden stood. The door was buried beneath a cage of ivy so thick that it was almost impossible to find. At least, if one didn't know where to look. But beneath years of overgrowth, a heavy lock waited, the iron blistered with rust and age.

After the accident that had taken her twin's life, her father had sealed the entrance. He didn't know that she'd been sneaking in ever since.

Of course, she'd tried to be strong as everyone had told her to do. *Be strong for your parents*, they'd all said. And by the time of her fifth birthday—her first without him—she had learned what an accomplished actress she was by putting on a brave face. And she had continued to do so every day.

But her nights had been a different story.

The nursery—which had once been filled with giggles and whispers past bedtime, followed by twin sleepy heads sharing the same pillow till morning—had become a room of yawning quiet and dark shadows hovering over the empty bed across from hers.

There had been no one to share secrets with about stolen biscuits from the kitchen, frogs that escaped pockets at dinner or splinters from slides down the banister. No one to creep beneath the covers with when the house creaked and the wind wailed through branches that scraped against the windows like unearthly claws.

During those endless months, the loneliness had grown too great to bear. So she'd crept out of bed and gathered up his coverlet, breathing in his smell—a fragrant mix of wonderful things like puppies and meadow grass and mud puddles. Then she'd padded outside and up the hill toward the family plot to curl beside his mounded grave.

But even with the blanket over the two of them, it had felt too cold. Too final. She'd needed to be someplace he had lived. Someplace he had loved.

That was when she'd first started coming to the garden.

She'd stolen the key that Father tucked away at the back of his desk drawer. When she was old enough to bat her eyes at the blacksmith, she'd had her own made. And just in case someone checked on the entrance, she kept the timeworn patina on the lock, but the inner chamber was well-oiled.

Plunging her hand beneath the curtain of ivy, she found the lock. The key turned with a decisive click. Then, casting one glance over her shoulder, she squeezed in through the narrow opening, careful not to disturb the underbrush.

Even after all this time, she still kept her visits a secret. She couldn't tell her parents. It would only break their hearts all over again, and she knew this because no one ever talked about Ernest or that terrible day. And all the lack of talking about it weighed on her heart.

Honoria dragged the door closed behind her and stepped beneath the low-hanging branches of a hawthorn tree and into the garden, the walls edged with roses, hollyhocks and climbing clematis. Spears of sunlight shone through the clouds, turning the last remains of mist into a cascade of crystals. And she smiled as if this were proof of her brother's presence here.

Breathing out a heavy sigh, she reclined on a cushion of dewy clover, beside the hexagon base of stone where the fountain had once stood.

"Do you remember when I mentioned that man I met in Paris?" she asked without preamble as though they were always in the middle of a conversation. "No, not Lord Holladay. The other one. The gambler."

She waited for Ernest to consider this. Even though he wasn't present in physical form, that didn't stop her from sharing her deepest secrets as they'd always done.

"To be clear, even though I may have mentioned him on occasion, that doesn't mean I ever wanted him to appear on my doorstep. Quite the opposite. Remember that trip to Brighton Beach when we were little and came away with all those pesky sand-flea bites? Well, he's like those, a constant source of irritation."

Unfortunately, her vehement declaration only reminded her of last night and the way his eyes had darkened, his hands flexing on her hips. And since she had been on her toes, all it would have taken was one small tug and her mouth might have collided with his. Accidentally.

Not that she'd given the matter any thought.

"I suppose one might consider him somewhat attractive. If one preferred the tall, dark and dangerous sort. Which I do not. At all. And no, I'm not crossing my fingers. That's just how I hold them when I'm thinking." Casually, she uncrossed her fingers, then scoffed as if in outrage of a ghostly accusation. "*Someone* is rather impertinent today. Very well, I may have kissed him once in Paris, but only as a means of escape. And no, I am not—absolutely not— obsessed with the notion of kissing him again. Oscar Flint can go to the devil, for all I care."

A breeze rustled against the decaying silk and wood frame of a forgotten kite, tangled in the branches. To her, it sounded like mocking laughter.

"Fine. He's the only one who's ever given me moths. There. Are you happy?"

The kite rustled again, and she stuck out her tongue at the cloud-dotted sky.

She was quiet for a while, absently plucking the leaves from a stem of clover.

Years ago, she'd made a vow in this very garden, to live life for two because Ernest never had the chance to live one. She intended to keep it. Therefore, she couldn't— *wouldn't*—allow this unfortunate attraction to Oscar Flint stand in her way.

"Though, to be completely honest, I'm worried that it's more than moths," she said quietly, half-afraid of the words coming true. "He sees through me in a way that no one ever has. And if this blackmailing scoundrel ever displayed a true redeeming quality, I'm afraid that I could actually begin to . . . like him."

She expelled a rush of breath as if the confession stole some vital force from within her.

"Oh, Ernest. Please help me send him away before I do anything foolish."

⚞

"AND WHY DID we have to walk into the village on the hottest day of the year?" Thea asked, trudging along the road beside her, a parasol in one hand and a fan in the other.

"To distract us from the insufferable heat, of course."

The misty morning had cleared away in time for the sun to steam the earth like a pudding in a copper pot, and Honoria was a sweaty plum in the batter.

Though, unlike Thea, she decided to forgo wearing a hat in addition to carrying a parasol. And if she happened to freckle, she would consider the blemish a badge of honor, a salute to her decision to be away from home in case Oscar paid a call.

"We might have waited for Mother to return with the carriage," her sister grumbled.

Honoria blotted her forehead with a lacy handkerchief. "She is with Lady Broadbent plotting your debut and will likely not return for hours."

Thea groaned. "Pray do not remind me."

"I thought you were eager for your first Season."

"I was until Mother told me there would be no pockets in my ball gowns. What will be the purpose of going if I cannot list my observations for future plays?"

"I believe the purpose is to dance and enjoy oneself."

"I thought you didn't enjoy your Season," she said, her dark brows lifting as if in question.

Honoria considered her response. "It was . . . entertaining. However, because of the scandal, there were many members of the *ton* who'd made it clear that the sole reason I was invited to parties was because of my beauty." Which had been rather tiresome to hear. Repeatedly. "There were also gentlemen who made offers for me that were—shall we say—less than respectable. And I tell you this only because the black mark upon our name is not completely scrubbed clean. Therefore, you may encounter the same. Just be on your guard. Though, I highly doubt Lady Broadbent will permit you to be in the company of such men."

"In other words, I am not to encounter any man interesting enough to inspire a future character."

Honoria shifted her parasol to her other hand and laid

an arm around her sister's shoulders. "Trust me, in London you shall encounter a multitude of characters."

"It's too warm for placating," she said, shrugging out of the partial embrace. "Ugh. How I wish the weather wasn't so—Oh, look! Our saviors have arrived."

Thea waved merrily to the Culpeppers, Percy on horseback with Peter and Carlton in the phaeton. The three of them lifted their hands in greeting.

But then they stopped and exchanged looks between them. And for some peculiar reason, they turned around on the narrow road and went back in the other direction.

"That's odd." Honoria felt her brow pucker. "I wonder why they did not come toward us. Perhaps they are returning with a more suitable conveyance for all of us?"

"I wouldn't hold my breath, if I were you."

"Whyever would you say that?"

"I saw Vandemere talking to them by the pond yesterday. Then the Culpeppers left directly, and they looked rather pale, too, as though someone—and I'm not saying who—might have dangled a threat over their heads if they should happen to flirt with a certain someone betrothed to him."

Honoria was already shaking her head. "Oscar would not have done that. And before you romanticize whatever it is you're thinking, he has no cause to put on a pretense of jealousy, for that is all it would be, a pretense. We are barely acquainted."

"I don't understand. What about the letters? Not to mention the fact that, for years, you've turned down countless proposals, citing your betrothal to Vandemere as the excuse."

"I wouldn't call it an excuse." It was absolutely an excuse. "Furthermore, I have no intention of marrying him just because he happens to be here. For all I know, he'll be gone next week."

Oh, please let him be gone next week.

"But you have to marry him."

"There is nothing in the contract stating that I must marry, only that *if* I do, it will be to him. Otherwise, he means nothing to me whatsoever."

"If you say so." Thea slid her a dubious look. "Though, to be honest, I cannot imagine why our parents allowed our grandmother and his to set the contract in place. It is all so very archaic."

"Believe me, I've asked that question countless times. The only answer I've received is that one day I will understand."

"Whatever the reason, we'll never discover it since we'll soon be reduced to nothing more than puddles beneath listless parasols. Unless . . ."

Thea turned toward the sound of wheels trundling on the road behind them. And Honoria closed her eyes on a brief wish that it wasn't Oscar.

Her wish came true. Turning, she saw Mrs. Brown, the baker's wife, along with her two sons. Twins with mops of curly brown hair. She hadn't seen them since they were infants, but they must have been nearly five years old by now. The same age Ernest had been.

At the thought, a sharp ache pierced the center of her chest.

Somehow, she summoned a smile as the horse cart stopped beside them. The back was filled with empty breadbaskets and two rambunctious boys who were hanging over either side to watch the wheels turn. "Mrs. Brown, what an unexpected pleasure to see you. I hardly ever have the chance to see you out making deliveries."

"Good day to you, Miss Hartley and Miss Hartley. Aye, Mr. Brown went to see his brother. Our little Charlie and Henry are . . . *assisting* me with deliveries. Ain't ye, boys?"

In response, the boys giggled and proceeded to tell all about their adventures in being chased by geese, climbing trees, dusting off every loaf they dropped—except for the ones that landed in horse dung—and how they'd fooled their mother into thinking they disappeared when they were hiding inside the baskets all along. After recounting their tales in a great rush, they both leaped up and began a sword fight with two baguettes, making the cart jostle from side to side.

With the patience of a saint, Mrs. Brown let out a breath. "Oh, but it's a dreadfully hot day to be out for a stroll. If you'd like, I could drive you into town."

Honoria shook her head. "We wouldn't want to be a bother."

"We'd be in your debt," Thea said over her.

"Think nothing of it. There's not much room up here, but plenty in the back."

"That would be lovely," Thea said, tugging her sister along. "Thank you."

By the time they reached the bakery, Honoria was eager to be home again. Not that she minded the bumbling cart, for it was fun to dangle her feet over the road as she'd done as a child when her father had driven them into the village for a ha'penny sweet at the merchant's.

And her reason wasn't because she found Charlie and Henry too rambunctious either. Quite the contrary. Their exuberance reminded her of all the fun that she'd had growing up in a house with an eldest brother who rode the stairway railing all the way down, hoisting a sword above his head and daring his sisters to battle to the death. On stage, of course.

But it was the combination of those memories, along with a host of others, that only served as a poignant reminder of the life that had been cut short.

The life that Ernest should have had.

The carriage rumbled onto High Street. They passed the ice cart, the back heaped with straw. Immediately, the twins started begging their mother for a chance to get a sliver of ice.

"No," she said as they stopped in front of the bakery. "You've bothered half of Addlewick today. I'll not have ye beggin' for an ice chip."

But then her sons turned their big brown eyes on her, clasped their hands to their chests and said *Pleeeeeease* so prettily that Mrs. Brown rolled her eyes and handed them the last quartern loaf to trade with the ice man. Then she shooed her hands in the air. "Off with ye now. But come back straightaway."

Charlie and Henry darted off in a flash, while Honoria and Thea helped carry the empty baskets into the bakery.

When Honoria came out the second time, she saw the boys lingering by the ice cart, happily slurping their slivers . . . until one brother bumped teasingly into the other and made him drop his ice. A tussle followed, and both lost their prizes in the dirt.

Ah, the joy of siblings, she thought with a grin.

While the ice man was inside the shop, the boys searched the cobblestones beneath the cart. And they must have found only one ice chip because a tug-of-war over it ensued. Back and forth, heaving and tugging.

No one heard the mail coach until it was too late.

Honoria's gaze darted down the street. To her horror, the frantic driver was reaching for the ribbons that had dropped from his grasp, and the four black horses galloped untethered.

Her attention veered to the boys. Charlie shouted in victory as he tugged the ice free . . . and staggered back into the street.

A nightmare unfolded before her eyes.

In her mind, the flower-boxed shopfronts turned into a walled garden. And it was Ernest with his halo of golden-blond curls, laughter bubbling out and echoing around her, bright as the sun.

A light snuffed out too soon.

Honoria tried to shout, to move, but she couldn't break free of this nightmare. A raw and gaping terror trembled inside her, opening the void like a dark chasm. Her blood turned to ice, freezing her to the pavement.

"No!" The scream that was lodged in her own throat came from Mrs. Brown beside her.

The four horses continued to charge down the lane, the loose reins just out of the driver's reach, his face a mask of dread.

A sudden motion blurred in front of her. A shape sprinted into the path of the horses—a man dashing into danger.

Oscar, her mind whispered as she registered the color of his hair, the outline of his form.

A new terror filled her when she knew there would soon be two casualties that day.

She wanted to look away, to cover her eyes, but she remained frozen in place, watching as he scooped up the boy under one arm and then—

He disappeared.

As the horses rushed on, she couldn't see him any longer. Was he . . . ? Were they both . . . ?

What had to have been mere seconds seemed to pass like eons as the coach went by.

Then she saw the huddled, lifeless forms on the other side of the lane. Saw the stricken, haunted expression on the twin who survived.

A bleak, choked sound came from Mrs. Brown. The driver slowed his horses. And Honoria still couldn't move. Still couldn't look away.

Only then did one form move, a slow unfolding from a crouch to a stand.

Only then did Oscar lift the boy to his feet, turn and offer a jaunty salute.

Only then did the villagers, who'd poured out from shopfronts, cheer with gladness as the twins tightly embraced.

Honoria couldn't breathe. Her chest ached. It felt as though she was trapped at the bottom of the sea and she'd never reach the surface.

But then a breath shuddered through her, that first gulp of air burning her throat. And suddenly she wasn't frozen any longer. Raw emotion scorched her insides, threatening to erupt in a torrent of the pain she'd kept locked away for so long.

So she did the only thing she could do . . . She ran.

Chapter Twelve

Oscar DIDN'T REALIZE he was uncomfortable with praise until the moment he deposited the wayward ragamuffin and his brother in their mother's arms, and she called him a . . . a hero, of all things.

Him? The same ruthless man who'd cheated, lied and stolen for his entire life?

No, he wasn't a hero by any means. Far from it. He was the type of man who mothers stared at crossly and warned their children to never follow in his footsteps.

He was a callous, self-serving, arrogant devil who had no qualms about taking over another man's life and title to suit his own purpose.

So after shrugging off all the backslaps and the good-natured accusations of being humble, he slipped away to find the one person who knew him. The real him.

Beyond the village square, he caught a glimpse of Honoria's blue frock as she skirted around a corner. Not wanting to be obvious about his pursuit, he pretended an interest in window-shopping. Then, when the summer sun had forced the villagers either into the shops or on their way home, he stole around the corner, too.

Oscar found her standing alone behind the haberdashery. Facing away from him, her head was bent toward the collapsed parasol in her grasp.

"It appears I've discovered your meeting place for assignations. Shall I leave you alone to slay one of your besotted followers with those come-hither gazes you like to unleash on the unsuspecting?"

He meant the words to sound like one of their usual barbs, but they came out in a growl instead. And he didn't know where this inner beast had come from or why he couldn't seem to shove it back into its cave.

"You know me so well." She offered a light laugh, the sound of it tinny to his ears.

Had he been right? Was she meeting someone?

He strode forward, his gaze scanning the surrounding shrubbery beyond the verge. It was quiet here, secluded. The ideal location for a clandestine meeting. "Who is he?"

She scoffed in response. However, when he reached her and turned her around, he noticed that something was wrong. Though her countenance was perfectly composed, there was a slight reddening at the tip of her nose and her damp lashes clustered together in spikes.

"What happened, Honoria?"

She shook her head and flitted her fingers. "I don't know what you mean."

"You were crying, and I want to know why." All the gruffness had gone out of his tone as he reached out to smooth away the last trace of dampness at the corner of her eye.

Her chin trembled ever so slightly. Yet even then, even when he was staring directly at her cards and they both knew she was bluffing, she still tried to sound flippant. "I thought I'd finally gotten rid of you, and in such a convenient manner."

"Ah, I think I understand," he said gently. "You are thoroughly vexed by the knowledge that you'll still have to kill me yourself."

"Precisely."

"Let me guess. Death by parasol?" Taking the frilly accessory from her, he leaned it against an empty crate. "There. I have disarmed you. Now you'll have to find a new method."

She followed his actions, staring vacantly at the parasol. When she spoke, her voice was almost too quiet to hear above the distant clamor of horse hooves on the lane and the soft susurration of the wind through the leaves.

"It all happened so fast. One minute he was beside his brother, laughing and teasing. The next he was stumbling into the street." She gestured with her hand as if the tableau were playing out again before her eyes. "Then you just . . . appeared. If you hadn't, I shudder to think about the outcome."

He didn't want to think about it either. So he simply shrugged. "Sometimes all we have is a moment."

She looked over at him quizzically. And, without a word, she moved toward him.

He watched her warily. After all, he never knew what to expect with this one.

Reaching up, she put her soft gloved hands along his jaw. Then, holding his gaze all the while as though she feared he would vanish from sight, she lifted up on her toes and pressed her lips to his.

He went still, his mind utterly blank. His heart stopped midbeat. Then a startled breath stalled in his lungs. One moment she'd seemed on the verge of tears and then she was . . . kissing him.

Again.

But this was not like the first kiss, that bold-as-you-please claiming she'd done in Paris. No, this was a hesitant tasting as if they were passing something fragile between them, back and forth in a silent communication. *Don't let it fall. Gentle now. We must be careful or this thing will shatter.*

He felt a tremor in his hands as they settled on the slender curve of her waist, the enticing flair of her hips. Then her soft sigh fanned over his lips, her eyes drifting closed, and Oscar wondered if he might be the thing that she feared would shatter. Because he was certain something cracked inside him, a fissure opening that sent a quake through him.

He staggered back a step, grateful that he met with the haberdashery wall. Those bricks and her lips were the only things keeping him upright.

What was it about her? What power did she yield to make him weak at the knees?

That was how she'd gotten away from him in Paris. She'd turned his legs to jelly, leaving him without the strength to run after her. And now she was taking more from him by continuing these shy, tender kisses that he would never expect from a femme fatale.

She was positively diabolical, taking no prisoners as she slanted her mouth beneath his and her fingers coasted up the nape of his neck.

He would dream about this for the next year. And quite possibly, for every year after that. In fact, he was beginning to understand why the Trojans opened the gates and let in that suspicious horse.

Of all the times he'd kissed women—and there had been a great many in every port and city—he had never in his life been kissed like this.

This was more than covert warfare. She was wearing him down with her tender assault. The untried fervor in each press of her lips undid him. It seemed to reach inside him to an unexplored crevasse, taking hold of some hidden . . . *thing* that was long forgotten and buried.

His fingers flexed, drawing her into the frame of his body. The contact jolted through him in a swift, cataclysmic bolt of lightning. A raw and ragged sound rumbled in his throat as their hips aligned and her supple breasts met the unyielding hardness of his chest.

He curved a hand around her nape. Felt the sublime surrender of her lips beneath his, the shy parting as the tip of his tongue tested the plump seam.

Then he tasted her, the sweet essence that had lingered long after she'd escaped him in Paris. He'd thought of this moment for a year. This supple feel and flavor had haunted his nights no matter how many other women had tried to obliterate it with their skilled seduction. But there was only one woman who tasted like her.

He delved into the inner softness, and she gasped when his tongue touched hers. The innocent response made him pause. Then he felt a tug at the corner of his mouth as realization took hold, and a surge of possessiveness for his bold little thief flooded him.

Gathering her closer, he coaxed her with slow, languid kisses. She offered only an instant of shy stillness before her own tentative touch found him. Then a pleased mewl purred in her throat. The vibration tunneled low inside him, reaching a primitive place that wanted to claim, to slake, to devour.

He pulled her flush against him, his pulse thickening, his blood hot. Their lips locked, tongues twining with searching strokes. She gave back every ounce of passion he gave her.

Then she upped the stakes by raking her teeth over his bottom lip. Damn. This woman would be the death of him. But oh, what a way to go!

Her fingertips curled against his scalp to pull him closer. Her throat emitted a greedy sound as she gently sucked on his tongue. He sagged back, certain his knees had again turned to jelly, and she began to pepper him with fervent kisses . . .

Until a throat cleared.

The kiss ended with an audible smooch as they broke apart. Or rather, as Honoria shoved away from him at once. His own reaction, on the other hand, was a bit slower, his head—and other parts of him—still lost in a haze.

He was only too thankful that it was Thea Hartley standing there instead of Ladrón.

Even so, her scowl was rather formidable, her arms crossed, one mahogany brow arched at her sister. "No interest in him whatsoever, hmm?"

"This was just—"

Her sister raised a hand, effectively cutting off Honoria's explanation. "I will be directly around the corner, prepared to declare that I saw nothing and never speak of it again. However, if you make me wait in this insufferable heat any longer than ten—I repeat, *ten*—seconds, at dinner this evening I'm going to mention what I stumbled upon. Then Mother will drive the two of you to Gretna Green by morning."

Then she turned on her heel and marched away.

"Devil's doorknocker. What have I done?" Honoria muttered to herself through her teeth as she snatched up her parasol and tried to open it. But the thing wasn't cooperating, and she growled at it.

It wasn't the most flattering of reactions.

Slipping the contraption from her hand, he opened it and gave it back. "What have you done? Well, I'd say you've shown your cards."

"Nothing of the sort. That was simply a reward for saving the boy's life."

"If that is true, my dear, then please look away while I toss a dozen other children in the street in order to save them all."

The corner of her mouth twitched as she attempted to school her features. "Hmm . . . I'm afraid, Mr. Flint, that my moment of gratitude is over. Moreover, I have absolutely no desire to reward you again. Ever."

"Liar," he said with smug triumph as her gaze darted to his mouth. Since her cheeks were already pink, it was difficult to tell if she blushed. Though, he was fairly certain she did.

But as she walked away and disappeared around the corner, he felt as though he'd been cheated out of something. He wasn't sure what. All he knew was that he wished she hadn't started this new game of theirs.

Chapter Thirteen

॰৵৹

*H*ONORIA JOLTED UP in bed, panic hammering beneath her breast.

It was a dream, she told herself. Only a dream.

Though, just in case, she touched her hands to her face and her arms, ensuring that her skin was still intact. And finding it cool and damp with perspiration, instead of charred to a crisp, filled her with untold relief.

She never wanted to have a dream like that again. Ever.

It had begun ominously, with her standing in front of the chapel. She'd been garbed in a crimson dressing gown, the fitted bodice cut so low that she feared her next inhale would cause her breasts to spill over. Apparently, her dream self had visited Babette Fairfax's modiste.

Even so, Honoria's scandalous attire hadn't stopped her from reaching out for the long, wrought iron door handle. The feel of it was solid and smooth beneath her grip. But then it was wrenched away, the doors flinging open to reveal a chapel that looked very much like Addlewick's. With only one difference.

This one was red, all the way from the runner down the central aisle to the pews and even the walls. But not like red paint or even a red sash. No, this color seemed to glow as if alive. A living, breathing red.

She didn't want to go inside, but her feet left the ground, and she started to float toward the altar. That was when she saw Oscar, his lips curved in a smirk as the doors slammed shut behind her.

As she floated closer and closer, the air grew hotter.

Panicked, she suddenly realized that they were no longer in a church. They were inside an oven.

She called out to Oscar as the blaze encircled her. Her hem caught fire. Then her cuffs. And within seconds her clothes were incinerated, leaving her naked.

The flames licked over her bare skin, simmering inside her. She called for Oscar again, but all he did was watch her with hooded eyes. And she feared he was just going to stand there and let her burn.

Then he held out a hand. Blindly, she reached through the flames, hoping he would save her. Yet, when he pulled her through the glowing red inferno and engulfed her in his smoldering embrace, she realized it was too late. The fire was consuming them both.

That was when she woke up.

In the pink light of early morning, she threw back the coverlet and padded across the bedchamber toward the washstand.

She understood the symbolism. After all, she was an intelligent, modern nineteenth-century woman. And, clearly, she never should have kissed Oscar.

It only compounded the issue by making this betrothal nonsense seem far too real . . . and far too inescapable.

The problem was, since she'd decided against murder, there was no foreseeable way to rid herself of him. No stopping her family from pushing her toward the altar. And the last thing she wanted was to be married at all.

It seemed her only option was to tell her parents the truth.

"The truth," she said grimly into the washbasin, her voice bleak and echoing against her wavering reflection. Cupping cool water in both hands, she splashed it over her face.

Confession was the only way. Unfortunately, once word

spread, there would be another scandal. It was inevitable, but she could only hope they would forgive her.

On a resigned sigh, she rang for Tally and dressed for the day.

~~

PREPARED TO BARE her sins over porridge and toast, she practiced her speech as she left her chamber.

In fact, she'd just reached the top of the stairs when the front door of Hartley Hall crept open and . . . Verity stole inside.

Alarmed by the return of the very same sister who'd been married little more than a sennight ago, Honoria started down the stairs. But something made her hesitate.

It was clear by the way that Verity cast a surreptitious glance around the foyer, before taking pains to close the door quietly, that she wanted her arrival to go unnoticed. Lowering her valise, she ran a hand over bedraggled hair that looked as though her pins had been lost across several counties. And her puffy eyes appeared as though she hadn't slept in days.

But where was her new husband?

Honoria started down again, just as a series of howls sounded from the opposite end of the house. Verity blanched, clearly having forgotten about the Queen's Council.

Barrister and Serjeant-at-Arms weren't about to let her return go unnoticed. They came gamboling down the hall, voicing their exuberant *aroo*s of welcome, then proceeded to circle her skirts while nuzzling beneath her hands in demand of returned affection. Once that was settled, their attention abruptly turned to the tasty leather straps of her valise. And when Mr. Mosely appeared and tried to rescue the bag, Serjie and Barry dashed off with it. Their butler sighed, then followed.

Mother rushed in from the hall. "Verity, my dear, what is it? Has something happened?"

"Nothing of the sort. I simply . . . forgot something," she said, pretending as though her voice wasn't ragged from crying. But she'd never been very good on the stage.

Roxana Hartley, on the other hand, gave an exceptional performance at pretending to believe her. She offered a gentle smile and smoothed the matted hair from her daughter's cheek. "Ah. Whatever it is, it must be important as I've already sent most of your things to the Longhurst estate. Is Magnus waiting in the carriage, then?"

"No. He"—Verity looked away quickly and swallowed—"he had business matters to attend and stayed at his estate."

"I'm surprised he let you leave his side," Mother said and laughed lightly. "When he stole you away to elope, he was so lovestruck that I wasn't sure if he would let you out of his sight for the next year. Though, I had hoped he would have whisked you off on a honeymoon instead."

"Well, with the silver mine he's recently inherited, he had to settle up a few matters first."

"Ah. Then, you likely have your hands full with an entire household of servants to manage . . ."

Verity shook her head. "His mother sees to everything. She is . . . particular, and the servants are used to her methods."

"Yes, Geraldine was always quite particular," Mother said wrapping an arm around her shoulder. "Come, little finch. I'll help you find whatever it is that you're looking for."

When Verity's eyes flicked to the stairway, Honoria managed to conceal her worried frown with a mask of delight. "Huzzah! The prodigal sister has returned. Do not tell me you have actually missed our family dramatics and are eager to take part in Thea's next play?"

"If you have need of a potted ficus on your stage, you may call upon my skills," Verity said, attempting a wry smirk. But even that faltered, quivering around the edges.

Taking a page from Mother's script, Honoria pretended not to notice.

Being introspective and reserved was simply Verity's way, but it broke Honoria's heart to see all the pain she held inside. Her sister had spent so much of her life trying to maintain a level head, to keep the peace between siblings, and to bring a sense of sanity to this rather eccentric household that she never learned to express herself.

Honoria had hoped that Magnus would have brought her out of her shell.

She knew her sister loved him dearly. But clearly, there was something terribly wrong. Something that not even love could fix.

Then again, in Honoria's experience, love was the very worst thing that could happen to anyone.

THAT MORNING, OSCAR heard arguing through the open door of the dowager's sitting room, the discordant rumbles clambering up the staircase. The sharp, higher tones of feminine voices tried to drown out the low, unfamiliar baritone.

Standing, he closed the book of poetry and tucked it back into his inner coat pocket.

He'd been reading to Vandemere's grandmother every day. Sometimes from his own book and other times from the books of verse in the library.

He liked the collection. It made him feel . . . well, he didn't want to say that reading them made him feel closer to his own father. He barely remembered him. After all, he'd been five years old when his father had left without a backward glance. Even so, he did recall how much the little book of poetry had meant to his mother and how adamant she'd been that Oscar should keep it safe all throughout his life.

"That is all for today," he said, lifting the dowager's

knobby hand to bow over it. But when he tried to pull away, she held on with a surprisingly strong grasp.

"Here," she said with the *H* silent as though she had a cockney accent.

"Fear not, you haven't gotten rid of me, yet," he teased, believing she'd been asking him to stay. "I have other duties at the moment. But I will come again tomorrow, Grandmama."

He chose to call her that because . . . well . . . there was no reason not to. He had never had a grandmother. At least, none that he'd known about. And since Vandemere hadn't bothered to visit the one he had, someone might as well call her Grandmama. After all these years, she deserved that at least.

Still holding on, she looked down at his hand and gradually forced out one word and then another. "Rrrring . . . mmmine."

"I should like nothing more than to give this ring to you. However, I'm afraid I must keep it safe. I made a promise, you see."

At this, her mouth spread in a broad smile as if she approved. Or perhaps she knew that if he left it unguarded, it would likely disappear like many of the paintings throughout the abbey had.

He suspected that the widows or someone had started to sell them off over the years. Of course, he didn't know this for certain because he hadn't yet been granted access to the accounting ledgers. Apparently, Mr. Price had conveniently misplaced them on the day that Oscar requested to look over the accounts.

Lost ledgers aside, however, Oscar imagined that keeping a large estate such as this would cost a pretty penny. And it was really nothing more than curiosity that made him want to sneak a peek at the inner workings.

But that could wait. For now, he pressed a kiss to the older woman's knuckles and promised to return later.

On his way out the door, her nurse stood from the chair in the corner, setting her needlework aside. "Her ladyship always liked those poems. And her health has much improved of late. I do believe it is because of your visits, my lord."

He inclined his head and thanked her for her kind words. But as he left the room, he realized that, even in such a short time, he looked forward to these visits, too. It brought him a semblance of peace in the midst of the animosity forever brewing beneath this roof.

And speaking of animosity, he headed toward the raised voices.

He walked down one staircase and then another—still cringing at the sight of the cracked black lacquer on the railing—before the cause of the ruckus came into view.

Alfreda and Millicent were confronting a bull moose of a man, their arms wide like they were trying to herd him back through the open front doorway.

Algernon stood there, his hand on the door, looking completely oblivious as his cloudy gaze stared off in the wrong direction.

"I aim to see his lordship, and I ain't leavin' till I do," the bull moose said with a curt nod and a beetled brow, his barrel chest puffing out like a Watt steam engine ready to blow.

Alfreda put her foot down with a hard clap. "Mr. Brown, if you do not leave, I will be forced to send for my husband."

Oscar nearly laughed. The henpecked Shellhorn wouldn't know the first thing about confrontation. As for the matter of the bull moose, it took no toiling of the pia mater between Oscar's ears to discern that Mr. Brown was likely father to the two ragamuffins fighting over an ice chip the day before.

"And furthermore," Millicent added sharply, "laborers are seen to at the back of the abbey. Algernon, summon the footmen. Algernon!" When the butler merely stood there at his post, his hearing wholly undisturbed by the biting sound of harpies, she stalked off. "I'll fetch them myself, then."

Oscar bit back a grin as he surveyed the scene, walking down the last few steps. "It seems as though there's a commotion afoot."

Even though he spoke in a moderate tone, his voice not one-tenth the volume of Millicent's, he distinctly saw the corner of the butler's mouth twitch. That sly devil.

Mr. Brown peeled off his hat. "Are you the viscount?"

"I am Vandemere," he answered, taking no small amount of delight in seeing Alfreda's glower. "How may I be of service, sir?"

"But that's just it. You've already been. And a great service, my lord. The greatest, in fact. The missus and me owe you a debt for saving our little Charlie."

Embarrassed, Oscar wished he'd taken Mr. Brown aside and away from the hall. He wasn't used to gratitude. Now, if a man had charged through the door, accusing him of swindling him out of a fortune, that would have been something familiar. Then after a heated repartee, bout of fisticuffs or even a duel, Oscar would have realized he'd overstayed his welcome in that particular city, and in the morning, he would have been gone.

That was his life.

This was not.

This life belonged to Vandemere, wherever that truant was. And even though it had actually been Oscar who'd thrown himself into this by his negligibly noble act yesterday, he'd never felt more the charlatan than he did now. "It was no trouble. Any man would have done the same."

He took a step and gestured to the door. Unfortunately, there was no moving Mr. Brown from his spot until he'd had his say.

"But it was. Folks still be talkin' 'bout how you done tore down the street, risking life and limb to save me boy. I'm here to offer me humble gratitude."

When he bowed low, Oscar shifted uncomfortably. "Well then, it's all settled. I appreciate that you came all this way and . . . er . . . I'm sending you off to your family with my finest wishes for your future felicitations."

"Gratitude ain't all I brought." Mr. Brown flashed a broad, toothy grin of short, square teeth. "See, the gossips, they been talkin' about how you ain't had any proper victuals since you've come home." He paused to cast a disparaging glance at Alfreda and at Millicent, who was striding up like an avenging willow tree draped in black with two of her minions in tow. "So I brung all this for you."

As soon as he spoke, in walked Mrs. Brown and her two miscreants, toting baskets brimming with breads, pies and pastries of all sorts. Meanwhile, Algernon looked on, an amused grin on his rawboned countenance.

"Mr. Brown, I don't quite know what to say."

Oscar felt a peculiar, tight sensation in the environs of his chest. It made him feel closed in, his feet heavy on the floor as if they were sprouting roots. He wasn't sure what it was, though he suspected it was the green sludge at breakfast.

All he wanted to do in that moment was stride through the door and take in a big gulp of air. Or, better yet, get on his horse and ride until his hat flew off in the wind and—

"Well, I know what to say." Millicent flailed her arms in a shooing motion. "Be gone and take all this rubbish away at once. Dunnelocke Abbey needs none of your charity. We have food aplenty. It is not the fault of these kitchens if it doesn't suit every palate."

That snide tone was enough to chase away that uncomfortable constriction in Oscar's chest. Drawing in a deep breath, he silently thanked Vandemere's *dear sweet aunt*.

Alfreda motioned impatiently to the footmen. But then a most surprising thing happened. The footmen hesitated, sharing a look between themselves before directing their attention not to Alfreda . . . but to Oscar.

Before Alfreda could finish uttering "What are you waiting for?" Oscar cleared his throat.

"Rand. Perry," he said to the liveried men. "See to it that these generous gifts are taken with care to the kitchens, the contents unloaded and the baskets returned to my friends."

They bowed and said in unison, "Aye, my lord."

It wasn't until the instant he saw Millicent and Alfreda stiffen that the *my lord* registered. And he realized this hadn't been the first time that day either. The nurse had also addressed him with deference.

Apparently, there was a contagion running amok beneath this roof, starting with the servants.

He grinned at the aunts, filled with a sense of peevish delight.

"Oh, and one more thing," he said to the footmen. "Since Mr. and Mrs. Brown have been so generous, I believe it is only right that they should have a jar of the rose honey that Lady Millicent is forever declaring to be the best in all of England." His grin only widened when Millicent fumed. She was rather particular and protective about her hives. "And please escort Mrs. Brown through the rose garden and assist her with any cuttings she would like to take with her."

The men nodded without hesitation.

Mrs. Brown beamed, her hand splaying over her bosom. "Oh, your lordship, you are too kind."

When his kindness could bring misery to the pair of wasps glaring at him with stingers at the ready, yes indeed, he could be kind.

He inclined his head to Mrs. Brown and shook her husband's hand. The boys, in the midst of playing tug-of-war with their basket, were given a look by their father. They summarily dropped the basket, stood up straight as arrows and bowed at the waist like tin soldiers. And Oscar ruffled their heads, sending them off.

Once the hall was left with only the faint aroma of edible delights, he turned to the widows.

Alfreda crossed her arms beneath her black bombazine-bound bosom. "Mrs. Blandings will not be happy about this."

"I should think not," he agreed. "Doubtless, she will be embarrassed by the rumors that have been spreading about her cooking, and she will blame it all on you."

"How dare you invite them into my rose garden! And to share honey from my hives is unforgivable," Millicent sneered. "You have no authority here."

"So you say. However, it seems that the servants have other ideas. Except for the ever-loyal Mr. Price, of course. According to him, the accounting books have been misplaced. If that is true, I have to wonder what tasks keep him locked up in his office for hours on end." He pursed his lips, eyeing her with suggestive speculation. "You wouldn't happen to be popping by for a lengthy visit or a game of ribbon around the maypole, would you, Aunt Millie?"

She gasped. "Why, I never—"

"He's only attempting to provoke you," Alfreda interjected, her chin jutting forward. "Just leave him. He will soon have the noose around his throat when the cleric arrives with the bona fide baptismal record in hand. He will tell us all we need to know."

At the news, Oscar's countenance betrayed none of the disquiet suddenly churning in the pit of his stomach. He simply offered a salute to the pair as they stalked away. "Well, Algernon, this is turning out to be a rather interesting day."

"It is, indeed," the butler said. "My lord."

Chapter Fourteen

Ꮋᴏɴᴏʀɪᴀ's ꜰᴀᴛʜᴇʀ ᴀʀʀɪᴠᴇᴅ home in time for dinner that evening. And because Conchobar Erasmus Hartley possessed a silver tongue that had once earned him a place on the stage, his cheery "Halloo" boomed to all corners of the house.

His wife was the first to greet him with undisguised affection, no matter how uncomfortable it made everyone else. But they weren't the typical couple, especially among the aristocracy.

According to the tales spoon-fed to their children, theirs had been a fated match that no force in heaven or on earth could have stopped. And, after Con had wooed and married the toast of the *ton*—a debutante of famed beauty whose wit and skill in entrancing an audience matched his own—they started an acting troupe and toured the English countryside together. Which they had done, all the way up until Thea was born.

They'd settled into a quieter, mostly modest life, limiting their stage performances to the drawing room or the pit. And, even though society frowned upon dramatic displays that were typically seen as *common*, Con and Roxana had managed to retain the respect of their peers.

At least, until the scandal.

At the thought, Honoria wondered how his reception had been in town. He'd been in London ensuring that Truman was settled in new lodgings as he prepared to take a post in an architectural firm. But whatever concerns she had dispersed at the sight of the broad smile on her father's face.

He drew in a deep inhalation of the scents of home, as if all were right in his world . . . until his gaze fell on his eldest daughter, her eyes red-rimmed as she stepped into the foyer to greet him, and her husband nowhere to be found.

Whatever affection he might have felt for his new son-in-law extinguished in that instant.

"I'll kill him" was all he said before turning on his heel and ordering one of the grooms to saddle a fresh horse.

Verity rushed forward and tearfully clung to him. "No, please don't. Magnus did nothing wrong. The fault is mine alone. Please, Father."

After exchanging a speaking glance with his wife, he stroked his daughter's honey-blond hair and pressed a kiss to her forehead. "Very well, then. If that's what you wish."

"It is." She straightened her spine and smoothed her skirts before gesturing woodenly to the stairway. "In the meantime, I'd better return to my search."

He watched Verity with concern as she fled up the stairs, a hand pressed to her mouth. Then he turned to Mother. On an exhale, he bent his forehead to hers for a moment of unspoken communication. Then Mother stepped away to speak with the servants about readying a bath.

Knowing that the entire story must wait, he turned to Honoria in eagle-eyed appraisal. "According to the missive I received from your mother while I was in London, Viscount Vandemere has returned, and his first order of business was to see you."

"Then, you are well-informed," she said with careful evasion and pressed a kiss to his cheek.

Whenever possible, she tried not to lie any more than she had already done. After all, if the vicar was correct and there was a golden scale in front of the pearly gates, with one side bad and the other good, then St. Peter was surely only a pebble or two away from sending her bad-deed pan plummeting with such force that it would set all the good-deed pebbles flying.

Father stared at her for a beat as if expecting her to say more. In that fraction of a second she wondered if, heaven forbid, he'd seen the letter Honoria had written to Truman. The very letter with the first line in bold letters: *WHATEVER YOU DO, DO NOT LET FATHER READ THIS*, the contents including all of the details—well, *most*—concerning Mr. Flint and his unexpected arrival in Addlewick.

It had been a plea for advice. Though, as of yet, her brother had still not written a reply.

Since her father waited for her to speak, she decided a change of topic was in order. "What news of Truman? Did he find suitable lodgings?"

"He did, indeed." Father handed his coat and gloves to Mr. Mosely. "A flat of rooms on Bond Street near a tailor's shop, in fact. I daresay he'll be the sharpest-dressed architect London has ever seen."

"Splendid," Mother said, hearing this as she descended the stairs. "Your dinner will be sent up. Then, after you're settled, we'll have pudding in the parlor, and you can tell us all about it."

As the servants bustled the portmanteau away and Mother and Father went up the stairs hand in hand, Honoria breathed a sigh of relief.

Her father had always had an uncanny way of producing a line of Shakespeare that seemed inspired by the contents of his children's thoughts, the thoughts that none of them wished aired. And she had done her level best not to think about Oscar, the blackmail, the kiss—especially not the kiss—or the fact that Mr. Flint had the power to send the family into scandal. Again.

It appalled her to know that, even with all the power he held over her head, she'd still kissed him. What had she been thinking?

Clearly, she hadn't been thinking at all.

Turning, she saw Thea standing beneath the arched lintel with her arms crossed. "Clever evasion, I must say."

"You just hush," Honoria said in a whisper, casting a glance around the empty foyer. "Or I'll tell them I caught you kissing Carlton Culpepper."

"I was eight years old."

"Not the way I'll tell it."

Thea scowled. "Very well. Though, I don't know how long your answer will satisfy Father. Eventually, he will ask about your viscount."

"I know." Honoria was already fretting over future lies. *Prepare yourself, St. Peter. You'll need a steady hand.* "With any luck, something large and looming will fall from the sky and take everyone's attention away from Vandemere."

───※───

AN HOUR LATER, Honoria wondered if she had latent soothsaying abilities. Because, just when they were gathering for pudding, something large and looming crashed through the front door.

Or *someone*, rather.

It was none other than the Duke of Longhurst, darkly disheveled, road weary and eyes blazing.

Roused by the commotion, the family rushed into the foyer and heard him articulate only four words. "Where. Is. My. Wife?"

Upon seeing the towering beast in the doorway, said wife emitted a squeak of alarm, then dashed down the hall in the opposite direction.

Magnus fell into pursuit.

Any other family might have given them a moment of privacy. The Hartleys, however, never missed an opportunity for a bit of drama. So they followed at a discreet distance.

Verity ran all the way through the house, out the side door, through the birdhouse garden, over the hill and toward the pit.

"As if dashing off in the dead of night and leaving me to search frantically for you wasn't enough," Magnus bellowed after her, "now you're running away from me? If you think for one moment that I will ever stop coming for you, then think again, Verity. You are my wife."

"I am the yoke around your neck! Your mother said as much," she called back over her shoulder as she hastened down the stone steps. "I'll never be a proper duchess."

"I didn't want a proper duchess, I wanted you."

"That's a dreadful thing to say! You all but admitted that I fall short."

"Verity, you're being ridiculous. Come here, and let's settle this like sensible people."

Magnus growled and started down the steps after her.

Verity looked left and right, searching for an escape. Then she clambered up on the stage. "No. Your mother hates me. Do you know how hard it is to hear about the things I'm doing wrong all day long? She checks the clock each morning as I enter the breakfast room as if I've arrived late. Then she presents me with a list of tasks to be done that I'm not certain there's time enough to complete in one lifetime, let alone one day."

"My mother is merely afraid of being sent to the dower house, so she wants to seem useful. And she doesn't hate you. She doesn't know you yet. Give her time."

"Time for her to poison my tea, you mean," she grumbled. However, the acoustics from the stage were so marvelous that one could hear all the way to the terrace . . . precisely where Honoria and her family happened to be, all lined up at the balustrade, shamelessly watching the spectacle.

They had the best seats in the house.

Thea took out her ledger and made a note. "Verity is in fine form. I don't think she's ever performed this well."

"Because she isn't performing, dear," Mother said and gently covered the ledger so that her daughter would tuck it away.

Magnus vaulted to the stage, stopping only when Verity backed away. "Surely, that isn't why you left. Tell me."

At first, she hiked her chin, stubborn as ever. But as he neared, cautious as if he were approaching a wild animal, her shoulders slumped. In a shaking voice, she admitted, "I'm afraid of embarrassing you. I'm afraid the servants will never respect me. And I'm afraid that you'll see all my flaws and wonder why you ever married me."

"I married you because I couldn't live without you. You must know that by now."

She shook her head and sniffled.

"Come here," he crooned, pulling her into his arms as she buried her face against his chest. "I can recall each moment we've been together, and not one of them has left me embarrassed."

"Not even when I was dangling from a tree?"

"Quite the contrary. In fact, I have a rather fond memory of the dress you were almost wearing."

"What about the time I almost broke that priceless vase in the museum?"

"Do you mean the day you had on that delectably form-fitting green skirt with a mile of buttons down the back, and one of them caught on my watch fob? I wasn't embarrassed then either," he said warmly. "I adore you, Verity. As long as you are true to yourself and remain the remarkable, lovely and partly feral woman I fell in love with, that will never change."

She sniffed again and looked up at him. "What if society never accepts me as your duchess?"

"Then, we'll live on that little island in the middle of the river."

"Now you're teasing me," she said, trying to push free.

But he tugged her back to him and murmured, "I never

tease about the river, as you should know. Now, kiss me, my wildling."

"Come, children," Mother whispered, gesturing for them to go inside and give Verity and Magnus some privacy.

Father held the door and smiled. "Verity has definitely found her voice."

Mother paused to kiss his cheek. "And we'll have a grandchild by early spring, I should think."

Honoria walked in silence to the parlor, guilt dogging her every step. How could she possibly tell her family the truth now?

Verity had always struggled to find her place. But she'd finally found it at Magnus's side. Another scandal linked to the Hartley name would ruin her chance of happiness.

Not only that, but it would destroy Thea's chances to have a Season, too. And what about her brother and the new life he was trying to build? The previous scandal had already caused him to lose so much—his fiancée and all the dreams he'd had for his future. When he'd left to seek his fortune on the sea, it had been like losing another brother.

Holding fast to her locket, Honoria decided that she could not let Oscar's blackmail hurt her family. Even if she had to pay him every farthing she possessed and sacrifice her own future in the process, she would do it.

She wouldn't be happy about it. But she would do it, nonetheless.

Chapter Fifteen

❧

OSCAR PLANTED THE soles of his boots on a compass-shaped opus sectile in the marble floor of the library and considered his options for avoiding an early grave.

It wasn't until Mr. Brown and his baskets of gratitude arrived that he realized the importance of being Vandemere. Simply declaring it and hiding himself away in a small hamlet wasn't going to work.

In order for his *holiday* at the abbey to serve its purpose, he needed everyone to accept that he was the viscount. If he couldn't convince the widows that he belonged here, then they—and the cleric they'd sent for—would likely make a fuss. And a fuss would bring too much attention. Attention would draw Ladrón's notice. And since the Spaniard was fond of separating his enemies' heads from their bodies, Oscar very much wanted to keep that from happening.

Over the past year, Warring had tutored him on life as an aristocrat, including a list of viscounty tasks, like scrutinizing the accounts on a daily basis.

Unfortunately, Mr. Price was about as cooperative as a toad.

The steward even led him on a wild-goose chase through the abbey in search of the supposedly misplaced account ledgers. He put on a jolly good show, too, traipsing through the study, his own office near the servants' stairs, and even into the viscount's apartments in the west wing—currently inhabited by the Shellhorns—but the books were nowhere to be found.

Oscar knew better. They were hidden somewhere, doubtless by the command of the widows.

Frustrated, he scanned the library shelves, absently rubbing the scar beneath his cravat. What was the likelihood that Ladrón would simply forget about him? *Not very likely.* The man was obsessive in all his pursuits. There would be only one way to stop—

Something rattled sharply behind him.

He turned with a start to see Algernon. The old man was dragging a rickety old ladder with him.

Oscar immediately stepped forward to assist. But the butler barely spared him a glance as he kept plodding. He crossed to the far side of the room and propped the ladder against one of the burled wood pilasters that framed the slender floor-to-ceiling bookshelves. Then he began to climb.

Alarmed, Oscar followed and stood at the base of the ladder to ensure he didn't fall. He had no idea what the butler was doing. Perhaps the old devil had finally had enough of the widows and planned to do himself in by jumping from the top.

But then Algernon rapped the side of his fist against the smooth entablature beneath the crown molding, and Oscar heard a soft click. Wide-eyed, he watched as the butler opened a narrow hinged panel. A secret compartment. And inside, stood a row of black leatherbound books.

Algernon didn't bother to remove them, he simply started his way down the ladder. Once at the bottom, he turned to Oscar.

"I believe these are the accounting books you were searching for, my lord." And with that, the crafty old codger just walked out of the library.

Oscar shook his head. He was still getting used to the *my lord* honorific, as well as ordering other people around.

But it was likely better that way. After all, he couldn't return to his old life expecting people to bow and do his bidding. Well, not if he wanted to stay alive. And that was the entire reason he was here, wasn't it?

Climbing the ladder, he secretly hoped that he'd find a pouch filled with gold sovereigns at the back of the secret compartment.

He didn't.

However, he did confirm that those were the misplaced ledgers, and he took them to the study where he would have complete privacy.

Given his skill with numbers, it didn't take him long to see the discrepancies: a few pounds miscalculated here or there, larger sums gone astray beneath a purposely sloppy scribble or inkblot and an incorrect total carried over to the following page.

Interesting, he mused. But not altogether surprising. He'd suspected that there was a reason Mr. Price had hidden these ledgers.

What Oscar couldn't glean from the pages, however, was who else might have known about it. For all he knew, Mr. Price could have been working with one or more of the widows.

Yet, the only thing he could be sure about was the fact that he wasn't the only one at Dunnelocke Abbey with something to hide.

~~~

WHY WAS SOMEONE hammering?

Disoriented, Oscar lifted his head, his neck cracking with the effort. He blinked, the faint glow of embers revealing a paneled room and a dark expanse beyond the open window on the opposite wall. *The study*, he recalled groggily.

Looking down at the ledgers strewn across the desk, he realized he'd fallen asleep and that the lamp had gone out. Lifting the glass chimney, he attempted to light it, but quickly surmised that there was no oil. Yet another expense that was likely misrepresented in the ledgers.

Searching warped drawers that tended to give way in unpredictable increments—some lodging in place at barely a hand's width and others cracking open with the force of a battering ram enacted from the opposite end—he finally found a grouping of candles. But the instant the strong odor hit him, he muttered a curse. He hated tallows. They were greasy and foul-smelling and smoked excessively.

However, he knew they were cheaper than beeswax. He didn't have to look at the ledgers for that information. It was something he'd learned in his youth when his mother had held on to their last beeswax candle for as long as she could after his father left.

When it had burned out, it was like all the hope his mother had clung to had been snuffed out as well.

The knocking came again, pulling him from his thoughts with the realization that it was that sound that had woken him. And it seemed to be coming from the front of the house.

The clock on the mantel read a quarter past two. The odds that Algernon was still awake at this hour, not to mention able to hear the racket, were slim to none. So Oscar took the stinking chamberstick in hand, unlocked the study and went to the foyer.

A moment later, he slid open the judas hole and peered through to find a road-weary Cardew, wavering on his feet.

A breath of relief left Oscar. At once, he turned the latch, threw open the front door and pulled the man in for a hearty embrace.

"Cardew, you are a most welcome sight." Oscar slapped him on the back, disturbing the travel dust from his coat. Then he sniffed and wrinkled his nose, drawing back. "What is that horrendous smell?"

Cardew shook his head. "Let's just say that I was distracted by a particularly buxom tavern wench. Her husband came along at a rather inconvenient time, and I was forced to flee from an upstairs window and landed too near the chicken coop."

"When are you ever going to stop chasing the wrong women?" Oscar chuckled and shook his head. But he already had the answer, and they said in unison, "As soon as you find the right one."

But they both knew there was no such creature.

A bedraggled James Raglan appeared in the doorway. "I saw the carriage drive up. Shall I assist with the trunks, my lord?"

"Aye. Just set them in here. Then see that the driver has a bed and a meal for the night. I'll ensure that he's compensated in the morning."

When Oscar turned toward the stairs, Cardew cast an arched look his way and mockingly mouthed, *My lord*.

"Come along," Oscar said, rolling his eyes. "We have much to discuss, but it will keep until I can stand the smell of you."

⚞

AFTER CARDEW WAS settled in an attic room among the servants' quarters, Oscar returned to the study to finish perusing the last of the ledgers, taking time to pilfer a lamp from the parlor and build up the fire.

At his desk, he'd given up hoping to find a surplus of treasure and instead focused on the patterns, formulating a clearer picture of Price's bookkeeping.

Cardew entered the study in a fresh change of clothes, his trousers and shirtsleeves a bit wrinkled from the journey. With a wry quirk of his wiry white brows, he said, "A little light reading? I seem to recall you hating your schoolwork."

"No, just the pompous tutors." Oscar closed one ledger

and picked up another. "It took so long to get hold of these that I don't want to let them out of my sight before I peruse them all."

Cardew moved around the study with idle interest. "Changed your mind about raiding the coffers? As long as you're pretending to be an aristocrat, might as well behave like an entitled prig and take whatever you want."

"As I said before, we're not going to steal or draw any more attention than necessary. We're here for one purpose. And besides, there is no money in this estate. Even if there were, the widows and their loyal steward wouldn't allow me anywhere near it until they verify my legitimacy."

Cardew stopped short. "Surely, you showed them my letter."

"And they sent for a cleric of the church where Vandemere was baptized to verify it."

"That was my best work!"

A reluctant grin tugged at the corner of Oscar's mouth as he skimmed the figures. "You say that about everything you do."

"It happens to be true each time," Cardew said oh so humbly. "I suppose we're fortunate that Vandemere was born in Africa instead of Scotland as you were, or else their cleric would already be here. How much time do we have?"

"A month? Perhaps a bit longer."

Cardew cursed. Agitated, he withdrew a cheroot from the case in his pocket. Moving to the hearth, he lifted a stick to light it, puffing as the tip glowed orange. After he blew out a satisfied stream of smoke, he tossed the stick back into the flames. "That doesn't give us long. Or *you*, rather. Ladrón made it clear that he wasn't interested in me any longer."

"Surely, that cannot bother you," Oscar said looking up in time to see Cardew's shoulders lift in a petulant shrug. "I cannot believe it. You're pouting because a murderous villain is no longer after you?"

"I'm very good at what I do. It would be nice to be appreciated for once."

Oscar pinched the bridge of his nose to ease the sharp pain pressing against his skull. He wasn't going to remind Cardew that all this had begun because he'd tried to sell a forgery to a man known in the darker quarters as El Coleccionista. Or that Oscar had saved his life by offering to pay back four times the amount that Ladrón had originally paid for the painting. None of that mattered any longer.

The fact of the matter was, after losing the two thousand pounds he'd needed to pay Cardew's debt to Honoria, Oscar had proceeded to put himself in Ladrón's sights by using his particular skill with cards to win every franc he'd needed by dawn that very same day.

The problem was Ladrón had observed him in action and decided that he needed to add Oscar to his collection of rare objects. When Oscar had refused, he was informed by way of the sword at his throat that declining the invitation wasn't an option.

It was only due to Rowan Warring's timely intervention that he'd survived at all.

"I appreciate you," Oscar offered placatingly.

Cardew flicked his ashes. "You're just saying that."

"I'm not. And I'm sure that if Ladrón ever saw your series of Rembrandts, he would have wanted you for himself." When Cardew nodded and appeared suitably mollified, Oscar closed the ledger and sat back, returning to more pressing matters. "What news of Sonya?"

She'd been inconsolable after Ladrón attempted to use her as a means of coercion. But men like him were used to preying upon the frailty of others to get their way.

That night when Oscar continued to fight off his men, Ladrón had tied her to a chair and threatened to pluck out the eyes that had drawn his notice in the beginning—one a rare emerald green, the other a flawless sapphire blue.

When the monster didn't hesitate to produce the bejeweled dagger from his boot, Oscar had relented at once.

"Sonya was still unsettled when I left her in the care of Marie, Fiona and Helga. But I have every faith that the four of them will be good for each other," Cardew said as he strolled over to the window to stare out at the darkness.

"Leave it to you to have an entire harem living under one roof and at your beck and call."

He blew out a cloud of smoke as he looked over his shoulder. "As I said, I'm very good at what I do."

Refusing to think about that, Oscar walked to the sideboard and poured a dram of whiskey from the bottle he'd filched from Dudley Shellhorn. Tossing it back, he hissed as it burned all the way down. It wasn't the finest, but it wasn't the worst either. In other words, it would do. So he poured two glasses and crossed the room.

Cardew lifted his in a salute. "Have you heard from Warring?"

"Not yet. Therefore, I'm holding fast to the plan and trying to stay as inconspicuous as possible."

"What is this swill? Warn a fellow before you attempt to murder him." Cardew cringed and thrust the glass back at Oscar. Then he took a few deep pulls on his cheroot as if to cleanse his palate. "But tell me about your mustachioed charlatan. Have we any cause to worry on that front?"

Oscar knew that he was asking about the blackmail. They'd formed a plan, after all. Assume the identity of Vandemere, keep out of sight in the country until Ladrón could be dealt with, then steal away in the middle of the night.

Which was still the plan. And yet . . .

It felt more complicated than that. Damned if he knew why. And for reasons unbeknownst to him, he decided not to tell the whole truth. "Nothing to report. Everything is going along swimmingly."

"Good. However"—Cardew moved back to the fire to

flick his ashes—"if that changes, or if the cleric arrives, then we'll be left with only one choice."

Run, Oscar thought.

But he was tired of running. Even earlier, when the thought had crossed his mind, the notion of riding away had left him enervated and already imagining the first place he would go to rest.

The answer had startled him because it was Honoria's face he'd seen.

It meant nothing, of course. The only thing it had proved was how thoroughly she'd scrambled his wits the day before. He couldn't help but wonder how many other poor sods the siren had left in a similar state. Hadn't she said herself that she had scores of men falling at her feet proposing marriage? Pathetic. And if she thought one insignificant kiss put a ring in his nose so she could lead him around by it, she could think again.

"That won't be a problem, will it?" Cardew asked.

"No. I'll be ready."

Looking over his shoulder, Cardew's eyes squinted with suspicion. "You're not getting attached to this place, are you? Because you know what happened the last time. Complacency leads to sloppiness. A lesson you learned in Italy, I should think."

"I don't need to be reminded," he said tightly. "And there's no chance of becoming comfortable here. Once you meet the widows, you'll understand."

"And your femme fatale?"

"You already asked that question."

Cardew casually puffed on his cheroot. "I'll phrase it differently, then. You are Vandemere, right? She, for all intents and purposes, is your betrothed. I merely wondered if there is more than just blackmail between you."

Oscar thought again about the kiss, about the way she'd held his face so tenderly and tentatively pressed her lips to his. And at the time, it had felt so . . .

He stopped before finishing the thought and remembered that she was a cunning, shrewd and intelligent vixen who knew precisely what effect she had on men.

Whatever happened between them was nothing more than a continuation of their charade. He would let her save her come-hither glances and slaying kisses for some bloke who didn't know any better.

"Miss Honoria Hartley means nothing at all to me."

Chapter Sixteen

❧

$\mathscr{T}$HE BUZZING OF the matrimonial hive reached Honoria the instant she stepped into the breakfast room.

She blamed it on Verity and Magnus. They were practically glowing as they mentioned taking a walk by the river on their way to visit Lady Broadbent. And, honestly, did they have to give each other such heated glances as they stood and abandoned their places at the table?

When they passed her—hand in hand—on the way to the door, her parents' collective gazes alighted on her.

Pretending not to notice, she chirruped, "Good morning, one and all," as she sauntered to the buffet. Tense and waiting for the first mention of the betrothal contract, she began to fill her plate with eggs, a rasher of bacon, halved tomatoes, a buttery scone, a slice of honey cake . . .

"Someone certainly has an appetite," Thea said conspiratorially as she retrieved the jam pot. "Or are you trying to ensure that your mouth will be too full to answer questions about our walk into town the other day and a certain vis—"

"Utter another syllable and I promise to stab you with a fork," she threatened through clenched teeth.

The imp grinned from ear to ear and practically skipped back to the table, her plait of mahogany hair swishing like a tale.

The worst part about having siblings who knew far too

much was that you couldn't murder them. At least, not without putting forth considerable effort to make it appear an accident.

To avoid any further attention about her appetite, Honoria put the honey cake back before she went to the table.

"So when am I going to meet this viscount of yours?" Father said the instant she sat down.

Thea snickered.

Honoria surreptitiously slid her fork beneath the table and brandished it at her sister. "He is certainly not mine, nor can I account for either his whereabouts or his plans. I have not seen him these past two days."

"That was the day Oscar rescued the baker's son, was it not?" Mother asked, drizzling honey on her toast. "You never mentioned whether or not you spoke to him afterward."

"Hmm . . . I cannot seem to recall."

"Well, with all that transpired, I imagine it was a rather eventful afternoon."

Thea coughed to hide her laugh and then—"Ow!"

"What is it, poppet?" Father asked, his tawny brows furrowed.

"Oh, nothing. Just assessing your reactions to a sudden exclamation," she said tersely, rubbing her leg just above her garter ribbons. "Research for a play I'm writing."

Since this was scarcely different from any other day, the rest of the family continued without surprise. Thea even pulled out her pocket ledger to make a note with the stub of her pencil . . . before brandishing the lead point back at Honoria beneath the table.

In a gesture of faith, and because she was wearing skirts of pale yellow, Honoria put her fork back beside her plate, then stirred a nip of sugar into her tea. But she would hate to be forced to spill the cup all over Thea's lap if she suggested anything about the *events* of that particular afternoon.

"From what your mother tells me, Vandemere popped by every day since his arrival. At first."

"If Mother says it, then it must be true. I wasn't paying much attention."

"But now that I learn he hasn't returned since the day of play rehearsal, I'm concerned that we might be rather more eccentric than he expected. You did . . . tell him about us, did you not? In your letters, I mean."

"Of course," she lied. "And I'm certain he has his reasons for staying away."

"Did the two of you have a falling-out, dear?" Mother inquired with a tsk as she dabbed a napkin to the corner of her mouth.

"There is nothing to fall out over. He likely has a great many responsibilities that have been keeping him away." After all, even a charlatan would have to put on a convincing show. At least, that's what she'd been telling herself. Otherwise, she might have become rather vexed that he hadn't bothered to acknowledge her existence after they'd kissed.

Not that she needed any sort of acknowledgment from the likes of him. At all. It was just rather rude of him to simply disappear after such an unimportant and not-life-altering kiss.

And besides, she was grateful that he hadn't darkened their door. She had no desire to see his absurdly handsome face ever again.

Her father chewed thoughtfully on his bacon, gesturing with his knife and fork when he spoke. "Perhaps you are right. It would be difficult to acclimate oneself to a new home and new responsibilities in just a few short days. Not to mention, the Fairfax widows haven't exactly been known for their hospitality."

Mother punctuated that comment with a dry "Ha!"

"Therefore," he continued, "I'll invite him to dine with us. It is important that a man feel welcomed when he's in a new place. As for our part, we must all gather him into the bosom of our family."

Unable to contain it a moment longer, Thea let out a rolling laugh, then quickly darted from her chair before Honoria could pinch her.

"Good heavens, Althea!" Mother sputtered as her teacup clattered to the saucer. "Whatever has gotten into you this morning?"

"Nothing at all," she said, her eyes dancing with mirth as she gamboled to the buffet for a buttered crumpet. "I was just thinking about Romeo's last line and how amusing it could be if told in different context."

"*Thus with a kiss I die*," Father intoned, considering as his gaze slid from one daughter to the other. "What do you think, Honoria?"

"I think anything, in the right context, could be amusing. Even murder," she said sweetly, smiling at her sister.

～

OSCAR HAD ACCLIMATED to the way of things at Dunnelocke Abbey. His days began predictably with a disdainful tête-à-tête with his valet; the presentation of a meal fit to turn the stomach of a mongrel that regularly feasted on its own excrement; a few scathing glances from the aunts and Cousin Cleo; a ride over the grounds; then a visit with the dowager.

Aside from the welcome arrival of Cardew—albeit with some rather unwelcome news—nothing really altered.

Except for this morning, when someone tried to shoot him.

Just minutes before, he'd set off on a ride with Cardew to be well away from prying eyes and ears.

They'd stopped along the ridge that overlooked the tree line and the lake beyond. As Oscar surveyed the vast woodland and rolling hills, he wondered how Vandemere could have all this waiting for him and yet didn't seem to want it.

Or want his betrothed, for that matter. A betrothed who could turn a man's knees to jelly with a single kiss, slay

him with a single glance and bedevil his dreams every . . .
single . . . night.

Aye, Vandemere was one lucky bastard.

Oscar loathed him.

"It's been a few decades since I've ridden. Thankfully,
this old girl prefers a more sedate pace," Cardew said, stopping next to him. He leaned down to pat the dappled mare's
neck, then looked out over the ridge. "Not a bad prospect."

Oscar nodded. "It could earn a tidy profit if well managed. Unfortunately, Shellhorn has taken over most of it,
and he doesn't have enough sense to put his boots on the
correct feet. His son is even worse. As far as I can tell, the
only thing he does is follow Miss Dunne around all day
making sheep's eyes at her."

"If Miss Dunne is that voluptuous vixen I saw leaning
out the window to spy on us this morning, I can well understand that."

"That was Babette, widow of the third son, Frederick.
By all accounts, she's a veritable man-eater."

Cardew grinned. "And I just happen to be a man."

"Not in this world, old chap. I am sad to report that you
are a servant and, therefore, beneath her ladyship's notice."
He chuckled at Cardew's affronted scowl. "It was your idea
to masquerade as a gentleman's gentleman."

"We were sailing the Atlantic after our narrow escape,
and I was under the influence of a good deal of rum, if
you'll recall."

They'd both been imbibing a great deal of rum during
that voyage. Perhaps that was the reason Oscar hadn't anticipated things becoming more complicated than a little
blackmail while hiding out of sight.

He could lay the blame for that at Honoria's feet as well.

"I have a proposition for you," he said. "This morning, my valet offered to assist you in your duties. This was
likely due to the fact that you'd told him to sod off when
he'd attempted to wake you this morning."

Cardew grumbled. "I'd been abed for barely an hour before he came knocking. And I don't need that nuisance following me around all the bloody day."

"That's what I thought you'd say. For that reason, I've decided it would be better if you gave up your dedicated service as my valet and retired."

"But I—"

"Here me out," he said, holding up a hand. "The abbey requires quite a few repairs, first and foremost paint in several rooms. Not to mention, the splintered black lacquer on the railing—"

"A sacrilege."

"—and I thought you could take care of that," he said. Seeing Cardew's eyes twinkle at the prospect of picking up a brush, Oscar was reluctant to continue. "However, there's just one caveat. You cannot be good. And don't even think about touching up the murals. The widows and Cousin Cleo are a crafty bunch, and it wouldn't take much for them to see your skill and begin to wonder about that letter. Not to mention, if word gets out about an artist suddenly appearing in Lincolnshire, we might as well slit our own throats and save Ladrón the trouble."

Cardew considered this for a moment and looked askance at him. "Before I answer, I'd like to know why you would bother making repairs at all. We're not going to stay. Unless . . . you are having second thoughts."

Oscar scoffed at the speculation. "I'm merely offering you the chance to do what you enjoy instead of shining my boots while we figure out our next steps. But if you'd rather sh—"

The shot rang out.

The horses reared, forelegs pawing at the air. Oscar's heart stopped beneath his chest, his hands gripping the reins, but Hermes was quick to steady with a few low commands.

Settling his mount, he looked over at Cardew, whose color had gone ghostly pale. "Are you hurt?"

"No. You?"

"No." His sharp gaze quickly scanned the tree line in time to see a blur of bright red within the deep shadows of the forest. "But I think that was the intention."

Spurring Hermes, he raced down the steep path in hot pursuit.

In the back of his mind, he was thankful to his mother for the years of riding lessons she'd forced him to take. It had been costly. There had been times when Cardew had come up short. But she'd been stubborn when it came to his education and always found a way, scraping together enough coin even if that meant they had to do without and she had to darn and mend garments that should have been castoffs.

Still to this day, he didn't know why she'd been so determined. But mothers had their reasons, he supposed.

At the bottom of the hill, he bent low, giving Hermes his head, tearing up the damp earth beneath them with hard, thundering hoofbeats. He raced toward the trees, surrendering his hat to the wind. And that's when he saw the culprit.

Or rather, he saw *someone* moving toward the edge of the forest, a musket raised above his head.

"Show yourself!" he commanded, drawing Hermes square with the tree line.

"Aye, my lord," a man called out, emerging from the mass of pine, oak and elm.

At once, Oscar recognized the bewhiskered face and ruddy cheeks of the stocky gamekeeper on the estate. "Mr. Holcombe? Devil take it, man! Were you trying to kill me?"

"Not I, my lord. And neither was Master Toby," he said as red-haired Toby Shellhorn appeared, the musket slung over one shoulder and his boyish face chalk-white. "The boy thought he saw a fox. I told him it weren't hunting season till October, but he got the shot off before the warning, even if he did miss the quarry."

Sheepish, Toby nodded vehemently to this, appearing too tongue-tied to communicate.

Suspicious, Oscar asked, "If it isn't fox hunting season, then what were the two of you doing out here with guns in the first place?"

Holcombe bristled, the shoulders of his green coat thrusting back. "A gamekeeper always has a gun when checking the traps. It's up to me to keep the vermin population down, but there are times when poachers set traps and a deer will step a leg in the wrong place and need to be put down. Thought I'd let the boy tag along since he has no other occupation, if your lordship approves, of course."

Oscar heard the sarcasm and realized his brusque manner might have given Holcombe the impression he was trying to undermine his authority. "As you know, I'm still acquainting myself with the estate. If you can find time in your schedule, I'd be grateful for your assistance in surveying the grounds."

"I can manage that," the gamekeeper said shrewdly.

"Much appreciated, Holcombe." Seeing that he'd smoothed some ruffled feathers, he turned to Toby. "And, young Mr. Shellhorn, it appears that both of us could use a bit of target practice. Perhaps one morning, with Mr. Holcombe's assistance of course, we might try our hand at it."

Toby's color returned on a whoosh of relieved breath and he nodded. "I'd like that, sir . . . I mean, Vandemere. And my father, as well?"

"As long as he isn't planning to shoot me instead."

"No. That'd be Alfreda," Toby said, then blanched again. "But not really. I mean, I don't think she even knows how to load a musket."

"I suppose I should be thankful for small favors." Touching his gloved fingers to his forehead in a salute, he bade them farewell.

However, as he rode Hermes up to the ridge where Cardew waited, he wondered if he faced more of a threat from Ladrón or from his supposed family.

Either way, he should watch his back.

Then as if he didn't have quite enough people who were likely to kill him once they learned the truth, Algernon informed him that he'd been invited to dine at Hartley Hall this evening at Baron Hartley's special request.

Oscar felt a prickle of uncertainty about attending. From the information that Warring had given him, apparently Baron Hartley had known Vandemere's father.

This would be a test. If he couldn't convince the baron that he was Vandemere, then his ruse would end abruptly.

And yet, it wasn't the prospect of being outed and losing the concealment his disguise provided against Ladrón finding him that bothered him most of all. For some strange reason, it was that he wouldn't see Honoria again.

That alarming realization was even worse than being shot at.

Chapter Seventeen

꩜

FROM THE AGE of fifteen, Honoria had never been in want of admirers. In fact, she kept a cache of polite refusals or stern setdowns at her disposal to keep the number of devotees to a more manageable level.

Much of the time, she was able to thin the herd by explaining the paltry amount of her dowry. Pretty though she might be, she knew a gentleman required something more tangible than mere looks.

For those who had ample funds and were more determined to possess her—as if she were little more than an objet d'art—she resorted to explaining about her betrothal to Lord Vandemere.

Some weren't deterred by that either. Which was why she'd learned to defend herself.

But what was she supposed to do with a man who cared nothing for how she looked and, apparently, spent no time even thinking about her?

Oh, the Fates were having a jolly laugh at her now, because for some inexplicable reason this shortsighted, unscrupulous man was the only one who she couldn't stop thinking about.

She growled at herself the instant she realized she was gazing out the parlor window, waiting for Oscar.

It was so unfair! The moths were determined to flutter whether he was near or not. All she had to do was think about him, dash it all!

It made her positively ill to know that he'd reduced her to this state.

Where was her feminine power? Her sense of agency? Her knowledge that she could have any man she wanted, even though she'd never wanted any of them?

By the time she heard his carriage on the gravel drive that evening, she was flustered. And she was never flustered. And when he appeared in the drawing room doorway, her nerves were on tenterhooks.

It vexed her to no end that he looked positively delicious in his slate-gray coat and trousers. The high points of his collar and the slim precision of the mathematical knot on his cravat only enhanced his chiseled features.

Her lungs cinched tight beneath her crimson bodice, waiting for his gaze to fall on her.

But the cad didn't even bother to glance her way as her parents greeted him. In fact, he appeared perfectly content to linger just inside the doorway and chat with them all evening.

The waiting continued as they introduced him to Magnus and Verity. He stopped to greet Thea. Then he even met their tenant, Ben Lawson, who was always willing to even out their numbers for a dinner party. The men paused in unhurried conversation. It was maddening!

In the meantime, the pulse at Honoria's throat threatened to burst through her skin. And if she died of this dreaded anticipation, she vowed to haunt him every day for the rest of his life.

By the time it was her turn, she pretended great interest in rearranging the bric-a-brac on the side table.

"Honoria, dear, are you not going to greet our guest?" Mother asked.

Turning, she feigned surprise. Or rather, she feigned a pretense of concealing her surprise, which took far more skill. "Ah. You have arrived. Pray forgive me for not greeting you at the door. I didn't recognize you, Vandemere. It's almost as though you were another person altogether."

"Clearly, you were distracted by the figurines and what-not," he said with a passing glance to the little shepherd and shepherdess on the table. "I shall endeavor to make a grander entrance next time. Perhaps wear voluminous mustachios and pinch a monocle to my eye."

Speaking of eyes, hers slitted briefly on a murderous glare. "I'm not certain your countenance could support such embellishments."

"Yes, well, it does take a certain type of face that requires so much disguise."

Then as if they weren't having an all-too-revealing tête-à-tête in front of her parents, he reached out and took her hand to bow over it. His gaze raked over her in swift, thorough appraisal, sending a flare of heat through her. When he lingered overlong on her lips, she felt a wash of color rise to her cheeks.

As if her unbidden response were a game he'd just won, he smirked. *Smirked!* The cad.

"Con, would you open the window a bit wider? It's rather warm this evening." Mother smiled as she exchanged a speaking glance with Father, who nodded in agreement. "And I'll just fetch the claret, shall I?"

As her parents left them alone, Honoria could see clearly enough that they were reading far too much into a simple blush. It meant nothing.

Though, when she drew her attention back to him and saw the scorching appreciation in his gaze as he took another, more leisurely perusal over the bare expanse of her shoulders, exposed above a ruffle of lace adorning the bodice that flawlessly skirted the line between modest and brazen, she felt rather vindicated.

At least, until he spoke.

"My darling, Signore. You look positively delectable in red. Forbidden fruit has never been so tempting," he said, his voice low. "However, while you are exercising your feminine wiles, you do not want to play the *I can reveal your secrets* game. That is one you will never win. Not with me."

A frisson of warning replaced the enticing heat. And she felt like an idiot.

While she'd spent the last two days thinking about a kiss, she'd forgotten the reason he was there in the first place. Money. He wanted her money—her future, the only security she had.

Oscar Flint was a ruthless scoundrel. And she would do well never to forget that.

***

THE INSTANT OSCAR saw the change in Honoria, he regretted his callous threat. Why couldn't he have simply flirted with her this evening?

But he knew the answer. He'd been on edge since the gunshot, and having her dangle his secret in front of her family made him feel . . . exposed. Defenseless.

In fact, *she* made him feel defenseless. Not only because of what she knew of him but what she did to him.

She made him want. Made him feel like a boy begging on the street, willing to do anything for a farthing. Made him feel as if he were peering through a kitchen window at a life that could never be his.

He hated it.

He especially hated that, the instant he'd delivered his threat, he'd wanted to beg her forgiveness.

But he didn't do that. Instead, he escorted her into dinner and let the tension linger between them like a splinter wedged deep beneath the skin.

It was better that way.

He had too much at stake, having dinner with a man who'd actually been acquainted with Vandemere's father. Any hole in his research could expose him for a fraud at a moment's notice.

The tension coiling inside him didn't lessen after dinner either. When the men were left alone to linger over port, the buffer that the women had provided left with them.

This was his true test.

Oscar directed the conversation to a safer topic. Namely, by telling the Duke of Longhurst that he was acquainted with his younger brother. Rowan and Oscar had contrived a carefully scripted history of how they'd become friends in the event that the ostensible Vandemere came face-to-face with Longhurst.

It was supposed to establish Oscar with a history and solidify his claim to the viscountcy. However, Longhurst was so distracted by the desire to return to his bride that his attention to the conversation was split between his checking the clock, a brief conversation with Lawson regarding the construction of the birdhouses that Verity liked, and then glances to the dining room door. So even if Oscar had erred in his locations or dates, the duke wouldn't have caught it.

When Mosely came to announce that the women were waiting in the drawing room, Longhurst nearly upended his chair from standing with such haste.

Hartley ambled down the corridor and issued a chuckle behind Longhurst's back, who walked with a purposeful stride ahead of them. "I remember those days, when being apart from Roxana for even an hour felt like a year in prison."

At the eerily specific comparison, Oscar shot a glance to Hartley. Could he know? Was this a trap waiting to spring shut?

But there was nothing sly or suspicious in his countenance, only a good-natured grin. So Oscar relaxed. Or tried to.

"Of course," Hartley continued, "you couldn't say that to Magnus. Lad's too proud."

"To admit such a weakness is to show your enemy where to sink the blade," Oscar said. It was a good reminder, too.

Because the one time he'd allowed himself to get too close to a woman, he'd ended up in prison. After that, he'd vowed never to let his feelings for a woman cloud his judgment again.

"Uncanny," Hartley said, drawing Oscar's attention to the searching gaze. "I remember your father saying something to that effect after I married Roxana. Titus was as cynical as a man could be. At least, until he was struck by Cupid's cunning arrow." He clapped Oscar on the shoulder. "But Titus Fairfax was a good man, too. Kicked up a bit of dust in our day. I'll have to tell you some of the stories." However, as they entered the drawing room, Hartley looked askance at his wife. "But another time, perhaps."

"I'd like that, my lord."

"Ach, no need for such formality, lad. We're going to be family, after all. Call me Con, or Hartley if you prefer."

Roxana breezed over to them, pausing briefly to smile as Longhurst crossed directly to Verity and took her hand as if their time apart had been centuries. Oscar would never be that pathetic.

"I didn't mention this before, but I wanted to say that I saw your mother perform," Roxana said to Oscar, her expression resplendent. "She was divinity itself."

"Aye, the pair of them were a marvel to behold," Hartley added.

"Pair?" Oscar felt his brow furrow, then inwardly kicked himself for revealing his surprise.

"Her sister."

"Ah, yes. Of course. I wasn't thinking," he said and allowed his gaze to travel to Honoria, ensuring that her parents believed him to be love-addled instead of clueless. He knew next to nothing about Vandemere's mother, other than she was an actress.

Hartley chuckled. "Though, with their father owning a theater, it was only natural that they would both take to it like ducks to water."

"My mother rarely mentioned her time on the stage," Oscar explained quickly. "Then again, even if she'd wanted to, I was not a son who sat still long enough to listen."

When Roxana had laughed lightheartedly at this, citing her own son's inability to linger in one place, he knew he'd offered a passable explanation.

But passable wasn't going to keep him from being discovered.

He was impersonating an aristocrat. Such a fraud could have him exported at the very least, or earn him a short drop from a hangman's rope.

That was, unless Ladrón found him first.

Either way, his neck was on the line, and he would prefer to keep it intact.

The evening drew to a close after a rousing game of charades, which he'd never played before. It was no surprise that the ladies trounced the gentlemen soundly. Oscar rose to bid adieu.

But before he could, his hostess prevailed upon him to take her daughter for a stroll. "It is far too lovely an evening to squander."

Agreeing, he proffered his arm to Honoria, and only he had heard the begrudging exhale she emitted when her hand curved over his sleeve.

She was still mad at him—a point made clear by her continued silence after they'd been walking for nearly a quarter of an hour.

This was another game, he supposed. And the first one to break the silence would lose.

"You seem rather cross this evening," he said, willing to forfeit.

"And you seem rather distracted," she countered as if they were playing a rapid hand of Snip-Snap-Snorum and she was determined to match card for card.

He laid another. "You're angry about what I said earlier."

She ignored the comment and made her own observation.

"I thought you were going to jump out of your skin when the footman appeared at your side with the soup terrine."

Had he? Well, it was no wonder. By rule, he never sat with his back to the door. "Bisque always sends me into fits of alarm."

"If I suspected for one minute that you were telling the truth, I would follow you with soup-filled crockery day and night," she snapped, stopping beneath a bower of heavy-headed white roses.

"Day *and* night, hmm? I do admire your commitment to winning, whatever the cost."

"Oh, you have no idea what I'm capable of."

By the lethal glare she shot him, he had a fairly good impression. Like the flowers, she was beautiful and armed with a plethora of thorns.

He preferred her this way. He would much rather fight with her than take the risk of her opening another fissure in him.

"But tell me one thing." His voice dipped low as he openly admired the way the moonlight caressed her skin. "Will you be wearing this gown? Because that would be worth any torture."

Her manicured nails curled toward her palms. "No."

"Even better," he purred, circling her like predator to prey.

As she fumed, her breaths drew his attention to the upper angles of her scapula above the back of her gown. He couldn't resist tracing the delicate line, watching as goose-flesh bloomed over her flawless skin beneath the lazy pass of his fingertip. Her breath caught, he noticed, but she did not ask him to stop.

"I think I'd rather bash you over the head with it—the terrine, not my gown," she said, the venom in her tone had taken on a breathy quality. "What are you doing?"

He wasn't entirely sure. All he knew was that he had to put his lips on the crest of her shoulder, to feel the satin of her skin. Though, he noticed something peculiar. When *she* kissed him, his knees turned to jelly. The other way around and his bones remained solid and steady. The knowledge opened up a world of possibilities.

"You started a new game the other day," he said, brushing his lips over her bare skin, breathing in her scent. "I'm merely playing my hand."

"And what makes you think I wish to play?"

"Because you always want to win. And the only way to win is to play. In that regard, we are the same." He slid his arms around her waist and drew her back against him, and for a moment, he felt her melt. But then she shook her head and moved away.

She turned to face him, her eyes lit with blue fire. "I play because I want to live. To have control over my own life. To have a future. Just as I told you in Paris. But that future is in jeopardy because of you."

Oscar had to force himself not to close the distance between them and haul her back. His arms felt empty.

She was making him want her again.

He closed his hands into fists. "I'm not the only one playing."

"But you are the only one playing for yourself," she said, flinging an accusatory arm at him. "You did your research, and you know about the scandal. Because of the shadow it cast over our family, my sister arrived at Hartley Hall, after having only been married a week, and she was crying because she feared she would never find acceptance as Longhurst's duchess. Do you think I could live with myself if I let *another* scandal fall on her head? Or on my parents for that matter? Or Thea?"

This was not an act. He could see in the way her eyes shimmered with incipient moisture and in the way her voice cracked. She loved her family. It was clear that she would do anything for them.

They were more alike than he cared to think about. Didn't they both keep secrets to protect themselves? Disguise, deceive and scheme in order to take control of their own fates?

Everything he did, every action he took, was by his choice. No one had ever forced him to pick pockets when he was a lad. But he knew that he didn't like being hungry. Just like he knew that he couldn't stomach the consequences of being a boy on the streets, at the mercy of the men who'd flashed their silver. So for years after, he'd made a choice to steal instead.

In fact, every decision he'd made had been of his own choosing. Because of that, he understood Honoria's bitterness toward him.

The more time he spent with her, the more he could see that people had likely underestimated her. They saw only what was on the surface, a shell. But he could see the struggle she faced just to be seen as a whole person. Not only that but after witnessing the effort she put into her characters, he wondered if she sometimes wished to be someone else altogether.

And seeing this vulnerability did strange things to him. Like make him question his own judgment.

But he'd put his faith and trust in a woman before, and he still bore the scars from her betrayal.

Even so, it wasn't the cunning Josephine standing with him now. It wasn't Josephine with unshed tears in her eyes, swallowing him up in a sea of blue.

"Devil take it." He raked a hand through his hair.

She simply stared back at him, those fathomless eyes still glistening.

"You don't have to worry about the scandal hurting your family," he said on a resigned breath.

"You . . . you'll keep my secret?"

He was making a choice, one that wouldn't take away hers. "Aye."

"So"—she held her breath and took a hesitant step toward him—"you're not going to tell anyone about Signor Cesario?"

"Didn't I just say that? You don't need to repeat it." Bloody hell, it was like playing a losing hand all over again. "And lower that beaming smile of yours before you blind someone."

Her smile only widened. "I cannot control it. You have just given my life back to me. And the best part is when you leave, no one will ever expect me to marry. They'll think you treated me abominably by abandoning me."

"I never said that I—"

"It's the perfect plan," she interrupted, lost in her false assumptions. "Oh, I'm so happy that I could kiss you."

And before he could clarify the misunderstanding, she surged up on her toes and her lips found his.

His legs gave a warning quake.

His arms closed around her, and her body fit with unerring precision against his. It was as if the heat from their previous encounter had created a perfect mold of each other in interlocking pieces.

He felt his heart quicken in time with hers. His hands roved along her back, one splaying low in the dip just above the curve of her bottom, the other caressing the bare silken skin above her fastenings. And when she nudged his lips apart and shyly licked into his mouth with a hum of hunger, he wasn't certain he would ever be the same again.

She proved it by gently sucking his tongue into her mouth. He felt a corresponding tug in the vicinity of his cock, his blood pumping thick and hot through his veins. And all he wanted to do was sip from her lips, tug down the front of her gown, taste her breasts, feel her welcoming heat slick his fingers as she quivered beneath him . . .

Bending his head, he nuzzled the side of her neck, drawing in her delectably sweet scent. He wanted to devour her for hours on end. "Are you hiding a parcel of biscuits under your skirts, by chance?"

Her soft laugh vibrated against his lips. "Is that all you ever think about?"

"Yes," he said, whether or not she was referring to biscuits or to the paradise hidden beneath yards of muslin and cambric. "You smell all sweet and buttery, like you've been freshly baked in sunlight."

"I'm sure I should be insulted. Aren't men supposed to compare women to flowers?"

"You're not insulted. I can feel by the jump of your pulse beneath my lips that you like being irresistible . . . and edible."

Her neck arched on a sigh, her soft hands drifting to his hair. "And will you next tell me that that I am crumbly, too?"

"No, that's the best part. You're the kind of biscuit that stays all in one piece. The kind I can keep eating and eating and never be full." He nibbled his way along her throat to the salty perspiration gathered in the diamond-shaped hollow. "Damn, Honoria. I've been craving you. This."

"For two whole days?"

"No. For more than twelve miserable months."

She drew back. "Cad! I knew you remembered."

He could have continued to deny it. But when her eyes met his and held, the truth came out instead. "Signore, you are quite impossible to forget."

She kissed him again—exuberant, passionate kisses. But then she was laughing against his mouth, cradling his head in her hands, her fingers weaving a magic spell through his hair, and he was suddenly breathless. Breathless and aching with a different kind of wanting. A wanting that he couldn't form into words. And worse, a crevasse seemed to be splitting apart his rib cage.

"I don't know why I'm kissing you," she said with that infectious laugh, panting, her cheek pressed against his.

He swallowed, fighting the urge to press a fist against the center of his chest, but held her tighter instead. "Because you find me irresistible?"

"Certainly not." She smiled against his temple, then proceeded to kiss his brow, his nose, his cheeks and chin. "I'm actually quite furious with you for all you've put me through."

"Then, why are you laughing?" he asked, coasting his lips over hers, part of him wanting to silence the sound that was doing terrible things to him, and part of him wanting to get drunk off it.

"I like winning."

"And what do you think you've won, precisely?"

"Our game. You said it yourself. You'll keep my secret. Which means that you aren't using that information to blackmail me, and without that leverage, you'll soon be gone from my life. Ergo, I win."

Then that cunning whisp of a female tried to slip out of his embrace. But this time, he wouldn't—*couldn't*—let her go.

He pressed his mouth to hers once more, her lips surrendering beneath the pressure, her body supple in his arms. And in the brief shattering moment that followed, her hands slid from his chest to his nape, her fingers tangling in his hair, nails biting into his scalp as she stroked her tongue into his mouth.

Oscar welcomed it. Reveled in the heat and potent ardor of her hips cradling his. Drank in the delicious sound of her wanton purr when he splayed his hand over the lush curve of her bottom. And savored her reflexive hitch against his tumid hardness as he slowly rocked against her.

"There's only one flaw in your reasoning," he said against the purring pulse on the side of her neck. "I never said I would leave."

He felt her conflicted response as the words sunk in, her body still pliable and supple in his arms as her hands untangled from his hair.

She swallowed and drew back marginally. "But you just told me . . ."

"That I wouldn't reveal your secret." He nibbled at the corner of her mouth. "But you said it yourself that day at the abbey. With the betrothal contract, our wedding will make Vandemere's return quite official."

"You're still threatening to marry me?" She pushed out of his embrace, her flashing eyes reflecting the torchlight in the garden.

He shrugged, ignoring the gnawing ache that filled the distance between them. "If you want me gone, you know the price. Or else you leave me no choice." Purposely misunderstanding her incensed silence, he opened his arms. "Come, my love, and give your future husband a kiss. You know you want to."

"Know this, Mr. Flint. I will never marry you and will never, *ever* kiss that unscrupulous mouth again!"

And with that, she flounced off in a fury.

Chapter Eighteen

~*~

"WHERE IS THAT blasted betrothal contract?" Honoria grumbled in the stuffy attic air.

She'd already spent half the night and early this morning searching the library and her father's study but had come up empty-handed. That left only one place to look: her grandmother's trunks.

Unfortunately, after sifting through the contents, inspecting every hatbox, reticule and portmanteau, she'd found absolutely nothing about the betrothal. And for a woman who'd apparently saved every possible letter, playbill, calling card and invitation, it irritated Honoria to no end that the contract seemed to be the only thing missing.

But she had to find it. The solution to her current dilemma could be within the wording of the document. And if it weren't? Well, she'd destroy it.

Of course, there were likely two copies of the contract—one here and the other in the abbey—which meant that she'd have to return there and risk Oscar discovering what she was up to. Doubtless, he would use any means necessary to keep her from gaining the upper hand . . . even kiss her to distraction as he'd done last night.

Yes, she might have started it, she admitted. But he'd waited until she was drunk on passion before revealing his cards.

Declaring to never kiss him again had seemed the perfect setdown given the circumstances. After all, she had felt the way his body had responded to her. Felt the intriguing hardness that he'd pressed against her. And she, as an intelligent adult woman, knew what that meant.

He had been aroused by her. Wanted her. Just as she had known that the clenching weight low in her belly and the insistent pulse that thrummed between her thighs meant that she'd been equally drawn to him.

But after waking in the middle of the night from a lurid dream of him taking her out of an oven and devouring every naked inch of her as if she were a biscuit, she'd already found herself wavering with indecision.

She'd never felt more alive than when she'd lost herself in his arms. And that frightened her.

She'd lain awake in the darkness wondering if she would ever feel alive like that again . . . Until she remembered that Oscar was a lying, sneaking scoundrel who needed to be put in his place.

And that place was far, far away from her.

Frustrated, hot and grumpy, she slammed down the lid of the trunk and continued her search.

"There you are," Verity said as she climbed the stairs. "Tally said you'd gone to the attic, but she didn't know why."

Which was precisely the reason Honoria couldn't tell her. No one could know that she was looking for the betrothal contract or else they'd start to ask questions.

She wiped her damp brow with the back of her hand. "I just think it's far too warm for puffed sleeves, cinched waists and full skirts. Summer demands flimsy muslin with capped sleeves. So, I thought I'd look up here for the older fashions we've packed away."

"Since I left my new wardrobe at Magnus's estate, I'll help. We could both use a change of wardrobe."

Thea popped up behind Verity, her hair frizzled with humidity. "Here you both are. Tally said you'd gone to the attic."

"We're on safari," Verity said as she tossed a straw bonnet in Thea's direction. "In search of cooler attire."

Donning the hat, Thea joined the hunt with alacrity.

As the minutes ticked by, it was difficult to concentrate. The long, narrow room was stifling with only one window at the far end. The servants' rooms were on either side, lined with the dormer windows that would be beneficial on days like this. Honoria was half-tempted to strip down to her chemise, and it wasn't even midday yet.

Of course, if she could keep her thoughts from returning to last night and the feel of Oscar's mouth grazing along the column of her throat, her skin might not be beaded with perspiration.

She stopped after the third trunk, fanning herself and rustling her skirts for ventilation. "Any luck?"

"No, but I found some costumes," Verity replied.

"Same," Thea added before closing her trunk with a thud. "Though, I'm tempted to go down to tea in the pantaloons from when we played pirates in *Pericles*."

"I'm sure Mother would love that," Honoria said wryly.

Then she spotted a mysterious square shape beneath a holland cover in the corner. To get to it, she had to dance a pair of dressmaker's dummies in Elizabethan costumes— a gent in blue and gold window-paned breeches, and a lady in a flattering indigo bodice, tapered sleeves, and starched ruffs that were impossibly itchy—out of the way.

Believing she'd found the trunk she was looking for, she lifted the cover only to find paintings. An entire stack of them.

A glance at the familiar signature told her that they were her mother's watercolors, beautiful and bright. A vague memory sifted through Honoria's mind, of a time when the family rooms of the house had been filled with them. But why had they been tucked away?

She had her answer when she reached one toward the middle.

Her throat closed as she gazed upon the walled garden, vined with flowering clematis, slender, leafy trees standing in the corner, a sea of blossoms underfoot . . . and a fountain with two children splashing, both with pale blond curls.

For an earth-swallowing moment, she was lost in that day, the sound of laughter tinkling like rain falling into a deep well, echoing in ghostly chimes.

Look, Ernest! I can blow bubbles with my face underwater. See?

I bet I can blow more bubbles than you.

Cannot.

Can too. Watch me.

Watch me . . . The words haunted her even now.

"That's rather pretty. Is it yours?" Thea asked, peeping over her shoulder and nearly startling her out of her skin.

Honoria took a breath and slid the painting behind the others before issuing a practiced shrug. "Oh, just one of Mother's."

"I've seen her sketch before but didn't know she had actual paintings up here."

"Well, you know how she is. If her latest endeavor doesn't excite her passions, then she will abandon it and move on to something new."

"Speaking of passions," Verity said from the other side of the narrow room, "look what I found."

Thankful for the distraction—really, *any* distraction would do—Honoria turned.

Both Thea and she groaned at the sight of the little puppet theater that their mother had used to perform a sock puppet play, informing them of the supposed pleasures that awaited them in marriage. Flanked by rose satin curtains, the stage was dressed as a flowery bedchamber.

"I had nightmares for a month about Lord Turgid," Thea said, stalking across the room and searching through the trunk for the puppets. Finding two of them with an *aha!*

she held them aloft. "I mean, just look at the size of him. He's a veritable monster compared to drooping, wrinkly Lord Flaccid."

She proceeded to move the puppets in a pantomime of Mother's play, walking the bumbling Lord Flaccid across the stage.

"I'll just be two shakes of a lamb's tail, my sweet," he lisped, disappearing behind the miniature dressing screen in the corner.

Then out popped Lord Turgid with a low, comically sinister chuckle. "Where are you, Lady Content, my little rosebud? Don't be shy. Not with me, your husband."

Honoria and Verity stifled a giggle.

Thea returned to the trunk and found the puppet dressed in the petals of a silk flower. Her voice became high-pitched and trembling. "Oh my! Lord Turgid! How big and strong you are. I feel so dewy in your presence."

And then Lady Content fainted onto the bed with a sigh.

By the time she finished, Honoria and Verity were doubled over with laughter, tears streaming down their cheeks.

"I don't see why it's so amusing," Thea said, staring perplexedly at the puppets. "Lord Turgid is clearly the villain of this play. Just look at how he's proportionately larger than the painted doorway and more than twice the size of Lady Content, which left me to wonder if I was watching a tragedy. Do you think Mother was trying to frighten us?"

Honoria dabbed the wetness from the corners of her eyes. "We could ask our resident expert on the matter. Well, Verity? As the only married woman of the three of us, did Mother exaggerate?"

"I am not—*absolutely not*—answering that," she said with a gasp, her cheeks poppy red.

Turning away, she draped the holland cover over the stage once more. However, when she turned around, her lips were pressed together to hide a telling grin.

Thea didn't see this look or the perceptive eyebrow

waggle that Honoria cast her eldest sister. She was too busy putting the puppets back into the trunk when she said, "And no matter what Mother professes, I cannot imagine how all the kissing and plundering that Lady Content endures could convince her that she was in love. Then again, I never understood why Romeo didn't simply wait a few minutes— *before* gulping down a vial of poison—to realize that Juliet was still breathing. If he had, they both would have survived."

"He did make a great number of assumptions in the span of a few seconds. Not very sensible, if you ask me," Verity said wryly, and Thea snickered.

But this time, Honoria didn't join their amusement. She moved to the window and looked out over the garden, her attention distracted by the words *kissing*, *convince* and *in love*.

She'd forgotten that had been part of Mother's lesson, too. That a woman, who wasn't necessarily in love, could be convinced by pleasure that she was. Essentially, falling in love against her will.

Which was the very reason Honoria had decided not to marry at all.

She didn't want to fall in love. Love was painful and wretched and empty. It was half of her gone and gone forever. And it certainly wasn't necessary to experience life to the fullest. To feel every single beat of her heart as if for the first time, to taste every breath as if it were her last, and to live inside the moment that fell in between.

Unfortunately, the only time she'd felt that way was when she was kissing Oscar. She'd felt something bloom inside her like a star in the heavens, beautiful and destructive all at once.

She wanted to keep her distance. But she was drawn to him by a force that she couldn't explain, even to herself.

He was calculated and ruthless. But he was also a man who'd run into the path of danger for a boy he didn't know and who'd been swayed by a woman's tears. And, for reasons unbeknownst to her, she was curious about him.

Not curious enough to want him to remain here, of course.

She just needed to remember that for the next time she was with him. Because she knew that, unless she found the contract, there would be a next time.

Therefore, she made a vow to herself. There would be no kissing. Absolutely no more kissing.

Chapter Nineteen

❧

"*I* BELIEVE YOU OWE me one kiss, Signore," Oscar said the following afternoon as they sat beneath a shade tree, attempting another picnic. He had the audacity to sigh and shake his head as if he were wholly blameless. "You drew the Queen of Hearts, after all, and I don't make the rules."

She glanced down at the card in her hand. The Queen looked back at her archly as if fully aware of her inner struggle.

She squinted at him. "This is your game. You just made up the rules two minutes ago."

When they'd first settled in their shaded spot, before she'd set about unwrapping the contents of their picnic, he'd stayed her hand and oh so casually suggested they make a game of their meal.

The winner would be the one most satisfied in the end.

Intrigued in spite of herself and welcoming a distraction from her thoughts, she had agreed. Then he'd deftly withdrawn a deck of cards from his coat pocket, shuffled and fanned them out for her to choose first.

The rules were simple: black cards allowed him to choose what she would eat; red put his fate in her hands.

But the only trump card was the Queen of Hearts.

When she'd balked at his proposal of making it worth a kiss, he'd accused her of being intimidated by the prospect of playing for such high stakes.

Of all the nerve! He knew very well she couldn't back down from a direct challenge. It left her no choice but to accept and make him eat his words.

And yet, she'd *mysteriously* drawn the trump card on her first turn? Ha!

"I highly suspect," she continued, "that you devised a way to make me choose this card."

"I am wounded, madam. That is a completely unfounded accusation. I've never cheated at this game in my life."

"Because it has never been played before." She threw the card back at him, and the cad caught it between his teeth, flashing a grin.

Next time, she would throw a rock.

He tucked the card back into the deck with a sigh. "I'm afraid the rules of forfeit are two kisses."

"Rules seem to be swarming this game faster than flies to horse sh—"

"Sit back down, Miss Hartley. I promise there will be no additional rules." He crossed his heart.

She glanced at the spot dubiously, suspecting the black-guard had no heart at all. "Then, give me your hand. After all, there was no part of the rule that mentioned the kiss must be on the lips."

There. She showed him, she thought.

"I will remember you said that." His low promise sent a wayward thrill through her.

Too late, she saw the glimmer of heat in his gaze. Brief, unbidden curiosity made her wonder where he might kiss her. But she quickly banished the thought from her mind. *Mostly.*

Oscar presented his hand like a king expecting a pledge of fealty over his ring. Pushing off from the blanket, she pressed a brief peck to his knuckles. It wasn't a real kiss, therefore she was still holding fast to her declaration.

When it was clear that he intended to wait until she paid the two-kiss forfeit, she leaned forward, fully intending to bite him. But then she had a better idea. Something assured to make him regret this game of his.

Honoria licked his finger instead. Slowly, and much the same way that he'd licked hers in Paris. She wanted to tease him. To taunt him. And she felt a measure of triumph when his stormy eyes darkened as he watched her, his lips parting on a breath.

He shifted toward her.

Knowing that she could affect him as much as he affected her filled her with a sense of feminine power.

She sat back, a feline grin on her lips. "I do believe that round went to me."

"It isn't about a single hand, my dear," he said, "but who wins in the end."

The diabolical shimmer in his gaze reminded her that she was dealing with a rather ruthless gambler. There wasn't anything he wouldn't do to win.

She ignored the unbidden thrill that coursed through her as she cast an uncertain glance down the hill. "We should throw away the Queen of Hearts. If my maid or your driver sees us, my reputation will be ruined, and that is not part of our bargain."

"Clever attempt at skirting the rules, but I'm afraid your point is invalid," he said. "Because, while you were up here arranging the shawls and pillows, I was pointing out a rather tasty grouping of blackberry bushes around the bend of the creek, which just happens to be in the shade and not in direct sight of the top of the hill." He grinned. "Though, if you are concerned, I have another solution."

He proceeded to borrow her parasol and wedge it into the side of the basket. Then he moved the basket nearer to the log and balanced his hat upon a stick so that it looked as though her parasol and his hat were a respectable distance apart.

"You have quite the devious mind. And that is no compliment to your character," she groused.

"Perhaps not. Though, I highly suspect that's one of the reasons you're drawn to me. I'm different from other gentlemen of your acquaintance."

She scoffed. "*Reasons*, hmm? My, someone certainly thinks highly of himself. And to be clear, you are no gentleman."

"Truer words have never been spoken. I doubt there are many men at all who can boast of living in the number of cities I have done."

There it was again, that blasted curiosity. Putting on her most uninterested expression, she asked, "Did you travel greatly with your family?"

His mouth curled with bitterness. "My *family*, as you put it, consisted of my mother and a father who abandoned us when I was five years old. But even before then, we were stealing away in the middle of the night because we were unable to pay for our rooms. Scandalous, I know." He splayed a hand over his chest with comic insincerity, and yet there was something lurking in his eyes that made her heart ache for the boy who'd never had a home. "Flit forward three and twenty years, and I'm hying off to a small hamlet in Lincolnshire because a bloodthirsty Spaniard wants to sever my head from my body. So you see, not much has altered. Like father, like son, I suppose."

A jolt of alarm sliced through her. "Is that true?"

"Do you want it to be true?" His brow arched with insouciant disinterest.

"Must you always be so aloof? I think waiting for a stone to deliver sap would be simpler than expecting you to say anything remotely personal." She huffed. "Then again, whyever should I care? If I knew more about you, I might be plagued with concern, and I wouldn't know what to do with that."

She saw the instant the shutters fell in place and he stepped into the role of the bored rake.

"I could offer a few suggestions, if you like," he said,

his voice suggestive as he absently shuffled the cards in his hands, his gaze skimming over her with prurient intent. "Or we could just play our game. I'm simply ravenous."

Against her will, her pulse responded to that slumberous look in his eyes . . . and something flipped in the pit of her stomach.

She ignored the sensation. "There are times when I hardly know what to make of you."

"I'd wager that bothers you exceedingly," he said, watching her with imperious amusement as he shrugged out of his coat and laid it aside.

Yes, she thought as her gaze skimmed over his broad shoulders and the outline of muscles beneath a tailored waistcoat, *you do bother me exceedingly.*

She had seen gentlemen without their coats on a number of occasions so she didn't know why she felt flushed. Then again, it was a rather hot day. She could not fault him for wanting to be cooler.

After all, she was garbed in the sprigged muslin she'd finally located in the attic, the capped sleeves displaying nearly every inch of her arms. Not to mention, her figure had rounded somewhat since she'd last worn the dress, and the rounded bodice that had once been modest now displayed a fair amount—albeit not unseemly—of her décolletage.

And she had caught him admiring her figure with a heated appreciation that did not offend her in the least. Nor was she offended that he was rolling up the cuffs of his shirtsleeves. As he gradually exposed the sinewy strength and dusting of dark hair along his forearms, she felt another wash of heat. But it was a hot day, after all.

Focusing her attention on the cards, she fanned them out for him to choose. When he drew a Ten of Diamonds—*her choice*—she contemplated the contents of the basket with devious intent.

"I think an egg for you, Mr. Flint, since you will soon have egg on your face."

She didn't give him a chance to respond with a taunt of his own but brought the offering to his closed mouth. When he did not open straightaway, she coasted the smooth white surface over his bottom lip. And for some inexplicable reason, she felt a tingling sensation on her own lips.

She saw the hint of a snake curl at the corner of his mouth as if he knew. Her gaze met his, but all she found there was simmering heat. Then his lips slowly parted, and he sank his teeth down into the soft flesh.

She withdrew the other half of the egg, only to have him capture her wrist. His lips parted, taking the remainder *and* the very tips of her fingers into the humid interior of his mouth. His tongue flicked over her flesh, tasting her as tingles chased up her arm and scattered over her skin like errant sparks from a Catherine wheel.

She slipped free. He wasn't playing fair.

"Delicious," he said with erudite satisfaction before reaching for the cards.

Refusing to reveal any of her unwelcome responses, she primly slid an Ace of Spades from the deck. His choice, dash it all.

"Hmm . . ." he murmured, peering into the basket. "A radish will certainly suit your spicy temperament today."

"You have no idea."

"Now, close your eyes." When her eyes turned flinty with suspicion he said, "It's just a radish."

He was asking her to trust him, and since he'd trusted her a bit, she could do the same.

Closing her eyes, she felt the fan of her lashes resting on the upper curve of her cheek as she waited. She expected a nudge against her lips an instant before the offered bite. But he kept it just out of reach. She knew this because she caught the peppery scent. It hit her at the back of her throat and caused a small pool of anticipatory saliva to gather just beneath her tongue.

She understood at once that he was doing this by design. He wanted her to be wholly absorbed in this one bite. This one moment.

Reflexively she swallowed, becoming aware of the sinuous glide of her own throat and the supple texture of her lips as she wet them with the tip of her tongue. She heard his sharp inhale, and her pulse kicked up a notch, her lips tingling and plump. And when he finally nudged the smooth root against her lips, she felt a corresponding sensation deep in the pit of her stomach.

He dragged it slowly over her bottom lip, and her own breathing faltered. She bumped it with the tip of her tongue, gauging the size, then opened her mouth a bit wider. As she sank her teeth into the firm flesh of the radish, the full flavor burst on her tongue.

She opened her eyes to find his gaze on her lips, dark and hungry as he took the remaining half into his own mouth. And she was thankful he finished it, because she wasn't sure her hammering pulse could survive another bite of radish.

This was nothing more than attraction, she told herself. Perfectly innocent animal attraction. And she was strong enough to resist it.

His turn came next. Eight of Clubs. And he wickedly declared that he would like to feast on tongue. The scoundrel.

In the basket, the beef and lamb were in slender slices within a shallow earthenware dish. She lifted out a long sliver of spit-roasted tongue. Shifting to her knees, she leaned forward to dangle the tip for him.

But he surprised her by closing his eyes. He tilted his head so that she was obliged to feed it to him, bit by bit. Distractedly, she watched the muscles of his jaw flick and the way his throat worked on a swallow.

Then he suckled the juices from the tips of her fingers with a hum of pleasure. And, she realized belatedly, he wasn't holding her wrist captive. She was lingering all on her own. Dash it all!

When her cheeks flushed with color, he chewed with relish. "Your turn."

She could just imagine that he was tallying up points for that round as well.

Gathering her composure, she drew the King of Spades.

His choice. Again. It seemed that every hand had given him the advantage.

He withdrew a peach the color of a perfect sunrise, a soft pinkish orange. She'd been waiting for the fruit to ripen in their orchard and had yet to sample this year's crop. The aroma was so sweet her mouth watered in anticipation.

But he didn't offer it straightaway. Instead, he held it to his own mouth, his nostrils flaring as he drew in a deep breath. "I'm tempted to keep this for myself. There's only one in the basket."

"Don't you dare." Her hand curved around his wrist. She wouldn't put it past him to devour it himself.

But this round would belong to her.

She felt the jump of his pulse beneath her fingertips, the masculine strength of hard bone and sinewy muscle beneath the taut layer of heated skin. He allowed her to draw his hand to her mouth, and she held his gaze as she parted her lips.

The light furring of the fruit tingled against her skin. The ripe fragrance assailed her nostrils, teasing her tongue. Then her teeth sank into the flesh.

Her eyes closed on a moan of pure ecstasy. Nectar, lush and sweet, flooded her mouth with so much decadent juice that it dribbled down her chin. She tried to catch it with her fingertips before it dripped onto her bodice. But Oscar was faster.

As her mouth fastened on the fruit, his other hand cupped her chin, collecting the syrup before bringing it to his own lips, sipping thirstily before coming back for more.

She took another bite, the tender, succulent flesh melting on her tongue, and his hand returned to her chin. And she didn't know if it was gluttony, an insatiable appetite or something else altogether, but she took another greedy bite.

A river of nectar surged forth, and Oscar leaned in, his mouth opening over her chin. The flat of his tongue laved the vulnerable skin beneath, licking along the runnel of juice to the corner of her mouth. And then he sealed his lips on the other side of the peach, his eyes dark with desire as they both devoured the fruit, making hungry sounds as if they were animals ravaging their newly felled prey.

When the pit was all that was left between them, he took hold of her hand and licked away the sticky sweetness from wrist to fingertips. A prickle of gooseflesh danced over her skin. Her nipples tightened. A pulse rabbited through her body, exciting nerves along the way before settling low between her thighs.

Thrumming, she leaned closer to skim her thumb over his lips and capture the glossy traces and suck them into her own mouth.

He growled and drew a card without looking. Then urged her hand into the basket.

She wasn't even sure what she chose. It didn't matter. After the peach, their picnic turned rather salacious.

Before long, they were dipping into jam pots and suckling the sweetness from each other's fingers. They were not taking their time to select with care but delving into the basket blindly, sharing whatever they found—a wedge of sharp, tangy cheese; rich, succulent roast duck; currant scones; clotted cream; pear tarts; ripe plums—their mouths only a morsel apart.

In the back of her mind, she knew that this was far more dangerous than kissing. And yet, it made her feel so alive. Every taste, nibble and sip made her acutely aware of the pleasure in each moment until she wasn't even certain she'd been living before at all.

It was her turn, and her heart was racing in anticipation.

Her gaze fell from the cards to the hedonistic remains on the shawl. One would think a bacchanalian orgy had taken place. Panting, she searched through cards in a frenzy, tossing the wrong ones out of the way. But she couldn't find it.

"Looking for this?" He held up the Queen of Hearts between his fingers.

When the corner of his mouth curled with the smugness of victory, her fevered skin suddenly felt chilled as if she'd been buried beneath an avalanche of snow.

This had been a game. A mere game to him. And she was mortified to realize that, somehow, it had started to feel like something more to her. What that *something* might have been, she refused to think about.

"Congratulations, Mr. Flint," she said coolly. "It appears that I'm the one with egg on my face."

"That wasn't my intention."

"You intended to win. That was the purpose, was it not?"

"The prize wasn't to make a fool of you, Honoria. I wanted—" He growled, raking a hand through his hair.

Refusing to reveal her curiosity by prodding him, she went about cleaning up. They had certainly made a mess of things.

"Damn it all, I wanted you to kiss me. More than that, I wanted you to *want* to kiss me."

"Forgive me if I doubt your sincerity. After all, I already kissed you on two previous occasions."

"And you said you wouldn't ever again, and that . . ." He scrubbed a hand over his mouth, his words muffled when he added, ". . . bothered me."

She was not so angry or embarrassed that she couldn't see that this confession was difficult for him. Nor did she revel in her own sense of triumph—well, not too much—at the fact that the threatened withdrawal of her kisses had been the catalyst of his actions.

He had done all of this, inventing a game not simply to

lord a victory over her but to ensure that she kissed him? What an idiot.

She felt the tug of a smile at the corner of her mouth but quickly subdued it. "I didn't quite catch that last part."

"I said, Miss Honoria Hartley," he growled, "that you bother me. Exceedingly."

Facing the hamper, she gave in to a small grin. "You bother me, too."

Chapter Twenty

OSCAR WAS STILL bothered the following morning.

He was ruthless when it came to gambling. So why hadn't he just taken what he wanted? Or let his mouth naturally drift to hers? He knew that she had wanted the kiss, too.

But that wasn't the game they played.

What might have begun with Honoria and him pitted against each other, both holding secrets over the other's head, now felt more like a partnership.

The secrets they kept from everyone else had somehow forged a bond between the two of them. He wasn't sure how he felt about that.

Unsettled, he supposed.

So then, why was he wondering what Honoria would think if she knew the whole truth about him, even the things he hadn't shared with anyone, not even Cardew?

Hoping that a morning ride would bring him clarity, he set out on the bridle path, then spurred Hermes onward toward the ridge, where the rising sun turned dew-dappled grass into jewels and the air was sweet as clover nectar on the tongue. A man could get used to this.

Yet, as he gazed out over the expanse of tree, rolling hill and jutting rock, he thought of the real Vandemere and wondered if *he* would have to plot and scheme for Honoria's kisses.

No, he thought. Vandemere would be worthy of them.

He wouldn't have done the desperate things that Oscar had done to survive.

Beneath him, Hermes shifted and expelled a hard breath through his nostrils as if weary of the burden he carried. Oscar could relate.

Still thinking about Vandemere, he rode toward the fenced graveyard on the hill. Oscar left his horse to munch on tall grasses, then stepped through the squawk and judder of the old iron gate.

Headstones the dull color of tarnished silver stood like thrones in a row of descending years, father to sons. A rage-induced heart seizure had claimed the patriarch in 1800—incidentally the same year that his youngest son eloped with an actress. Opium claimed Sylvester in 1804. A mysterious accident, while ensconced in his hunting cabin with his mistress, claimed Hugh in 1815. Passion claimed Frederick in 1815. And apparently, debtors were the death of Titus in 1807.

That year was another thing he had in common with Vandemere. Whereas the real viscount had lost his father to death, Oscar's had simply walked out the door.

He remembered his mother sinking to the floor after they'd sold the last of their possessions to pay rent for one more week. She had looked so lost and afraid. And even though Oscar had been only five years old, he'd sensed that her tale of sending their draperies and bedclothes to the laundress wasn't the truth. It was something one did when left with no other choice.

"Papa isn't coming home, is he?"

Mother had forced her mouth into a smile and blinked to pretend there weren't tears shimmering in her eyes. Then she'd pulled him down onto her lap. "Of course he is. He will come back for you. Always. You are his son and the most precious creature on earth to him."

"And you are precious to him, too," he'd said with certainty, his years of knowledge on the subject of mothers and fathers seemingly infallible. But this had made those tears spill down her cheeks, and so he'd wrapped his arms around her neck to console her.

Lost in grief, she'd mumbled something he would never forget. "He will always love her. Always see her in his dreams. But he was my dream. So I loved him enough for us both."

He knew she didn't intend for him to pay attention to her garbled sobs. Yet, as he'd grown older, he'd often wondered if his father had taken a mistress and run off with her. But he'd never asked.

She'd had her own worries. Her days of singing opera had ended when she'd developed a cough that had left her voice shredded. She'd done her best to find work as a dressmaker, but too many years of stitching by candlelight had strained her eyes.

That had left her only one option.

Even though Oscar hadn't known at the time why she would come home with her dress torn and sometimes with a bruised cheek or red marks on her neck, he'd known it had something to do with the hollow look in her eyes and her sudden ability to purchase a few scraps of food.

That was the reason he'd started begging on the streets and in dark alleys. It hadn't taken him long to understand what vile acts his mother had had to perform.

For a few coins, she'd had to sell her soul.

And that was when, already jaded at the age of seven, Oscar had started hating his father.

"He isn't there, you know."

Startled, Oscar turned to find Cleo standing beside a leaning obelisk shrouded in ivy, her frock and bonnet the same dusty green as the foliage.

"That's merely a marker," she said, gesturing to the headstone for Titus. "His actual grave is somewhere in France or Naples or wherever he was killed. But you would know that already, I'm sure."

She didn't bother to conceal the blatant suspicion in her arched look, her arms folding beneath her breasts.

In no mood to rise to the bait and weary from the constant battle, he expelled a resigned breath. "I'm not your enemy, cousin."

"I'm certain that's what the man in King Henry IV's court tried to say when he demanded this property, then imprisoned, starved and kidnapped my ancestor. But some men believe they are entitled to whatever they want and use whatever means they can to get it."

"You think I'm trying to take away your home, but that is the furthest thing from my mind," he said. "I know what it's like to have your roots ripped out from beneath your feet. To have your history vanish in the blink of an eye. Believe me, I would not wish that on anyone."

Much to his surprise, she didn't immediately dismiss his comment and march off. Instead, she scrutinized him shrewdly, lips pursed. "There might be some truth in your declaration. But that still doesn't mean you're entitled to be here."

And *then* she turned on her heel and marched off.

Not surprisingly, young Mr. Shellhorn had been waiting nearby and walked behind her.

The eighteen-year-old was forever slathering at her heels, seemingly with no direction in his life. Though it was no wonder with his father content to linger on the estate without any occupation other than to nod his head in agreement at whatever Alfreda said.

From what Oscar had gleaned from Timms, none of the widows even dared to take a holiday or travel away from the abbey. It was a commonly held belief among the servants that they were all waiting for the moment the dowager kicked off so they could grab whatever they could.

All Oscar knew was that if the real Vandemere ever intended to come home, he'd better make haste before there was nothing left for him.

⤚⤙

AT THE STABLES, Oscar left his horse in Mr. Raglan's care. The young man had truly turned around in the past week and come up to scratch. His appearance was tidy, the carriages impeccable. With Oscar's permission, he'd even taken a younger groom under his wing.

The older coachman and stable master were still trying to make up their minds about him. But they had started to greet him with deference, especially when he'd showed interest in their discussion of fodder crops. And he was interested. After all, what did a gambler do when not gambling but consider other ways to make a fortune?

Not that anything would come of it. He would be gone soon enough. But he enjoyed the prospect of making improvements to the abbey. Better yet, he knew that any mark he left behind, no matter how small, would vex the widows greatly. And that made all the difference.

In the grand scheme of things, a few painted walls and an unvarnished railing weren't much, but the changes might give some life back to this grand old giantess.

With the intention of having another crack at getting Mr. Price to speak of the discrepancies he'd found, Oscar walked with a clipped stride to the front of the house.

Just as he rounded the corner, he heard a rider approach. His surprise instantly turned to wariness as he imagined it was a messenger from Rowan Warring, who'd said that he would send a missive only if there was cause to worry about Ladrón's whereabouts.

But it wasn't a messenger. It was Baron Hartley.

He should have felt relief in that. However, according to the tutelage given to him by Warring on life in the upper classes, he knew that social calls were not made before ten o'clock. So at once he thought of Honoria and worried that something had happened to her.

"Good morrow, lad. I see that we are both early risers." Hartley pulled back on the reins and frowned. "Your face is pale as stone. Whatever's the matter?"

Oscar took hold of the bridle. "Honoria . . . is she well?"

"Ah. Now I see. Rest assured, my daughter is perfectly hale. If she weren't, I'd hardly be leaving her side to pay a call, would I?" He chuckled and swung his leg over to dismount. Then, with a good-natured grin, he clapped a hand on Oscar's shoulder. "Allow me to offer you a bit of marital advice, which is to know your audience. Being sharp-eyed will save you from many an argument in the future."

Oscar felt like a nitwit. Until now, no one had ever accused him of being less than observant. But in the case of Honoria, he was forced to acknowledge that his thoughts frequently became muddled. And that irritated him as he handed the reins off to the groom.

"Think of it like gambling," Hartley continued companionably as they strolled into the abbey. "You do play, don't you?"

"On occasion."

"Well, you'd hardly wager your fortune against an opponent who is grinning from ear to ear. Then again, proficient gamblers are usually cleverer than we care to find. Much like women. They may be the fairer sex, but they're wily, too. Will have your heart tucked away in a jar before you've realized you've lost it."

Oscar wasn't worried about that happening. Only a man who had a heart to begin with need worry about it being stolen.

"Sound advice," he said, trying not to read his current opponent, and wondering just how much Hartley knew about him.

Pausing in the foyer, they handed off their hats and gloves to Algernon. "And to what do I owe the pleasure of this visit?"

"Perhaps we might go into your study for a more private discussion."

When Hartley's expression turned serious, the tension of uncertainty clamped a fist around Oscar's nape.

Without revealing so much as a facial tic, he turned to Algernon and requested a tea tray for his guest.

"Very good, my lord," he said with a bow.

Entering the study, Hartley crossed directly to the slender casement windows, a view of the verdant countryside through the mullioned panes. "Fair prospect."

"It is, indeed," Oscar said with an unfounded measure of pride.

Reminding himself that none of this was his, he felt an unexpected twinge of longing, a pinch he hadn't felt since he was a boy and tired of moving from place to place, craving the feeling of belonging somewhere. He'd become so numb to it over the years that the sensation took him off guard.

Sensing Hartley's attention on him, he shoved the thought aside and closed the door.

"As fond of loquacity as I am, there are times when a man needs to be direct," Hartley began ominously. "With that said, have you looked over the betrothal contract?"

Wary, Oscar shook his head. "To be honest, it has been something of a challenge to locate most of the papers within the abbey."

"I'd thought as much." He glanced over the shoulder of his green riding coat. "Servants tend to gossip."

"I'm sure you've discovered a great deal, then."

"Enough."

Oscar's nerves were taut as piano wire. Bloody hell. Even his palms were starting to sweat. Couldn't the man just state his reason for coming here and end this interminable wait?

"You came to discuss the betrothal?"

"In part," Hartley said, refusing to give an inch. "It was my mother's doing. The contract, I mean. My mother and your grandmother had a romantic notion when they drew it up."

Romantic? Oscar thought it was archaic. In fact, as of

this moment, he considered it a medieval torture device, as excruciating as the iron maiden.

"I, myself, thought it rather Shakesperean," Hartley continued. "The most we could hope for was a comedy of errors. Though, like my mother, Roxana had thought it was romantic as well, not to mention essential. Therefore, I agreed."

"Essential?"

"Well, as you know, your grandfather didn't approve of your father's marriage," Hartley said. "He then proceeded to destroy every trace of his youngest son, cutting him off completely. In fact, he even made certain that if anyone in the family ever assisted Titus, they would be cut off as well. And he wasn't allowed to return to the abbey under any circumstances."

"Tenderhearted soul, my grandfather."

Hartley nodded, thoughtful. "He had a particular plan for each of his sons and didn't want any of them to be without direction. As you might imagine, he did not approve of my friendship with your father either. He believed my parents should have tightened the reins." He waved a hand dismissively in the air. "Be that as it may, he did everything he could to ensure that your father would regret disobeying him. Then his heart failed him. Shortly following his death, your grandmother tried to locate Titus, but to no avail. Then, four years after that, her eldest son died. She became utterly despondent."

Oscar's gaze lifted in the direction of the dowager's sitting room. He'd been unaware of all the details but felt sorry for the woman upstairs who'd endured so much pain in her life. And he didn't want to be the cause of any more.

"Naturally, my mother was concerned for her friend and tried to console her," Hartley continued as Oscar swallowed down a lump of guilt. "Then, during one of her visits, a letter arrived. It was from your mother with news of your birth. I believe it was in the hope-filled days that followed that the kernel of a notion was first planted."

"The betrothal contract," Oscar concluded.

"Aye."

"Even so, to force your own daughter to marry a stranger seems like relying on false hope. After all, Vandemere could very well be—" Catching himself, he stopped, then clarified. "I might have turned out to be a disreputable scoundrel."

The baron's mouth twitched. "I knew you wouldn't be. After all, your mother, rest her soul, was as fine as could be."

Oscar nodded distractedly, thinking of his own mother. She hadn't always approved of what he did at the gaming tables, but she also knew that they had to live. Even so, she'd often said that she'd wanted more for him and that he would have the life he deserved once he found his father. What would she think about him masquerading as Vandemere?

But he knew the answer.

"Besides," Hartley continued, "there's nothing in the betrothal contract *forcing* my daughter's hand. Or yours, for that matter. It clearly states that death or elopement renders the contract null and void. So if Honoria ever fell in love and chose to elope, there would be nothing any of us could do."

Oscar had a sense that Hartley wouldn't have minded at all if Honoria had simply flitted off to Gretna Green with one of her many admirers. "You're a romantic, too."

"As the Bard once wrote, 'Love looks not with the eye, but with the mind—'"

"'And therefore is winged Cupid painted blind,'" Oscar finished.

Hartley chuckled. "Aye. 'Tis true, as well, lad. Though, no man gazing upon Honoria has ever lamented that he was stricken by an arrow against his will."

Oscar frowned, his thoughts returning to their picnic. If he'd just kept his smug mouth shut, she would have kissed him and he could have crowed about her surrender after. Instead, he was left only with an infernal craving that had not been satisfied. "Perhaps. But isn't an overabundance of beauty a fault in and of itself? After all, what man wants to contend with a sea of admirers wherever his woman goes? And she is far too sharp-witted and sharp-tongued for any man to gain the upper hand."

"And stubborn, too."

"As stubborn and cross as a pair of mules with their tails tied together." Then, remembering who he was talking to, Oscar cleared his throat. "If you'll pardon me for saying so."

"No need to apologize. I felt the same about Roxana."

"And what did you do about it?"

"I made her fall in love with me. It was either that or threaten to murder every man who gazed at her adoringly."

Oscar felt the full force of the older man's piercing blue eyes and shifted uncomfortably. "For the record, I did not threaten to *murder* the Culpeppers. Not exactly."

"They're good lads, but you needn't worry about them stealing Honoria's affections," he said. "And you may have done them a service by *encouraging* them—shall we say—to court other young women. Regardless, that's water under the bridge. It's time to discuss the dowry." As he spoke, he crossed toward the desk, reached into the inner pocket of his coat, withdrew a sheaf of papers and handed it to Oscar. "Perhaps this will help to smooth your path into the bosom of your family."

"Your daughter told me that she had no dow—" He broke off at the figure written in a tidy scrawl. "That's quite a sum."

"It is, indeed," Hartley said. "Though, mind you, £5,000 is not a great fortune. However, I do believe the sum would provide—"

A crash sounded in the hall, just outside the study door.

Crossing the room, Oscar opened the door to find Millicent, who'd apparently collided with the servant carrying the tea tray.

"Beggin' your pardon, my lady," the maid said, dropping to her knees to pick up the shards of the broken porcelain while frantically trying to mop up the spilled tea with her apron. "That was ever so clumsy of me. I didn't see you there at the door, all crouched over and such."

"Crouched over, indeed. I don't know what you are insinuating, but I'll speak to the housekeeper about your impertinence."

Oscar noticed twin patches of color rising to dear, sweet Aunt Millie's cheeks. And when she was flustered, her Scottish brogue peppered her speech generously.

He sent the maid to the kitchen for a mop. In her stead, even though he knew it wasn't done by the lord of the manor, he bent down, picked up the remaining broken pieces and stacked them on the tray.

Standing, he looked archly at his aunt. If he were to hazard a guess, someone had been peering through the keyhole. "Popping in for a visit with your favorite nephew, were you? Though, you might wish to try rapping on the door next time."

"I was informed that we had a guest," she said, attempting to sound overjoyed as if the widows regularly welcomed visitors to their doors. And he wasn't sure if that was supposed to be a polite grin on her lips or if she was about to be ill. "And since Baron Hartley will soon be family, I thought it only polite to greet him."

"How kind of you, my lady." Hartley offered a genial bow, but there was a twinkle in his eye that suggested he knew precisely what she'd been up to.

Oscar wondered if Millicent had heard the amount of the dowry. Likely so. It made him smile to himself thinking that, if he were the real Vandemere, she'd be kicking herself for continuing to deny his claim.

"So very kind of you, Aunt Millie."

When her eyes slitted on him, he flashed a grin and watched her storm off in a flurry. It was like watching a willow tree caught up in an angry tempest.

"I ken what you mean about the frosty welcome. That

one could freeze the Thames at a glance," Hartley said with a wry chuckle as he chafed his hands over his biceps. Then he sobered. "But I've no doubt, they'll warm to you. Give them a bit more time."

Time was not a luxury he had, especially not with Ladrón in London. After all, the man wouldn't search there forever.

"I suppose I should count myself fortunate that they haven't tried to murder me." At least, other than trying to starve him to death and young Shellhorn supposedly misfiring his firearm, he thought to himself.

The baron chuckled with grim amusement. "Not yet, lad. But better sleep with one eye open, just in case."

It was meant as a jest, but little did Oscar know that a few minutes later it would prove to be prophetic.

"Well, I'd best be off," Hartley said with a heavy sigh after they'd had their tea, with a generous splash of whiskey. "'Tis the ladies' day for callers. Doubtless, there'll be gentlemen by the dozen crowding into our parlor."

The news pulled furrows along Oscar's brow. "Surely not for Honoria."

"Oh, aye. She'll have her share, indeed. And then some." Hartley clapped him on the shoulder again. "At least until she's wed, good and proper."

They headed to the door, but Oscar's mood darkened, his thoughts plagued by the audacity of other men.

She was his . . . as far as they knew.

"Perhaps I'll ride over with you," he said as Hartley mounted his horse. Ordering Hermes saddled, he turned and stepped back inside for his hat and gloves . . .

Just in time for the chandelier overhead to come crashing down.

Chapter Twenty-One

❧

"DAUGHTER OF MINE, is there something you'd like to tell me?" Roxana said from the bedchamber doorway, her voice silken as syllabub and her delicately arched brows hinting at only the barest degree of suspicion.

Honoria pretended complete innocence, blinking owl-eyed as she lifted the flounced hem of her green skirts and sank a foot into a waiting slipper. "Hmm . . . No. At least, nothing that I can think of at the moment, other than the fact that you look positively radiant this morning."

That much was true. Dressed in russet and gold, Roxana's skin fairly glowed. But with her chestnut hair pulled back into an elegant chignon, it drew attention to her dramatically dark features. Especially the look of knowing in the impish tilt at the corners of her eyes.

"And I suppose if I were to tell you that a dozen octogenarians were waiting in the parlor, the news wouldn't surprise you a whit?"

Honoria affected a stageworthy pout. "Only a dozen? How sad. I'd sent out seventeen invitations. Either I'm losing my appeal, or some of them weren't able to make the journey. I should make a note of it and visit those who couldn't be here."

"There is also an ample supply of suitably aged gentlemen in attendance."

"Well, I certainly didn't invite *them*."

At the moment, she was only interested in interviewing

candidates for elopement. The more aged and infirm, the better. She would also prefer him to have plenty of sons so no one would expect her to conceive.

Until now, she'd never really given the thought of elopement fair consideration. But it was time to rethink her options. After all, marriage might not be too unbearable as long as it was on her own terms. And the fact that she'd come to this decision after her picnic with Oscar had nothing to do with it whatsoever.

"No, I don't imagine you did," Mother said. "The others are likely here because word has spread about Vandemere's return, and the fact that the banns have yet to be read has given them a semblance of hope." She lifted a hand to her temples. "Consequently, the entire house is beginning to smell like a hothouse from all the bouquets they've brought, giving me a megrim. And Verity and Magnus have fled to Swanscott Manor to spend the day with his grandmother."

An Aubusson rug in rose and ivory muffled Honoria's steps as she crossed the bedchamber. Dutifully, she pressed a kiss to her mother's cheek. "I think the solution is to send all the younger gentlemen on their way."

Roxana slanted her a look of omniscience that motherhood had honed to perfection.

But Honoria refused to feel guilty. So she offered an offhand shrug. "Unless, of course, Thea wishes to entertain them."

"Your sister's primary interest in the horde waiting below is to cast them in a Homerian epic, then have them entertain *her* on the stage. She has already asked if she could borrow the servants to throw pails of water on the men drawn helplessly to the sirens for the shipwreck scene."

"Oh, that's actually quite"—Honoria faltered when her mother's look darkened—"clever, isn't it?"

"I'm more concerned with the cleverness of my middle daughter at the moment, or lack thereof. I just hope you know what you're doing."

Honoria swallowed. "Of course I do. You've always taught us to let our hearts guide us, and that's just what I'm doing."

Because her heart was telling her to stay far, far away from Oscar Flint.

BY THE TIME Honoria entered the overwarm parlor, her dozen octogenarians had dwindled to seven. She discovered that two had been caught up in fits of sneezing from all the flowers. A third had an attack of gout. The last two had fallen asleep and were taken away by their nursemaids.

Those who remained were fading fast in the summer heat. It seemed an hour of plying the men with strong black tea to keep them awake had backfired somewhat. Five of them required the use of the retiring room. Four of those never returned. She imagined them lost somewhere in the house, ambling endlessly in the corridors and stopping to chat with a marble bust.

Stifling a giggle at the thought, she trained all her wiles on the final three.

She was thankful that Thea had been willing to take the younger men to the music room, with Roxana as chaperone. Honoria didn't want their mother to witness what she was about to do.

But as every woman knew, desperate times called for . . . décolletage.

With a graceful lift of her hands to touch her hair, she pretended that she had no idea that the action offered her breasts a little boost in their gusseted cups. And when she lowered her arms, the firm swells strained against the pink beribboned edge of her bodice.

"More tea?" she asked as she bent over to pour a cup for Baronet Roth who was, incidentally, a perfect candidate at eighty-nine. His wiry brows lifted as he followed the gesture, a tea-drunk grin on his lips. Then his eyes glazed over, and a dribble of saliva pooled over his bottom lip.

Oh, dear. Perhaps she'd gone a touch too far. Losing another, she rang for Mr. Mosely.

Just as the butler and one of the footmen were helping Lord Roth back to his carriage and his traveling physician, a white-haired termagant stormed in on a huff.

She went directly to the portly Lord Windrow and slapped his plump, ruddy cheek. "'Just going for a drive, my pet,' you said. 'Won't be but a minute,' you said, only to find you in the company of this . . . this harlot." She cast a disparaging glance to Honoria and her mostly modestly covered bosom. "Ain't I given you the best years of my life? Baked your bread? Washed your stockings and drawers? Gave into your slap and tickle for nigh on twenty years now? Said you'd make an honest woman of me. Well, no more. I refuse to be strung along. And, mark my words, I'll never cook or clean for you, or rub that belly when you've ate too many Banbury cakes, ever again."

As she stormed back out, Lord Windrow shot to his feet. He stumbled after her. "Pudding, don't go! You know that you and your Banbury cakes are all I've ever wanted. Pudding, please . . ."

A door slammed in the distance.

And then there was one, Honoria thought with a sigh and closed her eyes.

But in the next breath her eyes sprang open when she heard her father's stage bellow coming from the foyer. "What the deuce is going on here?"

"I'd lay odds that your middle daughter is behind it," an all-too-familiar voice of raw silk replied.

Devil's doorknocker! What was Oscar doing here?

She whirled around to her one remaining octogenarian and clasped her hands over her rabbiting heart. "It is such a lovely day. I wonder if you might escort me for a stroll in the garden, sir."

Sir Russel Covington—ninety in September—eyed her blandly with two slow blinks over cloudy blue eyes. Like a pillar of beeswax left overlong in the sun, his face was long and narrow, with a sloping nose and a wide mouth tipped down at the corners toward drooping jowls.

When her question was met with that blank stare, she recalled that he was hard of hearing and tried again a bit louder.

"I'm not one for flowers and such," he answered after a third attempt, his voice a cool monotone. He cast a withering glance to the bright bouquets bursting from the vases and pitchers that crowded every flat surface.

Hearing footsteps on the stairs, she took two more steps into the room. "Then, perhaps the library."

"Too much reading addles one's thoughts."

She hid her disapproval of that statement and briefly thought that she would still have the option to smother him in his sleep on their wedding night . . . if she could simply get him to stand up and walk with her. Perhaps she could shove him into his carriage and hie off to Gretna Green this afternoon.

But the instant a footfall stopped behind her, she knew it was already too late.

She caught the scents of amber and sandalwood beneath saddle leather, horse and sweat, and hated that the mélange of fragrances set her moths aflutter. Stupid moths.

"Why, Lord Vandemere, what a pleasant surprise," she said without turning to face him.

He came up beside her and settled a warm hand against the small of her back. "Is it, my dear?"

No. No, it most definitely was not.

"I should have thought you'd be busy plundering the abbey's coffers," she muttered through gritted teeth, all the while keeping a smile on her lips for the sake of her guest.

"The abbey had other plans for me," he said. "Would you care to introduce me to your . . . caller?"

She despised that amused *I can see all your cards* tone of his. "Sir Russel Covington."

"Eh?" Covington asked, his waxen features nudging into alert confusion.

Honoria raised her voice. "I was just introducing you to Lord Vandemere."

"Puppeteer, you say? Bah!" He sneered and pushed a gnarled hand through the air. "Never been one for puppets. Childish things. No man . . . should . . . waste . . ."

Apparently, the sudden burst of activity exhausted him, and he nodded off, the sagging lids over his rheumy eyes drifting shut. As his chin melted against the voluminous folds of his cravat, he let out a snore.

"And then there were none." She sighed. "I hope you're hap—"

Turning to glare at Oscar, she startled at seeing a thin red cut over his left eyebrow. "What happened?"

When she reached up, he covered her hand and drew it down. "It's nothing. A wayward chandelier. Thankfully no one was hurt."

"You were hurt." Hearing the tenderness in her own voice and realizing that her hand was resting over his heart, she stepped back and issued a shrug. "Of course, I would have preferred a fatal accident."

He smirked and seized her hand, tugging her out of the parlor. "For that cruel remark, I believe you owe me a walk." And when she tried to pull free, he added, "Unless you'd rather speak with your father. I believe he's in the music room making inquiries."

She ended up allowing him to curl her hand around his sleeve. But she wasn't happy about it.

"Where are you taking me?" she groused as he steered her away from the house and past the gardens.

"I don't trust you, Signore. The minute I release you, you're likely to load Covington into a wheelbarrow, toss him into his carriage and abscond with him."

The fact that he was uncannily accurate vexed her to no end, and she jerked her hand away. "You don't know as much as you think you do."

"I know a desperate play when I see one. You're betting all your fish tokens before the cards have been dealt."

"Perhaps I have complete faith in my hand. Did you ever think of that?"

"What I think is that you like to be in control, and it scares you when you're not."

She scoffed, but her pulse scurried in a panic. It felt as though she were dressed as a target and he had just struck the red eye in the center.

She hated being so transparent to him!

Of all the gentlemen she'd met in her life, not one of them had ever seen past her beauty. Until Oscar. He saw through all her disguises and deeper still, leaving her vulnerable. And yes, it was frightening. But she refused to tell him that.

So she stayed silent as they walked the winding path through the meadow, the air sizzling with the rustle of tall grasses, the droning buzz of honeybees, the crackle of grasshoppers and the distant susurration of cicadas.

The pompous blackguard beside her didn't bother to hide the smug arch of his brow as if he'd read every one of her thoughts. Before she could tell him to go to the devil, her gaze drifted up to the angry red slash on his forehead, and something pinched in the center of her chest.

"You should apply salve. Otherwise, you'll have an unsightly scar."

"It will just be one more to add to all the others."

"*What* others?"

The shoulders beneath his coat lifted absently. He ambled over a stile and held his hand out to assist her. "Where is the woman who planned to murder me in my sleep?"

"Still perfecting her poison," she countered, choosing to ignore his open palm.

But he refused to let her proceed on her own and set his hands on her waist before slowly lowering her to her feet.

The churning maelstrom of unwanted feelings made her want to run in the opposite direction. Either that or wrap her arms around him, hold him close and reassure him that she would keep him safe. *Him*, the very man who'd been blackmailing her.

It was absolutely ridiculous.

Before those all-seeing eyes could read those thoughts as well, she shoved away from him and stormed off, around the bend.

Her steps faltered when she saw where they were.

She rarely walked by the river. Even though it was a hot day, seeing the sun glinting off the surface of the water gave her a chill.

She chafed her hands over her arms. "Why did you have to lead us here?"

"I thought we might enjoy a change of scenery. We haven't strolled by the river yet, and it's hot as blazes. Hot enough to take a swim."

Behind her, she heard the splash of water. Her blood suddenly ran cold. As if caught in a bog, she turned slowly. She saw him remove his coat. Saw him walk toward the river's edge. Saw him lose his footing and sink down—

"No!"

Without thinking, she bolted. Charging toward him with her arms outstretched, she caught him around the waist just in time to knock him—drag him—back onto the path.

He fell with a hard thud, her body sprawled over his.

"What in blazes, Honoria! One minute, I'm bending down to wet my face and the next you're—"

He broke off, his scowl abruptly fading into concern as he looked up at her.

That was when she realized what she'd just done. She'd barreled into him, for heaven's sakes. Just launched herself at him out of the blue. And she felt like an utter fool.

Mortified, she tried to push herself off him, but her limbs were too weak.

"What is it? You're whiter than my backside, and you're trembling." Oscar sat up, pulling her onto his lap, his hands cradling her face.

Her entire body shivered, her teeth chattered. And she wished she could will herself to stop.

But when she closed her eyes to concentrate, all she saw was a vision of him, face down in the water. "I thought . . . you were . . . falling."

"I wasn't, but even if I were, I don't think that's the reason you're crying right now."

Was she? Devil's doorknocker, she was. How humiliating! She could feel the wet runnels on her cheeks as he wiped them away with his thumbs. Could this moment get any worse?

Then she sniffled so hard that her nostrils closed, making a snorting sound at the back of her throat. And she had her answer.

When she tried to scramble away, he held her close. "Shhh . . . Whatever it is, you know you can tell me. I am the keeper of your secrets, after all. And you are the keeper of mine."

"Oh, why must you say such tender things? It makes it so difficult to hate you."

"All part of my diabolical plan."

Her head found the niche between his neck and shoulder that seemed formed just for her, and she felt the press of his lips against her hair.

"I had a twin," she said softly. "His name was Ernest, and he was"—*the other half of my entire world*, she thought—"lovely. We were still in the nursery, still climbing into the other's bed at night. We'd never spent a day apart. Until the day he drowned."

Oscar's arms tightened around her, and he cursed softly. "Forgive me. I didn't know."

"You likely think the way I behaved just now was foolish."

"You're wrong," he said. "I know all too well how a loss at that age can change everything. It's hard to have the world you know crumble beneath your feet."

Those words, that simple acknowledgment and understanding, meant more to her than he would ever know. She closed her eyes, feeling the damp press of her lashes, hearing the reassuring beat of his heart, strong and steady.

"I still think of that day," she said. "We were playing a game, blowing bubbles in the water. The pure delight of laughter echoing in the garden like raindrops plinking down a well. We were forever challenging each other. Everything with us was always in halves. When I finished, he crouched down to begin.

"I still remember his dimples and the way his eyes turned to crescent moons when he smiled, the way his flaxen hair looked like curls of sunlight and how they fanned out like threads of a silken halo around his head when they touched the surface of the water. And he said, 'Watch me . . .'"

A breath shuddered through her, and Oscar held her closer, his lips brushing her forehead. "But I'd heard a strange sound, a cry or shout of alarm. It came from my grandmother. She'd stood up from the bench. Then, just as suddenly, crumpled to her knees, her eyes wide and confused in a way that frightened me. So I climbed over the side of the reflecting pool and ran off to find the nurse who was fetching flannels for Ernest and me."

Honoria remembered everything, every moment: the shouts of her grandfather to summon a surgeon from the village, the commotion of the servants, the strange and terrible chill that had crept over her.

She shivered, and Oscar rubbed his hands down her back in soothing passes. "I think I knew even before the nurse screamed. Even before the gardener lifted his limp body out of the water. Even before I saw that his pink cherub's mouth was tinged blue. And the last thing I remember about that day was the howl of anguish from Grandfather as he fell to his knees holding my brother's limp body and Grandmama in his arms. And all because I didn't watch—"

"No," Oscar interrupted, his tone hard even as his hold remained soothing. "It wasn't your fault. You were a child and saw the world through a child's eyes. There was no way for you to know."

"But if I had just—"

"Stop. No amount of guilt or regret can alter the past. Those pages of our stories have been glued in place. Trying to pry them apart and rewrite them so they have a different ending is not only impossible but leads to misery." He tilted up her chin and forced her to meet his gaze. "You will never learn to live your life—truly live it—until you stop trying to change what happened and let yourself mourn for what was lost, not for what might have been."

She wanted to shove away from him. Wanted to ball her hands into fists and pummel his chest for his audacity. Wanted to rail at him for daring to think that he knew anything about her. But when she opened her mouth to do just that, a cry came out instead.

It was an angry sound. Almost a shout, hard and bitter, her eyes slitted. She almost convinced herself that it was only anger. That all she had to do was yell at him. She didn't know that releasing it would break the dam that had been holding back years of the agony and utter loneliness she'd been hiding for most of her life.

When the emotions rose up in a sudden torrent, she wasn't prepared. They streamed from her eyes, stuttered from her throat and drained her of the strength to hold them back.

Oscar held her tightly as she sobbed. She couldn't stop the torrent. Not even the reminder that she was humiliating herself in front of her adversary could stop her. And he simply let her cry, holding her all the while.

Wrung out, she allowed herself to sink against him and heard him breathe in as his lungs expanded. Gradually, her own breathing slowed to match his, his comforting scent reaching inside to soothe her.

Oscar's lips brushed her temple. "You've had that locked inside you all this time, haven't you?"

"We never talk about Ernest in my family. And I refuse to force it because I don't want to upset my parents. But he should be talked about, remembered. He's still part of this family."

"It was the same for my mother," he said after a while. "She lost her sister, her twin, before I was born. But she said it was too difficult to talk about her because she felt as though half of her had died."

Honoria looked up at him in surprise. "That's precisely how it feels."

He pressed a kiss to her forehead. "I think I understand you better now, the loss behind the reason you keep yourself guarded. We are alike in that, as well."

She didn't argue. Even so, it seemed impossible that this vexing, blackhearted man could know her better than anyone. And even more impossible that all she wanted to do was burrow closer to him, to let him fill that emptiness she carried with her.

But that wasn't something she was willing to do.

Therefore, she stood and brushed out her skirts, attempting to make herself look presentable. He did the same, moving around behind her as she carefully avoided his gaze. Now that the moment was over and she was no longer in his arms, embarrassment crept in again.

"Don't," he said gently, settling a hand beneath her chin to tilt up her face. Her mouth opened on an argument, and he pressed his damp handkerchief to her lips, silencing her. "Don't start building your walls again, believing that I won't scale those, too."

Then, holding her gaze, he proceeded to tenderly wipe away any residual traces of her tears. And whatever diatribe that waited on her tongue for his impertinence simply dissolved away.

She put her hair back to rights, setting a few loose pins in place before brushing the dust off his shoulders. She even reached up to comb back the wayward dark curls that had fallen against his forehead, which seemed to amuse him.

With a grin tucked into the corner of his mouth, he captured her hand, then tugged her along the towpath, their fingers interlaced. She kept pace beside him but inwardly wondered how this had happened.

She didn't have the answer. Then again, it wasn't a question she wanted to spend too much time thinking about either.

He stopped at the old ash tree, its trunk as wide as a carriage. "Look at this grand beauty. I've yet to see its equal on the abbey grounds."

"We used to climb this as children. Reaching the top became sort of a rite of passage for us." She traced the names they'd carved just above the first knothole. "It began with Truman, of course. Not to be outdone, Verity soon followed. You wouldn't think it by looking at her, but she climbs a tree like a monkey. Then came me and"—she swallowed as her fingertips skimmed the letters—"Thea."

But there was one name missing. Ernest never had the chance to climb this tree. She still remembered the day she'd carved hers, and that night, how she'd cried herself to sleep.

Oscar gave her one look, just one, then reached down into his boot and withdrew a dirk.

When he stepped behind her, one hand anchored on her waist, she asked, "What are you doing?"

"What should have been done long ago." He stuck the tip of his dirk into the soft gray bark, exactly beside her name. Then he wrapped her hand around the hilt and covered it with his own. "We'll do this together."

Together.

By the time they finished, her eyes were swimming with bittersweet tears. That painful pinch in her heart suddenly gave way to something else. Something that she wouldn't think about until much, much later.

Chapter Twenty-Two

⁂

THE FOLLOWING MORNING, Oscar rode out across the estate lands with Mr. Holcombe.

The gamekeeper was a quiet man, keeping his cards close, but his keen gaze made it clear that he was always thinking. Doubtless, a vole couldn't make it onto the property without the man knowing about it.

As they headed east toward the ridge, Oscar was struck by a peculiar rush of amusement. Not for any particular reason. It was just that never in his boyhood dreams had he imagined himself a country gentleman. And yet, there he was—or, at least, Vandemere was—his interest piqued with every grunt and frown the gamekeeper made over various animal tracks, a crooked fence post, or strips of bark scored from the trunk of a tree.

He'd even perused the library's shelves and found a first edition of *The Gardener's Labyrinth* by Thomas Hill. The widows had been quite cross when he'd mentioned the improvements he planned to make to their cutting garden—extending the flagstone pathway, expanding the rose bower, adding additional beehives.

It pleased him to no end to drop little nuggets like that for them the grumble and grouse over. And he was beginning to suspect that their genuine dislike of him was more show than fact.

Then again, thinking back to the chandelier . . . perhaps not.

Oscar and Holcombe were just approaching the ridge when the gamekeeper stopped and turned his mount. Oscar followed his gaze as another rider approached. A beautiful rider, in fact.

Honoria Hartley by morning light was definitely a sight a man could get used to.

Today, she was garbed in a burgundy riding habit buttoned all the way up to the neck. A jaunty hat sat perched to one side of her luminous flaxen hair as she rode toward him with unsurprisingly fluid grace atop her side saddle.

When she reached them, she beamed. "Good morning, Vandemere. And Mr. Holcombe, aren't you looking ruggedly handsome this fine day?"

Even though the gamekeeper's impassive countenance did not alter when he issued a nod of greeting, his cheeks suddenly looked a bit ruddier than usual. Oscar actually felt sorry for him. No man stood a chance against Honoria's charms.

"And to what do we owe this unexpected pleasure, Miss Hartley? Or is it that you came all this way to speak to Mr. Holcombe? If so, I'm afraid I would be forced to challenge him to a duel. Unfortunately for me, he's a crack shot, and my chances of survival are minimal at best."

She tapped her gloved finger against the side of her pursed lips, her gaze drifting coquettishly to the gamekeeper. Then she sighed. "Oh, I suppose we cannot have that. Not yet, at any rate. Therefore, my reason is that I accompanied Mr. Lawson to the abbey."

"And my list of rivals is growing by the minute. Doubtless, I will be forced to spend your entire dowry on an arsenal of weapons and building high walls to surround the abbey and shield us from besotted invaders."

"Perhaps." The imp flashed a grin, not realizing that he was partly serious. "However, today he came to have a look at your chandelier. Father would have come as well, but he and Mother had a prior engagement for breakfast with

Lady Broadbent before my sister and her husband leave on their honeymoon. So I decided to tag along with Mr. Lawson and ensure you hadn't taken a spill down the stairs or something."

"Waiting to push me yourself?"

"You know me too well." And yet, when her gaze collided with his, he detected a kernel of truth revealed in that Aegean blue. She looked away quickly, her cheeks coloring as she gestured with an absent flick of her wrist. "Be that as it may, Mr. Lawson began his inspection, and when the groom said that you were with Mr. Holcombe, I decided to find you."

Oscar was glad she had, but he didn't tell her. Confess such things to a woman like Honoria and she would win every hand.

"I regret to inform you that we were just concluding our tour of the estate," he said. "However, since you're here, might as well take in the best view from the top of the ridge."

Without hesitation, she spurred her horse and dashed past them. Over her shoulder, she issued a taunting laugh. "Race you!"

Oscar didn't know if the grin he wore as he charged after her was one that appeared on his face the moment he saw her or if it was a new one because she'd managed to surprise him yet again.

If he wasn't careful, he might actually start to like surprises.

She beat him to the ridge, triumph glowing in her lifted cheeks. And when Holcombe joined them, Oscar could have sworn he saw the ever-impassive man smirk.

The view from the ridge had become Oscar's favorite place. Sloping hills, blending into forest and fen, and green as far as the eye could see. And sitting on his mount with Honoria beside him, he almost felt like Vandemere.

"It is quite a lovely prospect." Honoria lifted a hand to

the brim of her hat to shield her eyes from the sun that rose higher in a sea of cloudless blue.

Oscar nodded, feeling a surge of pride, unfounded though it might have been.

"What about that outcropping of rock over there"—she pointed—"peeking out just beneath that copse of trees?"

"That's the old keep, or what's left of it," Holcombe offered. "Twelfth-century or thereabouts. Most of the timber and roofing were scavenged around the sixteenth century to begin building the abbey. The rest just crumbled away. When it rains a spell, you can see where the moat was." He grinned, his gaze turning distant with reminiscence. "The young masters used to wage wars over who could be king of Awildian Palace."

A shiver tightened Oscar's scalp, lifting the hair at the back of his nape. "I beg your pardon?"

"Awildian Palace," Holcombe repeated. "Ach. But that was just something master Titus invented. The actual name is Bramslea Castle."

Awildian Palace. Just like the book of poetry his father had read to him.

"I should like very much to see it," Honoria interjected, casting sidelong glances to both men.

Holcombe cleared his throat, his cheeks flame bright. "It's a fair pace away, Miss Hartley, and I have a fence to repair."

"I'm sure Lawson is expecting me," Oscar said.

She clucked her tongue, pouting prettily. "What a pity."

Oscar knew that tone. Knew that look, too. Her politeness was a mere formality. She fully intended to do whatever she wanted, and no one would stop her. But when he saw her gaze slide down the steep incline as if to ride down the treacherous path—perched on her sidesaddle, no less—he had to intervene.

"You're not going alone, so get that notion out of your head at once."

She peered over the ridge. "It isn't so very steep. I'm sure I could—"

Before she could finish, he sidled his horse up to hers and secured the bridle. Then he turned to the gamekeeper. "Holcombe, if you wouldn't mind letting Lawson know that I will attend to him shortly. Apparently, I'll be escorting Miss Hartley to the ruins to ensure her safety. We shan't be long."

Holcombe's gaze flicked between the two of them, and it was clear in the small shake of his head that he understood that Oscar was dealing with a headstrong female. Only, one of these days, she might end up getting herself into real trouble.

"Aye, my lord," he said with a tug on the reins and left them alone.

"Clever. You are attempting to reinforce your pretense of authority. Indeed, that was quite the *lord of the manor* display." Her brows flashed flirtatiously. "But we both know that I fully intend to traverse that slope."

Oscar's grip on her horse didn't lessen, and he leveled his gaze at her. "That wasn't a pretense. You are not—and I repeat *not*—risking your neck. We are riding back the way we came and around to a safer path. And don't even think about arguing over my right to command you. If you so much as glance down the slope again, I will lift you off your saddle, sling you over my knee and escort you to the abbey to have tea with the widows."

Her eyes blazed fire as her nostrils flared. But his glare was just as lethal, and his tone brooked no argument.

He was about to add that he'd throttle her backside, too. However, the instant he remembered how that shapely rounded part of her fit against his hand, his mind started to veer off in another direction. It was best to keep his focus where it mattered.

"Fine," she said after a moment. "But it's only because I want to see this Awildian Palace for myself."

So did he.

It was strange, but in all the times he'd looked over the ridge, he'd merely thought it was an outcropping of stone, which was not an uncommon sight. He had yet to explore all of the property. The land here was so varied with woodlands, hills, rocks and marshes, and he was often overwhelmed by the beauty of it.

He'd spent so much of his life moving from city to city that, if it weren't for seeing the countryside through the window of a carriage, he might not even believe places like this existed.

Not for the first—and definitely not for the last—time, he thought Vandemere was one lucky bastard.

"Are you through with pouting yet?" he asked as he urged Hermes forward and matched the pace of her mare until they were side by side across the fen. Thus far, she'd been keeping ahead by two lengths, her back stiff as a pole.

Her chin jutted out. "I could have handled the slope. You know nothing about my horsemanship, and I don't like being underestimated for the sake of your ego."

"It has nothing to do with my ego. You said it yourself. I don't know anything about your horsemanship. And I wasn't about to stand idly by while you attempted to prove yourself," he said, his voice rising. "If you haven't realized by now, I stopped underestimating you when you left me weak-kneed and stunned in Paris. And I'm not the kind of man who needs to learn the same lesson more than once."

"Then, why wouldn't you let me?"

"Because I don't want to see you hurt! I should have thought that was obvious."

She looked over at him, quiet and considering. "Fair enough, I suppose."

He arched a brow back at her. "And this is where you confess to coming here because you were worried about me."

"Hardly." She scoffed. "My primary concern is that your death would force me to invent a new viscount."

"Ah, yes. Wouldn't want to inconvenience you."

He saw the corner of her mouth twitch just as one gilded curl slipped free of the coil and rested on her shoulder. It reminded him of a sumptuous dream filled with images of silken limbs tangled with his own, of Honoria's pale hair falling in a golden curtain around him as she kissed him, rising over him to sink down onto him, her neck arching as he filled her again and again . . .

"Oscar?"

Hearing his name, he realized he'd allowed his attention to drift and lifted his eyebrows in silent query.

"I asked about your plan."

"Plan?"

"To pay your gambling debt. At least, I presume it is a matter of money. And since you're no longer holding secrets over my head, and you are intelligent enough to know that I won't be forced into marriage," she said and paused to cast him an arched look, "I'm wondering what your plan is."

He shifted in the saddle. Clearly, the only undulating happening here was in the sway of the broom shrub as yellow flower-tipped branches bent and bowed in the cool breeze that swept over the fen, stirring the air with a sweet fragrance. "First of all, I always pay my debts. And second, it's a little more complicated."

"Then, enlighten me," she said. "Oh, come now, Oscar. I am the keeper of your secrets, as you are of mine, remember?"

She was diabolical, using that soft look against him. What man stood a chance?

"It began with one of Cardew's paintings."

"Cardew?"

For an instant, he caught himself wondering why the two most important people in his life hadn't been introduced. But just as quickly, he cast that thought aside as a mistake because Honoria wasn't in his life. Not really. Therefore, she couldn't possibly be important to him.

"Ignatius Cardew is something of a mentor to me," he explained. "After my father . . . left, Cardew stayed and provided for us in his own unconventional manner. He's an artist. A rather exceptional artist, but one whose skill lies primarily in replication."

"In other words, he's a forger."

"A very good one," he clarified. "He just made the poor decision to use Ladrón's mistress as the muse for his Titian . . . while she was wearing the ruby necklace which she'd stolen from Ladrón's wife."

Honoria considered this for a moment. "I don't understand. If Cardew was the one who cheated him, why is Ladrón after you?"

"That's where it gets a bit muddy. When the bloodthirsty Spaniard had Cardew by the co—" He coughed. "Let's just say that he threatened to relieve Cardew of his favorite appendage. That was when I made the not-altogether-brilliant boast that I could quadruple the amount that he'd paid Cardew and settle the debt. The bargain earned a temporary stay of execution."

"And you were to pay that debt the night we met," she surmised.

"Most memorable night of my life."

A frown knitted her brow as she stared ahead toward the ruins where white stones were heaped in parallel piles, as if it might have supported a wall or drawbridge. Off to one side, a massive moss-shrouded sessile oak stood guard like a ghostly sentinel.

"By winning, I set this entire debacle in motion," she said. "Not the least of which was putting your life in danger."

"Careful, Signore. You wouldn't want to give the impression that you care about the state of my neck."

She sent him a glare in response and assumed that if she looked away quickly enough it would mask the worry in her eyes.

But witnessing the truth for himself sent a warmth that

threatened to spark to life in the center of his chest. He tamped it down, of course.

"But you had been winning most of the night, up until then. I've given this a good deal of thought, and I think I distracted you and made you lose count."

His jaw slackened with shock. "Lose . . . count?"

"That is what you do, isn't it?" she asked with a shrug as if she hadn't just floored him. "Though, to be perfectly honest, I didn't put the pieces together straightaway. It's only been since knowing you and seeing the way your eyes change when you're remembering something that gave me the first clue. Your reaction, just now, merely confirmed it."

She truly was an astute observer.

When they reached the shallow trench—the likely remains of the moat from ages ago—they stopped. Dismounting, he stepped over to hand her down.

"You are a dangerous woman, Honoria Hartley."

"So then, it's true," she said hollowly as he lowered her to the ground. "You are running for your life because of me."

"No." Tilting up her chin, he stared directly into her eyes. "No, it isn't. I've been in scrapes all my life. When I wasn't dodging trouble, I was looking for my father and winding up in trouble all the same. And making a living as a gambler doesn't keep a man in one place for too long."

"Surely, it wasn't always like that for you. It couldn't have been."

He knew she wasn't doubting his word. It was clear enough in the tender concern in her expression that she simply didn't want to believe it.

So he was gentle when he said, "I don't even know my real name, Honoria. One of my last recollections of my father was when we'd had to leave our rooms in the middle of the night in order to escape creditors. The names my parents went by would change from one city to the next. My surname of Flint is a shortened version of Flintridge. Which was the last alias we had before my father left."

He lowered his hand, but not before she reached out and took hold of it. Even through the layers of their gloves, he felt the jolt of contact.

"I'm sorry," she said softly. "For what it's worth, I wouldn't have wanted anyone else to blackmail me."

"You're only saying that because I'm no longer blackmailing you."

"Well, you're no longer blackmailing me because you're attracted to me. So it's a wash."

That wasn't the reason. But it was amusing that she thought so. And why not let her go on believing it?

Threading her arm through his, he escorted her toward the foundation stones of what had once been a curtain wall and between a pair of crumbling towers. As they approached, he thought again about the uncanny coincidence of the book of poetry his father had read to him.

"*The tumbledown mystic of castle walls,*" she whispered, as if hearing his thoughts.

He stopped and met her gaze. "You read my book."

"Well, you're the one who left it on your bedside table for anyone to stumble upon." She issued an unapologetic shrug. "Did you already know about this castle, then? And the name Titus Fairfax had given it?"

"Not until today. My father used to read those poems to me."

Honoria's lips parted on a soundless gasp. "I thought the book came from the abbey's library."

"No. And I'm just as puzzled. The book was printed, and yet there appears to be no author named. Either that or it has worn away over time. All I know is that my mother told me to keep it safe."

"Perhaps the author was someone who knew Titus Fairfax and spent time here." She stepped toward him, her hands lifting to his lapels, her eyes glowing with excitement and possibility. "Or, better yet, perhaps your father was the author, and he knew the family. He might have grown up nearby. There's a chance that his home—*your* home—is not far from here . . ."

As she spoke, that unsettling warmth filled his chest. This time, it came on too fast, and he couldn't guard himself against it with his usual cynicism. It was as if her every breath was a spell blowing over ashen coals, stirring the sluggish embers until they caught fire.

Why was she forever doing this to him? Making him want all the things he'd convinced himself long ago he was better off without?

"Stop," he said, taking her by the shoulders.

"But surely you want to uncover the mystery of it at last. There could be someone here who met your father," she continued, her words blazing inside him. "Someone who knows his surname, where he was born, and where he is now. Together, we could—"

He kissed her into silence, sealing his mouth over hers.

His shoulders sagged with relief when she stopped spinning her enchantment. All he needed was a moment to think, a moment to remember that he was a nomad without any roots to a place or family, and he didn't need anything or anyone . . .

But then he tasted magic on her sigh of surrender. Felt her sweet breath kindle the blaze inside him, her body melting against him like candle wax.

Her lips moved in a wordless incantation that burned inside him to the point of agony as her palms glided over his chest, up along his cravat to cradle his face. He tried to steal himself against it. Tried to hide the secret yearnings he'd had as a boy behind the jaded facade he'd developed over time.

It was no use.

She'd pushed him too far. She'd started a conflagration that consumed his barriers, turning them to cinders as her arms wrapped around his neck and she held him, clinging and vibrating with fierce tenderness.

He never had the chance to warn her. To tell her that the barriers he'd kept carefully in place for most of his life weren't only there to protect himself. No. They were also there to protect anyone who might breach them and unleash what he'd locked away.

But now, because of her, there were no walls to salvage. They were all burning to ash.

Crouched in the center was a hungry, needy thing, feral and raw. And when it felt the thumping of her heart against the wall of his chest, it growled, *Mine*.

Chapter Twenty-Three

❧

$\mathcal{K}$ ISSING OSCAR AGAIN was a terrible idea.

He was like the last bite of cake. She should resist. She wanted to resist. *Mostly*.

But unlike the last bite of cake, leaving Oscar's lips seemed impossible.

Her body and will were at an impasse, negotiating, bargaining, then bending with a final concession as his hand slid along the sensitive curve of her throat to cup her nape. As his tongue teased past her lips, stroking slowly into her mouth, she felt heat drop into the pit of her belly. The intensity of it made her arch against him. And when her hips met the thick hardness of him, she gasped.

Needless to say, she was no longer thinking about cake.

Turning her head, she rested her cheek against his, panting. "I didn't give you permission to kiss me."

"Then, give me permission," he said, nuzzling the corner of her mouth, his hands splaying over her back, drawing their bodies chest to chest, belly to belly, hip to hip, awakening every pulse beneath her skin.

Entranced by the skilled caress, she practically purred.

He took the sound as capitulation and captured her lips again in a toe-curling, moth-singeing kiss. His hands glided along the cage of her ribs, grazing up her sides then down again, her breasts taut, her flesh aching. Wanting him to ease the tender fullness, she arched against him.

He growled into her mouth. In a quick, jerky movement

he lifted his hand and bit the tip of his glove, ripping it off. The other met the same fate, falling away like the last of her denials.

She wanted his mouth on hers, their bodies flush. Couldn't remember a time when she didn't.

The truth surged through her when their lips met again, feasting and tugging, his hands skimming up from her waist.

He paused beneath the ripe swells, the heat of his palms burning through the fitted layers of her riding habit, corset and chemise, and her nipples tightened beneath the cambric. Lips parting, she drew in a breath, her pulse thrumming in anticipation.

"Yes," she rasped, and his thumbs swept over the sensitive peaks. The sensation spiraled down, clenching low in her body, strumming at the heavy thud of a pulse between her thighs.

He took her lips in long, drugging kisses, his hand closing over her breast. "Mine."

Honoria might have argued if she hadn't felt suddenly lightheaded. Instead, she clung to him, the sensations overwhelming her.

They sank together onto a cushion of soft grass within the curtain wall as fluidly as sugar melting into steaming tea. His kisses burned sweetly against her lips as he settled alongside her, his hard thigh insinuated between her own. And wanton that she was, she turned toward him in welcome instead of shying away.

But how could she deny that this wasn't everything she'd been craving? The only thing that made her feel this alive?

So she gave herself over to the kiss, dimly aware of her hat falling away, his deft fingers in her hair, working in soothing circles where her scalp was tender from the pins of her tight chignon. His lips brushed her cheek, her brow, her chin as his fingertips skimmed through the tresses of her hair, down her neck and along the rolled lapels of her riding habit.

He nipped at her breasts through the layers, the teasing sensation almost tickling and driving her to distraction.

But surely, they shouldn't tarry here. They were expected at the abbey.

"Just a few more minutes," Oscar said, reading her thoughts.

When their mouths touched, tangled and tasted, she realized kissing Oscar wasn't like the last bite of cake. It was like the first: sumptuous and decadent, melting into her in a way that made it impossible not to close her eyes as pleasure danced in pulses where their hips met. And when his hand slid to her lower back and he rocked her against his thigh, a heady breath stuttered out of her.

It was only then that she realized she could breathe because he'd unfastened the row of buttons along the front of her stiff-boned jacket, revealing the habit shirt beneath. It was a simple, sleeveless garment that fastened along the back and ended just beneath her breasts. But because she was so warm, the fine lawn was transparent, the fabric clinging to the rise and fall of her perspiring flesh.

Irises the color of a stormy sky darkened to midnight as he gazed down at her. His fingertips traced the swells rising above the gusseted cups of her corset, his palm covering the pebbled tip. She arched reflexively, thrusting her breast into the cup of his hand.

He obliged her command with a low, possessive growl, kneading the tender fullness as he took her lips again. And when his thigh shifted against her, she felt as though a bolt of lightning crashed into her, igniting every nerve ending.

Her fingertips flexed into his coat, but her hands felt clumsy inside her gloves. So she peeled them off and let them fall. Then her bare hands were in his hair, sifting through the cool silken layers to the warmth of his scalp. As if he were a big cat, a deep, guttural purr vibrated in his throat.

Something primal within her flared to life at the sound.

Knowing that she had done something that pleased him made her feel territorial. That was *her* sound. It belonged to her.

Hungry for it again, she nudged her mouth against his, as her fingernails gently raked through the thick strands. He gave it to her, his hand sliding to her nape.

She had never felt like this before, so lost to pleasure. So wild and uninhibited.

Dimly, she became aware of him unfastening her buttons. Her breath quickened as his lips coasted over the exposed skin of her throat.

"We should return to the abbey," she rasped. But then his mouth drifted to the place—that secret, newly discovered heaven on the side of her neck—and his warm tongue laved the vulnerable flutter of her pulse. "I mean, shouldn't we?"

She felt his lips curve in a smile.

"Let's play a new game, Signore," he said, peeling away her habit shirt.

The summer breeze offered her fevered skin cool relief as he bent his head over her. "What kind of game?"

"It's called Pleasuring Miss Hartley." His fingertip circled the budded center of her breast through the corset and chemise. "Until she confesses that she rode over here this morning because she cares about me."

Before she could respond, he dragged down the cup and chemise in one swift tug and closed his mouth over her bare flesh.

She arched on a gasp. Her hands gripped his head as he drew the ruched flesh into his mouth. The clever flicks of his tongue, the long, sinuous pull felt so good she had to close her eyes.

A helpless, garbled sound rose from her throat.

She should push him away. She really should. There were so many reasons she should. But the sensations curled so exquisitely in the pit of her belly that, surely, there was no harm in lingering just a bit longer.

His thigh pressed between hers, undulating to the rhythm of his pulls on her flesh. Her ardent pulse answered in kind.

Lady Content never mentioned this. And good morning, Lord Turgid, she thought saucily, feeling the large shape pressed against her hip.

But thinking about the puppets suddenly reminded her of the paintings in the attic and the vow she'd made to herself.

"Wait," she said breathlessly, feeling the weight of her locket between her breasts. "I . . . I need a moment."

He instantly lifted away, but without straying. His hair was mussed from her fingers, his color high on the crests of his cheeks, and his lungs labored for each panting breath.

Eyes dark with unfulfilled passion studied her closely. After a moment, he appeared to have come to a conclusion and tenderly brushed his fingers over her flushed cheek. "You don't need to be afraid. It's perfectly natural to feel this way. The shortness of breath, racing heartbeat, the tingles—"

A laugh bubbled out of her. "Do you honestly think I have no idea what desire is? I am three and twenty, after all. And I have, on occasion . . . explored these feelings."

"With whom?" he asked darkly, a muscle jumping in his cheek.

"Are you jealous?"

"Answer the question, Honoria."

Though she would never admit it, there was something tantalizing about his hard, commanding tone. It sent a heated shiver through her. There was also a sense of danger lurking in the steel banded muscles of his forearms when he flexed his fists as if he were planning to slaughter every adult male in the parish.

Propped on one elbow, she brushed a curling lock from his forehead. "With no one other than myself, silly man. A warm bath, a splash of scented oils, a bit of brandy and . . . well, I'm certain a scoundrel like you can gather the rest."

It was strange how swiftly a murderous glower could transform into primal lust. And yet, it only took a blink and his intentions became abundantly clear when he shifted closer.

Before he could gather her in his arms again, which would only bring them back to this exact place, she splayed her hand over his chest, keeping him at arm's length. "I don't intend to have a dalliance with you—or any man, for that matter—when it is my understanding that tender feelings will sprout from sexual congress, whether one wishes them to or not."

"Who told you that?"

"My mother. She has always been rather forthcoming about such matters. According to Roxana Hartley, a woman should embrace her own desires. But she should also guard herself against the illusion of love. Passion, while potent, is also fleeting. And Hartleys only marry for a deep and abiding love."

His brows crowded in confusion. "In Paris, you said you weren't interested in marriage. You said you wanted to—"

"Live," she supplied, touched that he remembered. The moths attempted to flutter toward her heart, but she swallowed to stifle their upward trajectory. "That hasn't changed."

"Then, I cannot see the problem."

"I don't want to fall in love with you," she blurted, showing her cards. "Even if it's only a temporary illusion."

He held her gaze for a moment. "We're not blindfolded adolescents. We both know what we want out of our arrangement. And right now, I only want to make you feel good."

His sincerity surprised her as much as it caused her body to clench with sweet longing.

Looking down, he delicately traced the outline of her hand on his chest before turning it over to do the same with the lines on her palm. She wanted to curl her fingers around the tickling sensation, but he held her open to his touch, forcing the sensation to tunnel through to the center of her body.

Unable to help herself, she closed her eyes and absorbed it all.

Tempted. Oh, she was dreadfully tempted, and the arousal he incited in her body wasn't helping her think clearly.

"Why?" she said, waiting for him to make some shallow observation about her beauty and to fuel her with enough indignation to push out of his arms.

"There must be dozens of reasons," he said. "Because you're bold. Because your confidence is utterly tantalizing. Because you know what you want and you're not afraid to go after it." He brushed his lips over the surprised, fluttering pulse at her wrist. "Because you want to seize your life with both hands. Because you know that living is the difference between merely breathing in and out and actually drawing in the scent of the air, the perfume of the earth as sunlight warms it. Because I want to show you how to ring out every ounce of pleasure from each moment. Because you smell like biscuits and—"

Somehow she was in his arms again, her lips pressed against his in wordless yearning. She just couldn't take it any longer. Every word he spoke threatened to tunnel directly into her heart, and she had to stop him.

In return, she expected him to kiss her, hard and demanding, a lewd thought-scattering kiss that would erase all the things he'd said.

But he was tender instead, slowing her down, his lips coaxing and mesmerizing her with small nibbles as he eased her back onto the bed of grass. He brushed the wayward locks from her cheek and kissed her there, cradling her jaw as if she were precious to him, cherished.

The idea caused her heart to thud in panic, her arms trembling as she held him.

"Shh . . ." he crooned softly, his mouth trailing down her throat, between the gold chain to press a kiss over her heart, just above the locket. "Shh . . ." he said again, and the hard thumping beneath his lips quieted as his hand caressed in soothing passes along her sides, her hips, her thighs.

Then his mouth was on hers again, his kiss languorous and unhurried. She fought against it, tried to pull him deeper, but he remained deliberately patient, the tip of his tongue teasing and retreating, making her want. His hand splayed over her belly, warmth seeping into her as he moved in slow circles until she accepted this gentle seduction.

It was no use. She was clay in his hands, and he knew very well that she couldn't stop craving his kiss, his touch. Her breath came out on a sigh, her body welcoming the slow simmer of this passion.

He deepened the kiss as his hand slid down to the juncture of her thighs. He cupped her there, and she sucked in a gasp. The feel of that large hand was so foreign, so . . . masculine that a small quake trembled through her bones. Her hips hitched reflexively, and he murmured a sound of approval against the corner of her mouth. So she did it again on purpose.

But his hand lifted away, gliding to her hip. She nearly moaned in frustration, not understanding the rules of this scandalous game.

Then, lifting her knee, he followed the heavy folds of fabric down to the hem. A cool breeze brushed against the damp saturation of cambric between her thighs. And at the first touch of him against her stocking above her half boot, her leg trembled.

But not with shyness. With need. She wanted this, wanted him so desperately that she ached with it.

"Let me," he said, raking his teeth over her bottom lip.

She gave her acquiescence with a kiss, long and deep as a calloused fingertip traced the bare skin above her stocking and beneath the lace hem of her drawers.

His touch trailed along the inner seam, higher and higher. And when he reached her center, his breath came out ragged. "You're wet for me. So wet."

"I'm sure you shouldn't say such things," she said on a gasp as his fingertips grazed the thatch of honey-blond curls.

He grinned against her throat. "I'd wager you like it. In fact"—he followed the swollen seam of her sex—"I'd wager that you secretly enjoyed the bawdy talk of men when you were disguised as one of them."

She refused to answer. But yes, it had thrilled her to hear the words, knowing that men had a secret language, and learning it had given her a sense of power.

His mouth found her breast again, and she arched into the pleasure of the tug and flick, her hands in his hair as his finger delved between her dewy folds. She knew it was scandalous. But she only had one life and had promised to live two. So there was no thought of stopping, not while her blood was singing with life in her veins.

And yet she wondered, as he traced the outer edges of the tight bud with prurient skill, if being pleasured by Oscar might be the death of her.

The tip of his finger nudged inside the tight constriction, and he let out a groan as if the breach pained *him*. But she knew it was only her skin that burned, stretching taut around the invasion.

"Oh, why does it never feel this good when I touch myself?"

He growled against her breast. "I would give a fortune to watch you make yourself shatter."

"You don't have a fortune," she reminded, panting.

"Then, I would give my soul."

She moaned, her neck arching as he slowly stroked into her, the slick walls clamping around him in a ripple of sensation.

An imprecation passed her lips, a prayer, a plea.

She had explored her own body and knew that a few light brushes over her nipples, a delicate pass around the tender bud beneath the hood of her sex felt delightful. But this? This was too intense. Her body was coiled so tight she wondered how she would survive.

"Open your eyes, Honoria. I want to see you come apart."

She couldn't ignore that low command. It did terrible things to her. Her pulse leaped against the heel of his hand, and when she met his dark gaze, she was sure he knew it, too.

Then the blackguard withdrew and slowly pushed two fingers into her. The fullness was nearly too much to bear. "Now, I want you to think of how it will feel to have my mouth on you, my tongue inside you, licking all this hot honey flowing from your impossibly snug little qu—"

"Don't," she said over him.

His words were too wicked. His touch too scandalous. It was heaven. Then he hooked those fingers and rubbed a secret place with each thrust as the heel of his palm pressed in glorious circles that—

A strangled breath caught in her throat, back arching off the ground, her body locked in suspended pleasure . . .

Until he brushed her once more and she broke. Pieces of her scattered through the stormy sky of his irises and to the stars beyond. Worlds exploded inside her on a torrent of spasms. And he chased every ripple, drawing out her pleasure until the very last tremor.

It had never been like this before. Her own touch had never made her feel this sublime.

She melted against him, boneless and breathless. "You are utterly"—she paused to catch her breath—"wicked."

He kissed her tenderly, his fingers slowly withdrawing and leaving her with the tender ache of emptiness. "Yes, but you like me that way. Admit it."

"Any confession you coerce from my lips right now would be considered cheating."

"I never said I was above cheating to get what I want," he said with a grin, smoothing her skirts back in place.

Then he pressed one final, lingering kiss to her breast, the flick of his tongue shooting sensation directly to her womb.

She gasped at the quickening, the flutter, surprised that he could kindle her desire again so swiftly. But then he lifted his head, a smug grin on his lips as he put her corset to rights.

"Cad," she said, flustered. And even more so when she shifted and noticed the large shape straining the fall of his trousers. "Shouldn't I do . . . something . . . for you?"

She stared down at it, curious, though somewhat intimidated. These were uncertain waters, after all.

He chuckled. "Like I said, I just wanted to pleasure you."

"I wouldn't mind. Truly. In fact, I am rather—"

He pressed his lips to hers, silencing her. Then in a warning voice, he said, "If you continue to tempt me, I'm going to put you in the dungeon of this palace and keep you here forever. And you're not ready for that."

Knowing it was a hollow threat, she smiled up at him but felt her heart give a little lurch at the warm affection she found mirrored back at her.

Devil's doorknocker! This was alarming to say the least.

"Hmm," he murmured with intrigue, and a snake tail curled at the corner of his mouth. "Do my eyes deceive me, or am I about to win this new game of ours?"

"I have no idea to what you are referring."

A dark brow arched in challenge. She ignored it.

Deciding that a change of subject was required, she sat up and tried to bring a semblance of order to her hair, hunting for the pins in the grass. "Now that you know your father had some sort of connection to the abbey, what will you do?"

"There's no proof that he had a connection. It's likely just another coincidence. Just a map to a treasure that only leads to an empty trunk buried beneath a tree."

She shot an exasperated look over her shoulder. "The book of poems about Awildian Palace—about this very spot—has to mean something. At the very least, someone in the abbey will know who the author was."

"Perhaps."

It was the offhand shrug of his shoulders that revealed the tension in the gesture, and she realized that it did matter to him. But he clearly didn't want to talk about that. He only wanted to win the wager by having her confess that she cared about him.

Well, he was in for a very long wait.

She moved on to her next question. "What do you plan to do about the man who wants to kill you?"

"My, aren't we curious?" he practically purred, his eyes the color of a storm approaching instead of the soft aftermath she'd witnessed moments ago. "Here, let me fasten your buttons before I ravish you again."

He tugged the jacket from her shoulders and deftly re-fastened the gaping half shirt.

Her shyness reappeared. How strange that the act of dressing seemed almost more intimate than undressing had. It was rather domestic. Something a husband might do.

Honoria jolted at the thought, her spine stiffening, heart hammering.

"What's the matter?"

She shook her head. "Nothing. Nothing at all."

"Hmm . . . I think I know," he murmured, lifting the downy hairs from above her collar and trailing his lips in a tingling caress over her nape. "You're ticklish, aren't you?"

Breathing a sigh of relief for his misunderstanding, she allowed herself to be pulled back against him, his arms a strong, sinewy band around her waist. And in that instant, she vowed never to allow such musings to enter her mind again. "Perhaps."

"Alas, we'll have to explore that another time." Finishing, he stood and brought her up with him. He made quick work of her jacket buttons, as well, then took hold of her lapels. "Now, are you prepared to pay the forfeit?"

Only then did she remember the so-called new game they were playing and the true reason she'd ridden here this morning.

"You did not win," she said. "After all, how could I care about a man who refuses to discuss his plans with me?"

His jaw hardened, all the warmth extinguished from his gaze. "We are not discussing Ladrón."

Then, as if the matter were settled, he bent down and swiped up her hat from the ground.

A moment later, he was handing her onto her saddle, his expression inscrutable. And if not for the lingering tenderness between her thighs and the thick shape still outlined against the front fall of his breeches, she might have wondered if their stolen moment on the grass had been part of a dream.

Even so, her head felt heavy as if she'd just awakened, her mind hazy. And the only thing clear was the fact that he didn't want to include her in his plans. For reasons she didn't care to think about, that wounded her.

But he had given her something: the name of the man who was after him. *Ladrón.*

She would have to write to her brother to see if he knew anything about that villain. Then perhaps she could do something to ensure that Oscar could leave here safely and *before* she did something utterly foolish . . . like fall in love with him.

Chapter Twenty-Four

ℰ✦

OSCAR HAD NOT been raised in the shadow of a church. His mother had stopped attending, had stopped toting him along each Sunday with his face scrubbed clean, after the church had turned them away when his father had left and they had nowhere else to go.

He remembered little of that day other than overhearing one of the veiled women on the stone steps outside the chapel doors, sneering about an unholy union just before she'd spat at his mother's feet.

But he remembered walking. Walking endlessly, the soles of his shoes already worn thin and soaked with gutterwash, before finding an alcove to huddle in his mother's arms for the night, sitting atop all their belongings tied up in a shawl.

No, he'd never been one for churches or prayers or even wishes that would cost a copper penny when dropped in a well. He could never afford wishes.

And yet, as he watched Lawson and Honoria ride away, he would have made a wish or even fallen to his knees in prayer—if he'd known how—just to go back to who he'd been inside the tumbledown walls within the castle ruins when Honoria was in his arms. Back in time to those blissful moments before he'd remembered that he was a man with no roots, no family and no future . . . until he knew he was beyond Ladrón's reach.

All he had was a questionable surname, a book of poetry with mysterious origins and three women who wanted him dead. Because, according to what Lawson had said when he'd pulled him aside a short while ago, there was a chance that rope holding the chandelier hadn't frayed. It might have been cut.

Peculiarly, Oscar's first reaction to the news had been amusement. The widows were a crafty bunch, to be sure. And any man who'd made the choices he'd done in order to survive had to admire their determination.

In fact, he actually respected them all the more for the effort. If they weren't careful, he might even start to like them.

So when he turned around and saw the three of them at the upper-gallery railing in their widow's weeds, he tossed them a grin and touched two fingers to his forehead in a salute. "It's a glorious day, isn't it, aunties? Makes a man glad to be alive."

Alfreda and Millicent scowled down at him. Babette, however, laughed and waggled her finger at him before they all turned their backs and skulked off to their coven.

"Well, Algernon, I think I'm beginning to win them over."

The old butler decided it was better to feign deafness in that moment, but his mouth twitched.

Oscar crossed the entry hall in search of Cardew. Since he wasn't in any of the rooms marked for painting, or removing the hideous lacquer from the railing, Oscar went belowstairs. Yet, after checking the servants' hall, scullery, cleaning room and laundry—believing he might have required holland covers or turpentine—the task still came up empty-handed.

Growing tired of mysteries to solve, he mounted the stairs again and tried the portrait gallery. No Cardew. But he did find the dowager countess.

Her nurse was pushing her in a wheeled wicker bath chair, and when Vandemere's grandmother saw him enter the long, sunlit hall, her eyes brightened, and she smiled in instant recognition.

He couldn't quite explain why that made his heart feel like it was in the basket of a Montgolfier balloon. Perhaps it was just that her greeting was a welcome change from what he usually received beneath this roof. Whatever it was, it made him smile in return.

"You are as pretty as a picture this afternoon, Grandmama," he said, bowing over her hand in greeting.

She sniffed in amusement and looked askance at him. Her reply took effort, the sound a slow susurration like the first hiss of steam from a kettle. "Sssss-stuff."

"I'm deeply offended, madam. You look quite fetching in that periwinkle frock. In fact, I daresay there isn't a portrait among these that can compare."

She managed an arched silver brow before she turned to her nurse. A silent communication commenced whereby the nurse nodded and then proceeded to wheel the chair to a portrait on the far wall above the black marble fireplace.

Framed in mahogany was a lovely young woman in white with a pile of Titian hair spilling out from beneath a broad-brimmed feathered hat. She had a fair complexion and a daring grin that lifted one corner of her mouth.

Feeling her gaze on him, he glanced down to find that same grin, and her chin lifted proudly. "What a saucy little minx! I'd wager you had gentlemen eating out of your hand."

She didn't deny it. Just offered a slow, self-satisfied breath.

He laughed and, unable to help himself, leaned down and pressed a kiss to her vellum cheek.

She blushed a soft watercolor pink and waved her hand in a shooing motion. But he knew she didn't want him to leave when she reached up and grasped his hand. So they stayed that way, staring at her portrait as if it were a window in time, and all they had to do to capture the moment was to lift the sash and let it breeze in.

"'Ere," she said in her occasional cockney accent.

"I'm here." He gave her hand a delicate but reassuring squeeze.

She smiled like someone who had a secret. "R-ring."

It was only then that he followed her gaze to the portrait and noticed the gold cannetille earrings that dropped down from a star of black onyx.

Oscar felt his heart miss a beat. He glanced down at the star of black onyx on his ring. Then he looked at the portrait again.

His heart picked up the missing beat and added forty more, his pulse racing on the side of his throat. *Surely, it couldn't be . . .*

He didn't finish the thought. He couldn't allow himself to.

Drawing in a deep breath, he let logic take over as he turned back to her. "The shape. You're noticing that the shape is similar, aren't you?"

Her smile faltered as she worked on speaking again. "My . . . ear . . . r-ring." And then, after a small hesitation, she said, "Give . . . son."

Guilt churned in his gut as he realized that he was confusing her. This woman had already lost so much: her husband, her children and her health. She didn't deserve this or the heartache that was destined to befall her.

Suddenly, the cost of playing Vandemere seemed far greater than when he'd first thought up the scheme.

Or perhaps he'd known all along, and consequences hadn't mattered to the jaded, ruthless man he'd always been. He'd always done what he'd had to do in order to survive. Always kept people at arm's length.

But this wasn't just about him and Cardew. Not any longer.

As he covered her frail hand with his own and looked into her shining, hope-filled eyes, he knew he had to do right by her. Even if that meant finding the real Vandemere.

"Fear not, my lady. You will have the grandson you deserve."

―

It wasn't until midafternoon that Oscar finally found Cardew. He was walking down the corridor from the direction of the servants' quarters in the garret . . . and he wasn't alone.

Beside him, Babette looked flushed and tousled as she trailed an index finger down the buttons of Cardew's gray waistcoat. She pressed a kiss to the air between them just before she turned and left him standing there with a satisfied grin.

Passing Oscar, she trilled her fingers in greeting and winked. "Good afternoon, nephew."

"Auntie," he said with a nod and heard her giggle as she sauntered away, hips swaying boldly in fitted black silk, the rustle of a red crinoline peeping out from beneath the hem.

Cardew watched her sashay down the hall, clutching his heart as he grinned with appreciation. "That woman could bring a man back from the dead."

"Except for poor Uncle Freddie."

"Ah, yes. She told me about her first husband and that they were in the midst of *faire l'amour* when he shuffled off this mortal coil and, sadly, left her unfulfilled." He clucked his tongue, then slid a glance to Oscar. "Don't give me that disapproving glower, cub. I was merely performing my duty as a gentleman's gentleman by consoling a woman who hadn't been properly pleasured in over a decade."

"Did you have to choose a woman beneath this roof? For all intents and purposes, I am the head of the household, and they are under my protection."

A pair of wizened white brows lifted. "My, aren't we taking the role of nobleman to heart. Shall I polish your gleaming silver armor? Saddle your white steed?"

Oscar knew very well that he was about as far from a

knight-errant as any man could be. And it was no secret that
the women—with the exception of the dowager—held little
affection for him. However, that didn't mean he wanted
Babette to become another in a long line of Cardew's con-
quests, ones who were quickly cast off and replaced with
the next.

But he didn't want to argue either. So instead he walked
to the nearest doorway and peered inside. By the looks of
the moth-eaten curtains, dusty little table and pair of small
beds with moons and stars carved into the headboards, it
was the nursery.

He gestured for Cardew to follow and closed the door
behind them.

Without preamble and wanting to get to the bottom of
the Awildian Palace mystery, he asked, "Did my father
know Vandemere?"

"And what's put that question into your noggin?"

"You said you were his friend. So do you know if he
knew Vandemere?"

Cardew turned to a cobweb-strewn shelf and set a tiny
rocking horse into motion. "The truth is I didn't know your
father for very long."

"But you've always said he saved your life."

"Aye, and in turn, I vowed to look after his son before
he"—he gestured with a dismissive wave, the breeze bending a corner web like a sail—"went away. Aside from that, I
knew little about him."

"Damn," Oscar said. He was afraid of that.

To be honest, he'd suspected as much over the years.
Cardew was a man who knew how to spin a good yarn,
but when it came to his friendship with John Flintridge
he'd never had much to say. Then again, Oscar had spent
so many years hating his father that he hadn't cared to ask
about the past. The only thing he was interested in was the
present whereabouts of the bastard who'd left his wife and
child behind.

So this didn't surprise him. Not really. Where his father was concerned there were always questions. Never answers.

But what else could he do? Give up? Ignore the promise he'd made to his mother?

The answer was simple. No.

"What has you thinking about this?" Cardew asked with careful scrutiny. When Oscar explained about the book of poetry and the castle ruins on the estate, Cardew shook his head in dismissal. "I don't see why it should spark your interest. It isn't as though you're going to continue this charade."

"It matters because Awildian Palace was a name that Titus Fairfax invented. The inspiration for every line in the book can be seen from that very spot. What I want to know is how my father came into possession of this," he said, withdrawing the tome from the inner pocket of his coat.

"I cannot answer that. But when we find him, we honor the promise you made to your mother."

Oscar expelled a deep breath but nodded. There was nothing for him to do but wait for news on his whereabouts. Having a friend who'd once served king and country in the military meant that Warring had many connections.

And, unbeknownst to Cardew, he'd asked Warring to look into the matter as well.

As for the promise he'd just made to the dowager viscountess, he decided to go down to his study and pen another letter to Rowan and see what his friend could unearth on the real Vandemere.

Tucking the book away, he felt the ring catch on a thread. He paused at the threshold, considering. "You always told me that you won this over a game of cards."

"Aye. That I did."

"As I recall, you'd won other such baubles over the years. But when we needed the coin, you never hesitated to sell them off. Except for this one. You kept it safe all these years. Why?"

"Does a man need a reason for everything he does?" He issued a flippant shrug and set the horse to rocking again. "I just wanted to keep it. I'm an artist, and it was different from any of the other men's rings I'd seen."

Different, indeed. And yet it matched the earrings worn in the dowager's portrait. The coincidence of it, coupled with the book of poetry, felt like it had to mean something.

Even though he hated himself for the thought, he wondered if Cardew was withholding information from him.

But Oscar was tired of chasing dragons. So for now, he would push those things to the back of his mind.

"If that's the reason, then so be it," he said and set a hand on Cardew's shoulder, his gaze steady. "After all we've been through over the years, there's no need to argue over a piece of jewelry, is there?"

"Who's arguing? At my age, I'm certainly not."

"And just how old are you exactly?"

Cardew grinned. "Older than your left boot."

Chapter Twenty-Five

❧

*H*ONORIA LEANED OUT the sitting room window in hopes of catching a breeze. But beneath the hazy summer sky, the morning air was already thick and sticky as orange marmalade bubbling on the stove.

What they needed was a good storm to break over them and cut through the stifling heat. Or perhaps all she needed was a few moments of lying on the cool grass beneath Oscar's scandalous touch. Her breath fell out on a sigh at the memory.

July was most decidedly a month of heat and sweltering kisses. The scorching moments were seared into her like a brand. But even though Mother had warned her that pleasure could make a woman forget herself, it wasn't true for Honoria.

She remained clearheaded. And if Oscar thought that he could simply shut her out and order her not to worry about the man who was trying to murder him, then he was in for a surprise.

As soon as she'd ridden home yesterday, she'd penned a letter to Truman asking if he knew anything about a man named Ladrón. She knew her brother wouldn't let her down.

Through the window, she saw Verity drive up in Lady Broadbent's horse cart, the dogs rushing out to greet her. Both she and Magnus would be leaving this morning for a lengthy holiday in Marseille, their coach loaded with the trunks sent from the Longhurst demesne. And yet . . .

"That's odd. Our sister appears to have misplaced her husband again," Honoria said. When Thea didn't respond, she turned to see her leaning out the adjacent window while holding a stick with a red ribbon dangling from one end. "What *are* you doing? You look as though you're holding an angling rod. Trying to catch a breeze and pull it inside?"

"No. But that is likely a better occupation. I was actually contemplating the life span of a ribbon and wondering if it, like me, would endure an entire existence without so much as a whisper to stir its soul."

"And the award for overly dramatic soliloquies is presented to Althea Hartley." Honoria laughed when Thea stuck out her tongue.

Mr. Mosely appeared at the doorway and cleared his throat. "The Duchess of Longhurst requests an audience with her sisters in the side garden."

Honoria and Thea shared a look, both of them shrugging as they rose.

On the way, they speculated over the reason for this peculiar request. But they never suspected that their serious and sensible sister was playing a trick on them.

Not until it was too late.

Honoria gasped the instant the shock of cold hit her. Thea shrieked.

"Have you gone mad? What is this?" Honoria demanded on a surprised laugh as she performed an awkward jig while fishing an icy shard from beneath her bodice.

Verity took a few careful steps back in case of retaliation, all the while grinning from ear to ear. "Merely a souvenir from a visit to Lady Broadbent's icehouse. I thought you might like to cool off."

"You are wicked!" Thea laughed, too, and reared back as if to throw her ice at Verity.

A half-hearted chase ensued. The dogs, caught up in the excitement, bounded happily around them. Then enervation took hold, and Thea stopped to palm the shard against the back of her neck on a sigh instead.

Honoria fished hers out to do the same, and for one blissful moment, she felt the cooling pleasure of ice against her nape, melting in meandering trickles down her back until it evaporated in the heat of the day.

As they walked together up the hill toward the shade tree, Honoria realized that this was the last time they'd be together like this. Everything was changing.

Even though Verity had already eloped and left the house, today's farewell felt more permanent. Thea would soon be having her first Season and could possibly be married by next spring. And Oscar . . . well, he was always expected to be temporary.

So whyever was her stomach twisting itself into ridiculous knots at the thought of what it would be like when he was gone?

Exasperated with herself, she looked over at Verity and saw a piece of straw sticking out from her chignon. Pulling it free, she held it out. "A souvenir from your visit to the icehouse . . . with your husband?"

Verity flushed crimson and snatched the straw away. Plucking it absently between her fingers, she grinned and gazed off in the direction of Swanscott Manor. "One does what one can to escape the stifling heat."

Seeing her sister so contented warmed Honoria's heart. "Are you glad you came home?"

"I am, actually. For some reason, I had it in my head that I had to be a perfect copy of my mother-in-law in order to be accepted by her, by society and by my husband. But after observing Mother and Lady Broadbent, I can see that they don't give a fig about what society thinks. And there's something altogether liberating in that. And it doesn't hurt that Magnus loves me exactly as I am, flaws and all. And if my mother-in-law and all of society wish to earn the condescension of the venerable Duchess of Longhurst"—she straightened her shoulders and adopted a haughty air—"they will simply have to take me as I am."

"Brava!" Thea cheered.

"Spoken with the mettle of a true duchess," Honoria added and threaded her arm through Verity's. "I'm going to miss you, you know?"

Instant tears began to gather along the lower rims of her eyes. "You are?"

"Of course, you goose," she said with a pinch to her sister's arm. Then feeling the prickle of her own tears, she turned to blink them away. "Everything is happening so quickly. Isn't it peculiar? We spend so much of our lives waiting to live, that when we finally realize we are actually living, it feels as though it's already the end."

"The end of one thing is merely the beginning of something else."

"Now you sound like our mother."

Verity's smile softened with fondness. "Do I?"

"I suppose there are worse things," Honoria teased and glanced over her shoulder to where their sister flopped down beneath the tree and arranged her skirts, Serjie and Barry sprawling beside her, tongues out and panting. "You could sound like Thea."

"I heard that," Thea said. "Just wait. I'm going to turn you into a bride in my next play."

"That is no longer a threat for our sister," Verity said, her gaze seemingly filled with their mother's uncanny knowing, too. "Me thinketh the fair Honoria doth dream of being wed to her viscount."

A sudden swell of warmth rushed to Honoria's cheeks as she thought about last night's dream.

"Mmm . . . Quite the telling blush, sister."

"It's hot," Honoria groused to the pest beneath the tree.

"Aha! So it *is* true!" Verity skirted away on a laugh before Honoria could pinch her again.

Thea, too perceptive for her own good, tapped the back of a pencil against the side of her mouth and studied Honoria. Then she scribbled something in her pocket ledger, her eyes glinting with devious intent.

"It isn't true. I am as determined as ever to live a life of my own choosing. In fact, I would be immensely glad if he simply went away and never returned."

"Hmm . . . Well, you may get your wish, if what Mr. Lawson said holds true."

"What do you mean?"

"According to Magnus, last evening when the gentlemen lingered over port in the dining room, Mr. Lawson mentioned that he wasn't entirely convinced that the rope had been frayed from age."

Honoria stilled. "Are you suggesting that someone might have cut it?"

"The plot thickens," Thea murmured as if she were a Greek chorus.

Verity shook her head. "That seems rather far-fetched. I know the widows tend to be disagreeable, much like my mother-in-law," she added wryly. "But they wouldn't wish him harm. In fact, after meeting him, I cannot imagine anyone who would."

A certain Spaniard sprang to Honoria's mind. That man definitely wished Oscar Flint harm. Though, as Vandemere, he had a chance of evading Ladrón. Just as long as no one else made the connection.

"Though it is rather peculiar," Verity continued, "that news of his return hasn't spread far and wide. Geraldine hadn't even heard of his return until Lady Broadbent wrote to her. Both Geraldine and Olympia are wondering why Addlewick hasn't been flocked with society who wish to make his acquaintance."

The knots in her middle were back, and they were

steadily climbing up to Honoria's throat, choking her with panic. "Surely they wouldn't . . . write to their acquaintances about Vandemere?"

"I wouldn't doubt it," Verity said, oblivious to her sister's unease as she absently tossed the straw over the fence. "The way my mother-in-law sees it, I am at fault for not informing her of Vandemere's return straightaway. She accused me of secrecy and said it was 'not done in respectable families.' Doubtless, this will remain a thorn wedged between us until the end of time." She dusted her hands. "However, if that woman expects me to take her into my confidence, then she must earn that right by proving she is no longer holding a grudge against our family."

"Hear! Hear!" Thea called out, using the ledger to lazily fan herself, her pencil tucked behind her ear. "Though, after hearing about all this discord—not only with you and your mother-in-law but between Vandemere and his aunts—I am determined to find a husband who hails from a perfectly amiable family."

Verity chuckled. "Best of luck with that. You'll be hard pressed to find any family who doesn't have at least one skeleton in the cupboard."

"Hmm . . . An actual skeleton might be interesting. Certainly playworthy. Honoria, do you think there are any skeletons at the abbey?"

"Your morbid interest in the macabre is alarming, to say the least," she replied, trying not to think about it.

And yet, if there weren't a skeleton at Dunnelocke Abbey, then—between the mysterious accident and the man trying to murder Oscar—there might very well be one in the near future.

                              —✑

THAT AFTERNOON, AFTER Verity and Magnus had gone, a messenger arrived with the letter Honoria had been waiting

for. But the news Truman sent did nothing to quell the fears
that had been plaguing her.

Dearest sister,

   *In regard to your query about the mysterious Spaniard
you mentioned, out of your supposedly 'mere curiosity,'
my answer is to rid yourself of any and all curiosity
about him. I've had dealings with the man—though
I knew him as El Coleccionista, the Collector. A truly
dangerous fellow, driven by obsession. You must not trifle
with him! Promise me, dear sister, that both you and
your ostensible friend Cesario will not. Only then will I
see to your request.*

Signed,
Your all-seeing brother

Her blood went cold, her heart thudding in panic. Ladrón
sounded more dangerous than she'd feared. The Collector.
What did a man like that collect? And more importantly,
what did Oscar have that he wanted?

She swallowed. No matter what the answer was, the
important thing was devising a plan to keep this man from
finding Oscar.

But Truman knew her too well. It was apparent that she
would have to be a shade less than truthful if she intended
to glean any more information out of him.

So with the fingers of her left hand crossed, she wrote:

Dearest brother,
   *This once I shall heed your advice, banish my
curiosity and stay near Vandemere.*

"Devil's doorknocker," she muttered. She'd meant to
write *Addlewick*, not *Vandemere*.

At the door, the messenger cleared his throat. Hearing

his impatience, she didn't bother with a new scrap of fools-cap but merely struck a line through the mistake and wrote the correction beside it. Surely, her brother would think nothing of a meaningless error.

She finished the letter with her appreciation for his prompt reply and signed it *Your ever biddable sister.*

Sanding the ink, she then folded the missive carefully and pressed the family crest into the red wax. After paying the rider, she went back into the parlor and penned another letter. This one to Oscar, inviting him to dinner.

One way or another, she was going to winkle out more information on *El Coleccionista.*

Chapter Twenty-Six

❧

THE INSTANT OSCAR received Honoria's sweetly worded invitation to dine with her family at Hartley Hall, he knew she was up to something.

By the end of the evening, when she'd oh so subtly slipped in a question about Ladrón, he knew what it was.

But he had no intention of letting her win this game. He did, however, play his hand just enough to procure another invitation for the following evening, just to see how creative she would be.

This gameplay continued—the back-and-forth, from subtle query to clever evasion—for four evenings in a row that week. And he wondered if she realized how much she was revealing to him with her concern for his welfare.

Admittedly, it was rather nice having her worried about him. Nicer still that she found some reason to reach out and touch him. Just simple, casual gestures—brushing a speck of road dust from his shoulder, tugging a loose thread from a waistcoat button, sliding her arm through his without waiting for him to proffer his own. And this evening, she'd even smoothed a lock of hair from his forehead.

She was likely trying to lull him into acquiescence, wanting to put him so at ease that he'd accidentally reveal more information.

"And what has you grinning all of a sudden?" Honoria asked as he escorted her into dinner that evening.

Glancing up from his sleeve where she had brushed away

one of her blond hairs, he looked at her heart-shaped face tilted toward his, her gambler's eyes searching for some sort of tell. "No reason. Just pleased to be here, I suppose."

"After my father threatened to have you sing for us one evening, I should have thought you wary."

Oscar shook his head on a wry laugh. "As I told him, none of you should wish that torture upon yourselves. Cardew claims that I can startle the feathers off a chicken."

"In my family, that skill is all the more desirable. Imagine how pleased the cook would be for you to belt out a few bars," she said, smiling as he left her at her chair and crossed to his on the other side of the table.

It was strange, indeed, to have a customary chair. To know that each evening he dined here there would be a place at the table. For him.

From the age of seven, his life had been spent in various taverns, hotels or rented flats. There had been some evenings where Mother, Cardew and he had sat around a table to share a meal. But it wasn't commonplace. There was never any routine that he could settle into.

Of course, he had a place at the head of the table at the abbey now, but it wasn't the same.

No, the Hartleys had something different. Something special that men like him only glimpsed through a pane of glass.

He had never been part of a traditional family. Not to say that the Hartley clan were at all traditional. They were something else altogether. Yet, somehow, it worked. Their household, while eccentric and surprising, was also welcoming.

Each evening this week, he'd watched them, studying the way they interacted with each other, and he wondered if they possessed some sort of magic.

He was growing used to the baron spontaneously offering Shakespearean wisdom. So it didn't surprise him that Hartley fell into character during the soup course.

Hunching over his creamware bowl, he took a pinch of

salt and sprinkled it over the surface. In a gravelly cackle, he said, "'Eye of newt, and toe of frog, wool of bat, and tongue of dog.'" When the wolfhounds lifted their heads from where they sprawled at the foot of the buffet, he addressed them with assurance. "No one you know, lads."

As if in understanding, they settled down, resting their wiry gray muzzles upon their paws.

It really was magic, Oscar thought. What other explanation was there to be among these strangers and not feel like a stranger?

So when he felt his guard slipping, like autumn leaves drifting from breeze-tickled branches, he attributed his overall ease and enjoyment to some power the Hartleys possessed.

They were spellcasters, weaving incantations. And whatever magic this was, he knew that the widows didn't possess it. They were more like the witches stirring the cauldron, muttering, *"Double, double toil and trouble . . ."*

But what did it say about him that he felt more deserving of their scorn than of the Hartleys' acceptance?

⋘

After finishing out the night with cards—whereupon Oscar sensibly lost every hand—he took his leave. But not before graciously accepting Lady Hartley's invitation to return on the morrow, even at the risk of being forced to demonstrate his singing skills.

Then, as he had done the previous three evenings, he bade farewell to Honoria at the door.

He purposely abstained from asking to walk with her in the garden, knowing full well the eventuality of a kiss. Even though he craved her lips like a man bespelled and bewitched, he left her staring after him with a delightfully furrowed brow in the foyer.

He was playing the long game, waiting for his opponent

to make her move. Waiting for her to admit to herself that there was something between them.

But she didn't stay him with a beseeching hand on his sleeve. She did not follow him out into the dusty purple of twilight, the air singing with the chirrup of crickets.

So he stepped into the carriage and tapped on the roof for Raglan to drive him home.

The horses barely managed to trundle around the crescent drive before he saw an elegant hand grip the door through the open window. And then Honoria's face appeared, flaxen curls tumbling from their pins and her expression fraught with vexation.

"Just so you know, running after a coach is much easier in trousers. I think I lost a slipper, drat it all."

Oscar suppressed the grin that threatened to reveal his hand, ignored the sudden wild beating of his heart and blandly asked, "Would you like me to unbolt the door?"

"If you would be so kind."

Gripping her hand so she didn't lose her footing, he opened the door. The instant she tumbled inside, he pulled her onto his lap and sealed his mouth over hers.

This, he thought when she met him halfway, her hands already in his hair, body arching into him. *This is what men cross continents to find. This is why men wage war, write sonnets and sing ballads. It's all for this.*

He had never experienced such passion and yearning in his life, and he desperately wanted to take her, to claim her as his own. To order Raglan to keep driving and never stop.

The elixir of her sweet scent filled his head, making him dizzy with want. He could get drunk on this woman, on her heady kisses, on the way she raked her teeth over his lower lip before soothing it with her tongue.

Growling, he deepened the kiss, angling her mouth beneath his. But she was hard to hold onto in her yellow satin gown. When her perfectly rounded rump started to slip down between his thighs, he lifted her at the waist, situating her to straddle him.

They both groaned as the heat of her settled against the straining fall of his black trousers. Their frenzy from an instant ago seemed little more than a stroll through a shaded lane compared to the galloping heat that consumed them now.

She clawed at his cravat, deft fingers unknotting it, his pulse racing beneath the hot press of her lips. Lost in pleasure, he arched his neck, one hand tangling in her hair, the other drawing her hips flush.

"I knew it, Signore. I knew that if I waited just long—" His hand settled on a thick leather pouch strapped to her thigh. "What's this?"

"Hmm?" Honoria nibbled along his jaw, purring against his skin.

For a moment, he was distracted as her hips undulated, rocking with the motion of the carriage. But when he nudged her thighs wider, wanting more of her heat, his fingers grazed the leather again.

Coming up for air, with her cheeks flushed and mouth swollen from being admirably kissed, she glanced down at where his hand enveloped her thigh. "Oh. Well, that's . . . actually the reason I rushed out to your carriage . . . in the first place."

It took a moment to clear his head enough from the haze of lust to understand what game she was really playing.

When she tugged on the leather laces, fingers fumbling in her attempts, the leather pouch fell open.

A fan of bank notes spilled out. And everything inside him went cold.

He hid his anger behind a slow smirk. "My, my, Miss Hartley. This seems like a great deal of money to ensure your satisfaction. But your manner of delivery is incorrect. The way most aristocrats like to treat this sort of favor is to use the money as a lure. Only once you are satisfied do you toss the money in the gutter and watch me scurry after it."

She shook her head, the flesh above the bridge of her nose furrowing.

"Do you see this?" he continued, tugging the collar and shirt neck aside to reveal a silvered pucker of flesh in the once-tender skin. "This is what happens when a boy refuses what's expected of him for half a crown. And this"—he held open his hand—"was from my first attempt at pickpocketing."

She recoiled from the venom he could not keep out of his tone. Then he saw the shimmer of tears in the lantern light as she discerned the reprehensible truth of his admission.

"That isn't what I wanted. I didn't know. I just—"

"Didn't want to think about the way a boy grows into being a ruthless and despicable scoundrel? A man capable of blackmailing a woman for money?" Then he dragged his thumb across the wet trail on her cheek. "A man who even threatens to marry her by pretending to be someone he's not?"

"But that's not who you are."

"Correct. That's not who I am," he said, setting her apart from him. Then he rapped his knuckles against the hood. "Raglan, turn around. Miss Hartley would like to return home, where she belongs."

In the ensuing silence, she managed to set herself back to rights before the carriage stopped at her door.

"You need to pay Ladrón. Please, Oscar. Take it."

He clenched his teeth and kept his face averted toward the descending darkness. "If you don't wish to see what other vile things I'm capable of, then you will flee this carriage at once and take your almsdeed with you."

When the carriage shifted and the door closed, he told Raglan to drive on, and he never looked back.

Chapter Twenty-Seven

✕

SOMEONE HAD BEEN in his bedchamber. And it hadn't been Timms.

He knew this because his valet had gone to the village on an errand just before Oscar had gone down to breakfast. As usual, he had eaten alone. However, unlike his standard routine of leaving directly following his meal—thankfully, sans gray gruel and burnt toast—he went back to his chamber for his gloves.

That was when he saw it.

The door of the wardrobe was slightly ajar. Which was something the surprisingly fastidious Timms wouldn't have allowed. In fact, he'd been the one to inform Oscar of the warp in the door and had come up with a solution to keep it from swinging open by itself. And there on the floor was the scrap of linen he always tucked between the gap.

That could have been easily explained away, of course. Perhaps it was mere forgetfulness on Timms's part, the lingering dampness in the air and resulting expansion of the wood, or even a sudden gust of wind blowing down through the chimney. But that wouldn't account for the book on his bedside table.

Years ago, Oscar had developed the habit of always laying his book flipped over with the front cover down. In his observations, he'd found that people assume a book was laid face up. It was just a natural inclination. Therefore, someone who might have been waiting for the opportunity to rifle through his belongings in a furtive search tended to lay a book down with the cover facing up.

Which was the way he found the volume of *Faust* he'd tried to distract himself with last night. But that was not the way he'd left it.

His brow flattened as he scanned the rest of the room, wondering what the widows were after. They'd already been through his things. Twice. And he knew it wasn't the servants. Cardew said that most of them—aside from the steward—respected him. A small triumph, though little good it did a charlatan who'd soon be gone.

There was no reason to stay. He knew that now, especially after seeing the look on Honoria's face.

A man could never outrun his past, his choices. They were part of who he was and always would be. He'd been a fool to think otherwise, no matter how briefly.

So he would leave sooner than planned. He'd send word to Warring and, perhaps, by then Ladrón would be in Spain. Regardless, he could still keep his promise to the dowager by finding her grandson, but he doubted he'd find the answer here.

Swiping up his gloves, he left his bedchamber with every intention of riding off the tension that gripped his neck and shoulders in a vise. But halfway down the stairs, he turned, deciding to inform Cardew first.

If they could arrange it, why not leave by first light tomorrow?

Yet, as he turned to climb the stairs, he caught a glimpse of Mr. Price through the railing. The steward was a floor below, walking swiftly in the direction of the old nave.

Curious and just irritated enough to confront the man who'd hindered him at every turn, Oscar followed.

But by the time he crossed the hall, moved through the nave and gained the winding corridor where Price had gone, the steward had vanished.

This part of the abbey—the cloister—had fallen into disrepair over the years. A musty, stale odor of disuse hung heavy in the air. The rooms along the narrow corridor were situated close together, almost utilitarian in design with small windows set high on the outer wall for light but little else. There were no window seats for daydreaming the way that most of the rooms were designed at Hartley Hall.

He shook his head to rid himself of the thoughts that would wend their way back to Honoria.

But a headshake wasn't enough because the image of her gripping the door of the moving carriage flashed in his mind . . . Then her face surrounded by a tumble of curls . . . Her eyes drowsy and dark . . . Her lips wet and swollen from his kiss . . .

And that leather pouch spilling open.

Bile rose to the back of his throat at the memory. His fists clenched at his sides as he wondered how she'd dared to look so shocked, so hurt by his reaction.

Though, the logical part of his brain reminded him that the money was the reason he'd come there in the first place. Or, at least, that's what he'd told her.

But that was before, he argued internally. Before she'd kissed him. Before he'd carved her brother's name into the old ash tree. Before he'd held her trembling body within the walls of Awildian Palace. Before he'd found his place at her family's table across from her. Before he'd been foolish enough to imagine that she cared for him . . .

He could kick himself for what he'd revealed to Honoria last night. And with his admission, he had ensured that whatever tendre she might have felt was utterly destroyed.

Though, why should that matter when nothing would ever come of it? It wasn't as though she ever would have married someone like—

The faint shriek of a hinge interrupted his thoughts, and he knew Price was close by.

Just around the corner, he saw a fan of pale light fall across the dusty stones beside a partially open door.

According to the old ledgers and diagrams he'd found, this room had originally been the old library. However, during the persecution of Catholics in the sixteenth century, the abbey had been raided, priests and nuns forced to march on foot, leaving what little they had behind. But then the patriarch of the Dunne family—a Catholic himself—was bequeathed this estate by the king for his support of the new Protestantism.

Oscar stepped closer, cautiously peering inside. Only to find the room empty.

Then again, as his gaze homed in on the cold stone hearth, perhaps it wasn't empty, after all.

A priest hole, he mused as he saw the concealed door in the dark paneling beside the fireplace. Apparently, the Dunne patriarch had sympathized with the old religion and kept it a secret from king and country.

And now Mr. Price was using it for his own purposes.

But before pushing through the door, Oscar caught himself. Why was he even bothering to chase after Price? It wasn't his concern. It was Vandemere's.

So he pivoted on his heel and walked away.

⤙

A SHORT WHILE later, he found Cardew in the garret by spotting the discarded turpentine and rags he was supposed to be using on the railing. Not that it mattered any longer.

Without knocking, he opened the door . . . and summarily closed it, squeezing his eyes shut.

On the other side of the door, he heard Auntie Babette's giggle followed by the patter of bare feet on the hardwood and the rustle of clothing.

When she came out, she grinned up at him through her lashes, trailing a fingertip along his shoulder. "No need to be prudish, nephew. It's all for the sake of art. And I just happen to be his muse."

She sauntered off, caring nothing for the fact that the back of her dress lay open, revealing her lack of undergarments. Then again, he had seen that for himself just a moment ago when she'd been posing for Cardew. *Posing!*

His irritation vaulted as he stepped into the room and closed the door firmly behind him. He clenched his jaw, taking considerable effort not to raise his voice when he gestured to the canvas on the easel. "You were supposed to keep this quiet."

"Fear not, cub. I explained to my lovely muse that I've never even considered painting a portrait before in my life . . ."

"Until you met her," Oscar concluded, knowing that particular speech was a favorite method of Cardew's. "And by some miracle she brought out the hidden artist within?"

He grinned. "Coincidentally, it has always been a dream of hers to become a patron of the arts and be memorialized on canvas. And I think it's my best work yet. Just look at the way the brush loves all those delicious curves. She is a feast for the eyes."

Well, Oscar had certainly had an eyeful.

"I call it *Venus in Summer*. The bed will be an altar draped in vines. Meadows and orchards beyond the open terrace. The warm glow of the sun rising over the—"

"We need to talk," Oscar interrupted.

Facing him, Cardew's excitement over his current painting dimmed from his eyes, and his smile fell. "Did you receive word from Warring?"

"Nothing yet. But there is no reason to stay."

Cardew regarded him thoughtfully. "I'd heard a rumor among the servants that your debutante's dowry is considerable. I thought, perhaps—"

"What? That I would marry her for her fortune? Spend

the rest of my days groveling at her feet to be deserving of it—of her—while she looks down on me with disgust?" It turned his stomach to realize he was tempted to do just that. "No. That is not an option."

"Then, we'll leave before first light," Cardew said matter-of-factly.

The easy acquiescence took him off guard. It was like slamming face-first into a lamppost. He needed a moment to reorient himself and glanced absently around the room.

"Your canvas is wet," he said. "And we cannot leave it behind without risking a trail leading directly to us. So, we'll stay until it dries."

"Or I could simply burn this one and start again somewhere else. It isn't as though we haven't done as much before." Cardew shrugged, wiping his paint-spattered hands on a rag. "Unless, of course, you have a few loose ends to tie up before we depart."

The artist's gaze casually surveyed him as if *he* were painted on canvas.

Oscar's spine stiffened. "There is nothing keeping me here."

"It's for the best." Cardew laid a hand smelling of turpentine on his shoulder. "In a few days, it will be like it always was, and you'll hardly ever think about this place."

Oscar only nodded before he turned and left. He needed that morning ride more than ever.

But as he descended the stairs, still cringing at the black lacquered railing, he knew that he would think about this place. That was the way his memory worked. Every place he'd ever been was inside his head like cards stacked all neatly in a deck.

Even so, he feared that Honoria would be more than a mere memory. She would haunt him, a ghost rattling around inside his mind, her kisses permanently etched upon his soul.

He expelled a hard breath, foolishly wishing to bury this

part of his life, to put it to rest in a way that made it easier to leave behind. If he had time, perhaps—

He didn't have the chance to finish that thought.

An urgent knocking fell on the door, and Algernon opened it to a messenger.

Oscar knew, even before he saw Rowan Warring's distinctive scrawl, that he was out of time.

Chapter Twenty-Eight

HONORIA HATED THAT changeable, foolhardy sapskull! If he wanted to refuse her money and keep a murderer hot on his heels, then so be it. She didn't care a whit.

Not. A. Single. Whit, she thought, brushing her hair into submission.

"Perhaps a calming blue muslin today, miss," Tally suggested.

In the looking glass, Honoria could see her maid's concerned and slightly wary expression at the furious swipes of the brush. She set it down and fixed a smile on her face. "No. I think red would suit my mood. Besides, it is our at-home day, and I want to look my absolute best for the gentlemen callers."

She pinched her cheeks for color. Though, to be honest, her color was already high. It climbed higher still when she thought about the two thousand pounds she had tucked away beneath the false bottom of her wardrobe beside Signor Cesario's hair and monocle.

But Oscar could go to the devil for all she cared. Which was not a single whit.

With a decisive nod, she rose from her vanity table and prepared to make an entrance.

~

IT WAS SO refreshing to return to her former carefree self. Honoria laughed and flirted with the gentlemen who—

even though they knew she was betrothed—refused to give up the hope that she would run away with one of them. And she was more than willing to oblige this fantasy for one afternoon.

She knew very well that it was a game for them as much as it was for her. Gentlemen were hunters by nature. She knew from firsthand experience of attending a fowling party as Cesario that men simply enjoyed the pursuit and camaraderie, whether or not they bagged any birds.

"What an honor to have so many handsome gentlemen pay calls on such a sweltering day. You all make me quite giddy," she said, fanning herself with coquettish skill.

There were a few of her octogenarians among the lot, as well. She wondered if they'd driven here this afternoon or if they were stragglers from last week, left behind to wander aimlessly about the halls until someone rang for tea.

Dimly, she recalled that was the day Oscar had arrived with a cut on his forehead from a falling chandelier. No, she corrected, a cut chandelier. That man was forever inciting people into murder. Not that it mattered to her.

In fact, she couldn't wait to be rid of him for good. The sooner Ladrón found him, the better.

A shiver chased down her spine at the thought. Likely the last vestiges of any possible concern she might have had for him draining away. Besides, Oscar was far too clever and would be gone well before his life were in danger. She was sure of it.

"Isn't that right, my dear?"

Honoria blinked at the sound of her mother's voice and saw her curious expression.

"I was mentioning to Lord Barker that you would love to hear the sonnet he wrote in your honor."

"I have it memorized," Barker offered, his eyes the soulful brown of a basset hound puppy. *"Your beauty shines greater than the heavens. Your beauty doth make the roses jealous. Your beauty . . ."*

Standing at the door behind him, Thea dramatically clutched her heart and laid the back of her hand against her brow. Honoria had to bite the inside of her cheek to keep from laughing.

Yet, as the *beauty*-full sonnet continued, she was starting to take offense.

It shouldn't bother her. From an early age, she had learned many individuals never looked beyond the surface of anyone they met. Those same individuals preferred to make categorical judgments on whatever they believed they found. And though she'd struggled for a number of years to prove herself as something more than just pretty, it never altered the consensus.

Her mother had taught her to simply smile politely. *One should never be cross with those who only see and do not possess the gift of noticing or knowing.*

Her father, in turn, told her to pity them. *I'd wager a sixpence that they were dropped on their heads as infants and were left a few currants short of a scone.*

However, being gaped at and having the confidence that her parents instilled in her had led her to throwing herself into acting on her family's stage. As a character, an audience expected her to be someone else. They even waited for her to reveal it. There was something altogether thrilling about being free to express the different aspects of her own personality through the parts she played.

But there inside the parlor, on another too-warm afternoon, and with Lord Barker's sonnet droning to an end—which, incidentally, compared her nose to a rose in the final couplet—she was tired of pretending. Tired of being nothing more than a porcelain figurine to the majority of these gentlemen, aside from a rheumy-eyed octogenarian who'd spent a good deal of time having a conversation with an Argand oil lamp.

Fortunately, she was saved from Lord Barker's adamant desire for a discourse on the merits of the work when Mr.

Mosely appeared at the door with a silver salver. The instant he looked at Honoria, she felt the heavy th-thud of her heart and instantly wondered if the letter resting on the surface was a farewell from Oscar. After last night, she could well believe it. And she should be glad to be well rid of him at last.

So then why did she feel so cold all of a sudden? Why were her hands trembling?

Setting down her cup and saucer, she rose and went to the doorway. Dimly, she heard Mother take over as hostess and inquire if any of the gentlemen would like Thea to slice more cake.

That was when she saw the letter was from Truman. But there was only one reason Truman would be writing to her again so soon.

She broke the seal at once.

Dearest sister,
  Ladrón was spotted leaving London. I tell you this only to serve as a warning to stay away from Vandemere.

She didn't finish the rest. Crumpling the letter in her fist, she picked up her skirts, dashed down the stairs and out the front door. Without thought or care, she untied the nearest horse, sank the toe of her slipper into the stirrup and hauled herself up into the saddle.

Hem high and stockings bared to the world, she raced off pell-mell toward the abbey.

The seven miles seemed to take an eternity. When she'd finally arrived, she dismounted and stormed straight inside without even knocking.

She nearly fell to her knees with relief when she saw Oscar stopping at the far end of the entry hall.

His eyes widened with undisguised shock. Then that look abruptly altered, shuttered and turned cold. Just like it had last night when she'd offered him money.

"I'm not here for that," she said, shoving a hank of hair from her forehead. "I'm here because—"

Suddenly, when she lowered her hand, she caught sight of a movement in the gallery directly above him. Right before her eyes, she saw a heavy urn on a pedestal begin to topple forward. Then it fell.

There was no time to call out a warning. All she could do was run toward him.

They collided in a bone-jarring jolt, momentum tipping their bodies toward the floor. She felt a hard blow to the back of her head. And then everything went black.

Chapter Twenty-Nine

❧

HONORIA WAS DEAD. She was sure of it as she became aware of a sharp, stabbing pain. She groaned. One would think the afterlife would feel more pleasant than this.

Blinking into the eternal darkness, she felt her lashes tug against something that rested on her cheek. No, not just on her cheek. There was something stretched over her brow, too. And her chin.

It felt like cloth. Her burial shroud?

Curious, she tried to lift her hand to investigate, but her arm was trapped at her side.

"Try not to move. It will only hurt."

"Oscar?"

"Stop moving."

She bristled at his quiet command. But the throbbing pain radiating along her skull was greater than her desire to argue with him. At least for the moment. "Where am I?"

"You're in the king's chamber inside the abbey."

So . . . not dead, then. She supposed that was a relief. *"King's chamber?"*

"Seventeenth-century king. Popped by for a visit. Never returned."

His words were short and clipped and did nothing to ease the disquiet brewing inside her from the question she was too afraid to ask. So she tried to answer it herself, straining through the piercing pain in her skull to remember.

It came to her in fragments: the letter, the mad dash on horseback, opening the door to find Oscar, and then . . .

Oh. The urn. "Are you injured?"

"No, you maddening little idiot," he growled. "What were you thinking, running toward me like that?"

"Well, there was an urn about to drop on your head, and I saw the perfect opportunity to be rid of you once and for all. I tried to position you directly underneath it. I miscalculated. Obviously."

"Pity for you, then. You'll have a hard time ridding yourself of me now." The words were a threat, but his tone had softened away the hard edge, revealing a trace of worry beneath it. "Close your eyes. I'm lighting a candle."

She did but frowned and felt the cloth shift against her skin with the slight movement. Then she heard the quick strike of flint and steel before a soft golden glow penetrated her eyelids.

She carefully squinted her eyes open, and a lance of fear speared through her at seeing white cambric fuzzing around the edges of her vision. "You're dreadfully domineering, I hope you know."

"After dealing with you, your parents, the surgeon and the widows, I believe I've earned the right," he said without looking at her, as if he *couldn't* look at her.

Working one of her arms free from beneath the tightly tucked coverlet, she tentatively touched the bandages, quickly discerning that they covered her entire head.

Hard beats of panic clogged her throat. What had happened to her?

She swallowed, not wanting to think about that quite yet. "My parents?"

"Of course your parents." He was back to being testy, his jaw set. "Naturally they were curious about the contents of the letter that would cause their daughter to flee a parlor full of gentleman callers and steal one of their horses, only to arrive hot on her heels and find her limp body in my arms after she was nearly crushed. To death. By an urn."

"I wouldn't have had to do anything of the sort if you didn't have a murderer after you. Which means that you need to leave here. This instant. He has already left London—"

"And is en route to Dover," he interrupted archly. "Where he will likely board a ship bound for Spain. You see, I also received a letter from someone who, I can only presume, is a bit more well-informed than your brother."

She glanced away, guilt overriding her unease for the moment. "I had to tell Truman in order to withdraw the money from my bank in London. He's the only one who knows. And we can trust him."

"Mmm . . ." he grumbled, clearly not convinced.

"What did you tell my parents? About the letter, I mean."

"I stayed as close to the truth as possible and explained that Ladrón was a man who I had done business with in the past and our parting was less than amicable. Then, I mentioned my regret in sharing this information with their daughter because I had no idea she could be such an idiot as to think that she could or should endeavor to intervene on my behalf."

"Well, it was clearly your fault for underestimating me."

When his nostrils flared and the muscle along his jaw twitched, she supposed that now wasn't the time to throw stones. Or urns, in this instance. The reminder brought a fresh wave of cranium-splitting pain, and she closed her eyes.

"Here. Drink some water," he said with surprising gentleness as he slid a hand beneath her nape and pressed the smooth rim of a glass to her lips.

As the first sip touched her tongue, she realized how parched she was and drank thirstily.

"Slow now," he crooned, and her eyes fluttered open, seeking reassurance. But he did not meet her gaze. He let her take two more gulps before easing away from her. "I'll give you more in a few minutes."

She wanted more now. Or perhaps it was just that she wanted to be close to him again. Wanted the comforting warmth of his partial embrace. Wanted him to look at her.

But he was staring down at the glass, rolling it between the cups of his hands.

She didn't want to think about the reason. "What did my parents say to that?"

"Hmm?" he murmured with an absent shrug as he set the glass on the side table. "Oh, nothing really. Your father spouted something Shakespearean about the heart. I believe it was 'Who could refrain, that had a heart to love, and in that heart courage to make's love known?'"

"My father has a quote for every situation, but they're not always accurate," she said in a rush.

"That was my first thought, too. And yet, it struck me that, while I was making up reasons to stay, you were stealing a horse to warn me about potential danger." Then, at last, he looked at her, holding her gaze with that ruthless gambler's scrutiny. "I think it's fair to say that we are both suffering from a stronger regard for each other than we'd anticipated."

"It will surely pass." Her pulse quickened in panic. And now she wished he would look away. "Besides, I'm likely hideous underneath these bandages."

"Fear not. You are still beautiful," he said on a sigh of indulgent exasperation.

"Then, why haven't you looked at me until now? How badly am I hurt?"

"It could have been much worse."

That wasn't an answer, and his evasion only amplified her worry. "Just tell me."

"Fine. I'll tell you," he said. "Since you decided to hurtle yourself recklessly toward me, part of the urn glanced off the crown of your head. It bled. A great deal. And every time I think about it I want to—" He shook his head, then closed his eyes. Drew in a deep breath, exhaled slowly. "The surgeon claimed the bleeding was normal for such a wound but added that you would have a sizable lump on your head for a few days. Your parents, in turn, decided it best for you to remain under my roof. Chaperoned, of course."

He gestured toward the opposite end of the room. And, for the first time, Honoria noticed the dowager's nurse recumbent on a chaise longue, her head lolling to one side as she slept, oblivious, the faint sound of her snoring evenly rusting in and whooshing out.

Confused, Honoria turned back to him. "Then, why is my face covered in bandages?"

"Partly because the position of your wound made it necessary to anchor them . . . *and* partly because the surgeon was afraid you would scratch yourself." He shook his head, issuing a half shrug as if the town surgeon were a dunderhead.

But there was something Oscar wasn't telling her. She could read it in his eyes. He'd never looked at her this way before.

"Tell me the truth. No matter what it is, I can bear it. If I'm disfigured, then there's no need to coddle me."

"Very well," he said blandly. "I think you're being ridiculous. You are far more than a collection of lovely features, you also possess exquisitely ripe breasts and taut, firm b—"

"Oscar."

The corner of his mouth twitched, clearly satisfied that he'd made her blush. He was trying to distract her. And it was only making her worry all the more.

Seeing this, he sobered at once. "Would you like me to wake the nurse and have her remove the bandages so you can see for yourself?"

Her throat went dry. "No. I don't think I'm ready yet."

"There is nothing to be afraid of." Leaning closer, he

took her chin gently in his grasp, his gaze steady and sure. "You are the most brave, clever, daring and stubborn woman I've ever met. You've never let anything or anyone stop you from doing precisely as you please, which also means that you're determined to overcome any obstacle in your path. I admire the woman you are, as well as the woman you're destined to become. And as every day passes into years and into decades and your face wrinkles and softens with age, I will still think you are beautiful. I will *always* think you are beautiful."

Honoria wasn't sure what frightened her more—the idea that she would be scarred for life or the way his tender admission burrowed directly into her heart.

Unable to deal with either at the moment, she burst into tears. And because it made her megrim all the worse, she cried some more.

He took her hand in his own, enveloping it in his reassuring strength and warmth. "Now, what's all this blubbering about?"

"I don't know wh-why"—her breath staggered wetly—"you're being so kind to me all of a s-sudden."

He leaned close to wipe away her tears, then pressed a kiss to her lids before easing back into the chair and taking her hand again. "Oh, Signore. I think you have the answer already, and that's what truly scares you. But at some point, you're going to have to face it."

Reflexively, she shook her head, only to wince from the effort. "I'm tired. I don't want to think about anything. Not now."

"Then, I'll leave you to rest."

"No," she said at once, curling her fingers around his. "Don't go. Please."

His stormy irises were eclipsed in the shadows of his lashes as he studied her. Then he softly clucked his tongue. "First you cannot wait to be rid of me. And now you want me to stay. Which shall it be, my dear?"

She knew what he was asking. The blackguard obviously had no qualms about taking advantage of her weakened state. Even so, her heart thudded so hard against her ribs that she was sure he heard it.

However, she also knew that she could feign ignorance later and that gave her the courage to say, "Stay."

And when she awoke a few hours later to the pink light of dawn filtering in through the windows, he was still there.

At some point in the night, he had fallen asleep with his head resting against her midriff, every ounce of jaded cynicism erased from his countenance. If not for the shadowed scruff, he would have looked rather boyish with those dark lashes fanned against the flush of sleep on his cheeks.

She brushed his hair away from his brow, a silken lock curling, clinging like a vine around her finger. And, all at once, the heart she kept safely tucked away behind high garden walls did the one thing she never wanted it to do.

It opened the door.

Chapter Thirty

༄

IT WAS STILL early morning when Oscar left Honoria's bedside. Early enough to catch fingers of morning light wending through the trees to shimmer across a sea of dewy grass and kiss the stone facade of this grand giantess.

And to think, Oscar might have missed all this and so much more if he'd kept to his plan to leave with Cardew.

But it was too soon to think about the future. There were still matters in the more recent past to contend with . . . and when he saw a shadow skulking through the nave toward the old cloister, he knew he wouldn't have to wait long.

He caught Mr. Price carrying a bulging valise through the opening of the priest hole. With the steward holding a chamberstick, he didn't see Oscar in the shadows by the door until it was too late.

The weasel-faced man startled at first. Then, seeing who it was, he sneered. "If you do not mind, sir, I should like to pass."

"I'm sure you would, indeed." Reaching out, Oscar snatched the valise and peered inside. "Mere silverware? I admit, I'm a bit disappointed. Then again, you've likely stolen all the most lucrative trinkets by now."

"Are you accusing me of thievery? I'll have you know I planned to take this into my office and polish it today. With so few servants, I have been more than willing to perform the duties that are otherwise beneath my station."

"We'll see if the magistrate believes that tale."

Price scoffed. "If you dare make such a vulgar accusation, I will tell him that you put the silver in my valise."

Thoughtful, Oscar crossed his arms and studied him. If he were sitting across the table from this arrogant arse, he might require a moment to consider the cards he held. Price was good at appearing affronted and proud of his elevated status in the house. It was easy to imagine how the widows were duped.

At one time, Oscar had imagined they were all in on it together, but not any longer. The widows were tired of being embarrassed by the state of the house and their lack of funding to see to its care. Their gardens were proof of how much they wanted beauty surrounding them, in addition to the fact that they usually had tea on the lawn.

Oscar might have thought they were all trying to keep the world outside the doors of Dunnelocke Abbey. But the truth was they'd started to see themselves as part of this house. It wasn't just grabbing hold of their rightful portion of it when the time came. It was the feeling that they'd failed in taking care of the old place and the fear of the unknown outside these walls.

He knew all too well the power that the fear of the unknown held. It made a person linger in misery for far too long. So long, in fact, that you began to wonder if you ever deserved anything more.

Understanding the widows better also made his fury toward Price all the greater.

"You may try to tell the magistrate your fiction." He shrugged. "However, nothing will change the figures in the books I found in the storeroom."

Price's gaze darted down to his waistcoat pocket where he always kept his key.

"Fear not. It's still there," Oscar said and reached out to withdraw it, the brass glinting in the low light as he held it up. Then he closed his hand, turning his wrist with a flourish before it vanished. "Or is it?"

Price swallowed. "Give that back to me."

"I don't think you'll be needing it where you're going. You see, I know you've been stealing from the abbey for years. Not just trinkets and baubles, but servants' wages and tenants' rent. You may not have started out a lying, swindling thief. It's my guess that the first discrepancies were honest errors. But when you got away with it, you felt a surge of superiority. Arrogance like that tends to lead men toward gambling in other ways, like over a gaming table." He arched a brow at the telltale guilt draining the color from Price's complexion. "Just as I suspected. But you never developed a head for cards. You're the type who believes it's a matter of luck rather than skill. After all, any ignorant arse can tumble a cup of dice, right? Toss a few quid onto the table for a pair of Kings?"

As Oscar paced the floor around him, Price shifted from one foot to the other but said nothing.

But Oscar didn't need him to. "Then, you fell in over your head at the tables and thought you could just perform some clever bookkeeping. No one needed to know. They're your books, after all. It's all part of the place you've earned above the rabble that work beneath you. So, what would it matter if you pointed the finger at one of the servants if a pair of candlesticks were to go missing? All you had to do was fire them and inform the widows that you took care of the terrible thief in their midst. I'm sure they were grateful."

He thought of Honoria with her eyepatch, telling him of how impossible it was for the widows to keep any servants over the years, and it only added to his anger.

"None of this is true," Price said. "And I don't have to listen to any more of your accusations."

"I'm afraid you do. You see, through all your conniving, scheming and stealing, you forgot about one thing." Oscar stopped in front of him, his voice deceptively calm, his fists clenched at his sides. "That there's always someone better at being a monster. And beneath this roof, that happens to be me."

"Are you"—Price retreated a step, the candle flame trembling in his grasp—"threatening me?"

Oscar stepped forward. "I am."

Before Price could dart away like the weasel he was, Oscar grabbed him by the lapels and shoved him against the wall. The chamberstick clattered to the floor, snuffing out. "You were seen yesterday."

"I—I don't know wh-what you're talking about. I wasn't even here. It was my off day."

"I repeat, you were seen. In the upper gallery. Right before that urn fell on Miss Hartley."

Bleary light filtered in through the old slitted windows as his face shifted from indignation to denial to pale fear. "It wasn't me, I swe—"

Oscar shook him once, hard.

"It w-was an accident," Price stammered, eyes wide. "When the d-door burst open, I was at the top of the stairs with one of the statuettes from the king's chamber. I didn't want anyone to see me. But when I dashed out of sight, I m-must have bumped the urn. You have to believe me. I never meant for anyone to be hurt."

"You could have killed her, you bloody bastard!" Oscar lifted him off his feet, ready to strangle the worthless life out of him.

Somehow, through his rage, he felt a hand on his shoulder. He turned to see Baron Hartley.

"Release him, lad. Let him not turn you into the better monster," he said.

Oscar dragged in a breath and lowered Price to his feet. With the rage still running hot through his veins, he had to step away.

"Oh, thank you, my lord," the weasel said. "This man is positively barbaric. He is certainly no gentle—*Auuugh!*"

Hearing Price groan, Oscar looked over his shoulder to

see him doubled over, his mouth agape like a trout gasping for water.

Hartley dusted his hands together and shrugged. "The better monster just happens to be me, at the moment. She is my daughter, after all."

AFTER HARTLEY AND the magistrate carted Price away, Oscar decided to personally deliver Honoria's breakfast tray.

It wasn't that he was worried the kitchen would try to serve her that foul gray sludge—well, mostly not. He wanted to ensure she had the best of everything. And with that thought in mind, he decided to adorn her tray with roses.

But no sooner had he cut the first blossom than Millicent appeared, her widow's weeds embellished by a large floppy hat.

"And just what do you think you are doing?" she snarled.

He cut another and jammed the stem into the vase beside the other. "If you must know, I am taking these to Miss Hartley."

"*Men*," she muttered, that hint of brogue revealing her frustration. "You cannot give her those."

"I can and I will." He snicked another just to prove his point.

She surprised him by snatching the knife. For a skinny old bean, she certainly was quick. "Each blossom in the garden is a symbol, a language all of its own. And you cannot offer a woman who is staying beneath your roof a bouquet of flowers that signify passion, passion and only passion. It is unseemly. Imagine what the servants will think."

He felt the flesh of his brow pucker. "I just thought they were pretty."

"Heaven spare us all from such ignorance." She sighed and shook her head, shoving her basket into his hand. "Follow me. Now, you'll want bluebell for constancy. Weigela for faithfulness. Some fern for fascination . . ."

As she was clipping to her heart's content, he stopped by a bright orange cluster. "What about these?"

She scoffed. "*That* is butterfly weed, and it would tell her your wish for her to let you go."

"No butterfly weed, then."

"And while we're on the subject, no marigolds or dahlias either." She pointed to each in turn. "But some garden sage for esteem, I should think. This way. Don't dally."

Then she blew by him toward the kitchen garden. He had a hard time keeping up with her. But she was in her element, fussing and finagling all the leaves and blossoms into a perfect little bouquet. To tie them all together, she withdrew a lace handkerchief from beneath her sleeve.

"There. I think that will do quite nicely. Oh, and I suppose . . ." She took one of the roses he'd already cut and slid it into the center, her cheeks coloring. Clearing her throat, she pursed her lips dourly and handed the cluster to him. "Just so you know, I was dreadfully worried about your Miss Hartley."

"Admitting that you wish I was struck instead?"

She narrowed those dark eyes. "Nephew, if I had pushed an urn down atop your head, I wouldn't have missed."

"You just called me *nephew*," he said, just as shocked as she was.

"You are mistaken."

"I'm not. And what's more, I think you like me, Aunt Millie." He waggled the bouquet at her. Then, before she could deny it, he pressed a swift kiss to her cheek and sauntered away.

He could have sworn he heard her call him a *scamp* as he stepped inside.

Carrying the breakfast tray, he climbed the stairs and heard threads of an argument.

With a glance across the gallery to the archway leading toward the west wing, he saw Alfreda and Dudley in the midst of a heated discussion, scowls met with finger-pointing.

Oscar did his best to appear invisible and took inordinate interest in the silver dome he carried.

"I am my own man, Alfreda. Though, little you would know of that, considering the fact that you are always judging me for the crimes of another."

"What am I to think when you refuse to tell me why you *claimed* the need to speak with the surgeon privately? And immediately afterward you suddenly had an errand in the village?" She scoffed. "I never knew you to be so secretive, but after sixteen years of marriage, your true nature has been revealed to me at last."

"Unfortunately, I know your true nature all too well, and it's intolerably suspicious. And I have tolerated it long enough. Too long, I should think."

"If that is all you have to say, then I see no reason for you to linger in my"—she paused, drawing in a shuddering breath—"presence a moment longer."

"Do not involve yourself," Oscar muttered under his breath, even when hearing the slight tremor in the hard-hearted Alfreda's voice gave him pause.

But just as he reached the top of the stairs, Dudley tromped directly into his path.

Oscar offered a brief nod in passing, believing that the older man would continue on.

But then Dudley halted, turning to him, his color high. "If I could offer a bit of advice, man-to-man, it's to never involve yourself with a distrustful and heartless woman."

"You have some nerve!" Alfreda spat from farther down the corridor. "This has nothing to do with him."

"She is right on that account," Oscar said carefully. "So I'll just be going."

Before he could turn away, Dudley leaned over the tray between them and lowered his voice.

"All I did was have one word with the surgeon about a certain"—he glanced down to where his own hand fluttered just below his waist—"uncooperative appendage without wanting to inform my wife, who has always regarded me as rather virile. The surgeon recommended a certain powder that hails from the Orient and . . ."

Wanting to be anywhere else in the world, Oscar dutifully inclined his head in a nod as Shellhorn concluded his all-too-informative diatribe.

"Surely, it isn't unreasonable that a man be allowed a measure of privacy."

Realizing that he'd become involved, whether he liked it or not, he stepped over to the narrow console table in the corridor and set down the tray.

He clasped Dudley's shoulder. "I completely understand your desire to address this issue without informing your wife. Odds are, however, she has already noticed that something is amiss. She has been rather testy lately," he added as if he'd ever known her to be otherwise.

"And I take full blame. You see, I haven't had the stamina to, well, pop her buttons, so to speak. Why just the other day, we were in the music room when she did this trilling thing with her fingertips right underneath my—"

"Don't say it. I beg of you."

"Right, well, it was all over before it had begun."

Oscar wondered if the tea on the tray was still hot enough that, if he were to pour it directly into his ears, it would make him forget ever hearing this. The mental images alone would give him nightmares for months.

"Perhaps," Oscar suggested, "you might discuss some of this with her. Not many wives are fond of secrets, I imagine. And, considering that her first husband died in an opium den, I'd gather he kept a few."

Shellhorn grumbled. "Of late, a day has not passed without her remarking on her belief that I'll take after him."

"So it is possible—wouldn't you say?—that secrets make her think of death, and she is worried about you?"

"Crackers! I think you might be onto something," he said, his gray brows lifting. "And we haven't had our cuddle time lately."

"Again, I don't . . . need . . . to know that," Oscar said haltingly, shaking his head. He drew in a breath to quell a sudden bout of queasiness.

Dudley looked over his shoulder with hesitation at Alfreda, pacing on the other side of the gallery. "The problem is, old chap, I've said some rather terse things, and my Freda isn't altogether quick to forgive. Do you think you could ease the way a bit?"

"*Me?*" he balked. "I'd only make matters worse."

"Not true. You have a way of cutting directly to the heart of a matter. And I fear she's ready to close the door on me, once and for all."

Devil take it! He should have walked away or, better yet, gone up the servants' stairs.

He heaved out an exhale. "I am only going to ask her if she would be willing to speak with you. That's all."

Resigned, he walked across the gallery, Dudley watching with the hopeful gaze of a dog waiting for a scrap at the dinner table.

Oscar lightly rapped on the doorframe of the sitting room. "I am here on behalf of Mr. Shellhorn, who begs an audience with you."

"I don't care what either of you have to say." Alfreda crossed her arms, immovable as a mountain.

Oscar would have accepted that and walked away, if not for the strain of uncertainty and worry around her eyes.

So he kept his tone gentle. "And that is your prerogative. All I want to offer is that sometimes a man finds it difficult to reveal any weakness to the woman he loves. He wants to be strong for her."

"And I have never doubted that. Not once. But that is no excuse for secrets and lies."

"Quite true." Oscar hoped he wasn't standing too close to the chapel or any stray bolt of lightning that might smite him. "However, it may be a bit more difficult for a man to be completely forthcoming when, say, his wife compares him to her first husband."

"I do no such thing. They are—or were—complete opposites, until recently."

"And yet, by wearing black every day, aren't you refusing to release the memory of Sylvester?"

She blinked, owl-eyed, her bottom lip close to pouting as she uncrossed her arms. "Did Dudley say that he doesn't like my dresses?"

"Nothing of the sort. He completely adores you. All I'm suggesting is that, instead of mourning your first husband, perhaps you might wear a splash of color for your *living* husband to admire. Because he does—admire you, that is."

She swallowed and looked down at her stiff black bombazine. "I do have one gown tucked away. Babette gave it to me years ago. So you can imagine that the cut is rather bold, especially around the . . ."

When she gestured to her bosom, Oscar changed his mind about the lightning bolt. Let it strike him. He was ready.

"But the silk is a rather lovely shade of violet," she continued and glanced across the gallery. After a moment, she nodded. "Very well. I will grant him an audience."

Leaving that circle of hell, Oscar returned to Shellhorn. "Your lady awaits."

Without warning, Shellhorn reached out, snatched his hand and began pumping it up and down. "I'm overflowing with gratitude, Vandemere."

"My pleasure," Oscar said, feeling as though he hadn't

done a thing. Walking over to the tea tray, he sighed again, then picked up the flowers. "Wait. Give these to her. Apparently, they'll tell her everything you want to say."

"Mmm . . . And a rose for passion. Capital!" Dudley grinned, then clapped him on the shoulder. "No matter what their opinion may be, I think you're a right solid chap."

In that moment, as he watched the warring factions reunite toward a tentative cease-fire, he wondered if he actually might have done something, after all.

It felt almost . . . good, like something family might do for each other. Not quite the *I baked your favorite biscuits* type of family that the Hartleys had but more of an *I don't loathe you quite as much today* type of family.

The problem was, this wasn't his family. One day soon, Warring would write to him of news about the real Vandemere. And since Oscar had given his word to the dowager, he would make sure she had her grandson when he left.

But he felt a pang of yearning that only intensified when he stepped into the king's chamber and saw Honoria sleeping amid a tower of burgundy pillows in the center of a dark walnut four-poster bed.

He knew in that moment that she was the reason he'd started thinking about family. Just by being under this roof, she made this stark abbey feel brighter, colorful, alive . . .

She made it feel like home.

And he knew that he wanted this life—Vandemere's life—more than he had ever wanted anything before.

Chapter Thirty-One

※

$\mathcal{J}$T HAD BEEN four days and Honoria was tired of being stared at with pity. Four blasted days in bandages that the doctor insisted were "all for the best, my child." He wouldn't even permit her to look in a mirror when he redressed the wounds.

Additionally, Oscar saw to it that a maid stayed with her at all times. He claimed that it was in order to see to her every comfort, but she felt as though she were under guard.

If she didn't get out of this bed and out of this shroud she was going to go mad.

She felt well enough. Her megrim had vanished after the second day. She was no longer nauseous. Her appetite had increased, which was not necessarily good when one lay abed all day long. And, frankly, after four days of being swaddled, coddled and pampered to death, she needed a bath.

Thankfully, before madness tipped her over the edge and as she began to rearrange the pillows around her for the hundredth time that day, Thea arrived for a visit.

"Oh, fair sister! What news have you brought from the outside world?" Honoria asked in a death-scene voice as she reached out with a dramatically shaking hand. "Tell me, is the sky still blue? Do foals still frolic over field and fen?"

Thea chortled as she sank down onto the edge of the bed. "Be careful not to say that too loudly around Father or he'll start repeating it before every performance in place of our usual tongue-limbering exercise."

Together they both grinned and recited, *"Percival, Peter and Carlton Culpepper."*

"I think the Culpeppers would become quite bereft if we replaced them. They've always taken such pride in being part of our every performance," Honoria mused.

"But I think Vandemere would prefer it if you never spoke their names again."

"Ugh! Do not say his name to me. I'm thoroughly vexed with that man for keeping me in this pillowed prison. He treats me as though I'm made of glass. As though I'm incapable of taking care of myself."

It irritated her all the more because he'd told her that he believed she was capable and strong, but he was treating her as if she were the opposite.

"Perhaps it's because he loves you, hen wit."

Honoria shook her head, adamant. "It isn't that way between us. We understand each other too well for any genuine affection."

"I don't believe that for an instant," her sister fired back. "I've seen the way he looks at you. In fact, I've even taken notes for a future character in a tragic play."

"And why, pray tell, must it be tragic?"

"Because all the best plays are."

A shiver rolled over Honoria, reminding her not only of the man who wanted to kill Oscar but of the fact that he'd refused to take the money to save himself.

"Well, I hope your play ends happily when the hero escapes the villain's clutches."

Thea looked at her pointedly. "But do villains simply give up, head to Dover and sail away?"

Because of her foolhardy escape from the parlor and subsequent urn-to-the-head mishap, her entire family knew about the man who was after Oscar. Not everything, of course. He'd played it down as an old misunderstanding with the wrong sort of fellow. The kind of fellow who even her brother would have been wary of encountering. And she made certain to write Truman with a mention of this version of the truth, just in case.

But was she convinced that Ladrón had abandoned his quest for payment and vengeance so easily? No, she was not.

She'd wanted to say as much to Oscar, but the only time she'd been able to speak with him privately was that first night when the maid was snoring.

He stopped by to visit during the day. Short, *chaperoned* visits.

However, he had crept into her chamber at some point each night. She knew this because she would find him asleep in the corner chair beside her bed if she woke before dawn from a troubling dream. Seeing him there and feeling comfort in his presence would help her fall back to sleep.

But he was always gone before she woke up later, as if he'd never been there at all.

He was good at leaving, she thought grimly. Hadn't he told her that he'd spent his whole life doing just that?

"I plan to talk to him about it . . . if we can ever have a moment alone. I feel as though I've lived three lifetimes in this bed. And I really don't feel poorly at all. My head is sore when I touch it, but I saw the bandages when the surgeon removed them yesterday, and there was no fresh blood."

"Does your face itch? Mother always says that when a cut is healing it will itch, and we must not scratch it."

"Not on my face but definitely in my hair. It drives me positively insane. However, that could be because I need a bath."

"You definitely need a bath," Thea teased, pinching her own nose and earning a playful swat. Then she sobered and looked at her with concern. "Are you worried about what you'll find?"

Thoughtful, Honoria drew in a deep breath. "Strangely,

no. Of course, when I first woke up to find my head wrapped in bandages, I was alarmed. But then I saw the way that Oscar looked at me in the same way he has always done, which is to say directly through me—"

"That would be unnerving."

"In the beginning, yes. Quite. But in that moment, a sort of peace settled over me, calming the spiraling storm before it could sweep me away with worry. And then I remembered who I am," she said with a flippant shrug, concealing the fact that this one moment caused a monumental shift inside of her.

"Most annoying sister in the world?" Thea supplied sweetly, batting her lashes.

She laughed and took her sister's hand, noticing the worry beneath the dry humor. "I am one of many Hartley women capable of overcoming any obstacle. Like Mother has always said, 'We are made of ether and iron, the heavens and earth.' And whatever waits beneath these bandages, nothing will alter that."

She thought of Ernest, then of Mother. And she wondered if Roxana Hartley had always possessed such resilience or whether it was a skill she'd had to learn?

Something inside Honoria knew the answer. "Where is our mother, by the by?"

"Having tea in the rose garden with the widows. She brought over cakes and biscuits, in hopes of procuring some of the famed rose honey. Apparently, they've shared a good portion with Mrs. Brown, who has been selling out of Dunnelocke honey buns every day."

"I had no idea. That was rather sweet of them to share," she said. And she had a sense that Oscar had had a hand in this. "If they aren't careful, people will start to like them, and then where will they be?"

Her sister laughed as Honoria lifted her hand to gingerly touch the back of her head where it had begun to itch again. She was trying to be good and ignore it, just as the doctor suggested, but all she wanted to do was rip off the bandages and dig her fingernails into her scalp.

Frustrated that the instant she lightly scratched one spot, the itch would move to another, she dropped her hand to whip back the coverlet. "Thea, I need your assistance, but I must swear you to secrecy."

A pair of fabric shears slid out from her sister's pocket. "I came prepared, just in case."

⚯

EVER SINCE MR. Price had gone—and good riddance to him—Oscar had taken over the duties of the lord of the manner.

He knew from his tutelage under Rowan Warring that a gentleman's main goal was to ensure the longevity of his estate and produce an heir who would take on those duties one day. And yet—after visiting tenant farms; collecting rents; looking over the fields of wheat, barley and beans; learning about a potential problem of sheep rot, which he planned to research as soon as he found a book on it in the library; and hearing an earful about complaints and troubles that Mr. Price hadn't dealt with for years—Oscar didn't know when a gentleman was supposed to have the time to find, woo and bed the lady of the manor in order to produce the heirs for which he was trying to provide.

Oscar had pondered this conundrum several times over. But as soon as his mind pictured Honoria as the lady of the manor, brightening every room and leaving that sunlight-and-biscuits scent wherever she walked, he hated Vandemere all over again.

The promise he'd made to find him was like a knife twisting in his gut.

But Vandemere wasn't here yet. Oscar was.

So the first spare moment he was able to find, he went to visit Honoria.

When he rapped on her door, the maid informed him that she was in the bath.

The floor nearly dropped out from under him at the mention, the images swimming through his mind so heady that he had to prop his hand against the wall. And when the maid stifled a knowing giggle as she went back to her task, he realized he'd neglected to shield his cards.

The skills he'd learned as a gambler were slipping already. That was alarming. He was going to need those to be sharp again soon.

He forced his thoughts away from Honoria. A very naked Honoria . . . in a soaking tub . . . with scented oils . . . and those oh-so-inquisitive fingers she'd once told him about . . .

Then again, perhaps he should just go up to his bedchamber and think about it for a few minutes, in depth, just to take the edge off.

It was his own fault. He'd been leaving a Queen of Hearts card on her breakfast tray each morning and promising to collect on it later. But they'd never had a single moment alone. So with all these uncollected kisses compiling each day, his need to feel her lips on his had grown into something just short of madness.

Nearly at the stairs, he was just rounding the corner when the nurse hailed him.

"Good day, Lord Vandemere," she said with a smile, and he returned the greeting. "I was just on my way back to her ladyship's sitting room with this. I thought you might enjoy reading from another one of your father's books of poetry."

With his mind preoccupied, it took a moment for him to realize what she held up in front of him. But at the recognition of the slim red volume, Oscar went still. "Another?"

"Aye. Her ladyship has three of his books in her private collection. I thought you knew." When he took out his battered copy from the inner pocket of his coat, she issued a sorrowful smile. "Doubtless you thought the books were destroyed with all of his other things."

"I'd only heard that portraits and papers were destroyed."

She shook her head slowly. "Such a sad day for us all, especially for her ladyship. The late Lord Vandemere was in a tirade. You see, he'd chosen your father's bride. Said he was to marry an heiress, for the good of the family. But when Master Titus refused and married for love instead, your grandad just couldn't forgive him. Though, I suspect he didn't know about the books because your father was clever and kept his name out of them. Had them printed just for her ladyship, he did."

Oscar didn't allow himself to express the tumult of shock sprinting through him. And he couldn't simply ask if Titus Fairfax had written this. But comparing the two, it was obvious that—if his had been on a shelf for all these years instead of inside a pocket, day in and day out—the books would look identical.

"Show me," he said.

She beamed. "Right this way, my lord."

A few minutes later, Oscar stood in a drafty tower room and stared at a narrow bookcase with two other volumes. Four in all. Four books all written by Titus Fairfax.

It finally answered one question, but he still didn't know why or how his own father had attained the volume of *Awildian Palace.*

Not until he turned his head and saw the miniature hanging beside the mantel. And for the second time, the floor tipped and seemed to give way beneath his feet.

A miniature that held a face similar to the one that Oscar remembered from his childhood. "Did you know this man?"

"Aye. I was just starting as a housemaid at the time that Master Titus was still here, but I remember him."

"And are you sure . . . are you absolutely certain that this isn't a Fairfax cousin of some sort?"

She issued a soft laugh as if she thought he was a bit addlepated. "As you know, there are no male cousins in the family at all."

Oscar drew in a breath. Shook his head to clear it. And yet, no matter how many times he blinked he couldn't discount the fact that Titus Fairfax and John Flintridge could have passed for brothers.

He was already reaching up to study the miniature closer when he saw his hand shake. He lowered it again. Curling his fingers into his palm, he felt the weight of the onyx ring.

He had to ask. Had to know. "The earrings in the dowager viscountess's portrait. What happened to them?"

"The earrings?" She blinked, confused. Then her index finger pointed to the ceiling. "Aye. I remember it now. That was how it all began. Master Titus had sent a letter to his mother announcing his marriage. Her ladyship, in turn, sent him her earrings as a wedding gift to his bride. Oh, but when his lordship discovered what she had done for a son that he'd disowned, he flew into a rage. Such a sad day," she repeated, clucking her tongue.

Whenever he'd asked Cardew where he'd gotten the ring, his response was the same as it had always been: that he'd won it in a game of cards from a stranger.

Was Titus Fairfax that stranger who'd gambled it away?

The book. The ring. And now the similarities to the likeness in the miniature. Oscar shook his head, trying to make sense of it, much in the same way that he followed a hand of cards, calculating the next one played.

Perhaps this was just another in a series of coincidences. Or perhaps . . .

He didn't finish the thought. Not even a whisper. And yet, the ghost of it, a mere shadow flitted briefly like a filmy cloud crossing the moon, and he wondered if possibly . . .

"It left her ladyship's poor heart in tatters, it did. But when the first of your mum's letters arrived, she started to have hope."

He blinked. "Letters?"

"Went on for years, it did. They would arrive around your birthday. Lady Fairfax kept them tucked away in this box behind the—" The nurse stopped short when she opened the lid of the small casket, secreted away at the back of the shelf, and found it empty. "Well now, that's strange. Thought for sure they were here. I read them to her myself shortly before your arrival."

Her brow knitted, and her gaze turned distracted as she quietly retraced her steps.

First the misplaced ledgers and now missing letters?

To Oscar, it seemed that there was something more going on than three suspicious widows who believed he was a charlatan.

Chapter Thirty-Two

꩜

THEY WALKED THROUGH the garden after dinner. In the gloaming, clouds rolled up from the horizon like waves foaming onto a pale shore. The sky glowed silver, reminding Honoria of the color Oscar's eyes turned when he kissed her and his pupils spilled darkly.

Of course, she was forced to use her memory on this because he hadn't actually kissed her in nearly a week.

"We can turn back if you're tired," Oscar said, misinterpreting her sigh of frustration.

She fixed a smile in place beneath her bandages. "All I've done is lie about. If I don't stretch my legs, I'm likely to sprout roots."

"If you're certain."

"Oh, I'm certain."

He slid her a glance when her words came out a little testier than she'd intended. Then again, she hadn't really tried to hide it. Since he'd been so distracted all evening, she was sure he wouldn't notice.

She blew out a breath that was instantly snatched away by the breeze. "Very well, I am tired. But not the way you mean. I'm tired of being treated as if I'm made of glass. I'm tired of being under constant guard by the maidservants. And I'm tired of no one believing me when I tell them I feel fine."

"Anything else?"

"Yes, as a matter of fact." She stopped walking long

enough to jab her index finger in the center of his chest. "I'm tired of never collecting on those cards you leave on my tray each morning."

Those eyes darkened to match the sky as he stared at her. His nostrils flared on a breath as he took a step closer . . . just as rain-bearing clouds sent down a warning rumble.

Whatever he might have done in that moment was cast aside as the first drops of rain hit, sizzling against the torches on the lit path. "We should return to the abbey."

"The storm is miles off yet. Let's stay out just a bit longer. I feel as though I've just escaped prison and this is my first time—"

Before she could finish, the sky opened up in a deluge.

Oscar took her hand, and they dashed to the nearest shelter. Which wasn't much of a shelter at all, but more of a ruins with rows of empty window arches, framed in the same gray stone that formed the abbey. As they stepped inside the gaping doorway, she looked up at the vaulted ceiling—or at least, what must have once been a ceiling. The towering buttresses were blackened, scorched where there must have been a fire, and gave the overall appearance of the rib cage of a giant beast that had roamed the earth eons ago.

"What is this place?" she asked, feeling the need to whisper even as the rain still followed them, making the stone beneath her feet slippery.

"A century ago, it was the layman's chapel until a fire destroyed nearly everything flammable. Come. There seems to be shelter beneath the apse."

He guided her toward the domed niche at the far end and up three steps until they were inside the cozy, rounded space. The heavy downpour of rain faded to distant applause, and the air seemed to hold the faint tinge of incense.

Another growl of thunder sounded, followed by a flash of lightning that illuminated the mosaic tiles overhead. And peeking through the charred mat of smoke and age, white quartz glinted like stars, hanging above them in their own little heaven.

Smiling, she turned to Oscar only to find him frowning down at her.

"Damn. I shouldn't have taken you so far from the house. You're wet. Your bandages are—"

"A nuisance," she said, taking his hand that she still held and lifting it to her bandages. "Go on. Remove them."

"I shouldn't."

Sensing a resurgence of his recently developed overprotective nature, she did her best not to roll her eyes. "I want you to. Besides, I might catch a chill if you don't."

In the pale lavender light, his eyes held hers with steady assurance. His movements were tentative, careful in a way that made her heart ache.

She'd purposely avoided any such pains relating to the heart. Then again, that hadn't been difficult, because she'd never been plagued by moths with anyone else. But with Oscar, it was as though someone had lit a candle inside her and there was no way to blow it out.

She felt her lungs tighten, her breaths shallow and quick. And the beats of her heart were too fast and climbing higher. It seemed that the slower he went, the faster and higher her heart climbed. She tried to swallow it down, to keep it from reaching a terrifying pinnacle. To keep it from stumbling over the edge and out of her control.

He brushed his thumb across the lips he'd just uncovered. "I've never known anyone like you, Honoria. So bold and brave. I've admired the woman beneath all this wrapping from the very beginning."

"Even with my mustachios?" she asked, hardly able to breathe from all the feelings strangling her.

The corner of his mouth lifted as he continued to expose her. "Especially then. But, alas, you will never be the perfect woman without a large, hairy, mo—"

He stopped the instant he saw the mole that Thea had helped her glue to her cheek earlier.

Oscar threw back his head and laughed, the sound tipping her over that terrifying edge she refused to name.

Her heart felt so close to bursting that she was afraid she would die from it. Nervous, she started to ramble. "The doctor was being overly cautious over a little scratch, and it annoyed me that he saw only the flaw, that he had the gall to think that I would be so devastated by it that I'd have to shield my entire face."

"He was an idiot," Oscar said, coasting his lips over the small arching cut over her left eyebrow. A cut that almost mirrored the thin scar that he'd received from the chandelier. "You are so much more."

Then he kissed her lips so tenderly that she felt dizzy from it.

"You're shivering," he said. He shrugged out of his coat to settle it over her shoulders and tilted up her chin so that she would look at him. "What's the matter?"

Not wanting him to read all her cards—a lady deserved some secrets, after all—she executed a perfectly flippant shrug, drawing his coat closer around her. "Nothing. Though, I could ask the same of you, considering you've been rather distracted all evening. Some women might take offense."

"I've been thinking about you," he said in a serious manner that instantly riled her.

"I'm through with being coddled. There's nothing wrong with—"

"About what you would be like as lady of the manor."

Her breath caught, lodging in her throat, her pulse hammering in place with rapid tap-tap, tap-taps.

"I know what you're thinking," he continued as he tucked a curling tendril behind her ear. And she closed her eyes, leaning her cheek into his palm, glad that at least one of them knew. "You're wondering who the lord of the manor would be, the man standing by your side . . . sharing your bed."

She swallowed, picturing it. Picturing him.

"And I was distracted this evening because I could only imagine one man living that life with you."

He moved closer now, his nearness imploring her to open her eyes.

Honoria kept them closed, too afraid to let him see. Too afraid that he would see her falling end over end. Too afraid that he would catch her and hold her and she would never want him to let her go.

After a minute, he spoke again, his tone nonchalant as his free hand stroked her arm in soothing passes. "But it was just an errant thought. A thought that you would never entertain. Isn't that right?"

"I never wanted a life like that." Hating the threadiness in her voice, she dared herself to open her eyes. Dared herself to be honest. *Mostly.* "But if I had—ever thought about it, that is—I might have pictured you."

This time, *his* breath caught.

He didn't say anything for a moment. They just stood together in the stillness that fell around them, the rain like a curtain blotting out the rest of the world.

As she watched his chest rise and fall as he searched her gaze, she discovered that saying the words didn't scare her as much as she'd thought they would. Because she knew she wasn't alone in this.

"And in this imaginary life," he said, "would you kiss me good-night?"

Smiling, she rose up on her toes, cupped his face in her hands and pressed her lips softly, lingeringly to his. "Like this?"

"Yes. Just like that."

"I might," she said, feeling a sense of feminine power when he blew out a long, shaky breath. So she kissed him again, slanting her mouth beneath his.

His hand slid to her nape, and the kiss went from sweet to simmering in two heartbeats. A low sound vibrated in his throat, too quiet to be a growl, too hungry to be a mewl. It told her that he'd been needing this, too. Craving it. And yet, all these days, he'd masked this passion. The cad. Oh, but she quickly forgave him as his tongue licked into her mouth, searching and deep, making her come to life the way only he could do.

His lips trailed down her neck, his tongue skating down to the vulnerable pulse. "And would you let me kiss you here?"

She arched her neck to allow him better access. "Yes. As long as you did it just like that."

"Such a demanding lady of the manor." He smiled against her skin. His hands skimmed along her back, roving and possessive, drawing her against his frame. "And what if I told you that you look delectable this evening? All dressed in red like a berry ready to burst from your skin."

"I should say that you were too bold."

He chuckled, low and devious as if he heard her lack of conviction. She liked him bold, and he knew it. "If you were mine, I'd do so many wicked things."

His lips charted a path along the edge of exposed skin above the beribboned bodice. The fabric of her gown loosened, slipping down her shoulders as he slid the buttons free. And with one deft tug, the red silk gaped, exposing the creamy swells of her breasts rising above her corset.

She gasped, reflexively trying to lift the fabric to cover herself, even as her heart raced with wild excitement. "What if someone followed us?"

That devilish grin made an appearance as he lowered her hands, gently shackling her wrists with his fingers and drawing them behind her back. He held them both with one hand, while the other slowly traced the line of her corset, gooseflesh rising in its wake. "There's no one out here but us. And the lord of the manor has been waiting all night to have you to himself. He thinks you wore this dress on purpose to torment him."

Hearing the raw rasp in his voice, she thought he didn't sound like they were still playing their game of pretend, but like a man barely holding on to control. Even so, as she squirmed beneath his touch, she noticed that she could easily escape him . . . *if* she chose to.

For the moment, however, fleeing was the last thing on her mind as he bent his head to take her lips again. Branding her with his kiss, his hand stole beneath her corset and chemise to cup the weight of her breast, kneading the swell. Her flesh felt ripe and tender, her nipple taut with aching.

Then he nudged the gusseted cups lower. Bending his head, he closed his mouth over her flesh, laving the tender peak and drawing it deeper into his mouth with a firm, wet tug.

Her pulse quickened as he suckled her, and a helpless mewl tore from her throat as he raked his teeth over the tormented tip. She had never felt so alive, so present in her body. She felt every flick of his tongue, every scandalous kiss. And when he repeated the torture on her other breast, she was almost certain she could shatter even if he didn't touch her anywhere else.

"Not yet," he said, lifting his head to press a quick kiss against her lips.

"But how did you—?"

He grinned. "Because your legs are quivering, the way they do right before you come apart. I'd better sit you down before you fall."

And with that, he released her wrists and set his hands on her waist to lift her onto the flat stone altar, smooth as marble.

Stepping between her thighs, he took her mouth again in a kiss that ignited her blood, heating it, sending it throbbing in low liquid pulses where her skirts bunched between them. His hand brushed her hem, encircled her ankle, the touch sending a lick of fire up along her inner calf and thigh.

He traced the scroll embroidery of her stocking, coasting higher to her knee, to her garter ribbons and the bare flesh just beneath the lace cuffs of her drawers.

"Are you wet for me, Honoria?" he asked against her lips as his fingers skated in leisurely patterns along her inner thigh. "Have you thought about me touching you when you're alone in your bath?"

She couldn't catch her breath when he spoke to her in that scandalous manner. Every word elicited a wanton thrumming of the pulse between her legs.

He clucked his tongue softly, his gaze gleaming rakishly. "That's quite a telling blush."

"And what about you?" she asked, half-reeling, half-embarrassed. "Are you going to claim that you haven't thought of me . . . in that regard?"

"Having you, tasting you, is all I can think about."

Discovering the damp saturation of cambric near the opening, he made a guttural sound. His fingertips brushed the dewy curls. And she was so sensitive that even the light touch had her neck arching back on a gasp.

"*Yes*," she rasped.

All amusement fled from his countenance, replaced by unadulterated lust and the promise of intent as his kisses trailed down. He groaned as his hungry gaze feasted on her. With his shoulders in the way, she couldn't close her legs, but an unexpected rise of shyness compelled her to cover her sex.

But he took her hands and lifted them away. "Don't. You're absolutely perfect, like the plump petals of a flower, glistening with dew. And I"—he drew in a deep breath, a hum of pleasure in his throat—"I am a man dying of thirst."

Before she knew what to expect, his mouth opened over her cleft. A choked cry filled the night air as his tongue flattened against her, rising in one . . . thorough . . . lick. Then he hummed again, the vibration against the sensitive bud, flicking it lightly and sending a spear of sensation spiraling through her.

"I knew you would taste like ambrosia," he murmured as if to himself, then inhaled her scent deeply, his throat issuing another hum of approval. "I've been wanting to do this for weeks now. Tasting you, having you, is all I can think . . ."

His words trailed off as he opened his mouth over that private juncture again, his tongue searing along the swollen seam. The kiss was hot and wicked, and if anyone should come upon them in this ruin shielded only by a curtain of rain, her reputation would be destroyed. They would have to marry. But as his mouth ate softly into her flesh and his finger nudged inside her eager sheath, she didn't care. In this moment, she was a wanton goddess with ambrosia in her veins. So she let him feast on her.

She looked down, her bared breasts trussed up high beneath the folded cups of her corset. And lower, beyond the shelf of her skirts, her hands threaded in his curling dark hair as her hips tilted against the carnal flicks and swirls of his tongue and the skilled plunges of his finger.

Then two fingers pushed into the snug channel, and her head fell back on a moan. He was doing that thing again, hooking his fingers to rub that sensitive place on the upper wall, and she couldn't stop the garbled sounds of pleasure rising from her throat.

Lost to the moment, she lifted her hands to her breasts, pressing, kneading to ease the ache. She heard him curse, felt his heated gaze on her.

"Don't. Stop," he commanded, his eyes fever bright, his mouth wet . . . from her.

That only heightened her pleasure and made her feel more alive. So she didn't stop. Instead, she fondled and caressed her flesh. Pinching her nipples between her thumb and forefinger, she felt her body clench around his fingers.

He cursed again and greedily ate at her sex. Watching her, he suckled the ripe bud, her pleasure gathering in swirling tingles, collecting until she thought she might burst from her skin. Then he raked it with his teeth and, suddenly, her back arched on a gasp that rose to the vaulted ceiling. Chasing the rhythm of his thrusting fingers, her body convulsed on liquid spasms as his tongue replaced his fingers, darting inside, drawing out every ounce of her pleasure.

By the time he stood between her thighs, she felt drunk and boneless, grateful for his arms surrounding her.

She clung to him as she fought to catch her breath and felt the turgid length of him pressed against her.

His hand slid between them, fumbling with his fastenings. Then, for whatever reason, he stopped. Just stopped.

He lowered his forehead to hers. "We should return to the abbey."

"Now?"

"It's what a gentleman would do," he claimed, but the raw strain in his voice made it sound as if the words were being dragged kicking and screaming over gravel.

Then she understood. Honoria didn't know whether or not she should be offended or laugh in his face.

Neither, she decided and reached for his fastenings. "We both know that you are no gentleman."

"I should at least . . . make an attempt to be." But his eyes were glazed as he looked from her lips to her breasts to her parted thighs.

"Oscar, our game is not solitaire."

His lips parted as if he had a point to make, but whatever he planned to say came out on a strangled groan when her hand slid over his hard, heated flesh.

She marveled at her discovery, wishing she had better light to study him. But since she didn't, she chose to confine her thorough exploration to what she could feel as she maneuvered him through the opening.

"Your skin is scorching. Smooth as satin but impossibly

hard and so . . ." Big. Much bigger than she expected, she thought as her fingers wrapped around his girth. Or *attempted* to, rather. She swallowed down a rise of nerves as questions of capacity and choreography sprang to mind. "I had a notion that you would feel like a puppet."

"A *what*?" he rasped as her inquisitive investigation glided higher to the velvety crown, and she felt his fingers flex on her hips. His jaw was clenched, eyes closed tightly as if he were trying to focus on a complex equation.

"Never mind," she murmured against his mouth.

Tasting herself on his skin, she hesitated there. Then curiosity outweighed any trepidation. This was the taste of her desire, of the pleasure he'd coaxed from her body. A primitive thrill quickened her pulse when she kissed him again, wondering what *he* would taste like. What would it be like to kiss every single inch of him?

It wasn't until he groaned again that she realized she'd voiced that question aloud. And beneath her palm, she felt an intriguing flutter travel up the length of his shaft before he eased her hand away.

"It'll surely be solitaire if you continue, and a short game at that." He stepped between her thighs. Let out a hiss when the turgid heat of him met the slick heat of her. "We can . . . still go back . . . if you've changed your mind."

As he spoke, he slid his length down her swollen seam. A slow, decadent downward sweep, drawing her wetness up along the intimate path to tease the bundle of nerves beneath the hood of her sex.

Her breath hitched, her body clenching on nothing as he continued to torment her.

How could he make her feel so empty, so needy, when she'd been a pile of sated mush just a moment ago? The cad really wasn't playing fair.

Her fingers smoothed the damp locks from his forehead. "There's no going back, not for us. I want this. I want you, Oscar. Only you."

His exhale fanned across her lips in a rush. Then he took her mouth, claiming her lips, taking what she willingly surrendered.

The kiss seemed to encompass all they shared. It wasn't only fire, passion and hunger, but need. The need to touch, to taste, to fill and be filled. They were living, fully alive, here in this moment because sometimes that was all one had. So she gave herself over to the kiss and to him, wanting him all the more.

His shaft nudged the entrance of her body, edging inside. She bit her bottom lip at the burning sting of flesh stretched taut. Then he eased back on a gruff grunt. "You're so . . . snug . . ."

She was fairly certain that *her* dimensions were not the issue, but she kept her opinion to herself and braced for another attempt. He edged in a little more, her body clamping tight as if to expel him.

When he withdrew again, his breath was shaky. He was being so tender, so gentle with her that she knew this was more than just pleasure for pleasure's sake. This was more. Something greater that she didn't care to name even as her heart thudded with the answer.

"I want . . . want to make this good for you. But I need to . . . just this once . . ."

All at once, he thrust deep. She sank her teeth into his shoulder to stifle her cry, her flesh rending, stretching.

He held still as if in shock, as if he were the one who'd been impaled by one of the marble columns of the Parthenon. "Honoria, are you . . . Is this . . ."

She knew what he was asking, could hear the strangled strain in his voice. And she couldn't bear to tell him that she was being ripped apart. That it was too much and she was too full, her body struggling to accommodate him.

So she held him tighter, nodding against his cravat. "Good. So good."

Thankfully, the man who usually read her like no other

seemed too preoccupied to catch her in her lie. At least, that's what she thought until she heard him expel a low cough of amusement.

"I've no doubt that we are both clutching opposite ends of the same thread of agony. But I promise you, Signore"—he slid his hand to her nape and his dark eyes met hers— "before I'm through, I will deliver you to ecstasy."

Clearly convinced of his own prowess, he kissed her, long and deep. She, on the other hand, still clung to a few threads of doubt. And yet, she acknowledged that the pain had already ebbed. All that remained was the fullness, the grip of flesh surrounding flesh, of velvet over steel.

He began to move in shallow, languid thrusts, hips undulating against hips in a way that rubbed against that one place that sent a rush of liquid tingles down her spine, collecting low.

Her breath hitched. She felt something inside her give, yield to his patient rhythm. Felt his lips curl into a grin. Why, that smug scoundrel!

But she could hardly be mad at him for this. Even so, she hated being bested at any game. And with them, everything was a game where the winner took all.

He whispered, "Take me in . . . yes, sweet . . . let me have you . . ."

The rasp in his voice, the raw urgency made her body clench tighter around him as if to soothe him. The taut friction sent a sizzle of sensation through her, coiling deep, pleasure building on pleasure. She wanted to make this last, to hold on to him forever. When she tightened her inner walls around the welcome invasion again, he groaned, his rhythm breaking. It was that sound, the desperation to hold back from reaching the summit, that sent her soaring over the edge on a helpless cry.

He held on, driving in and in and in as she quaked around him. Only then, only when the very last tremor faded, did he withdraw. His arm moved in rapid jerks, his shoulders hunched as a guttural groan tore from his throat, and she felt the shock of heat coat her inner thigh.

He staggered against her, and she held on, clinging to him, her heart beating in wild disarray as she trembled. Then tears tumbled down her cheeks for reasons she couldn't quite explain. And she was thoroughly disgusted with herself for sniffling, her breath stuttering.

He put his hands on her shoulders, drew back and cursed, worry knitting his brow as his lips brushed away the dampness collecting on her lashes. "Forgive me. I was too rough. I was too—"

"It isn't pain. I mean, I expected something of that nature. But I didn't know how altered I'd feel afterward," she admitted shyly. "Or how much I already miss having you inside of me. It's just . . . new, I suppose."

He slid his arms around her, and he pressed his lips to her hair, his fingers stroking her bare skin.

It was ridiculous how much Honoria loved the way he looked at her. No, not *loved*, she thought, her heart stumbling in panic. She *enjoyed* the way he looked at her. This happy contentment wasn't love, she assured herself. It was simply the joy of being alive, of living her life to the fullest.

She pulled him closer, enveloping herself in this wonderful *not love* she was in.

Chapter Thirty-Three

That night, Oscar paced the length of his chamber for hours, in a wrestling bout between the man he'd always been and the man he thought he should be.

A gentleman, he decided, wouldn't plot a path to Honoria's bed. Wouldn't think of skulking down the servants' stairs to the floor below. Or imagine keeping to the shadows of the winding corridors in case Babette might be returning from a tryst with Cardew. Or know exactly which creaking floorboards to avoid outside Millicent's chamber. And he certainly wouldn't steal into Honoria's bedchamber with every intention of pleasuring her in a plethora of wicked ways.

A gentleman would be reprimanding himself for losing control in the first place, for behaving like the randy jackanapes who'd taken her on an old stone altar out of doors. A gentleman would feel guilty, if not sated. He certainly wouldn't be craving her like the desert craved rain.

But the man Oscar was could only think about the taste of her, the feel, the scent of her that still lingered on his hands and might very well be the cause of his death by asphyxiation if he continued to cover his face and breathe her in.

Lowering those hands, he walked to the door, curled a fist around the knob.

He told himself that he was only going to bid her goodnight. Press a kiss to her forehead. Perhaps lie next to her for a moment or two, just to hold her.

But he didn't believe his own lying arse for an instant.

He could already imagine all the machinations. The soft words. The *I only want to hold you* ploy. Followed by the *I just want to make* you *feel good* massage.

Oh, he knew all his own tricks. Bloody scoundrel.

But gentleman or not, Oscar wouldn't be the kind of man who'd use her twice in a single night. She'd been a virgin, after all, and her tender flesh would need time to heal.

So he released the doorknob, his ring scraping over the brass with a snick.

He looked down at it, wondering, speculating as he crossed the room again and sat on the edge of his bed.

The book. The miniature. The missing letters. And this ring. They were like cards in a deck: the Ace, the King, the Queen, and the Jack.

He still didn't know what the next card would be. Still didn't know if this was all nothing more than a coincidence. Or if John Flintridge and Titus Fairfax were one and the same.

Though, surely, his mother would have told him if that were the case. Especially if he was heir to an estate. And Cardew would have mentioned something as well. He certainly wouldn't have been chasing John Flintridge for the last twenty years if he'd known the man was dead.

Which led Oscar back to being a mere charlatan, pretending to be the man betrothed to Honoria. The man who had every intention of continuing this charade for the rest of his life, if he could convince her to have him.

But what did he have to offer her?

All his life he'd been little more than a thief, and he would continue to be just that if he forced her hand. Which was the reason he hadn't spilled his seed inside her.

After she'd told him about her brother, he understood that she'd avoided romantic entanglements because she was afraid to love, to give her whole heart and risk it breaking. Having a child—his child—needed to be her choice, not his. And he would do his best to ensure it remained that way.

So he wouldn't force her hand. But if he could *win* her hand by way of her heart . . . now, that was another matter altogether.

He was fully prepared to use whatever skills he possessed to woo and pleasure her endlessly until her heart simply fell into his open palm.

And when she was ready, he would—

The lock on his door turned, jolting him.

But he'd been so distracted that he barely had time to plant one foot on the floor before he saw a chamberstick, held by the nimble fingers of a fine-boned hand, emerge through the opening.

Honoria stepped inside. Wearing nothing but a white cambric nightdress.

He swallowed. Now would be an excellent time to say something chivalrous and remind them both that he had no intention of taking her a second time in a single night, his conscience told him.

But his throat was dry as dust. In fact, speech altogether was unlikely considering that all the blood from his brain had just descended south in a great exodus of want and lust.

The door closed with a soft click as she leaned back against it. The light of the candle flame shimmered in her eyes as she studied him shrewdly. "Since I've found you still dressed in shirtsleeves and trousers, I imagine that you were considering a visit to my bedchamber. And yet, because you are sitting on your bed, you were likely dissuaded by one of those gentlemanly impulses that have been a recent affliction with you. Do I have the right of it?"

"Something to that effect."

She padded silently across the room to set her lamp on the mantel, turning in a way that made her garment transparent in the crackling glow of the fire. The tantalizing silhouettes of her curves were on full display.

His mouth watered. As his cock swelled, pressing against the front fall, he made a quick adjustment to ease the discomfort.

She slid an impish glance over her shoulder, a slow feline grin on her lips. The minx knew precisely what she was doing. "What about now? Still thinking gentlemanly thoughts?"

"I . . ." He swallowed again, the pulse thick on the side of his throat as his heart sent another glut of blood south. "It would be better for both of us if you went back."

"Hmm . . . perhaps. But there's only one problem with that plan. You see"—she paused to prowl closer, then stopped at the foot of the bed as she toyed with the little white ribbon at her throat—"I'm not finished with you, Mr. Flint."

She gave the ribbon a tug and, with a sinuous shrug, the garment slipped off her shoulders, slid down her body and pooled at her feet.

He cursed under his breath. It was unfair. No woman should be that exquisite. There ought to be a law against it.

"For four days you kept me in a pillowed prison," she said, stepping out of the fallen garment, prowling toward him. Then she paused between his spread knees, her rosy tipped breasts enticingly close to his mouth as she stroked a hand under his chin, lifting his face. "I think it's only fair that I return the favor. I am your gaoler now."

A breath left him as she bent down to kiss him. But, taking him off guard, she shoved at his shoulders so that he flopped back onto the mattress instead.

Even before her laugh of triumph . . . Even before she straddled him and her hair fell in a curtain around him . . . Even before she pressed her smiling mouth to his, he knew that he had been imprisoned by her since the very beginning. And, quite possibly, had loved her since then as well.

"Aye. You are mine." As he slid a hand to her nape to welcome her soft plundering, he vowed to make it true.

Her fingers skimmed down his throat to the open collar of his shirt, over his shoulders and chest, every touch a caress that drew sensation to the surface and heightened the desire already thumping, hard and heavy, inside of him.

So he slid his hands down the silken sleek skin of her back to the firm globes of her buttocks and urged her hips down as his own lifted, arched, pressed. A shudder moved through both of them.

She raked her teeth over his bottom lip, then shook her head. "As tantalizing as it is to feel the friction of your clothes against my skin, I would much rather feel you. All of you, for I have some plans of my own."

Obliging her efforts to tug the shirt from his trousers, he lifted it off the rest of the way and let it fall to the floor.

"And just what do you aim to do to me?"

"Wicked things." She grinned down at him as she took hold of his wrists and set his arms over his head. "Now, keep these here while I see to the rest."

She took her time, humming with approval as her hands assessed every muscle along his arms and shoulders before splaying over his chest. When she brushed her thumbs over the flat discs of his nipples, the flesh gathered to small peaks.

Emboldened by this response, she bent to kiss him there, circling him with her tongue before flicking the center, her eyes studying the way his lips parted on a breath, searching for his tell. But there was no need. He couldn't hide anything from her if he'd wanted to.

Exploring the dark furring over his chest, she observed that it formed a T of sorts with an enticing trail down the center of his abdomen. His breath caught, the ridges of his muscles rippling, as she ran a solitary fingertip down that trail, all the way to where it disappeared at the waist of his trousers.

"You are being an exceptional prisoner," she mused as she outlined the shape of him. "But what, do you suppose, should I do about this?"

With plenty of ideas of his own, he began to lift his arms to surround her.

"Uh, uh, uh," she said, clucking her tongue as she set his arms back against the coverlet once more. "Not yet."

But her actions put her breast in proximity far too tempting for him to resist. So he didn't. And when he took the tender, ruched flesh into his mouth and suckled her, she arched her back on a gasp and let him feast. After a moment, she fed him the other.

Then she kissed him again, her hands still locked on his wrists, her luscious curves fitting the hard planes of his body like wax melting in the sun. And when the heat of her sex pressed against the engorged flesh restrained behind the front fall, a deep groan of yearning vibrated in his throat.

She made her way down his body. Worked the fastenings free. Explored him at length as she looked up at him through her lashes. But there was still something innocent in the way she regarded him. The flush of heat on her cheeks was not only from her desire but from shyness.

But the woman he knew, the woman who'd dared to come into his chamber, who'd dared to dress like a man or a servant to live a life of her choosing, the woman who had every intention of being in control, likely didn't want to admit that she was uncertain and didn't know how to proceed.

"As your prisoner, I would beg you to wrap your hand around the base . . . yes, like that . . . and a long, smooth stroke . . . aye, that's the way," he gritted, eyes screwing shut from exquisite pleasure. "And if you would but take me into your—"

He broke off, his back bowing as he felt the wet heat of her tongue, her mouth closing around the head of his cock. A shower of sparks traveled down his spine, gathering in a tight coil deep inside him, wanting release.

"Mmm . . . You taste like salt," she murmured as her pink tongue flicked the glossy dew at the tip.

Sweat beaded on his brow, his fists gripping the coverlet as her innocent ministrations continued. Hers was a simple exploration, but she was wholly absorbed in her task, trailing kisses down his shaft, gliding her tongue all the way up his length before taking him into her mouth again. And he was dying from pleasure, his throat constricting on choked sounds he couldn't contain.

In response, she moaned against his flesh, suckling him and swirling her tongue in a way that nearly sent him over the edge.

Unable to withstand any more without embarrassing himself, he drew her up and sealed his mouth to hers. As his hand delved between their bodies, he found that she was already wet and swollen from wanting.

He laid her flat on her back. With her arms above her head, he threaded their hands together. Then he entered her, the passage warm and slick but still impossibly tight.

Mindless from the pleasure of it, he thrust deep, filling her until he was buried to the hilt. Then he cursed himself for being too rough and held still, whispering endearments and contrition against her lips. "I'm a brute."

"No. This is better," she panted. "I felt too empty . . . aching for you."

The words were like oil on a hearth fire, adding flames to an already potent desire, but also kindling a new hope within him. They could have a life like this, he thought. All he had to do was convince her, wear her down if he must.

So when their mouths met again, tongues twining, Oscar matched the slow, sinuous rhythm to the mating of their bodies. He took her, thrusting in and in, showing her how good it could be—would be—between them.

"Then, wrap your legs around me and take more. Take all of me," he murmured, low in her ear and felt her heart quicken under his.

Tentatively, she vined her legs around his waist and gasped, neck arching as the position drew him deeper still.

He felt the change in her, the grip and pull of her body as he drove in, drove her to the first rise, then slowed again, drawing back on a mewl of protest.

He plundered her mouth and took her to another rise, higher, closer. Then slowed again, feeling her body tremble with unleashed desire.

He was shaking, too, restraint balanced on a knife's edge. But when he began another climb, another rise to the summit, her hips tilted, lifting to meet thrust after thrust. A garbled plea fell from the lips she coasted over his jaw, seeking his mouth with hers.

He felt it coming over her, ready to break apart. "Look at me."

And as their eyes met, her body arched and shattered on a hoarse cry.

Her pleasure went on and on, rippling around him in a torrent of spasms, nearly taking him over the edge. But he held on through the last tremor before he wrenched himself out of her body and spilled in volcanic rivulets, before collapsing to the side and pulling her, breathless, against him.

Within minutes, Miss I'm Not Finished with You was fast asleep. And he soon discovered that she burned as hot as a blacksmith's forge as she slept, her body draped half over his own and her head nestled on his chest. But he didn't mind. After all, she'd scorched the inside of him the night they'd met; why not let her brand the outside, as well?

Smiling from sheer contentment—whether he deserved it or not—he pressed his lips to the wild disarray of her flaxen hair and breathed in her baked-in-sunlight scent. She shifted, curling around him, her hand drifting to cover his heart as she let out a sleepy sigh.

"Nee too mah mimms," she murmured incoherently, but he understood it as her need for two more minutes of sleep.

He chuckled softly to himself. Tracing the outer edges of her fingers, over the neatly manicured tips, he remembered something his mother had once said. *Love is a flame*

*in the palm of your hand. It can warm or blister. But if you
snuff it out, it could be gone forever. So you keep the flame
alight no matter how much it burns.*

Hers, he knew, had been a one-sided love with his father. He had been remote and distant to her in ways that
he'd never been to Oscar. In ways that he'd never understood. And when his father had left them both, the pain
he'd caused had turned those short happy memories into
bitter ones.

Yet, even through all the suffering that followed, she
had still loved John Flintridge until her last breath.

Oscar had never comprehended her utterly foolish devo-
tion to a man he'd come to hate. But if what she'd felt for
his father was even half of what he felt for Honoria, then he
might have an inkling, after all.

He only hoped that his wasn't one-sided.

Not long after, she stirred awake on a sound that was part
hum, part snort. And when she lifted her head and shoved
back a fall of disheveled hair from her blinking eyes, he saw
a glistening drop of drool at the corner of her mouth.

Without putting on any airs, she swiped at it with the
back of her hand. "How long was I sleeping?"

"A full day. Everyone in the abbey knows, and we'll
have to marry. It's an anvil wedding for us, I'm afraid," he
said with a put-upon sigh as he tucked a lock of hair behind
her ear.

She rolled her eyes. "Think you're amusing, do you?"

"I have my moments." He kept his response nonchalant with a lift of his shoulders. But in his mind, he noted
that her usual alarm—that look of a rabbit flushed from a
warren—was absent from her face.

Did he dare hope that she might be leaning toward the
idea of a life with him?

"This isn't one of them," she said flatly and glanced to
the mantel clock herself, missing the way he shook his head
in answer to his own question. "I should leave soon. Return

to my own bed. The problem is, you've turned my limbs to jelly. And you're terribly comfortable."

"I should be flogged for these crimes."

"At the very least," she said, turning back to grin at him through her lashes.

As she remained draped over him, he stroked lightly down her back and wanted a life like this so badly he could taste it. Not stolen moments. He was tired of being a thief. He wanted a whole life, where he belonged to her and she to him.

Yet, for now, he would take whatever she willingly gave. And told himself that he still had time to woo her.

Lifting his other hand, she studied the jagged scar between his thumb and wrist.

"First attempt at pickpocketing," he answered to her silent query. "I was so frightened of being caught that I didn't pay attention to where I was going. Which, as it happened, was directly into the path of a better pickpocket who snatched the satchel from me with such force it nearly wrenched my arm clean off. But I held on as long as I could. The pain served as an excellent motivator to hone my craft."

She pressed her lips there as if to heal it, even after all these years. "And were you good after that?"

"Aye. But I always felt guilty, taking what didn't belong to me. So I chose my marks with care, stealing only from the wealthy nodcocks who flaunted their status while demeaning those around them," he said distractedly as she shifted over him, trailing kisses along his chest. "But I was grateful when I learned how to gamble. Because then, at least, men knew that they might lose. It seemed . . . fair, in a way."

"As long as they didn't see the way you counted cards, you mean?"

A wry smile tugged at his mouth. "Little good it did me in Paris."

She hummed, pleased with herself. Her lips coasted over

his shoulder and to the side of his throat, lingering tenderly at the silvered edge of a crescent-shaped scar. The memory of the cut felt distant, as if her kiss were a healing balm.

He realized that was what she was doing: healing him by accepting all that he was. Every part of him, from beggar to pickpocket to gambler to charlatan to . . . whatever he was now. And if he didn't love her already, he would have fallen for her all over again.

"I heard about Mr. Price," she said as he wrapped his arms around her. "It was nice of you to intervene on behalf of the widows."

"I had little choice in the matter. He'd been stealing from them for years," he said, carefully avoiding taking any credit as he hadn't had any noble intentions when he'd nearly strangled the man.

"But you did have a choice, and you chose to help them. The Oscar Flint I used to know might have caught Price in his scheme and chosen to blackmail him. You could have turned a tidy profit, I imagine. But instead, you chose to expose him and help the dowager and the widows. That's something family does for each other."

He issued a noncommittal grunt.

"That being said, one could easily see the correlation of how assisting someone who'd never turn to you, either for reasons of pride or sheer stubbornness, is actually better for everyone involved."

His scalp prickled with a sense of warning.

He knew Honoria too well to imagine she was still talking about Mr. Price. He felt the light brush of her fingertip along the horizontal pink scar beneath his Adam's apple. And then it struck him.

Oscar stiffened. "No. Absolutely not."

"You haven't even heard my plan."

"Whatever it is, put it out of your mind. I'm not having anyone else deal with Ladrón. He is my problem."

"Because of me. If it weren't for that night in Paris—"

He silenced her by pressing his mouth to hers. "Stop. It is not your fault."

"That isn't what you said in the beginning."

"As much as I wanted to blame you, the truth was you and your nimble fingers distracted me. You ended up with the better hand. Besides, if we were to go back to that very moment, you and I both know that nothing would be different. You would still have wanted to best me, and I would still be wondering what was behind your mustachios."

"You're wrong. If I could go back, I might have . . ." She frowned, although *pouted* was more accurate.

He knew that self-blame was one of the ways she kept herself safe and hidden. But it irritated him and made him want to bash down all those walls.

"Still trying to rewrite history, I see."

"No. I'm just—"

He kissed her again, rolling on top of her. "We are writing a new page. And I, for one, would much rather be here in bed with you than tussling in the Count du Maurice's garden."

"If you don't stop kissing me to distraction when I have a point to make, we're going to have that tussle regardless," she groused, narrowing her eyes even as her body softened beneath him.

His flesh responded. As much as he knew he would enjoy her delivering on that threat, he decided that now was not the time to test the theory. They had made love twice, and any additional bedsport would likely lead to . . . well . . . more bedsport. After all, there might have been an inch of her that he hadn't yet tasted. Unlikely, but possible.

Instead of embarking on another pleasure quest, he rolled to his back, tucking her against him, and drew the coverlet over her. "Very well. What is the point you'd like to make?"

She issued a mollified sigh, then rested her head on

his shoulder, her fingers absently drawing patterns in the thicket of chest hair above his heart. "Perhaps you don't have to run."

"Forgive me, but aren't you the same woman who risked her own neck to dash over here and tell me to do just that?"

"That was in the past. As you just pointed out, there's nothing we can do about the fact that you were being an utter clodpole," she said, and her shapely behind earned a playful swat. "All we can do is hope you've come to your senses and see that there's no need to handle this on your own. You have people who care about you. People who would intervene on your behalf."

"Why, Miss Hartley, are you actually *asking* me to stay?"

She scoffed but ruined the dismissive denial by pressing her lips to his skin. Perhaps he'd made more progress than he knew.

"I'm only saying that if you let someone help you, then you wouldn't need to rush off. Not straightaway. After all, it must be exhausting, running all your life. Never having a home. But you could, perhaps, have a home here. The real Vandemere isn't knocking on the door at the moment. And perhaps"—she paused, drawing another filigree over his heart—"you and I could write more pages like this one."

Oscar knew that look. No matter how soft her words, the determination in her eyes and in the set of her jaw were clear enough to him. She was still thinking about Ladrón.

He needed to get her mind off this topic and away from danger. So he slipped the ring off his finger.

As predicted, she went still as a statue, her eyes round as saucers. He felt the hammering of her heart against his rib cage and wondered if he'd gone too far in his method of distraction.

But there was no backing down now. Even so, he was careful with his words so she wouldn't bolt for the door.

"I'd like to ask a favor of you." He heard her swallow as he turned the ring, the stones glinting in the glow of firelight. "Someone has been in my rooms recently. I'm not certain who or what they were after, but I think it might have been this. Since it was entrusted to me, I don't want anything to happen to it. I'm wondering if you would take it, keep it with you."

"I . . . I'll be going home tomorrow." She cast a nervous glance to the mantel clock. "Or rather, later this day."

He nodded. "All the better, then."

She was quiet for a moment, her expression inscrutable.

Then, without a word, she sat up and reached across him to the night table for her locket. She opened the chain's clasp, gesturing for him to slide the ring onto the chain. When that was done, she refastened the necklace and slipped it over her head.

At the moment, it likely weighed heavily on her, where it rested over her heart with the lock of her brother's hair tucked inside the locket. But it would serve its purpose.

If she were to make a plan, then let it be for a life with him.

Chapter Thirty-Four

~∞~

$\mathcal{H}$ONORIA HAD THE perfect plan. And if Oscar thought he was going to see to Ladrón himself, then he was an idiot.

Before she left Dunnelocke Abbey later that morning, she found Cardew at the main stairway, running an oiled cloth over the newly exposed mahogany railing. Though they hadn't been formally introduced, she'd seen him from a distance several times. "Mr. Cardew? I'm Honoria Hartley."

"Ignatius Cardew, at your service." With those words, he smoothly swept up her hand and bowed over it, pressing a kiss to her fingers. "I must say, you quite steal my breath and my heart. Please, do me the honor of calling me Ignatius. Or simply whisper it once, and I will dream of it for the rest of my days."

She couldn't help but smile. "You are an unrepentant charmer, Ignatius."

He closed his eyes and laid a hand over his chest. "Like angelsong. Well, then, how may I be of service?"

"If you have a moment, I should like to speak with you privately," she said, gesturing to the receiving room. Knowing that Oscar was seeing to a matter of business, she knew she only had a few minutes. So the instant Cardew stepped into the room with her, she didn't hesitate. "I want to know more about this Ladrón. It's just that I don't want Oscar to spend the rest of his life looking over his shoulder."

Cardew studied her with the acute attention of a clerk

weighing coins on a scale. Then, as if coming to a decision, he offered a nod. "I don't want that for him either. Especially since it was my own fault that put him in this mess. Ladrón never would have set his sights on the lad if not for me. And I should have known better, but it's my nature to lose all sense when it comes to women. Just as it has always been Oscar's nature to look after everyone and make it right again." He issued a self-deprecating sigh. "That night was no different. There was a debt to be paid, and he swept in and took care of it."

Her brow furrowed in confusion. "But he lost that night."

"At the Count du Maurice's palace, aye. But then he went to a gaming hell, and much to my regret, Ladrón was there. He observed the lad play, fascinated by his uncanny skill, and decided that paying the original debt wasn't enough."

"I have the money to pay him," she said, feeling a sense of rightness course through her. "I just need a way to get it into his hands. To settle the debt once and for all."

Cardew shook his head. "You don't understand, my lovely. Ladrón is a collector of things *and* people. He wants Oscar to be his latest objet d'art."

Well, if anyone could understand what it was like to be treated as an object, it was Honoria. And if this collector wanted someone to gamble and make money for him, then she would put a stop to it.

"So you're telling me that Ladrón refused to take the payment as per your agreement." When Cardew offered something of a nod, she continued, "Then, all we have to do is ensure that he does so in front of witnesses, giving him no grounds to claim the debt wasn't paid. And I have the perfect plan. That is, if you are amenable."

He studied her again, his keen gaze turning thoughtful, his forefingers sliding against the pad of his thumb as if he were rolling an imaginary cigar. "And this exchange you have in mind would be on English soil, I presume."

"Yes, of course. Right here in Addlewick," she said.

"But the thing is . . . we would have to keep it a secret from Oscar."

She proceeded to give him a brief synopsis of her plan.

He turned away, stepping over to the window. "The one time I agreed to such a bargain, my boy was taken to prison for a year. I couldn't let that happen again."

"Prison?" A shock tore through her.

And yet, she'd suspected something dark lurked in Oscar's past that he still didn't want to talk about. She'd felt it in the way he'd stiffened when her fingers encountered the scars on his back.

"Aye," Cardew answered, gazing through the panes of glass. "Her name was Josephine. The lad was sweet on her. But one day, I caught her in the company of an aristocrat who bore a grudge against Oscar, ever since losing to him at the gaming tables. Before I could tell Oscar about it, she caught up with me and tearfully explained that she'd fallen into the gentleman's debt and was forced to pay it with her body for one night. She begged me not to say anything. Promised that she loved Oscar and couldn't bear the thought of her mistake bringing him pain." He lifted his hands in a shrug. "So I kept her secret."

A hot flood of anger burned in Honoria's stomach, already surmising the rest. "But she was lying."

Cardew nodded. "The man was her protector. He wanted Oscar out of the way. And she, lured by the polish of his pedigree, had willingly colluded with him. Together, they made up a fable regarding a debt that Oscar had refused to repay. The courts sided with the aristocrat and sent Oscar to debtor's prison. When he was released, he barely had the chance to bid farewell to his dying mother."

Burning tears pricked Honoria's eyes. She swiped them away, before laying a hand on Cardew's sleeve. "I promise, on the memory of my brother, that what I'm about to ask of you is to keep Oscar from harm, not put him in the path of it."

"I'm not agreeing to anything until I've heard every detail."

By the time Honoria finished explaining the plan that she and Thea had concocted, she had Cardew's support. *Mostly.*

Tilting his head to the side in appraisal, he added, "I want something in return."

"What?"

"I want to paint you."

She'd been asked this before, countless times, but had never sat for anyone other than the family's portrait artist. The last thing she wanted was to be hung on someone's wall and gawked at for all eternity. And yet, this man loved Oscar and was willing to agree to her scheme for such a small price.

So she nodded. "Very well. If you assist me in this matter, without informing Oscar, I will let you paint me."

They shook hands. Or rather, he kissed her proffered hand, and their bargain was struck.

A minute later, she was waiting in the hall when Oscar appeared, his eyes glowing with warmth as he strode directly to her. And she was plagued with a terrible desire to stay.

She shrugged it away and smiled at him.

He instantly narrowed his gambler's eyes. "You look like a cat who's gotten into the cream. Just what are you up to?"

"I don't know what you could possibly mean," she said, sliding her arm through his and turning toward the door where Algernon waited. And she thought she'd put on a rather convincing performance because he said nothing in response to that.

The instant they were inside the carriage, however, he turned to her, their knees bumping, his expression stern. "I've taken care of the matter regarding Ladrón. Promise me you won't be interfering."

It vexed her to no end that he could see through her

pretense of innocence. With an aggrieved sigh, she nodded. And in order to keep him from seeing that her fingers were crossed behind her back, she kissed him.

⊸

THE MOMENT SHE crossed the threshold of Hartley Hall and Oscar's carriage drove away, she turned to Mr. Mosely. "Has the rehearsal begun?"

"Already in progress, miss," he said with a stoic smile. "You'll find them in the pit."

"Splendid."

A few minutes later, Honoria stepped out onto the terrace and watched the proceedings.

Because it would have been impossible to keep a plan of this magnitude a secret from her parents, she'd told them the whole of it.

Well, *mostly*.

After all, she couldn't have told them everything without revealing her own part of how this all had begun in Paris.

When Mother and Father had visited her yesterday at the abbey, shortly after she'd talked to Thea, Honoria had explained that, during his travels, Oscar had dealings with a certain art collector, one who was left . . . unsatisfied with their previous dealings.

"This collector," she'd told them, "wants reparations that are far above and beyond their original agreement." To put it mildly. "Therefore, Thea and I have come up with a way to ensure that the matter is settled once and for all."

She'd laid out the details using a three-act structure, knowing that parents like Roxana and Conchobar Hartley would appreciate how it tied together in the form of a play.

"I say it's a grand plan," her father said with a decisive nod. "That boy has had a lifetime of dealing with things on his own. It's time that he had someone intervene on his behalf."

"Precisely."

"He's family, after all."

Honoria hadn't bothered to correct them. She'd wanted to, but for a woman who was excellent at delivering a line, she hadn't been able to think of a single thing to say.

The only thought in her head had been that Oscar would be leaving. One day. His charade wouldn't be able to last forever. But when that time came, she would ensure that he wouldn't have to look over his shoulder for the rest of his life.

"He most definitely is," Mother had agreed before issuing a fretful sigh. "And when I think of Oscar losing his father at such a young age, and what Marina must have endured in his absence without having anyone to turn to, it fairly breaks my heart."

Father had put an arm around his wife and pressed a kiss to her temple. "Which is why we'll do all we can."

Seeing the way Mother turned to him and rested her head on his shoulder made Honoria grateful to have such parents. She'd always drawn comfort from their easy affection. And while she hadn't always admired—and perhaps even resented—their acceptance of whatever the Fates brought, she saw it as one of their strengths.

Which was the reason she couldn't keep the possibility of the more dangerous aspects of the plan to herself.

"There is one more thing," she'd hedged. "From what I understand, this collector fancies himself a swordsman."

"Ah. Well, then." Father had lifted a hand to pull at a frown like a man worrying his beard, and she was afraid that he would call an end to it. Then he gave her a thoughtful look. "Our choreography would need to be spot-on, now, wouldn't it?"

Relieved, she beamed at him. "I have a plan for that as well."

"Thought you might, clever girl."

Chapter Thirty-Five

✍

$\mathcal{I}$N THE FORTNIGHT that followed, the plan took shape. They were able to sort out any pitfalls on the stage. And in the evenings, Oscar came to dine with them and didn't suspect a thing.

It was all moving along swimmingly.

The entire hamlet of Addlewick was in on the ruse. Well, *mostly*.

It was actually her father who suggested that the villagers wouldn't truly immerse themselves in their rolls unless they imagined they had a stake in the outcome. For that reason, they were told that the stranger coming to town was an important playwright, who'd sent the very script they were portraying to several villages as a sort of audition to discover the next sensation for the London stage.

A harmless little fib. At least, Honoria hoped it would be. After all, if all went as expected, no one would need to know that Ladrón was a bloodthirsty villain.

Then her mother suggested enlisting the help of the newspaper for authenticity. She was convinced it would create the impetus to compel Ladrón to suspend disbelief, should any other aspect of the play go awry. Since they were working with amateurs, as Father had pointed out, things had a tendency to go that way so it was important to make everything appear as genuine as possible.

And thus, the article about a "Titian Masterpiece Discovered in Local Woman's Attic" had been printed in the

Addlewick Gazette twelve days ago, leaving time to send copies to several port cities, in which a ship sailing to Spain might encounter it.

Truman had not been happy with this plan at all.

Regrettably, Honoria had accidentally informed him *after* there wasn't anything he could do to stop it. Such a thoughtless mistake, on her part. *Tsk, tsk.* Therefore, he had no choice but to agree to send word whenever his former seafaring acquaintances heard news of Ladrón returning to England.

That news had arrived yesterday. And just this morning, the Spanish ship *Venus* arrived at Port Grimsby.

The time had come. Everyone took their places.

Honoria—playing the part of Woman with a Breadbasket—surveyed the stage through the bakery's shopfront window.

Behind her, Mrs. Brown bustled from kitchen to counter. "'Tis all so thrilling, Miss Hartley. Do you think the playwright will stop in here? I've a fresh tray of Dunnelocke honey buns cooling. Oh, dear. Should I change my apron, do you think? This one has flour all over it from the morning."

"I'm sure the flour makes it all the more authentic. As if you've truly embodied your role," Honoria assured her and received a nod and sigh of relief.

As for herself, she swallowed down a rise of nerves. But quashed them just as quickly. This would work. It had to. She'd choreographed each scene herself. And, most importantly, this play of theirs would keep Oscar from having to look over his shoulder for the rest of his life . . .

As long as he didn't find out.

The last thing she wanted was for him to show his face in the village and ruin everything.

Thankfully, Mother and Mr. Lawson had volunteered to keep Oscar distracted at the abbey.

But here on High Street, the supposed Titian masterpiece was on display in the haberdashery. Then it would be whisked away at the perfect moment to incite Ladrón to chase after it.

From that point, Cardew—who refused to let anyone else manhandle his painting—would play his part as a curator for the National Gallery. While disguised, he would take the painting with him. And just as Ladrón arrived, his carriage would pull away.

Then, at a designated spot outside of the village, his carriage supposedly would hit a rut in the road, delaying him and thus allowing Ladrón to catch up with him.

That was when the great reveal would commence.

They'd practiced this part endlessly.

Cardew would strip away his mask, while handing over the leather pouch containing the two thousand pounds to pay his debt. However, as Cardew had explained to her, the money wouldn't satisfy Ladrón any longer. Which was where the painting came in.

However, after being double-crossed by Cardew once before, Ladrón was bound to suspect the painting was another forgery. The next lines he would say were absolutely crucial to the success of their plan.

As they'd practiced, Cardew would tell the truth. He'd claim to have painted the masterpiece, boasting with a healthy measure of uncertainty laced in his tone. This would pique Ladrón's interest, giving him reason to suspect that Cardew wasn't being entirely truthful, and he would want to investigate the painting for himself. Cardew would then shield the painting, as if trying to protect the great masterpiece from harm.

Suspecting that it was the genuine article, Ladrón would accuse Cardew of trying to hoodwink him. Cardew, in turn, would confess to having concocted a scheme to take possession of it, in the hopes of recreating Titian's work.

And finally, when Ladrón was thoroughly convinced and demanded the painting, Cardew would employ a King

Solomon tactic by holding a knife to the work and threatening to slice it in half because he couldn't bear to part with it. Knowing that Ladrón would sooner throw his own mother off a cliff than see a Titian destroyed should guarantee his safety and allow him to form a new deal where both he and Oscar would be free of him for good. No blood spilled.

It was the perfect plan.

The only problem was there were things that she'd learned about Ladrón that she hadn't shared with her family or else they never would have allowed her to do this in the first place. So she and Cardew had come up with an alternate plan, just in case the first one fell to pieces.

And if she were being honest, she hadn't been entirely convinced until she had seen the painting. It was remarkable. Even knowing the Venus depicted was actually Babette Fairfax, she still had trouble believing it. The oil and canvas even appeared timeworn as if it had spent centuries in someone's attic. Forgotten and shoved aside. What made it all the more convincing was using an actual sixteenth-century frame from the abbey.

Honoria held her breath as a coach and six rumbled onto High Street.

It was time.

A shiver rolled over her, and she chafed hands over her arms to ward away the chill of foreboding. But she refused to give in to any doubts. This would work. It had to.

And as long as Mr. Lawson kept Oscar occupied and Mother did the same with the widows, it would.

~⋙

WITH THE DAY'S first order of business concluded, Oscar headed toward the door. It was time for his morning ride, and he planned to take a direct path to Hartley Hall.

Hermes should know the way by rote. After all, they

had just been there the last fourteen evenings without fail. Though, leaving after dinner and without Honoria by his side, was getting more and more difficult.

He spent entirely too much time wondering which window might be hers so that he could scale the walls and steal inside. But he was done with stealing, he told himself. He wanted more than a collection of stolen moments. Even if some of those moments had been scorching—like the one against the tree, another beneath the rose arbor, twice on the bench behind the hedgerow . . . and when he'd borrowed the Culpeppers' phaeton, drove her down an empty lane, perched her on the springboard so that her hips were level with his shoulders, lifted her hems and proceeded to pleasure her most wickedly in the broad light of day—he still wanted more.

He wanted a life with her.

This morning, he planned to broach the subject. And considering the fact that she'd absently curled her hand around the ring and locket when they'd bid an all-too-chaste farewell at the door the night before, he hoped that meant she was longing for more, as well.

But whatever plans he had for the morning changed when he stepped down into the hall just as Algernon opened the door to Lady Hartley and Ben Lawson.

"Ah. Good morning, Oscar," Roxana said as she swept inside, the skirts of her emerald-green riding habit shushing over the floor as she pressed a kiss to his cheek in greeting. "You're just the man I wanted to see. Oh, dear, you weren't going out, were you?"

When her expression transformed seamlessly into one of embarrassment, he had no choice other than denial. It would have been rude, not to mention inauspicious, to make his potential future mother-in-law feel unwelcome.

So he returned the smile, bowing over her hand, and said, "I always have time for you."

"Splendid." Slipping her arm through his, she proceeded to steer him toward the back of the house. "Now then, where are your aunts? I should like to have tea while you and Mr. Lawson make a thorough sweep of the manor. You don't mind, do you? It would ease my mind greatly to know that there aren't any more potential hazards waiting to strike."

Oscar and Lord Hartley had already seen to the matter, along with every footman beneath this roof. However, understanding that Roxana would naturally be wary, he agreed. There was no harm in being exceptionally cautious.

"Of course I don't mind," he said genially.

After all, the matter shouldn't take too long.

⤙⤙

STANDING IN THE bakery, Honoria felt the rumble of horses underfoot as the coach and six thundered onto High Street. A rise of nerves pinpricked her skin while nausea churned her stomach.

As someone who had never suffered an instant of stage fright in her life, she refused to start now. So she drew in a deep breath and exhaled her vocal warm-up on a whisper. *Percival, Peter and Carlton Culpepper.*

After saying it thrice more, it was time.

Picking up her basket of bread, she strolled through the door. At her cue—the tinkling of the bell overhead—she paused to issue a cheery wave and say her line over her shoulder. "Good day to you, Mrs. Brown."

Mrs. Brown, flustered and fidgeting with her apron, forgot her line. "Um . . ."

Honoria stepped out onto the pavement, greeted by a cooler breeze, tinged with the first sunbaked hints of autumn. But the fact that she could hear the chatter of cicadas in the distance told her that the villagers were being far too quiet. The half dozen who were selected to stand on the pavement were supposed to be engaging in conversation, not simply smiling nervously, heads bobbing like hobby-horses.

However, she was relieved that the tall, swarthy man emerging from the carriage across the street didn't seem to notice. Dressed in impeccably tailored black superfine, he adjusted his high brushed beaver hat and read the spavined wooden sign on the pavement outside the haberdashery.

ENTER TO BE AWESTRUCK BY ELMIRA HORNCASTLE'S AMAZING DISCOVERY

Then, in smaller letters at the bottom:

FORGOTTEN TITIAN MASTERPIECE

The wording was supposed to have been the other way around. However, Honoria had made the mistake of leaving the task to Mr. Horncastle, who had obviously deferred to his wife's preferences. Or more likely, her browbeating.

Turning away from the breeze, she stilled her hat ribbons and prepared to cross the street just as a man approached on horseback. She'd never seen him before. Even so, the stranger was handsome with aristocratic features and wavy blond hair. So when he tipped his hat, she smiled in return.

But that was a mistake. She knew it the instant he goggled at her, eyes glazed with a sappy grin plastered on his face. The poor man nearly fell off his horse.

She glanced at Thea, who was standing in front of the milliner's, and they both rolled their eyes. *Men*, such helpless creatures. It was a wonder they were able to button their own waistcoats.

The moment he passed by, Honoria put him completely from her mind. She crossed the street as Elmira Horncastle bustled out of the haberdashery.

Elmira regally strolled to her mark, her chins held high

above a daringly cut plum-colored gown, displaying a wealth of matronly décolletage that proved her corset was surely fashioned of iron. As the breeze stirred, one of the long ostrich plumes sprouting from her broad-brimmed hat fell against her face.

Blowing out a pfft, she batted it away and smiled as she delivered her line. "Good morrow, sir. Have you come to see the picture?"

Miguel Ladrón doffed his hat as he sketched a bow. "*Buenos días, señora.* I have, indeed, come to see the *picture*, as you say." His words were spoken in thickly accented English, his tone as silken and seductive as a snake. "I recently read in your—*cómo se dice 'periódico'* . . . Ah, yes—*newspaper* about a woman who'd made an interesting discovery in her attic. A lost Titian, I believe."

Eavesdropping, Honoria thought that he was also quite skilled at playing a part. If she didn't know better, she could easily believe him nothing more than a refined gentleman with an interest in art.

"Why, that story was about me," Elmira said, splaying a hand over her bosom.

"Surely not," he said, all charm and ease. "For the article mentioned a mature woman and all I see before me is a flower in full bloom."

Keep to the script, Honoria thought when she saw Elmira blush and begin to fan herself at the compliment. All she had to do was make her apologies that the gentleman had arrived a moment too late, then explain about the gentleman from the National Gallery.

When Elmira finally managed to utter a semblance of her lines, Honoria issued a sigh of relief. Then, with a glance down to the milliner's shop, she gave a nod to her sister.

Thea—playing the part of Pedestrian on the Pavement No. 1, as well as stage director—signaled Cardew's carriage into motion with a twirl of her parasol.

"In fact," Elmira concluded with a wave toward the passing carriage, "I do believe that is Mr. Clarence now. Fear not, you'll see it again soon, hanging in London."

The scene wasn't perfect. But it did the trick.

Ladrón bid a hasty farewell and returned to his carriage, barking commands to his driver.

Yes, Honoria thought, all was going to plan.

⚜

"WON'T TAKE A moment of your time," Lawson had said before the hours on the hall clock slipped from morning to afternoon.

Oscar wondered if he should have the servants prepare a room for him.

Lady Hartley, on the other hand, had left after he received a missive telling him not to worry and that all was well . . . in a way that made him decidedly worried. But she'd declined his offer to accompany her home.

It left him on edge. In fact, this entire day just seemed . . . off. He couldn't quite put his finger on it.

Leaving Lawson to investigate the plaster ceiling in the ballroom, Oscar decided to ask Algernon about the note and who'd sent it. Yet, as he reached the gallery railing, he looked down and noticed that Algernon was not at his post.

Heading downstairs, he heard a gaggle of raised female voices drifting in from the garden, the argument indiscernible from this distance. But it sounded as though the widows were having a row. An ingrained sense of self-preservation advised him to stay clear of it.

He'd just planted a foot on the bottom tread when a knock fell on the door.

No need to stand upon ceremony, he thought and strode to answer it himself.

On the other side of the threshold stood a blond man

around his own age. He arched one eyebrow as he cast a swift, superior glance over him, condescension dripping from the epaulets of his military coat.

Oscar had seen such a look far too many times in his life, and he knew in an instant that he didn't like the man. "State your business."

The stranger blinked. Then, as if assessing the situation, his entire demeanor altered as he smiled and doffed his high hat, his brow lowering. "Is this Dunnelocke Abbey?"

"It is."

"I am relieved, indeed. I've been traveling on horseback for a number of days, ever since I arrived in England. You see, I've spent the majority of my life on the Cape in Africa," he supplied with a measure of expectation in his expression.

But Oscar had no time or inclination to inquire about it. He had other plans.

However, the unduly loquacious stranger continued. "I actually rode through the small hamlet's high street not a few minutes ago. I might have asked for directions, but I'm afraid that I became so thoroughly dumbstruck at the sight of the single most beautiful woman I've ever beheld. Nearly drove my horse into a grand coach and six," he said with a self-deprecating laugh. "Good job I didn't. Wouldn't have wanted to upset the swarthy fellow inside it."

A chill slithered down Oscar's spine. Ladrón, he thought. In Addlewick.

Panic clawed at his throat as his first thought was Honoria. Swallowing, he held up a finger. "Would you mind staying here for just one moment?"

He didn't wait for an answer. Pivoting on his heel, he strode toward the back garden in search of Algernon.

Oscar found him in the nave, carrying an empty platter from the widows' tea. "Could you send one of the footmen to find Cardew? It's a matter of urgency."

"I'm afraid Mr. Cardew stepped out early this morning, my lord."

Bloody hell. This was not the time for Cardew to go off on a another one of his strolls through the countryside for inspiration.

He raked a hand through his hair. "Very well. Have Raglan ready the carriage."

"I believe Mr. Raglan is driving Mr. Cardew."

"Driving Cardew? Why the devil would—"

He stopped as the pieces started to fall into place. The most beautiful woman. Cardew gone with the carriage. A swarthy man in town . . .

This was no coincidence. Especially since he'd seen Honoria talking to Cardew before she'd left a fortnight ago. And hadn't she been wearing a perfectly innocent expression when he'd found her? Oh, yes, she had. Which should have been his first clue that she was up to something.

But he'd been so distracted by his constant craving for her that he hadn't given it a second thought.

He should have known better! The little idiot had likely talked Cardew into some sort of scheme to pay off Ladrón without his interference. She thought she knew all about men from masquerading as one in society. And while society had its own dangers, she had no idea what monsters lurked in his world.

Cursing, he returned to the door. He had to get into town before she followed through with whatever harebrained scheme she'd concocted.

"I'm afraid this isn't the best time to pay a call," he said to the stranger, taking him by the elbow and escorting him to his horse.

"I'm not here to pay a call," he said. "This is where I live. At least, now it is."

Oscar closed the door behind them. Distracted, he shook his head. "I believe you've made a mistake."

Then, without another word, he turned on the gravel and headed toward the stables.

"I'm Manford Fairfax," the man called after him.

Oscar stopped. "*What* did you say?"

"I'm Manford Fairfax, Viscount Vandemere."

The ground seemed to dissolve from under his feet. His legs shook from the force of keeping himself upright as he looked over his shoulder. "Vandemere?"

"Correct. And you are?"

"Out of time, apparently," Oscar said and took off toward the stables.

Chapter Thirty-Six

❧

$\mathscr{I}$T WAS *NOT* going to plan, drat it all.

All the lines she'd written for Cardew to deliver at a safe distance were nullified when the two thugs with Ladrón overtook the carriage and dragged both Mr. Raglan and Cardew to their knees.

The confrontation was supposed to happen a mile up the road where dense woodland flanked either side *and* where her father and the men he'd insisted upon having with him were waiting.

Which meant that the *just in case* script was now part of the play.

Honoria slipped the spyglass into the breadbasket, then walked out from behind the copse of trees and onto the road.

A heavily accented voice carried on a limp breeze. "Where is your partner? I believe we have some unfinished business to settle."

"I have more money," Cardew said. "In the leather pouch inside the carriage."

Ladrón ordered one of his men to retrieve it for him. Then, he weighed it in his hand . . . just before he let it drop to the ground at his feet. "I did not ask about the money. Nor did I come all this way and risk the gallows by setting foot onto English soil only to leave with nothing for my collection. So I'll ask once more—where is Flint?"

When she came round the bend, she saw the tip of the rapier at Cardew's throat, his disguise in ruins. "He isn't here. We separated after Paris."

"Try again," Ladrón said, the neckcloth beneath Cardew's chin disintegrating with a flick of the wrist.

Cardew sucked in air through his teeth as a thin line of crimson appeared. "It's t-true. I . . . I stole the Titian so that I could earn a living without him. You'll never find him or put him in your collection."

Hearing this, Honoria gasped. She finally understood that Ladrón didn't want to find Oscar to pay a debt . . . he wanted to collect Oscar. Cardew had tried to tell her, but she'd been so determined to ensure that Oscar was free to live his life that she ended up putting him in danger with her foolish plan.

But panic and self-recrimination would have to wait. It was time to put on the best performance of her life.

Tugging on the ribbons of her hat, she continued down the lane, swinging her basket at her side. All the while, she hoped that Thea would keep the villagers offstage, as it were.

Then, as if the Fates were with her, Ladrón turned to see her approach just as her hat blew off and her flaxen hair tumbled free, cascading down around one shoulder.

As expected, he called one of his thugs to his side, murmured some directive and sent him after her. She feigned confusion, standing still on the path with her head tilted to one side.

The thug leered at her, eyes flashing with interest as his gaze openly perused her body in a way that made her ill. She couldn't wait to knock him in the head with his own sword.

It took effort, but she did her best to appear helpless, putting on a show of struggling to flee. There were times when being underestimated worked in her favor. She dropped her basket. *Oh, dear.* The thug relaxed his hold when she feigned a graceful faint, falling swaybacked against the iron bar of an arm across her lower back.

And that was when she made her move.

When he looked over his shoulder to Ladrón's command, she curled her fingers around the hilt of his sword. Then she sprang free, sliding the rapier from the sheath.

With quick feet, she maneuvered around him, feinting skillfully while he lumbered like a big troll. Catching the sword, he tried to wrench it from her grasp, but she slid it free, the blade slicing into his hand as he issued a sharp hiss and a bright line of crimson welled on his palm.

Angry now, he charged at her. But his anger only made him clumsier, and she swished the blade with a flick of her wrist, cutting an X through his trouser over his knee, drawing a point of blood on his leg. When he bent down to press a hand to it, she conked him on the head with the hilt of his own sword, and down he fell.

One down. Two more to go.

Applause greeted her actions. With a glance to her left, she saw the heads and shoulders of a dozen villagers peering over the town wall as if they were watching an outdoor matinee.

They thought it was all part of the play and had no idea how terrifyingly real it was. Not even Honoria wanted to think about that. She had to stay in character.

Holding on to her composure, she turned back in time to see Ladrón shrugging out of his coat. He discarded it with an absent toss, then strolled toward her in his shirtsleeves and trim waistcoat.

"You intrigue me, *querida*," he said with a grin, his features honed like a blade, hair dark as raven feathers. "Let us see how well you fence against a man who knows the blade almost as well as he knows how to pleasure his women."

Oh, please, she thought, fighting the urge to roll her eyes. But taunting him wouldn't suit her purpose. So she stood in first position and slashed her borrowed blade through the air in a salute. It was unfortunate that the weapon was much heavier than her own. Even so, she had faith in her skill.

But it wasn't long before she realized that she was outmatched.

For every thrust, he parried. For every lunge, he redoubled, his feet lightning quick. When she tried to retreat, he slashed. Not to her skin, but through every button on her spencer until it gaped, revealing the snug fit of her bodice. And when he grinned, his face devoid of perspiration, she realized he'd only been toying with her and tiring her out.

With her next riposte, he took her off guard, sliding his blade in a looping circle against hers and stripping it from her hand. It went sailing down the slope beside the lane as he caught her around the waist.

She did not feign her struggles this time but fought him like a tigress, all claws and teeth. He hissed when she drew blood on his wrist.

Then he jerked her against him, the force of it hard enough to knock her teeth together, his sword arm wrapping around her throat. He growled low in her ear, "That wasn't very sporting of you, *querida*. You need to learn some manners." As she struggled to breathe, his free hand slid up her body, parting the fabric of her spencer to cover her breast. "Mmm . . . I think I will enjoy teaching you."

Her heart thundered in panic, the force of it shaking the ground beneath her.

She tried to think as she clawed at the arm around her neck, her vision blurring around the edges. Through the haze, she saw a horse and rider charging at full gallop and realized that some of the quaking wasn't hers.

It gave her little relief, however, to see Oscar riding into the lion's den. And it was all her fault.

While she clung to the last shreds of her consciousness, she took advantage of Ladrón's distraction and stomped her foot down on his instep. On a grunt of surprise, his forearm went slack just enough to give her room to jam her elbow into his midriff. He groaned, relaxing his hold around her neck. She dragged in a breath and tried to slip free . . . but the bastard was too quick.

He spun her around with dizzying speed, capturing her with the other arm around her throat, leaving his sword arm free as Oscar leaped down from Hermes.

"Let her go, Ladrón! It's me you want."

"Ah, so this"—he gave her a teeth-rattling shake—"is why you came to England. She is what they call an *English rose*, is she not? I can well understand the temptation, and I look forward to exploring her in greater depth. Later. For the moment, you and I have a matter to settle."

"Release her, if you want to keep your head," Oscar said without a break in his stride.

Ladrón snickered. "You have no weapon."

"I don't need a weapon. I have yours."

In the blink of an eye—and Honoria wished she hadn't blinked—Oscar moved swiftly toward them, pointing to the sky as if the sword were falling from the clouds. Then he turned, making a single revolution and suddenly came away with the sword.

It was like a magician's sleight of hand. She was so dazzled by his maneuver that she was unprepared for when Ladrón flung her away. Actually *flung* her down the ravine.

Stumbling, she slid down the grassy embankment, losing a slipper on the way. By the time she'd pushed her hair out of her eyes and gathered in her breath, she saw the lumbering ox start to wake up.

"Oh, no, you don't," she said and whacked him with a rock.

Beside the carriage, Cardew and Raglan banded together to take out the other thug. Left without a weapon, Cardew had to sacrifice his masterpiece and whacked him over the head with it, splitting the canvas.

Oscar, apparently preferring fisticuffs to fencing, blood-ied Ladrón's nose. Eyes red with vengeance, the Collector sank down and reached inside his boot.

"Looking for this?" Oscar asked, holding a bejeweled dagger.

Ladrón lunged, but Oscar was far too quick, making her wonder how she'd ever bested him. Had her kiss truly weakened his knees?

But now was not the time for such queries.

Especially when her father came charging down the lane, followed by another man who seemed vaguely famil-iar and . . . her *brother*? But what was Truman doing here?

Yet, as she met his hard gaze, she had a sense that she was in a world of trouble.

Chapter Thirty-Seven

OSCAR WAS GLAD that Warring and Hartley arrived when they did. He'd had the blade to Ladrón's throat, and he wasn't entirely sure what he might have done because he couldn't stop seeing the image of Honoria being held against her will.

For a moment, just a moment, he felt his own monster deep within. But in that same moment, he knew that if he let it out, he would never forgive himself. And that wasn't the man he wanted to be.

All his life, he'd either been running from something or chasing after someone. He hadn't spent enough time in one place to figure out what he wanted out of his own life.

He knew it now. And he wanted her.

Unfortunately, there was a little matter of a betrothal contract and the real Vandemere to contend with.

"Couldn't have planned the timing better myself," Warring said with a wry grin that lifted a dark slash of eyebrows higher on his forehead. "Remind me to ask for Miss Hartley's assistance the next time there's a suspect guilty of piracy and murder to apprehend."

Oscar growled, his gaze traveling to where Honoria stood with her father and scowling brother, and looking as though she were getting a tongue-lashing. "Any man who underestimates her is a fool."

"I'd say any man who dares to love her is a fool, but I believe I'm looking at one right now."

"Aye. And unfortunately, her betrothed showed up at the abbey just before I left."

"What was that?"

Oscar shook his head. "I'll fill you in another time. For now, I need to speak with her. Alone. I know I've asked a great deal of you, but would you do me one last favor?"

"Do you have any idea how many accolades I'll receive for turning in Ladrón and his thugs? You can ask for favors until we're one hundred," he said, clapping Oscar on the shoulder. Then he gave him a little shove. "Go. I'll take care of the rest."

Grateful to his friend, Oscar strode over to Honoria, surprised that he managed to appear calm and collected when he had five thousand demons running amok inside him.

Turning to her father, he asked if he could take her away from all this. When her brother opened his mouth as if he might answer, Hartley cut in and gave his permission. Honoria had the good sense to appear sheepish when she looked up at him, but Oscar knew better.

Thankfully, Raglan was no worse for wear and managed to drive them away from the commotion as the villagers started clamoring, discussing *what fun* their play had been, without knowing the truth of it.

When their retreating carriage was met with a round of applause, he shot a glare to Honoria, his back molars grinding. "If you dare sketch a bow or even wave at your audience, I will throttle you."

Her sheepish facade faded in a flash, and she narrowed her eyes. "Try it, and I will remove your bollocks with a dull knife."

Damn, but he loved her. But that didn't stop him from being furious with her.

The instant they were away from the crowd, he unleashed all the worry and terror and dread her actions had wrought on him.

"You little idiot! Why didn't you listen to me? You shouldn't have been anywhere near Ladrón!"

"I was trying to save you, you ungrateful beast. And don't you dare underestimate me. I'm not just an ornament to hang on your arm."

"Save your outrage." He scoffed. "You know very well that I never treated you like a porcelain doll. More than anyone, I know how capable you are. But today you went too far, and you bloody well know it."

She threw her hands up. "Was I supposed to stand by and simply wait for him to kill you one day? No. Not when I could do something to prevent it. I couldn't have lived with it. Don't you understand? I cannot lose you. Not you."

"Why?"

"You know why! Aren't you the blackguard who always sees through me?"

"There's only one reason you'd be foolish enough to put your own life at risk." Reaching across the carriage, he took her by the shoulders and pulled her to him, even though he wasn't sure if he wanted to shake her or kiss her. "And that reason is because you love me."

She pushed at his chest. "You're wrong. I hate you."

"Try again, Signore. You love me. Say it."

"Stop. Stop it."

"Say the words," he commanded, shaking his head when she tried to cover his mouth with her hands. "Tell me you love me as much as I love you."

A growl of frustration tore from her throat, her eyes glistening with angry tears. She glared back at him in challenge, her lips clamped shut, her arms folding beneath her breasts.

But he knew what was there, behind her mulish silence. Knew that she was clutching at her own heart, trying to keep it from breaking free.

He gave her a tiny shake. "Do you know what I thought when I saw his sword at your throat?"

"You're a sapskull if you thought I'd let him hurt you!"

She grabbed him just as hard, then crushed her mouth to his.

All at once, they were lost in a frenzy of hard breaths and groping hands. Mouths devouring, tongues fencing and tangling. Teeth raking over tender flesh.

He tore off her spencer and threw it out the window. Then he dragged down the shoulder of her gown, tugged the corset and chemise aside and feasted on her breast. Her nails bit into his scalp as she held him there, neck arching.

They were too far gone for gentle love play. There was too much need and urgency. They had to feel each other, to drive away the memory of what might have happened. And they both understood that sometimes life was demanding and harsh, and the only thing to ease the ache of it was the connection of skin to skin.

Straddling him, she clawed at the fastenings of his breeches. Gripped his turgid flesh. Anchored him beneath her core and impaled herself in one slick slide.

He took her hips and drove deep, deeper still. As the carriage raced on, they ate at each other's mouths, feeding each other primal grunts and groans, abandoning themselves out of need, out of a love that neither one of them wanted or expected. But it was there in every fevered kiss and punishing thrust. It was there in every thundering beat of his heart and hers.

He felt her body clench around him, gripping him. Milking him as she shattered on a garbled moan of pleasure. The need to spill inside her, to claim her, was almost unbearable. But he held on and on, even as her climax threatened to rip out his soul.

"I'm close. I need to . . ." His hands tightened on her hips, ready to lift her the instant her spasms subsided.

But she took his face in her hands in the way that always undid him. "Stay. Stay inside me."

Then she pressed her mouth to his. And Oscar stayed, surging up on a choked shout, filling her again and again, even as she cried out and slipped over the edge, tumbling headlong into another quake that wrenched the life from both of them.

⤚⤙

HONORIA TRIED TO catch her breath as she sagged against Oscar.

She was still absorbing everything that had happened—how close she'd been to losing him, the desperation in their lovemaking, her command for him to spill inside of her.

She could still feel the pulse of his flesh wedged deep. Feel the ripples of pleasure running through her veins, even as the fear began to take hold.

What had she done?

She knew what that could bring. Her friend, Meg, had been belly-full after a single interlude in Italy. Her family had been understanding. Honoria's, however, believed in matrimony before progeny, even if that meant a mad dash to Gretna Green. After all, Truman's birthday fell barely seven months after the anniversary of her parents' nuptials.

But now, the children she'd been too afraid to have, too afraid to risk losing, were a possibility. Her only excuse was that she'd wanted, *needed*, to feel him, to celebrate being alive with him. In those moments, she'd felt so free, so open to the joy of living that she'd forgotten the pain and sorrow that could accompany it.

She had always kept her heart safe from that pain. But now? She felt utterly exposed to it. Instead of a reliable brick wall surrounding her heart, that traitorous organ had slipped through the cracks and sank kitten claws into Oscar, refusing to let him go.

And it terrified her.

"I need air," she said, easing up and away from him, wincing from the tender sting that sudden emptiness can bring. "Could we stop the carriage? I need to breathe."

An instant before he closed his eyes and blew out a breath, she glimpsed the frustration and impatience. Then he reached into his coat pocket, withdrew a handkerchief. Before he could tend to her as he'd done after their previous occasions, she took it from his grasp and discreetly cleaned the slick of their fluids from between her thighs.

Looking out the window and seeing the abbey drawing near, he cursed. Then he tapped on the roof and called up to Mr. Raglan. "Take us down by the lake."

The carriage turned, rumbling and bouncing over the uneven path as they regarded each other from opposite sides.

He was still breathing hard, taking up all the air she needed. His face was marked with the intensity of a thousand questions. Or perhaps just one. And she chose to turn her attention to the view beyond the window.

When the carriage stopped, she reached for the door latch.

He laid his hand over hers. "Come with me. Let's hie away to Gretna Green."

"Now?"

"I want a life with you. I may only be a beggar, a pickpocket and a gambler, but I'll work at making you happy all the days of your life if you'll have me."

"To be clear, you are asking me to marry you . . . now?"

"Yes, Honoria," he said with a small laugh as if she were the one going mad. "As my mother once told me, sometimes all we have is a moment. I didn't realize how true that was until today. And even though I've been offering wisdom to you on how to live your life to the fullest, I didn't know that I haven't been living until today. Because in order to live, to truly live, you have to risk it all—your heart, your soul, your past and your future. You have to lay all your cards on the table."

"I . . . I need air," she said and bolted from the carriage. She heard him follow, the crunch of his boots on the occasional twig not far behind her. "You're talking a good deal more than you usually do."

"I'm trying to make you understand."

"Oh, *I* understand," she said, pacing in a flurry of wrinkled skirts and disheveled hair. "I just don't think you grasp the enormity of the question you've posed. Otherwise, you wouldn't expect me to answer you now . . . after the day we've had."

"There will always be days like this." When she turned and gaped at him, he shrugged. "Well, not exactly like this. There will be difficult days ahead, however. No one can avoid them. But I firmly believe that we will weather them better together."

Honoria was scared. Terrified. As she listened to him tell her that she'd have to make herself vulnerable in order to live, and promised her difficult days ahead, she knew she should be running in the opposite direction.

And yet, she was rooted to this spot, gazing into Oscar's eyes and wanting more than anything to not be scared.

As if reading her thoughts, he reached out and took her hand. "You won't be alone at that anvil in the blacksmith's forge. I'll be there beside you, and for all the days that follow."

Devil's doorknocker! Why didn't she run screaming in the opposite direction when she had the chance? It was too late now. He'd pushed her over the edge, and her heart was no longer her own.

"Oh, Oscar. I suppose I do—" She saw a man enter the clearing between the trees and the lake and said, "Someone is coming."

Oscar turned, raking a frustrated hand through his hair. "You again. Look. I don't have time to deal with you. Honoria, I believe you were about to answer—"

"*You* are Honoria Hartley?" the man interrupted, agog.

With her hair in a wild tumble down her shoulders and her dress torn, she could imagine what type of woman he thought she was as his gaze turned from glazed to lurid.

"I am. And you are . . . ? Wait." She pointed, her brows lifting. "I saw you in the village earlier."

"Yes, I was on my way home. Here, at Dunnelocke Abbey, that is. I'm Vandemere. The real Vandemere. I don't know who this impostor is, but I've already sent for the magistrate."

Her gaze whipped to Oscar, and she saw the horrible truth written on his face.

"I planned to tell you," he said.

"Whatever you want to say to her, you can tell the magistrate. Doubtless you will be charged with fraud, at the very least. And if you're fortunate, you'll only be exported for your crimes."

"But I needed you to make your choice," Oscar continued as if the other man hadn't spoken. "It has to be your choice, Honoria. I won't take that from you."

"Gretna Green," she whispered in understanding and glanced toward the carriage where Mr. Raglan waited.

They still had time . . .

But the thunder of hooves beating on the long drive to the abbey drew her attention to the riders and carriages approaching in the distance.

"That will be the magistrate," Vandemere said smugly. "Before he is upon us, I'd like my father's ring, if you don't mind."

Reflexively, Honoria wrapped her fist around her necklace and his brows rose. Then he took a step toward her.

Oscar moved between them. "Don't even think about touching her."

"Toby," she said, glancing over Vandemere's shoulder at the young man's approach. "I'm glad you're here, for we could very much use your assistance. I don't know who this man is, but he's—"

"Take hold of his arms, Shellhorn." Caught by surprise, Shellhorn took Oscar's arms as Vandemere punched him in the gut.

Honoria rushed forward to shield him as he doubled over, coughing.

"Stop it. Stop it at once!" She pummeled Vandemere with her fists. But that was when he wrapped a hand around her necklace and yanked it free. "No!"

She tried to take it back, clawing at his fist even as he turned to walk away. But he shoved her to the ground, and she fell hard.

"See here, Vandemere," Shellhorn scolded. "You cannot treat a lady like that."

Without a word, Vandemere stripped the ring from the chain and slid it onto his finger.

"I think I can do whatever I want," he said, then he hurled the chain and locket into the lake before he strode back toward the abbey.

"No!" Honoria screamed again, her hand covering her mouth as her most precious possession fell beneath the surface.

Oscar suddenly shrugged out of Shellhorn's grasp and dove into the water.

She wanted to stop him, to call out. They still had time to make their escape.

But the moments ticked by, and he didn't surface. All she saw were ripples, bubbles rising from beneath.

"I didn't know, Miss Hartley," Toby said forlornly as he helped her up from the ground. "That Vandemere said he'd put us out on our ears if I didn't do what I was told."

As the horses thundered up the lane, she stood by the water's edge waiting for Oscar. And in those terrifying moments, she felt the utter aloneness and impotent fear that had been with her, locked inside of her, for most of her life.

Then she saw something—a blur of white just beneath the surface—and her breath stalled.

Chapter Thirty-Eight

𝒜 SCREAM RIPPED FROM Honoria's throat as she saw Oscar's limp body floating on the surface.

Her mind flashed back to her brother, to the way his hair undulated in a fan of silken tendrils on the surface. Sheer panic assailed her.

The unthinkable terror had her staggering into the lake. She didn't even feel the cold of the water seeping into her shoes, saturating her stockings and skirts. With every step, she fought against the constraints of the damp muslin twisting around her legs and then her hips, her waist, her breasts.

Only one thought was in her mind: *Get to him*.

She clawed at the water, trying to keep her head up, stretching out her arms, her neck. The reeds tangled around her skirt, slowing her down. But she kept plodding forward, her soles slipping through the insubstantial silt.

Then the water touched her lips. But she was almost there. Almost to the ripple of white fabric of his sleeve. If she could just . . . reach . . . a bit . . . farther.

She slipped under, water filling her nostrils. She swiped frantically at the lake, the air, eyes wide as she saw the sky through a film, the wavering sun and dissolving clouds growing dimmer as her feet scrambled beneath her.

Then, at last, the slap of her hand connected with something solid.

She didn't know how she managed it, but somehow she gripped the fabric of his shirt in her fist, then clawed her way to the shore.

Dragging him with her, she crawled up to the edge of the embankment and rolled him over, scrambling up to tap him on the cheek.

"Oscar. Oscar, wake up now." She kissed him, smoothing the hair away from his brow, his lashes spiked as they rested against his cheeks, his lips faintly tinged with blue.

"No. I won't have it." She shook her head. Her hands balled into fists as a sudden surge of rage filled her. "You cannot do this to me, you . . . you . . . blackguard! How dare you make me fall in love with you! I hate you! I hate you so much!" She pummeled his chest with her fist. "I'm not going to let you get away with it! You're going to wake up right this instant. Do you hear me?"

"Daughter," she heard her father say, heard the pity in his voice.

"Don't touch him . . . don't touch him! He's mine. He's all that I have in this world." When she felt her father's hand on her shoulder, she shrugged him off and shoved at Oscar. Hard. And when that didn't feel brutal enough, she shoved at him again. "Listen to me, you scoundrel. We're going to start a new game, you and I! You are going to marry me. Do you hear that? And this time, I'm going to die first! Let's see how you like it . . . being left . . . all . . . alone."

Sobs racked her body, her pummeling fists pitifully feeble. And then she collapsed, knowing that she had no more time left. That *they* were out of time.

"Pitiful excuse for a proposal, Signore."

The voice that rasped in her ear was impossible. She must have been hearing things. And yet, somehow it had broken through the sound of her own sobs.

She was nearly certain that something had broken inside her. That she'd gone mad. That she would hear his voice inside her mind for the rest of her life as she rambled around the attics of Hartley Hall.

"Shh . . ." he whispered before he coughed. Though why a specter skuttling about in her brain would need to cough, she didn't know. Then again, she was new to madness. So what did she know about it at all?

It wasn't until she felt cold lips against her temple, her cheek, a shaky hand smoothing away the tangle of hair from her face, that she realized she hadn't gone insane.

Or, if she had, she welcomed this vein of it. Welcomed the poison that leached into her brain. Welcomed the burn that woke her blood and opened her eyes to see the color of storms in his and the blue gone from his lips.

"Oscar!"

His name was a cry of relief and pure joy. Wrapping her arms around his neck, she felt her heart lift when he crushed her in his embrace. But she didn't mind. Anything less wouldn't be enough.

He coughed again. Then another inhale, and she knew in that moment the rest of her life would be spent joyously living breath by breath. His breath and hers.

"You're not dying first," he said as she blinked a half-dozen times to ensure she wasn't dreaming . . . or mad. But the warmth of his palm felt real as he cradled her face. "For if you do, I will drag you back from Death's clutches as you have done to me. And I promise you, I would drag you back to me time and time again until I win, and we are both centenarians, wrapped in each other's arms as we drift off toward our eternal sleep."

A laugh and the salt of happy tears clogged her throat. "Then, how will you know you've won, foolish man? Perhaps that's precisely what—"

A distant voice, hard and sharp, interrupted. "The impostor is down by the lake! Take him away at once!"

Until then, she'd forgotten about the real Vandemere.

But panic returned in a flood as nearly a dozen men broke through the tree line.

Scrambling to her feet, she pulled Oscar's hand. "They're coming. You must go. Make haste. Before it's too late."

"What's all this about?" her father asked, confusion and alarm furrowing his brow.

"I've no time to explain. But Oscar must go."

Yet, even as she spoke, four men rushed forward, corralling them at the water's edge. More men followed close behind.

There was nowhere to run.

Oscar looked over his shoulder across the lake to where Mr. Raglan still waited by the carriage. Then he looked down at her, and she knew what he was thinking.

"No," she pleaded. "Just run. I'll hold them off as long as I can."

He lifted a hand to her cheek, his thumb brushing away the hot tears that started to tumble over the edge again. "I wanted to tell you. The truth is, I was starting to believe our fiction. I actually thought that I belonged here, that I'd found a home. But my home is in your eyes, and for the rest of my life I will live there, no matter how far apart we are."

"Oscar, please. Just run. I cannot lose you again."

"Don't cry, Signore," he said as two men seized him by the shoulders. "You're fearless, remember? I want to think of you that way."

But she wasn't. Because right in that moment, she knew she'd wasted too much time being afraid instead of living. Instead of . . . loving him. And, heaven help her, she loved him.

"I love you." She wrapped her arms around him, wondering why the words seemed so simple now that everything was falling apart.

She heard his breath hitch. He struggled against the men's hold.

"Just give me one moment," he ordered them, but they refused and started to drag him away.

"Don't take him. Please, I can explain," she cried out, holding on to Oscar. Then one of the men pulled her off him. She tried to free herself, jerking against the vise grip that encircled her wrist. "No! Wait! You don't understand."

"Get your bloody hands off her!" Oscar shouted. "I'll go willingly, but leave her alone."

The moment the magistrate nodded, the man holding her wrist released her.

"No!" She tried running to Oscar, but this time her father wrapped an arm around her waist.

"Don't. You'll only make matters worse for him," Father said.

Knowing that he was right didn't stop her heart from breaking all over again. And when the men disappeared through the tree line, she turned and buried her face against her father's chest and cried once more.

AT HOME, SHE faced the wrath of Roxana Hartley. Which was to say there was a good deal of graceful pacing around the parlor, while at the same time stopping to fuss over Honoria to ensure she wasn't catching a chill.

"Well, what do you have to say for yourself?" Mother demanded as she gathered a shawl around Honoria's shoulders. Then she went back to pacing.

"There might have been one or two small things I neglected to tell you," Honoria confessed with a sheepish shrug as her thumb and forefinger pinched the air. Then, as both of her parents stared down at her with disapproval, she told the whole truth.

Well . . . *mostly*.

And yet, when she concluded relaying all her foibles, her parents didn't look as surprised as she anticipated. "You knew, didn't you?"

"Not about the blackmail," her father clarified. "I'll have

to speak to the lad about that. However, I did know about the disguise and that you were going about matters of business while using the moniker of Cesario."

"Didn't you wonder about the amount of your dowry?" Mother asked archly.

Honoria shook her head, a bit dumbfounded. "I thought it was a fabrication."

A tawny brow inched higher on her father's forehead. "The money is from each time a certain Signor Cesario purchased property and stocks from me. He was rather generous, that fellow, and I'd often wondered how you managed it all. But when I was in London with your brother, he confessed his part of it when I saw your letter to him. Now, don't be vexed with Truman. He thought he was protecting you."

Vexed? No, indeed. She was furious! Just wait until she saw that disloyal scoundrel of a brother. She'd like to remind him just how many secrets of his that she'd kept over the years.

"So, that's why you never questioned my plan with Ladrón? Because you were already exchanging correspondence with Truman, and you knew that there was a warrant out for Ladrón if he should set foot on English soil again?"

He nodded.

"I just thought you were being a dutiful father," she huffed.

"I've never been *that* dutiful." He set his hand on his wife's shoulder. She put her hand over his. "All that money was yours. Is yours."

"So you both knew all along, and you had resigned yourselves to the fact that I was gambling to secure my own future. Alone?"

"Well . . ." Mother hemmed, pursing her lips. "When your sudden enthusiasm about marrying Vandemere directly followed our first discussions about Seasons and wedding trousseaus, that gave me an inkling. Then there were the letters from Vandemere . . . which happened to coincide with letters from your brother and came from the same ports." Mother tsked as if she'd expected a better deception from one of her children.

Honoria expelled a sigh, feeling like a failure. "If you weren't fooled, then why didn't you encourage me to abandon the idea of Vandemere?"

"Because we knew that you thought you needed him as a crutch of sorts. A rather Shakesperean twist to your story, I should say," Father added with a proud glint in his eye.

If a child of Conchobar Hartley were going to fall apart, they should do it with dramatic flair.

Mother sank onto the settee beside her, rearranging the shawl around her shoulders. "We didn't yet know the reason but hoped you would come to us, in your own time. We just"—her breath hitched—"didn't know it was fear of loving someone . . . because of losing Ernest. Why didn't you tell us?"

"Because we never talk about Ernest. The garden is still locked. And I thought that it was too painful for you. I didn't want to make you sad."

Incipient tears shimmered in her mother's eyes, and she swallowed audibly. "During that time, I didn't think I would make it. I'd lost my child, and I hadn't been here. I'd also lost the mother of my heart when my own had turned her back on me for marrying against her dictates." She looked up at Father tenderly as he laid a hand on her shoulder, his eyes shimmering, too. "For those reasons and others, I didn't feel fit to be a mother at all. I didn't even know that it was grief blinding me to all that I still had. I could only see the loss all around me.

"I remember feeling so numb as I wandered through the house, listless for days, weeks. Never thinking of your father who had lost both mother and child, nor did I think of his father who had lost his wife and one of the lights of his life. I was dead inside. And it wasn't until I saw you through the window, sleeping on your brother's grave in the cold of night that I realized what I still had. And because of you, my dear one"—she took Honoria's face in her hands, pressed a kiss to her lips—"I remembered to live and to embrace each and every moment as if it were the last."

A fresh torrent of tears flooded Honoria's cheeks as she felt the welcoming warmth of her mother's embrace.

"It feels good to speak of him," she said after their hand-kerchiefs were damp and their eyes red but dry once more. "And you should know, I visit the garden."

Father bent down and pressed a kiss to the top of her head. "And you should have realized that the hinges are well-oiled and never creak."

"It seems as though we were all trying to protect each other." She smiled at that, then shrugged. "Had I known this before . . . if I would have just listened to my heart, I might have run off to Gretna Green, and none of this would have happened. And now I've lost him forever."

She thought of Oscar, imagining him cold and alone in a dark, dank cell.

Mother huffed and tucked a tangled curl behind her ear. "Now, that's a bit too dramatic. After all, we'll get him out of this, and the two of you will be married."

"But didn't you hear me? He isn't the real Vandemere. And the real one is a complete arse. Though, it serves the widows right to have to deal with the likes of him. Instead, they might have had Oscar. But they were too busy trying to prove his illegitimacy when he'd done nothing but try to help. They even sent for the cleric of the church where he was baptized because they didn't trust the letter Cardew had forged. But it was a very good forgery, I'm told."

Mother shook her head, confused. "They may not have trusted him in the beginning, perhaps. But surely that's changed. Besides, the cleric from Scotland would have arrived in a matter of days."

"I believe they sent for one in Africa. Or at least, that was where the real Vandemere was born."

Her father frowned, but only went to the window to gaze out across the garden.

A shiver rolled through her as if she were still fighting her way through the water to get to Oscar. And then it hit her all over again, and the torrent came.

She collapsed in a soggy heap onto her mother's lap. "I fell in love with a man I'll likely never see again. It's happened just like I feared all along—once you love someone, he'll be gone forever. They've taken him away. There will be a trial. And that horrible new Vandemere said that he planned to have Oscar h-hanged for his crimes."

"Shh . . . We won't let that happen, my dear."

⋙

SINCE ADDLEWICK'S MAGISTRATE had been preoccupied with the drama commencing in the village and then extraditing Ladrón into the hands of the authorities, Oscar was being held in a cell located at the back of a barn by the magistrate from a neighboring village.

A gelding one stall over was munching on some hay and studying him with bored wariness.

"I'm feeling a bit long in the face, as well," he said leaning against the bars and wishing he was on his way to Gretna Green. But that was just a dream.

"Charming the horses now, lad?"

Oscar startled and turned to see Baron Hartley striding down the aisle between stalls. He felt an instant of relief at seeing someone he'd grown to admire . . . until he remembered all the crimes he was guilty of, all the lies he'd told and all the ways he'd deceived him.

"You must allow me to beg your forgiveness for all that I've done. I never meant to hurt anyone with my deception, but the truth is I was only thinking of myself from the beginning."

"And blackmailing my daughter."

He cringed and knew that he deserved to be locked away even if only for that crime. "I apologize for that, as well. If I could start again, I would. I would live every day since I came to Addlewick all over again with only one goal in mind—to make your daughter happy. I love her, and that is the one single truth of my entire life."

Hartley studied him, his expression inscrutable. Then, after a long moment, he thrust his hand through the iron bars. "Conchobar Erasmus Hartley. And you are?"

"Oscar Flint," he said, gripping the offered hand. "My father is John Flintridge. He left us when I was five years old, and I have been looking for him ever since. I am a gambler and a charlatan, masquerading as a viscount."

"I'm glad to know you, Oscar," Hartley said with a cunning smile. "Did I ever tell you that I knew your father?"

Chapter Thirty-Nine

A WEEK LATER, HONORIA'S presence was requested at Dunnelocke Abbey by the real Vandemere. And the card actually read, *Your presence is requested by the real Vandemere.*

To make matters worse, the betrothal contract finally surfaced from wherever it had been.

It was a yoke around her neck, dragging her into despair.

As their carriage arrived in front of the abbey, Honoria's heart ached. "I cannot believe you accepted his invitation."

The invitation they received was in celebration of the betrothal between their families. But she already hated this new Vandemere. He'd sent her letter after letter, expounding upon her beauty and stating his eagerness to have her for his bride. The utter audacity!

It made her positively ill, and she couldn't believe that her parents had agreed to attend.

"We can hardly refuse to honor the word of our family. Besides," Mother added with a placating pat to her knee, "all we have to do is attend. You are not, and never were, obligated to marry against your will, no matter whose name is on the betrothal contract."

"Be that as it may," Father interjected, "if we didn't attend the formal gathering this evening, it would appear as though we were breaking the contract without considering the legalities. And the very last thing we want is to be embroiled in another scandal."

Honoria hated the guilt she felt. Hated that they were right.

"When we step inside, just remember that you can always refuse him."

Honoria nodded to her mother. But every step on her way to the door was weighted with dread.

When the door to the abbey opened, Algernon escorted them to the drawing room to wait.

Honoria didn't like returning to the abbey. It hurt her heart, remembering all too vividly the night she'd imagined herself lady of the manor. She didn't want to spend time with the widows. She was angry at them. And she didn't want to see that real Vandemere either.

In fact, she planned to give him a piece of her mind. But first she needed to gather her thoughts and her composure. In private. She said as much to her parents, and since the widows had not joined them yet, they encouraged her to take a few minutes out on the terrace in the night air.

Unfortunately, her desire to be alone was thwarted when she heard the scrape of a sole against the stones at the far end.

Her attention turned toward the shadows, just as a figure emerged. A figure who seemed to be made of shadows for how well he blended with them.

Her breath caught as Oscar appeared. And her heart leaped.

"Oscar!" she said in a stage whisper before she covered her mouth and glanced over her shoulder to the drawing room. No one seemed to have noticed. So she rushed to take his hand and drag him back into the shadows. "Before anyone catches you, we'll take my parents' carriage."

"Trying to save me again, are you?"

"Well, you're the idiot who escapes from gaol only to return to the people who had you carted away in the first place." She swatted his shoulder. "Why did you return to the abbey?"

"I had to stop you from marrying someone you don't love."

For that answer, she paused long enough to throw her arms around him and press her mouth to his. "Just so you know, I had no intention of marrying Vandemere. I only came here to give him a piece of my mind."

"Do you mean to say that you didn't appreciate the superfluous compliments and praise of your beauty?"

She sent him a glare. "And how did you—? Just how long ago did you escape? And why haven't you come to see me?"

He held up a finger. "Patience, Signore."

Lights illuminated the window near them, forcing them deeper into the shadows. At the end of the terrace, they took the stone steps down to the side garden, interrupting the cricketsong.

"Did I ever mention that I was born in Scotland?" he asked conversationally as if they weren't furtively skulking away from the abbey.

She looked askance at him. "I don't believe you did. Is that what you wish to talk about right now?"

"Actually, yes." He grinned. "Coincidentally, so was Millicent. She had even been betrothed to a farmer there, until her family insisted that she marry Hugh Fairfax. So she left the man she loved in order to honor the wishes of her family."

Honoria's steps slowed. "Oscar, you didn't escape from gaol to tell me to marry Vandemere, did you? Because if you did, I—"

He silenced her diatribe with a firm kiss. "As I said before, *patience*."

"Very well," she huffed and looked over her shoulder as they continued on.

"Now, where was I? . . . Ah, yes. So during this past sennight, Aunt Millie went to Scotland and reunited with her love. Coincidentally, he also happens to be the registrar who oversees the birth records and collects fines for those who don't bother to record the birth of their child. You see, Scottish law dictates that every birth must be recorded. They are very particular."

When they stopped to peer around the corner, she absently said, "Interesting."

"I thought so. Because this insistence is also helpful in matters of legitimacy," he paused. "You may not know this, but Scotland is one of the few places where a child's illegitimacy can be altered after the fact. So if . . . say a marriage certificate between two parties were to be presented well after a child was born, that child could then have the word *illegitimate* stricken from his birth record."

"Fascinating," Honoria offered and tugged him back around the corner when she heard voices. "But I don't know why you're telling me about Millicent and her former betrothed."

"As I said, I was born in Scotland. Illegitimately, because my father was grieving the loss of his first wife and child and was likely overcome with guilt when he sought comfort with my mother, who was also his wife's identical twin."

Her attention was snared at the mention of twins. "I remember you telling me that your mother was a twin. But I did not know that they were identical."

He nodded. "My mother was an opera singer, and her sister was an actress on the London stage."

"But that is just like Vandemere. You're not telling me that you're related to the man who had you thrown in gaol, are you?"

"No. Not to him, but that's a different story," he said. "You see, Cleo was rather protective of her home and decided to hire an actor to play the role of Vandemere in order to get rid of me. But her plan fell apart when the cleric from Africa arrived with the birth record stating the date of Manford Fairfax's birth and, regrettably, his death. Because both mother and son died in childbirth."

"So then, there is no heir? No Vandemere?"

He held up a finger. "But Titus Fairfax had another son . . . with the twin sister of his first wife."

"Oscar, are you saying that Titus Fairfax was John Flintridge, your father?" she asked carefully.

When he nodded, she could see the hurt and longing in his eyes as he was still coming to terms with it. All this time, he'd thought his father abandoned him. To know that he'd died must have been even more difficult.

And she wrapped her arms around him again. "Oh, my darling. And you have had to bear all of this on your own. Why didn't you come to me?"

He held her close, breathing in her scent. "Well, I've had a rather busy week. After all, I had to drive to Scotland with Millicent and an old cleric, who happened to look alarmingly like Cardew. But he arrived with a rather convincing wedding certificate between Titus and Marina Fairfax, which made my birth legitimate."

"I still don't understand . . ."

"I think you do, Signore."

She pulled back and gaped at him. "So you are . . ."

"Go on. You can say it."

"*You* are the real Vandemere?"

He lifted one shoulder. "In a matter of speaking."

"You wrote those letters, didn't you?" She swatted him when he flashed a grin. "I came here to throw that betrothal contract in your face."

"You still can, you know."

"Hmm . . . I think I will. But that still leaves one problem." She feigned a sigh. "There would still be a legally binding agreement. The only real way to get out of it would be to elope with the man I love."

"It just so happens that I sent a letter to the cook at Hartley Hall as well. Mrs. Dougherty adores me. And I have it under good authority that she packed a hamper and left it strapped to the carriage. Do you think there are any biscuits?"

She laughed. "I suppose we should find out."

"Then, what are we waiting for?"

Taking her by the hand, they made a mad dash around the corner toward the front of the abbey . . .

Only to have everyone waiting to bid them farewell.

As they climbed into the carriage, there was Millie in a rose-colored dress, standing beside a handsome man in a kilt. Babette was draped around Cardew, a hand resting over her belly. Alfreda and Dudley stood arm in arm. Her parents embraced and tearfully applauded with exuberance as if asking for an encore. And Cleo offered a wave and a sheepish shrug. Then, she took Toby by the hand and led him back into the house.

Honoria exchanged a look with Oscar. "I guess I'm not the only one determined to live my life to the fullest."

"And Toby is about to have a very good night," he said rakishly and tugged her over to his side of the carriage, arranging her on his lap. "Then again, I think I am, too."

He pulled her mouth to his, but their kiss was a tender thing. A new beginning. And her heart flooded with so much love that she was afraid she couldn't contain it all. But she knew that to truly feel alive, she had to accept all of it—all the pain and the joy—without hiding from it.

Easing back, she smoothed a lock of hair from his forehead. "I might be out of my depth. I'm not sure I know how to play this new game of ours."

"Then, we'll make the rules up as we go."

THE BEGINNING